INVISIBLE monsters

Invisible Monsters
By Michael Sutherland

Published by Less Than Three Press LLC

Edited by Michael Jay
Cover designed by London Burden

First Edition April 2013
Copyright © 2013 by Michael Sutherland
Printed in the United States of America

ISBN 9781620041963

INVISIBLE MONSTERS

MICHAEL SUTHERLAND

PrOLOGUe

From a faraway land, somewhere over a coal bing, many places since then in fact, the last being Berken-ed, a woman was on the run. And run she did in gingham and pigtails, with not even Toto for company, but a stuffed version in a breadbasket. To everywhere and anywhere between Chester and Bucky, and always with hope in her heart that somewhere over a rainbow there was a place she could be herself. But try as she might it was never to be and she ended up in Nuke-Assil instead, yet another place where no one knew her, another place where she only ever dared to go out at night.

And it would be the last place she would ever run from again.

Shirley was frightened because Shirley was different.

Shirley was an accountant. Shirley was smart. And tonight she wore a white miniskirt, black fishnets, white stilettos and a red boob tube. Shirley thought she looked good, in private at least, but always when she was on her own.

She glanced over her shoulder into her looking glass and teased the blonde curls of her new wig with her scarlet fingernails. It was the most expensive thing she had ever bought. Not nylon, not horsehair, but real human hair. It was her pride and joy. It looked convincing. Shirley had her doubts about the rest.

Her bangles clacked on her arms as she continued to poke and prod at her wig. She leaned into the mirror and teetered on her heels. She looked at her mouth with wide eyes and smudged her crimson lips together. A doubtful look clouded her plutonium-blue contact lenses.

If only it looked more … real.

She pulled back from her reflection. She licked her lip, tasted her strawberry flavored lippy and shrugged her shoulders. She just hoped as she tugged at his hemline that no one noticed the bad bits.

Last Saturday, as an experiment, she had stretched Lycra down her thighs and walked along the pavement under unforgiving streetlights to the bus stop. It was late. The bus had arrived. There had been a lot of drunks on the bus.

Shirley had stepped onto the gangway, paid her fare, and clumped upstairs in her six-inch heeled stilettos. She clamped her hands to the sides of her head. Her red talons disappeared into her blonde curls. Shaking her head side to side she had reminded herself to act natch, act natch, and there was not a seat to be had except at the back. Drunks sat gob smacked as Shirley tried to ignore their faces, their eyes, their incredulous looks.

Shirley sat down on the back seat and to her relief her knees didn't exploded through her fishnets like cannonballs through a spider's web either when she did. Everyone faced front once again. Shirley passed a crucial test.

Except in her mind where it mattered most.

Now she had packed away her life's dreams; the neatly folded plans, the portfolio of her designs, the pins and chalks, the pinking shears and swatches of material, the exquisite silks and handmade dresses that she worked her night hours away on as her heart sang with each stitch promising another step to the land she had always dreamed of.

She stepped elegantly over to the window, pulled the curtain to the side an inch, and looked down on the world that shunned her. Then she thought about the place where she really wanted to be, a place where she would never have to face the public in disguise again. In a hamlet by a river with lilac rhododendrons climbing the walls perhaps, a place where pink peonies edged a white picket fence as a willow tree wept over yellow and orange dried flowers hanging from the gazebo in the back garden. A little house with a chimney tracing wisps of pale-blue smoke across the evening sun.

She clutched the oversized Lulu beads around her neck as her heart ached at the thought of finally finding her perfect life of anonymity as she peered down at the street below. It was dark and quiet and looked safe, but inside Shirley knew of the dangers that lurked around every corner.

A bus raced by in the rain and rattled the glass in its frame, and when a drunk swayed along the street Shirley caught her breath and let the curtain drop back for fear of being seen.

After recomposing herself, she turned and looked over at the tailor's dummy standing like a silent old friend in the corner, for soon she would be saying goodbye to it and closing the door on her old life. Shirley would never run away again. And this time she meant it.

For the spirit that had kept her sane for so long was now waning, its light was dimming. The road she had followed faithfully since she was little was finally coming to its end and she was consigned to her fate. Born wrong in the wrong time in the wrong place in the wrong way, she would be brave enough now knowing, that at the end of the show that had been her life, the light inside of her would grow like the most incandescent star in the heavens. And even if she would be the only one to see it, it was enough for her to know that it was still there, even if no one else did, not her mother, not her father, not her sisters nor her brother.

They all hated her anyway. For to them, Shirley was a monster.

She walked over to the mantelpiece and traced her fingers over the tiles she had polished to perfection earlier then settled them on a photograph of her mother. She felt the silver frame, cold under her touch as a tear stung her eye and her mouth spoke the words that were silent. "I still love you, Mum."

She picked it up the photograph and placed down again beside an old black and white postcard of Shirley's heroine, Margareta Geertruida Zelle MacLeod.

She looked toward the window again.

No more drapes, she thought, no more curtains or blinds. No more barriers. No more hiding.

And a surge went through her heart. It was time, and it was to be the last time.

She walked across the room elegantly with lightness in her step as she dabbed the tears from her eyes, opened her sitting room door and looked back only once.

'Even if it means I will die at least I will be free,' she said looking around the room knowing that she was right.

No more fear, no more pulling back into the shadows.

No more living a lie.

CHAPTER 1

The arteries of the city hissed evening lifeblood a respectful distance from the garden of remembrance where a young man, wearing a thin blue jacket too big for his shoulders, stood before a yellow rose with his eyes closed to the dying sunlight as his lips moved silently in prayer.

Reaching up he wiped the back of his hand under his nose as one of the shopping bags at his feet crinkled and slumped over as he waited a few more moments before opening his eyes again and taking a deep breath.

"Needs must," he said, reaching down for the bags.

He would wait a little while longer before donning his cap again, but for now he made his way down the path, the bags tugging at his arms, towards the orange light of the evening sun bathing the spires and rooftops in the distance.

Why do things have to change?

Why can't things be the way they were?

Why did you have to die?

And then he thought of the story the old woman had once told him, of the fledgling forced out of its nest, of what might happen if it never left, if nothing changed, if nothing ever moved on.

His eyes stung as he walked out of the gate and into the deserted street, his fingers growing numb as he whispered to himself, "But why, Gran, why?"

"Because even wee baby birds have to learn to fly on their own, Alex," he remembered her saying.

He let the bags rest against his legs as he stood at the bus stop with only memories and the stories he would tell Jamie about her.

~~*

"Tell me some more, Eck," Jamie said slumping back on the sofa.

Alex huffed then twiddled his thumbs. "Suppose I could tell you some more concerning my gran," he said.

"Go on then."

"Okay, well, ' I could do with a bit fush,' Gran used say.

"Fush?" Jamie asked.

"Aye, fush," Alex said. "That's how she used to say it 'fussshhh'. Like with a long shush at the end ... fuh-hush. So anyway then I would say to her, 'Gran, don't you mean fish?' Cause her bottom jaw used to stick right out, right?" Alex demonstrated, thrusting out his chin. "Jusht like that. Fush, fuh-hush. Anyway, then she used to say to me, 'Ooo, Elex, you mean feesh?' That was her trying to sound right posh. 'No, Gran,' I said. 'I mean fush'... God now I'm saying it."

Alex wiped the back of his hand over his gob. "'Fish,' I said to her. 'Fish.' God, now I'm slavering everywhere. So anyway, 'Aye fish,' I said, 'Fish. No fush or feesh, but fish.' And I know I was only a bairn at the time, Jamie, but she also used to tell me that humans had three sets of teeth in their lifetimes."

"Oh aye," Jamie said resting his head back on the arm of the sofa.

"Temporary, permanent ..."

"Aye?"

"... And false."

Jamie rolled up his eyes.

"Derek used say it was because of her teeth that my gran talked like that," Alex said. "She had false ones, see? Wallies. But Derek told me that Gran's false teeth were better than the ones in the right olden days, though, like false teeth were different in the *olden* olden days."

"Different how?" Jaime asked.

"Derek said they were made out of different stuff when false teeth were first invented," Alex sniffed.

"What stuff?"

"Cement."

"Cement!" Jamie's head shot up off the sofa arm.

"Aye, cement," Alex said.

"Away you go."

"No, it's true. Derek told me."

"It must be gospel then," Jamie said, wriggling back into a more comfortable position, "if the Kelty klyper said it."

"I think he was having me on though," Alex said.

"You only think so?" Jamie said. "You mean you don't know?"

"You would think I would know though, aye?" Alex said. "Concrete falsers would be a bit hard on the gum line, would they no?"

"Aye, they would."

"I suppose," Alex said. "I didn't think of it at the time Derek first told me. But anyway, he also used to tell me that they would make false teeth in all different colors as well back then, when the National Health Service first started off that is. Like the time when they used to make specs out of pink wire just to make poor folk stand out like dense eejits. So they would make falsers in all different colors, like purple and orange, just to make sure everyone would know where you got them from. Anyway, that was before the ones they give folk nowhere days, before modern ones was invented."

"And you used to believe him too," Jamie shook his head. "I don't know, Eck, but you're awfully naive sometimes. You really are."

"What do you mean?" Alex jumped in.

"Cement falsers, that's what I mean."

"They were made out of cement," Alex said settling back. "Well, something close."

"Like?"

"Well—"

"Come on, come on. What?"

"Concrete!"

~~*

And now the air was still. The trees at the other side of the road stood crammed together behind a wall as if they had run into it, trapped, their sprint for freedom ended by carefully placed man made rocks. To Alex it seemed as if the trees had been penned in like wild animals in a zoo, only realizing too late how trapped they were.

A breeze passed through them and their leaves shook as if in protest.

He wondered of how trees would look if there were no walls in the world, where there was nothing to shut them in or out, their freedom being where they grew.

And would they be anymore more free if there were no walls anyway?

Something clicked inside of Alex then. That it was too late when you found out that your roots had grown their own prison sentence and that bars had grown up around you the in your act of standing still. Your freedom imprisoned when you were too busy growing, too busy looking the wrong way, too busy being distracted. Too blind to see how you were being nailed in place.

Maybe that was why the fledgling needed a nudge. But a nudge is a nudge and a push is a push. And with his grandmother now gone it had felt like neither of those but a painful kick.

Alex shook his head just as a wren, a tiny brown speck of a thing, flew out of the trees and landed on top of the wall on the opposite side of the road.

He watched as it stood sideways on, cocking its head to the side as if looking at him. Then it jumped up as if in indignation, its wings buzzing so fast Alex could hardly make them out. Then it flew up a few inches and landed back on the wall again, flicking it little tail up in the air before flying down to the pavement to bob along through the dust and grit, continuing to flick its tail all the while. Alex felt himself frown as he watched but before he could think of why he was doing so the wren was up in the air again, chirping as it flew over his head.

When the bus finally arrived, he climbed on board and staggered to the back, the bags catching on shoulders and silver poles before he finally managed to dump them onto the seat and sit himself between them. Then, protectively, to stop them falling over as the bus pulled away, he stretched his arms out over them and for all the world looked like a little emperor in his oversized jacket slumped between the bags as he was.

A young mother in the seat in front moved her baby from one arm to the other. The baby, in wide-eyed wonder, looked over his mother's shoulder at Alex. And since no one was looking at him, Alex lifted his hand and wiggled his fingers as if they were inside an invisible glove puppet. The baby's bright blue eyes followed the movements of Alex's fingers then back to Alex's eyes and smiled.

And settled for the time being, bus swaying, Alex gazed down the aisle, between hypnotically glinting rails, and drifted off into a revere with his grandmother's voice playing over in his mind.

~~*

"It, her, your sister," Gran said, "was like an Easter egg, only one made out of white chocolate. Though knowing your mother I found that a bit of a surprise, if not a shock."

"Eh?" an eight-year-old Alex said, perplexed.

Fit to burst after his grandmother's home cooked Sunday lunch, he slumped back in the armchair opposite.

"Never mind," Gran said her knitting needles clacking furiously as she sucked her falsers in and out faster than a fiddler's elbow at the MOD. "You're no auld enough yet to know about the fact that your mother was something that rhymes with a shed."

Alex frowned, cockeyed in concentration, tightening his mouth as he looked up at a corner of the ceiling wondering what she meant.

"Anyway—" Gran dragged out the word, "—she, it, her, your sister, whatever it is, looked like a big egg, only one with four matchsticks sticking out of it for arms and legs. And no difference between the neck and waist either. Hah! What waist? It was a head that was stuck on, if you'll excuse ma French here, Alex, a space-hopper.

"Still, it was a bairn. At least I think it was a bairn. And she still looks the same way from the back, if you get my drift. Only bigger, with a humph and a fat ark with pipe cleaners hanging out of it for legs. And those all buckled to boot under the strain of all that blubber. I'm surprised your mother didn't explode giving birth to it," she sighed. "Still, truth's stranger than fiction they say, until it comes to your brother and sister.

"But you're different, Alex," she leaned forward, face crinkling in a smile.

"Because I'm the bairn of the family?" Alex piped up slumping deeper into the big fat cushions, his eyes wide, egging on his grandmother for more of the same.

"Because you were a real stunner when you were born," she said glaring and tutting at the missed stitches of her knitting before going on. "You still are a stunner and always will be, mark my words. Though I had to check your name band just to make sure you really were who your mother claimed you were. It was that unbelievable. You were nothing like the first two, you see," she said, her voice dropping. "Nothing like your sister Thelma or that sleekit-eyed git, Derek, your brother. A stunner you were, aye. And come to think of it, the only way your sister ever stunned anybody was when she fell on them. Timber!" Gran cried out and Alex chuckled.

"No, Alex," she said, "you were different, are different. The bonniest bairn I ever saw. And to think you came out of something that rhymes with shed. Unbelievable."

Alex sniffed and looked up at the corner of the ceiling again. Shed, lead, bed... he thought of words that sounded the same as he sucked on his gob stopper. Red, bread ... hmm. He shook his noddle and tightened his mouth— nope, can't think.

Doesn't matter.

"... Your eyes," his grandmother spoke again.

Alex blinked and snapped his eyes wider. "My eyes, Gran?"

"Yes." She nodded knowingly. "You can tell a lot about folk by their eyes. And there's something special about yours. Not stuck on the one side of your head special, but ..." She lost herself in thought for a second. "Eyes full of innocence and awareness at the same time. That's what I mean about your eyes. Aye, and China blue to boot. Gorgeous.

"Now your brother," she sighed, "he has eyes like a snake. And Thelma, the one that looks like an elephant without legs because they've sunk into her with the weight of all the blubber they're holding up. Well she has eyes that look as if they're having a hard time catching up with the front of her head. Deep set! Any deeper and they would be sticking out the back on stalks, which would suit her to a tee."

~~*

Alex stepped off the bus and listened to it purr away into the distance before he dared to gaze up at the building before him, at the brass nameplate at the side of the door.

Seeing it now, he wished nothing more than to walk away, unseen, to slink off and hope it would all take care of itself. But the name etched into the brass was the same as that on the letter and he had already put it off for too long.

After giving the receptionist his name, he sat and waited, clock ticking as he looked around at the off-white walls. And after what seemed like an age, a telephone rang. The receptionist answered, nodded over at Alex and told him that he could go in now.

Once inside the office, he sat with cap in hand, feeling scruffy and threadbare in front of a man in a pinstripe suit, glad that the half-moon spectacles perched on the man's nose were aimed at the papers on his desk and not at him.

Words came at him, fluttering like moths to a light bulb, tapping against the glass, until Alex felt stunned blinking and wondering at what they all meant. Except for the part that Alex was to be the only one at the reading of his grandmother's will.

And everything, the solicitor said, was to be Alex's with only one condition; the trinkets, the photographs, the furniture, were to be sold off, or disposed of. Alex wouldn't have to worry about how it was done, as everything would be taken care of. It had been his grandmother's wish that Alex, would not be burdened with the wherewithal of the process.

Alex would have nothing to do except gain from what little there would be left when everything was sold off. His grandmother had come into the world with nothing and it was her wish that she leave it the same way.

Her reasons were quite simple, the solicitor read from the will. She did not wish Alex to be lumbered with the past. She did not want her grandson to hang on and mourn for things that would never return.

"Except for one thing," the solicitor said.

The walls seemed as thick as a safe's as Alex sat, eyes concentrating on the edge of the desk between them, at the dark mahogany, the grain of the wood. A smell of bee's wax wafted through the air, a half-forgotten undertone reminding him of his grandmother's polishing tin.

"'Alex has his own life now,'" the solicitor read, "'and he is to be freed of the burden of trying to keep alive the memory of an old woman.'"

Alex twisted his cap in his hands and looked up at this man, this stranger who seemed to have the power to take away everything from him, at his steel-grey hair, neat and trimmed.

Not like a vulture at all, Alex thought. Though why he should think that of the man Alex wasn't sure.

The solicitor's words continued to spill out at him.

If any money was left over then Alex would have it. Alex was the sole beneficiary. His grandmother had been emphatic.

Alex felt not only as if he had been kicked out of the nest, but that it had also been destroyed so that he couldn't return to it either.

It struck him then that his grandmother had been cruel. And as he listened, a lump pushed up into his throat. But he was determined he would not break down in front of this stranger. He was a man now after all, almost eighteen, and if any crying was to be done it would be done when he was alone.

Alex's thoughts began to wander off to all of the work he had put into Gran's house in the last few years, nothing much at first. Just sorting a few rickety shelves here and there, a fresh lick of paint where it was needed. Later he had become more adventurous, fixing electrical plugs, renewing wall sockets until eventually his abilities had extended to doing some rewiring, mending bits of plumbing and replacing some old floorboards.

And his grandmother had smiled as he did all this when he had given up his Saturday afternoons and sometimes Sundays too to do it all. Even when he had been covered in plaster and dust, she had continued to tell him her stories.

The solicitor's voice snapped him back to the present.

"There's only one thing you can keep and do with what you wish," he said.

Alex couldn't think of anything that could be left.

And as he sat there, his heart sank again as he thought of the old house, the one that his grandmother had rented for so long. Only now it would be passed on to strangers.

The lump in his throat swelled even bigger at the thought.

The solicitor paused with his words and looked over his spectacles at Alex and Alex felt himself shrinking under the man's gaze, shrinking into a world from the past, one that was safe but now no longer there. For the nest was now empty, Alex realized, and the shrubs surrounding it that he had trimmed to perfection, were now to be for someone else. It seemed unfair, a final insult to his grieving.

The solicitor laid Alex's grandmother's will down on his desk. Alex had now been forced to sail back to the present, away from thoughts of the house, his grandmother, the way she laughed, the way she had always made him laugh, at her bawdy humor, her stories, and for a few seconds he just sat there, unthinking, numb.

"Proceeds from after sales, minus charges come to one-thousand three-hundred and three pounds and twenty-six pence," the solicitor said. "And her bank accounts yielded a further two-thousand and six hundred pounds, plus interest."

Alex looked at the man in the eye for the first time and tightened his mouth for fear of blurting out his grief. He only nodded slightly, as tears threatened to well up in his eyes.

The solicitor cleared his throat and leaned back, the evening sun dying through the window behind him as he pulled out his desk drawer.

"This, however, is yours to do with what you wish, Mister McMullen," he said.

He pushed an envelope across the desk to Alex.

Not yet eighteen and he calls me Mister, Alex thought. The sound of it made him squirm uncomfortably.

He looked at the envelope, then at the solicitor again. "What is it?" he asked.

"It's yours," the solicitor said and leaned back.

Alex, intimidated by the unfamiliar and official, let the envelope lie there, unsure of what he was to do with it, as if something bad would happen if he reached out and touched it.

His cap dropped to the floor as he leaned forward, his fingers reaching out.

The solicitor spoke again. "My office will be pleased to take care of things, if and when you decide what to do," he said holding his hands together as if in prayer, the tips of his fingers touching his mouth.

He looked over his spectacles once more at Alex as Alex picked up the envelope.

There didn't feel like there was much inside it.

"All you need to do now is to sign here," the solicitor said with a sigh, pushing a form at him, his chair creaking.

Still clutching the envelope, Alex looked apprehensively at the man, for signing, he realized, would feel like the key that locked the door on his grandmother's life. And besides, the only other official thing Alex had signed before was a bail bond for his brother, Derek. And that had cost him a hundred quid when Derek had failed to turn up in court. Even then Alex had had to pay the fifty pound fine for him as well.

"And that's it?" Alex asked, swallowing hard, looking at the sheet of paper then at the man.

The solicitor nodded. "Yes, everything. Though I wish to say how sorry I am for the lost of your dearly beloved grandmother. And if you do need assistance with anything in the future, I will be only happy to take care of everything for you."

The solicitor pulled out a pen from his inside pocket, unscrewed the top and handed it to Alex.

Alex took it, felt the warmth of it between his fingers, but still unsure.

"Just here and here," the solicitor said pointing to two lines. "It's just my way of discharging my duties as executor to your grandmother's will."

Alex inched to the edge of his seat, reached out, clutching at the pen as he bit his lip.

He peered in closer at the page. "Here and here?" he asked, looking up.

"Yes, both lines, if you please."

Alex signed on the lines and laid the pen down.

At that the solicitor stood up sharply, smiled, leaned over the desk and held out his hand.

Alex picked his cap up from the floor, stuffed the envelope into his pocket, and shook hands with the solicitor before reaching down for the bags and saying his thanks before leaving.

And as he walked out of the office, past the secretary, the envelope in his pocket, the bags pulled down on his arms heavier than ever, a change had happened, Alex realized, but it was something for which he had no words as he climbed down the steps to the pavement.

The deserted street blurred as he walked along with the sun turning into a dying ochre beyond the rooftops and trees behind him. Taking a quick look back to make sure that no one was around to see him he reached up, bag swinging from his arm, and wiped his nose with his sleeve. Only that seemed to make it everything worse, a feeling from nowhere, a silent pain of emptiness where his heart had always been.

"Why, Gran, why."

And although he didn't know it yet, it had also been his last time at the Garden of Remembrance.

CHaPTer 2

Alex staggered through the kitchen door with his arms stretched to dislocation under the weight of the bags, past Jamie, who was leaning against the back wall his arms folded tight as high-tension coat hanger wire.

Alex stopped, looked at him, and then over to Derek, smooth as newly poured plaster over a hand grenade, slumped at the kitchen table.

Alex took a few more steps over to the table and set down the bags.

"What's going on?" he asked, weary, looking from one to the other and finally settling on Derek.

No one spoke.

"Well?" he prompted raising his eyebrows.

Still no one answered.

He looked at Derek. Derek looked at him and raised corners of his mouth, until they almost reached his eyes.

"Look, I'm tired," Alex said, "I'm knackered, and my feet are killing me, never mind my arms. So somebody talk, because I can tell something's up."

Derek lurched forward, slapping his hands on the table. "Watch out for the guy way the big shovel," he snapped then threw himself back with a self-satisfied smug.

"What guy way what shovel?" Alex asked wearily pulling the cap from his head.

"When you get to Amsterdam," Derek explained gleefully.

Alex dumped himself down on a chair glad the table was between them both.

"What guy?" he asked, trying hard not to look perplexed and anxious.

"The guy with the big green hat, big yellow rubber hands and a great big shovel," Derek let rip, then bit his lower lip in a bucktoothed grin.

"In Amsterdam?" Alex asked.

"Aye, when you get off the bus." Derek beamed knowingly. "The bus you get from the boat."

Alex rubbed his eyes then blinked at his brother. "So what does this geezer way the green hat, yellow grippers and shovel do?" he asked.

"Clobbers you over the head way his shovel." Derek smiled like a knowing snake.

"What!" Alex yelped.

"Of course it could be a rubber shovel. Or it could be a real one. But that's the trick, you see. You don't know until it brains you," Derek explained in terrifying detail.

Alex's eyebrows narrowed to a worried V. "And what's he doing bashing folk over the head for?" he asked, knowing he shouldn't.

Derek shrugged, nonchalant like. "It's Amsterdam."

Alex frowned and tightened his mouth.

Derek watched the effect this was having on his little brother and bit his lip in an attempt to stop his glee from showing. He widened his eyes slightly but caught himself in time before he looked too pleased. "And he shouts, as well!" He lurched forward again.

Alex jumped back and almost fell off his chair. "Shouts what?" he asked.

"Amsterdam yah bass!" Derek provided the elucidating key to the riddle. "Then he clobbers you over the head way his great big cast-iron shovel. Then he laughs, chortle chortle, tee hee hee. Amsterdamers think it's funny, they being clog-wearing weirdoes, like. It's just what you need after a long tiring journey, Alex, a flat head. Still, if you think it's worth it."

"You're talking rot," Jamie cut in from behind.

"I'm not going," Alex said, shooting a look at Jamie.

"Yar going!" Jamie said. Then to the back of Derek's head, "And you stop telling him rubbish. It's hard enough to get him to go anywhere."

"Should've got the plane then," Derek said, still looking at Alex.

"I hate flying," Alex said.

"You've never even been on a plane!"

"And I don't have to sniff cyanide either to prove I don't like it."

Jamie turned on Derek, waving a finger at him. "You just leave him alone," he warned.

"I'm only just saying." Derek said, sighing as he admired his nails chewed to the quick. He took another nibble. "You could've taken Sleazy jet. It would have been much faster than the boat anyway."

"Vomit comet," Alex said, pulling a face.

Derek shrugged.

"Anyway, planes crash."

Jamie jumped in. "And where have I heard that one before?"

"Boats sink, as well, Eck," Derek said reeling the bait out to his little brother.

"That's it!" Alex said, jumping up from the chair. "I'm not going."

"Yar going. It's paid for," Jamie said. "And you stop scaring your wee bra," he said to Derek. "I knew I shouldn't have let you in the door, yah creep. Alex and me need this holiday. So we're going and that's that!"

"What about the guy way the big shovel?" Alex nearly screamed.

"Stop being such a gullible bairn. There isn't any geezer with a shovel, big or otherwise. Derek's just making it up. He's never been and further than Kelty beach so what would he know anyway?"

"I was told," Derek beamed knowingly, looking at Alex.

"Told my toenails," Jamie cut in, launching himself a foot away from the wall.

"It was on the telly," Derek went on regardless.

"Awe aye, I forgot," Jamie said, "Everything's on the telly. And if it's on the telly then it must be real, right? That's if it *was* on the telly, and I doubt it."

"It was on that program, *EuroKrap*."

Jamie laughed. "And just about your level of understanding," he sneered. "I'm surprised you managed to pull yourself away long enough from your knocked off collection of the Tweenies."

Jamie walked up to Alex and put a hand on his shoulder. "We're going."

"But Derek said," Alex spluttered, then turned to Derek. "You wouldn't lie to your own wee brother, would you, Derek?"

Alex sat down again.

"I wouldn't lie to you, Alex," Derek said soothingly his eyes looking up, lids fluttering—flip flap.

"He's a liar all right," Jamie cut in.

"He doesn't tell lies, at least he says he doesn't," Alex said, looking at Jamie.

"He lies all the time," Jamie said, then to the back of Derek's head, "but you wouldn't catch him out on Hilary Bile's lie detector boo hiss show I can tell you that, because your brother's that good at it."

"And you don't watch the telly, of course," Derek said. "So is that before or after you've bashed in the lucky numbers on the phone for Midday Money?"

Jamie glared at the back of Derek's head.

Derek gave Alex a black-bordered condolence card look. "Alex, I'm your big bra," he said. "Remember that."

"At least me and Eck don't have our DNA on a criminal data base," Jamie said. "Which I have no doubt will come in handy one day, like proving that you two can't be possibly related. Yah *get*!"

Jamie only said it because he often hoped that Alex had somehow ended up in the family from hell as a matter of alien intervention. It was like finding a lamb born into the company of werewolves, and with Alex, the youngest, intimidated into looking after the older two when it should have been the other way around.

It was Alex who had held the family together when their mother had died. It was Alex who had left school and worked in one dumb job after another to put food on the table while his older siblings followed through with one disastrous lifestyle after another. It was always Alex who had bailed them out of trouble. It was always Alex who had provided food and shelter, a loving and a caring atmosphere. It was always Alex who took the flack with a shrug of his shoulders.

And now Derek wanted to throw the spanner in the works of them taking a short holiday. And Jamie could see why.

With Alex gone, who could they run to when things went wrong?

Why couldn't they stand up for themselves and leave Alex and Jamie alone and get on with their own lives?

Fury sprang up inside him as he paced across the floor, stopped at the counter, gripped it by the edge and tried to squeeze the wood into splinters with his bare hands.

Facing the wall he muttered under his breath, "We're going, going, gone. And that's it!"

"I'm not going," Alex said, sinking into his chair.

Derek's mouth turned up at the corners like the thin tight lips of a cobra.

Still facing the wall Jamie said, "If you don't go, Eck, I'll tell."

Alex twisted around looked at Jamie's back.

"Tell what?" he asked.

Jamie took a deep breath. "I didn't want to say this Eck," he said. "But I've had you googled."

"You've googled me?" Alex said.

"Interesting." Derek eyes flashed at Alex with renewed curiosity.

"What were you googling me for?" Alex asked.

"You can't be sure who you're living with these days, can you, Eck?" Jamie sniffed.

Alex's jaw dropped. Derek looked at him. Alex's eyes widened, his neck sinking into his shoulders as his head turned from side to side, lowering, until his nose scrapped at his collar.

Derek raised an eyebrow. His neck extended.

Alex slid further down in his chair.

"What are you hiding from us?" Derek asked his incredible shrinking wee brother.

"Aye, tell, Eck," Jamie said, turning around to face them and folding his arms, legs at ease.

Derek leaned further into the table.

Alex slid further under it.

"Tell what?" Derek eyes flicked wide.

Alex continued to turn his head from side to side as if he was trying to screw himself through the floor. His mouth sunk below his collar like a periscope beneath the waves.

Just then the foundations shook.

The door rattled in its frame.

"What in hell's name's that?" Jamie yelled, arm flying wide at the racket.

The kitchen door handle twiggled.

"I think somebody's trying to get in," Alex said, voice muffled by his collar.

"Or something is," Derek said.

The door sprung wide smashing into the wall.

Sharp intake of breath one and all as the trio looked on in awe.

There was a faint whirr of electric motors.

"Would you look it that," Derek said as the thing rolled in.

"What's with the wheelchair?" Jamie asked it.

"The Incredible Bulk meets the Matrix," Derek said.

The wheelchair rolled in. And sitting crow barred into it was Alex and Derek's older sister, Thelma.

"Something tells me I shouldn't be surprised to see *her* turning up," Jamie said. "Where'd she get it, the wheelchair?"

"I saw her eyeing it up it the jumble sale," Derek said.

"It must've coast a bomb if it can climb stairs as well," Alex said. "We're three flights up."

"It was being sold for a fiver," Derek said. "I fixed some extra gears on it. No bad, eh?"

"No bad if you could use your talents on getting a job, Derek," Alex said, "instead of sitting at home making toys."

"Know this," Jamie said. "When Madam Curry invented radiation, it didn't take some bright spark long to build a bomb with it instead of keeping it for radiating folk with for cures. Give Derek an innocent spanner and he finds a way to build a stair-climbing tank for transporting lard where it's not wanted."

"Stop picking on me," Derek whined.

"And you bought it for a fiver, Derek?" Jamie went on a renewed attack. "That wheelchair shouldn't even be on sale. It belongs to the National Health Service!"

The wheelchair stopped its relentless forward momentum.

Thelma's eyes scanned the room from behind dark glasses, Klatuu like (The Day the Earth Shuddered to a Crunch), as her thick-as-Fairtrade banana-sized fingers twitched on the joystick.

Motors whirred into action again.

The little fat wheels crawled forward.

Thelma's face remained tight.

"What's with the Hellraiser look," Jamie asked.

Derek raised an eyebrow.

Jamie sucked at the side of his mouth he saw how much the wheelchair's little fat wheels were flattened by Thelma's ample mass.

Thelma had a white face. She also had scarlet lips, insulating tape for eyebrows, black hair, and no neck. She looked like a cross between Davros and Jabba the Butt. She was also what Maggie the Cat might call one of '*tham thar no neck mansters*'.

"It's like something out of *Forbidden Planet*," Derek said. "Robbie the obese rowboat."

"Naw, it looks more like something out of that ancient film *Hellraiser*. Looks like a Cenobite." Jamie said as he thrust himself up onto the bunker, just in case some evil goo might flood the decks and see them all melt.

Derek had been fond of telling Jamie of the night Thelma had been working at the local newsagent, cum grocer, cum cheap-tacky-toys-that-fall-to-bits-as-soon-as-you-look-at-them, cum lottery and bingo-zingo cards, cum sell-anything-for-a-fast-buck shop—booze, cigs, lighter fluid, Yoo Hoo-in-an-empty-crisp packet. The kind of place that had electrified chicken wire draped over the Lucky Bags, as Derek told it.

It had been another one of Thelma's relentless pursuits to keep down a career, Derek had informed Jamie. They had struck up a sort of friendship back then. The kind of forced upon, captive audience friendship one has to put up with once in a while. Until you get so jaded and sick and tired of having to put up with it, and this being before the real rot, and Derek's scheming and lies had set in as far as Jamie was concerned, so he had listened.

But no matter, it had been one of many tales Derek would tell. Most of them lies, or fantasies, or truth and lies mixed up into a sticky alchemic yuck. The point was, to Jamie at least, Alex's big brother Derek couldn't, it seems, actually tell which from which. And to the point, it didn't seem to matter as long as Derek could convince himself, and anyone else daft enough to listen, that his stories were all, in fact, fact.

Right.

So Jamie had listened.

It had been nearing Guy Fawkes Night and the shop owner had been fretting about his fireworks going moldy before they could be sold. Something had to be done. And as any proper, little Hitler employer would do in his position, he thought up a brilliant plan. A very good plan to get sales going. It was an even better plan because he, the shop owner, Derek had said, wasn't involved in it.

"Thelma was."

So, every fifteen minutes the light in the shop would dim from brain stunning bright to darker and from darker to zero—blackout, which meant shoppers, and auld-granny-glue-sniffers, ended up colliding blindly into each other in the aisles.

It was then Thelma's job to stop whatever she was doing and jump up onto the big metal box, storing the fireworks therein for safety reasons. She then had to light two sparklers and wave them around in the stratosphere, as high as the weight "hanging off her fat armpits would allow," Derek had told Jamie. She was to paint big pretty circles in the dark for all to see and to ooh and aah at. Thelma had tried spelling *Stuff This For A Laff*, but she couldn't get her arms to move fast enough apparently. Too much wind resistance. The night before's radioactive vidaloo.

So one fated night, at the allotted time, the shop plunged into darkness, at which point Thelma stomped out her cig and whispered, "For Christ's sake, tot again," and dutifully did as she was bid according to the mysterious invisible contract she could never remember sighing, and to which it was alluded, she had to do whatever she was damn well told, "Or *else*!"

Everyone had turned to the sound of Thelma's bow-legged-with-the-strain stilettos screeching and slithering all over the metal top of the fireworks box, to the sound of it buckling under her bulk, and to Thelma's dulcet tones and poetic words: "Don't give me a hand then, will you!"

She held back on calling her boss by his *real* real name though—*Bastard Face*—as she had clambered her way up.

And after a few minutes of skint knees, burst tights, grunts and puffing, and hearing the magic words from the boss, "the hand that holds the dosh cracks the whip," Thelma had wobbled upright with her stilettos threatening to puncture the metal top of the fireworks box.

She then, Derek said, had lit two gigantic Nuclear Fairy Sky Blaster Sparklers (special edition Burn Down The Neighborhood For A Laugh Buckfast Bazookas) and waved her arms around like a seagull with a constipated smile. She painted light in the air. She wobbled and wibbled and her heels created yet more sparks as they screeched beneath her.

"You see," Derek had said, "Thelma was the only girl in town to sport iron seggs in her car-boot-sale, real imitation plastic Prada clodhoppers."

Then according to Derek it all went wrong. Whether the top of the box caved in under the weight of the Colossus of Kelty, or that it was in fact a trapdoor filled with dynamite, we shall never know, Derek had said with tears of laughter in his eyes.

It was never easy to get rid of rubbish staff, like Thelma, apparently, he told Jamie. Too many rules and regulations, the boss would complain. But the fact was, Thelma had last been seen to be dancing around on the box faster than Michael Fat Ark's Feet in the Fire Grate.

Smoke had begun to rise up alarmingly from the soles of her feet. The heat, it was said, melting her Pradas. And that fact alone had broken her. "I've been conned," she was heard to yell. "Leather doesn't melt." And Pradas don't cost a fiver a pair out the back of a Robin Reliant, either, Jamie had thought to himself as he'd listened. But he let Derek continue on with his fascinating diatribe.

A more likely explanation was that a spark had "dropped into her barrage-balloons-for-knickers, Christ knows," Derek explained with the scientific demeanor of the Nutty Confessor.

Although, it has to be said, Jamie took with a pinch of salt Derek's report of a crispy smoldering lump of lard found three miles away on Kelty beach with only two buckled sparklers in its mitts as a clue to its identity. Thelma, Derek said, was still waving her arms around even as they dragged her out of the crater, to the sound of her immortal words, "Get your shparklurzz here."

"The impact even registered on that Richter scale thingy as far away as *Edinburgh*," Derek informed Jamie in all sincerity. "Swung it right off its hinges, it did."

The fact that Edinburgh recorded earthquakes from the whole planet, as Jamie already knew, did not seem to register in Derek's noddle. It would seem, it was a subject too far out there, Jamie surmised wisely. Besides, Jamie had seen the damn Richter scale swingy-thingy for himself once when on a trip through to the big city with the boys from the home for himself. And it was Jamie's subjects at school—geography and geology—that he was good at that finally told him that Derek had porridge for brains. But nay matter.

And that was the saddest part of remembering the story that Derek had told him, remembering the boys' home he had been brought up in. On leaving it at the age of seventeen, a year ago now, and a long time in teen years, he had vowed to never think about it again, to block it from his mind. Yet there it had nipped in. And there was still too much pain that needed kept in place, pain to be avoided at all costs.

Thelma inched closer in her wheelchair to the table. A little fat wheel with a great big impact rolled over Derek's foot.

"Hey, watch it, Cast-Ironside."

Thelma fiddled with her joystick and rolled over his foot, two, three times, before she got the hang of it and slammed into the table.

"I'm depressed," something said.

They all looked around for the source of the weird sounding voice.

The electronic voice thing made some strange little phut phut noises before they realized it was coming from a gadget strapped to the front of Thelma's *Theeze-are-my-moun-taaaaaaanes* bazoombas.

"I'm depreooooossht!" it said again slowing to a stop.

"Awe God!" Thelma's scarlet and elastic-for-lips spoke.

"It speaks," Derek observed.

"Sounds like it's needing more coal," Jamie said as he slid off the bunker, safe in the knowledge that the thing Thelma was sitting in could do no longer do harm now that it was out of juice.

Alex jumped up from his chair, and called out, "Anybody for coffee?"

The evil spell had been broken for the time being, Jamie noted. And maybe Alex would forget about his fears of going on holiday. And with any luck Derek would also forget about being scared if his little brother Alex did.

Saying nothing as Thelma spoke to Derek, Jamie picked up the bags Alex had brought back from the supermarket. He did however counter the brevity of his miscalculated movements with, "Jesus Christ! What's in these bloody bags?" when he suffered their full weight.

With a struggle he hefted them up and dumped them on the bunker as Alex filled the kettle.

Lifting out the items one by one Jamie caught Alex looking at him, smiling sheepishly, as if Alex were asking for an unspoken truce. Jamie smiled back.

Suddenly Alex reached out and gave Jamie a quick hug around the shoulders. "Don't worry," he whispered close to Jamie's ear. "I'm still going with you."

Then all too quickly, Alex pulled away and busied himself with making something to drink for them all.

"Hey, lover boys, where's the *coffee*?" Derek called out.

"The kettle's no even boiled yet," Alex called over his shoulder.

"It's not the kettle we're worried about, it's the water that's in it," Thelma cackled. And as an afterthought: "Anything for eating in this joint, brother man?"

Later Alex asked Jamie what Jamie had found out about him, the googling.

"That you lied about your age for one," Jamie said.

"Eh?"

"Says you're ninety-four, a billionaire, and a author to boot, you never live anywhere for any length of time and that you're hard to pin down. A right mystery. Didn't find out much more because the boss came back in and I had to pretend I was working."

Alex sighed in relief. Sort of.

"But it wasn't really me, was it, Jamie?"

"Didn't find any pictures to tell me otherwise, Eck. You tell me."

CHAPTER 3

Rather than coal, Thelma stoked up on whatever Alex, her wee brother, placed in front of her: roast chicken, chips, beans, half a loaf of Mother's Pride—plain only, "None of that pan loaf crap"—(Derek shoveled in the other half), and a brick of Stork. Jamie, the outsider in this trio of familial slobbering, always refused to sit at the same trough as Alex's siblings and preferred to humph it in the front room and fizz with temper instead.

Which was where he was now.

The door opened a crack and Alex peeked around the side with an uncertain smile on his face. Jamie didn't turn away from the television even as Alex half stepped into the room.

"Not hungry?" Alex asked with an apologetic lilt.

"No!"

"Och Jamie, don't be like that," Alex said, sidling further into the room.

"Like what?" Jamie asked, still not taking his eyes from the television.

"Like that."

"I'm just watching the telly," Jamie said, throwing himself back on the old sofa, crossing his legs and arms defensively. Even from this far away down the hall he could hear the irritating clacking and scraping of knives and forks on plates. There was a resounding belch that sounded as if it could have come from the innards of elephant seal.

"Pigs," Jamie said under his breath, closing his eyes.

"You don't like them, do you?"

"Correct!"

"They're my brother in sister, Jamie. They're all I've got."

Jamie turned to him open-mouthed. "And what am I? Something the cat barfed up?"

Alex was confused. "But we don't have a cat," he said.

Jamie looked at him. "See what I mean, Eck?" he said. "You don't take me seriously."

"I know what you mean, Jamie," Alex spoke softly.

"No you don't know what I mean, Eck. They two are parasites. You do too much for them, and that's what bugs me." Then he thought about it and his arms shot up in the air. "What am I saying? You do *everything* for them!"

Alex sat down at the other end of the sofa and sighed. One of the springs made a disconcerting twang beneath him. "I just wish you would all get on better," he said. "That's all."

"They're pigs," Jamie snapped. "They're freeloaders. They're older than you and it should be the other way around. They should be looking out for you, not you looking out for them."

Alex was confused again. "That I should be a freeloading pig, you mean?"

Jamie gasped wide mouthed. "Now you're just twisting my words," he said. "You know what I'm talking about. They should be looking out for you, their wee bra, not you looking after them. That's what I mean."

Alex shrugged and huffed. Lips tight, his cheeks puffed up as he tried to smile, only his eyes weren't in it. There was no use pushing the situation when Jamie was feeling so bad. The best thing was to leave him be for a while, for Jamie to settled things in his own way in his own time.

Alex pushed down on his knees and stood up as if with some great effort, and turned away. It had been enough of a day without this. He was still under the sadness he had experienced at the Garden of Remembrance. The yellow rose was still in his mind's eye, the rose he had picked out in his grandmother's memory, a rose he had paid for to be looked after and tended for the next ten years. Not a long enough time, he'd thought, given that his grandmother had lived more than seven times longer. The yellow rose, a lonely thing in the dying light, one rose amongst many, like trees trapped behind a wall.

His grandmother had been right, he'd supposed, to have everything she owned sold off, that he, Alex, shouldn't be lumbered with material things, only to benefit from the proceeds of everything after it had been sold off, and that not much in the end. Not that Alex was concerned about material benefits, but he only wished that she had left him something to remember her by.

Memories are one thing, she had stated in her will, being chained to what an old woman had feathered her nest with would be a life sentence. She loved her wee Alex too much for him to suffer for someone who would never return.

Even now he couldn't bear to open the letter she had left him, the one the old solicitor had handed over. It was still inside his jacket pocket. Maybe he would never open it, too frightened that the emotional floodgates he never knew he had inside of him would open again.

Along the dark corridor, not trusting yet to walk back into the kitchen where his brother and sister sat eating as if the world had never stopped spinning, he locked himself in the bathroom, grabbed a towel and buried his face in its softness and screamed.

He was still suffering from the shock of having to arrange her funeral on his own, picking out her coffin, talking to the minister, a bald thin man, sympathetic and with swollen knuckles for worry beads.

The truth be told, no one liked his grandmother. She had no friends or family except for Alex, Thelma and Derek. But Alex had never known her to be otherwise kind and loving to him. It had saddened him that even after the notice he had put into the paper that so few had turned up for her funeral.

But true to his duty he had stood at the chapel doors and shook hands with the few who had.

Not one of them had included his brother or sister. He had told them, of course, date, time and place. But all they did was shrug. They hardly knew her, Alex was her favorite after all. They never got a look in. Their mother's mother or no, it made no difference to them. She was an old cantankerous woman to them. Thelma and Derek had said as much. Neither got along with her. Neither one had seen her since they were toddlers. Even then she had taken an instant dislike to them.

So they said.

In truth, as far as Gran had told Alex, they were always needy and destructive.

"A proper madam of a bairn, that Thelma, in no that wee when you took her girth into consideration," Gran had said. "Space-hopper comes to mind when I think of her. There's not a rocket strong enough to launch that amount of lard to Mars where it belongs."

And Alex would laugh and Gran would have a good giggle to herself too before she went on.

"See the cracks in the pavements, Alex? Ever wondered how they got there, the great big cracks in the paving slabs? Well, it's your sister that made them when she used to play at Pee-the-Beds, or Hopscotch, as they weird folk from south of the border cry it. Whatever it's called, Thelma's the culprit. A bairn born with hands and feet made of lead. Your mother wanted me to buy that weather balloon of a daughter of hers new shoes when it was a year auld. But I didn't have the heart to tell her I didn't know of any deep sea diving shops where I could buy a pair of cast-iron bootees."

Thelma was always smashing things if she couldn't have what she wanted, Gran had said. And since Thelma herself never seemed to know what that was then no one else did either.

~~*

"Derek wasn't much better," she had told Alex. "Both were terrors from an early age … I tried, Alex. We all tried. But your mother would just dump them here and off she would go, to God knows where. So I looked after them … No Alex, I don't know what your mother was up to. I never asked. And she never told me. But I saw a lot of her in Thelma and Derek. Then when I found out she was pregnant with you, the blood fair drained from me. Two like that was bad enough. But a third?

"Anyway, you were entirely different. I didn't mind looking after you. A real draw you were too. I would take you out to Slay Drive Park there up at the end of the road, pushing you along in that old rickety pushchair of yours. Proud as punch I was, the proud grandmother. Nothing could take that away from me. Except the wheels on that pushchair of yours were always falling off the thing. Still, a spanner in a hammer and I fixed it up myself.

"Your big beautiful blue eyes would sparkle, Alex. Everyone admired them. Even that auld crab Martha Mowbray two doors down from here, at the other side of the electrified razor wire fence, over there. Aye that's her house, believe it or no, the one with the bars on the windows, on the inside. Anyway, that was a born witch if ever there was one. But when she caught sight of you, and your smiling big bonny eyes, she stopped trying to poison the ducks and swans way bamboo slivers in the Lofty Peak Dough balls she used to bake—well, tried to bake but always failed.

"But once she saw you Alex, well, she changed her ways in an instant. Not another petrol bomb thrown. Not another brick through another window either. She even stopped flattening the bairns' snowmen with rocks buried inside snowballs. And not another admission needed into that maximum-security unit she used to call home. Aye, you had that effect on a lot of people Alex. People changed for the better when they saw you.

"It was just a pity about your father."

And that's where it would always end.

Alex never really knew his father. No one ever told him about him either. His mother would always flutter her fingers as if they had been touched with a flame when he did. His grandmother would just sigh and tut tut tut, "Shame, a real shame." And that was it.

What you never knew you never miss, he would tell himself, knowing that was a lie. A lie that made everyone else feel better, less awkward.

His father was dead now. He had been since Alex was two. There were a few photographs, a tall lean looking man with fair hair, tanned, standing smiling by his mother's side. Happy.

But not that happy enough to stay.

Army, some whispered. Navy, said others. Killed in action. John Alexander McMullen. And sometimes he thought he could remember his father picking him up and hugging him. A thought, a dream, a need, a want. "A wee smasher!" he often thought he had heard his father say.

A waster. A drunk night in day out. A half wit, said Derek and Thelma.

And that hurt.

"He was a good man, Alex. Too good and too soft for a woman like your mother," Gran had said. "I only wish I had had a son like him. Pity was after I had your mum, I couldn't have any more. He used to call me Ma. I liked that. He loved you Alex. He really did."

The real truth only came out after Alex had found a note the night his gran had died.

He had gone back to her house hoping to at least catch some of the warmth and magic of her life still there. But it was only walls and furniture now, carpets and old pictures on the shelves.

It felt as if he were betraying her privacy as he had looked through her cupboards, taking out paperwork, official things he would have to deal with later.

And then, in an old tin full of photographs he had never seen before, he had found a letter.

Addressed to his grandmother, still in its envelope, Alex had taken it out and sat in his old chair, the one where he would sit on Sundays as she told him all her stories.

Everything seemed too big and empty now. Even the street outside had grown dark and quiet.

For a long while he had merely stared at the envelope wondering what to do.

Finally, even although he felt as if he was somehow betraying his grandmother's memory, he had pulled out the sheet of paper from its envelope and read.

She said Alex isn't mine, Ma. She said he was someone else's bairn. She said she's taken up with another man now. But I still think of Thelma and Derek as my own. I knew I would have been a good father to them. And I would have loved them both as much as I would have if they had been my own bairns. I know I would have loved them as much as I love Alex. And I know Alex is mine. No matter what Linda says, I know he is. She keeps going on about dates and times, but I was the only one with her then.

It breaks my heart, Ma, any time I think of him or look at his picture. And you know what? She wasn't even going to let me have that, a picture. But I took it, Ma. I stole it and now I keep it safe in a locket around my neck. And sometimes when I hold it, feel the warmth in it, I think of that warmth as if it's coming from him, my wee Alex. And when I lie here in my cot at night in the barracks, I open that wee locket and take a look at his smiling eyes. Did you ever see such bonny eyes on a bairn, Ma? And that smile, that wee toothless smile of his and it makes me so happy. But then I'm sad seeing him in that wee picture, knowing he's so far away.

Sometimes I'm terrified I'll lose this wee picture of his, the only thing I have of him, the only thing to remind me when I wake up that he isn't a dream, Ma.

Look after him for me, Ma. Please tell him his daddy loves him and that I'll never stop loving him. Alex changed my life when he was born. Everything changed when I held that wee bundle that was Alex in my arms. Something magical happened to me. Pure love, that's what made me cry for the first time in my life. And I don't care who sees or knows I did.

Now he's the only thing that keeps me going, remembering his bonny wee smiling face, and that daft wee laugh of his, a right chuckler.

Tell Alex his dad loves him like he's never ever loved anyone before, won't you, Ma? And if I never make it back be sure to let him know, that no matter what was happening, I was always thinking of my wee boy.

Love John

For days after his grandmother had died from a sudden brain hemorrhage Alex had walked around in a world of cotton wool. Everything a muffled mess.

At the last minute Jamie had turned up at the chapel just as the service had begun. And as the minister gave his short eulogy of Alex's grandmother's life from the pulpit, Jamie had sidled along the pew, reached out to Alex and took his hand.

"This is a time," Jamie had said as they sat there together in that little chapel, "when no man should have to bear sadness on his own."

It was the final act of kindness and Alex had sobbed uncontrollably.

And later Jamie had said something strange.

"Sometimes you really do get what you pray for," he had said that before looking away, as if he didn't want Alex to know something.

Jamie never did explain to Alex what he meant.

Jamie had reached out, put an arm around Alex's shoulders as he had wept, and pulled him close.

It wasn't until later that Alex realized that before meeting Jamie, he had gone through most of his life, day after day, and couldn't remember feeling the touch of another human being.

And now this. Jamie in a huff and Thelma and Derek eating them out of house and home. It was as if everything else didn't matter.

He went back to the living room.

"I'm away to make us something to eat," he said to Jamie, "I'll lay something out on the table for you, for after when they're gone. If you don't want anything just now you can just leave it and I'll heat something up for you later on."

And as he walked down the hallway he swallowed and sniffed quietly.

There was no time for sadness now. There had been too much of that lately and Alex didn't want to go though anything the likes of it again.

"The trick is," his grandmother had once told him, "be busy and keep busy. That's the answer. Let things take care of themselves and usually they do, pal."

Alex prayed that she was right.

CHAPTER 4

Jamie waited until Alex was out the room before bunching up his fists. He closed his eyes and tightened his mouth, willing himself to calm down, to count to ten. He only got to one before thumping the cushion in his lap.

When he opened his eyes again, the room had taken on a swimmy look.

"They are not going to stop us," he whispered through gritted teeth.

He threw the cushion to the side, leaned back.

He took a deep breath, let it out slowly and suddenly he felt lonely.

"And I thought I had left that all behind," he said. "It's true what they said. Sometimes you're better without families after all."

He picked up the remote control and pressed the mute button then looked over his shoulder, at the dullness of the room, the gaudiness of the wallpaper covered in years of grime. But as Alex had reasoned, it was all they could afford for the time being. Renting was the only option. Besides, it had at least got Alex out of that dump he had shared by his brother and sister, for most of the time anyway. That, at least was a small conciliation. But there was still the fear he felt whenever the vultures came pecking at their door, the fear they would drag Alex back to their Erie. And without Alex being there with him, Jamie realized, he would feel doomed.

It was a tug of war. Jamie could see that. And poor Alex was being torn between loyalties.

He put a foot up on the old coffee table with its history of all the others who had once lived here ingrained into it, a history of white rings from hot cups and cigarette burns.

And that geezer has a cheek to rent this out as a place fit to live in. He sneered as he reached out and picked up his packet of Scag and cigarette papers.

Alex hated it when he smoked, but Jamie wanted to feel good about something. Besides, Alex was addicted to coffee, so why couldn't he let Jamie enjoy his addiction. The only thing was Alex couldn't see it that way.

Everyone drinks coffee, Alex would say.

"Aye, but nobody drinks is much as you, though," Jamie would chide.

In truth, Jamie couldn't care less if Alex drank coffee or not. The only time it would rankle him was when they were out up town in the afternoon where it was like joining the dots, one place after another for "just one more coffee." And these days Jamie could only smoke outdoors anyway. So either he would stand outside and smoke whilst waiting for Alex to come out. Or he would go in and fume at the length of time it took Alex to drink up so that he could go outside for a smoke. Neither of them, at this point in time, knew where a compromise could be struck. Either Jamie should quit smoking, or Alex would have to quit his caffeine habit.

But not long after they moved in together, strange things had begun to happen.

Suddenly they had started copying each other, same number one crops, same clothes, same jeans and T-shirts.

But who was copying who?

And why?

Then Jamie had woken in the middle of the night after a really really bad dream called Single White Psycho.

Things had gone too far.

Things needed to change.

And then came the opportunity to put things back into perspective.

Could have gone better though, he thought now, still
...

~~*

The day came when they were walking down the high street, both with chests out, beaming pride for themselves, swaggering.

God only knew why.

"We're just like twins," Alex had said.

"Aye," Jamie said. "We could be for all that."

"Aye, twins," Alex had replied striding along with Jamie.

Until Jamie had said. "Except I don't have buck teeth."

There was a screech of what could have been tires, only it was really Alex cheap trainers slamming on the handbrake. Jamie walked on as Alex's feet slapped up to him. Alex, like a crab walking sideways, had faced into Jamie and said. "But I've no got buck teeth."

"Never said you did," Jamie said, striding on.

"Aye, you did."

"No, I didn't."

"Aye, you did."

Jamie stopped. "I did not!"

"Aye, you did. You said 'I've no got buck teeth.' So that must mean that I *have*."

"Look, Eck, stop taking things so personally."

What do you mean, 'personally'? How am I supposed to take it?"

"See," Jamie said. "That's you all over, Alex. You think everything refers to you. And that makes you selfish."

"Selfish!"

Alex rushed over to a shop window and grinned at his reflection in the glass like something out of *Alien: Resurrection*. An old dear on the other side collapsed into a mush.

"I haven't got buck teeth."

Jamie sighed. "See, that's another problem of yours, Eck. You imagine things."

Alex was about to say something else when Jamie held up his hand. "Eck, kid, get a grip. There's nothing wrong with your ginormous yackers, except for a bit of an overhang."

Mortified and bug-eyed Alex screamed, "I don't have an overhang!"

"Okay, so there's nothing wrong with your pegs for teeth."

"Right," huffed Alex too easily.

They walked on. The crowds kept a safe distance. Then Alex spoke.

"At least my legs aren't screwed on the wrong way round."

"What!"

"Don't take it personally, Jamie." Alex strode on, smiling, nodding at the passersby, their eyes glued to the nut.

Jamie caught up. "At least I've no got a humph," he said.

Both slammed to a halt.

"I haven't got a humph!" Alex yelled.

"Just a fat back then," Jamie let rip. "A back that starts at your heels and ends at the flat bit at the back of your head. Lie down and the kids could use you as a seesaw!"

Maybe it was the nightmare and maybe it was their addictions kicking up a storm. For after that, Alex vanished into Starbucks and Jamie lit up and fumed in the street outside. But smoking didn't help Jamie, for he felt rotten for what he had said. Eventually he looked over his shoulder, in through the window, and mouthed to Alex, "I'm sorry."

Alex appeared on the street with a double-ultra-super stewed taurine-blow-your-balls-off Mocha in hand. "So, I've no got buck teeth then?" he said.

"No."

"Or a humph?"

"No."

Alex took a sip, grimaced, and threw what was left of his coffee in the bin.

"Still like me?" Jamie asked.

"No, Jamie, I don't like you. I've suddenly come to that conclusion. After what you said to me and what I said to you and the way we both reacted, it can only mean one thing.

Jamie's heart sank. "What's that, Eck?"

"That we don't like each other very much."

"Don't say that, Eck."

"Thing is, Jamie. If you were a perfect stranger I wouldn't have let it get to me, so ..."

"So?" Jamie had asked.

"It must mean that we mean more to each other than we've admitted to ourselves, or to each other, so far. Know what I mean?"

Jamie nodded.

"Sometimes folk who get close," Alex had said, "get scared and then they climb onto a battlefield. Still close, but at war. Don't let that happen to us, Jamie."

And Jamie knew then how much they had fallen for each other.

~~*

For now, he sat back, the springs on the sofa twanging, and lit his roll up, inhaled deeply, and blew smoke into the room, albeit with a sense of guilt.

"Too bad," he said to no one.

It didn't take the edge of his guilt though. In effect, he was smoking through protest rather than pleasure. He knew it wouldn't take long for the foul aroma to waft its way down the hallway and into the kitchen. He just wondered how long it would take for Alex to come thundering along and tell him to put it out.

He never had before.

Still there was always a first time, Jamie thought as he inhaled deeper this time, the smoke so hot and burning into his chest that he ended up choking and spluttering what was left in his lungs out into the room.

He fumbled forward for the ashtray, eyes red, coughing, and stubbed out the cigarette.

Before he had time to recover, Alex was at the door and quick as a flash. "What's going on?"

"Nothing," Jamie wanted to say dragging in lungs full of air.

Alex took another step closer.

"You've been *smoking*!" he said pointing at Jamie.

"So—" Jamie coughed, "—what. You've been drinking coffee. Right!"

"It's not the same thing."

"Quit your griping. I've put it out," Jamie said dragging in a lifesaving breath and flopping back.

"And thank God for that," Alex said. "Anyway," he went on in a quieter more conciliatory tone, "They'll be gone in a minute if you still want something to eat."

Jamie composed himself, red faced, as he was for nearly choking to death and with embarrassment for being ticked off like a naughty schoolboy. It made him feel even worse that it came from someone only a month younger than he was.

Might as well be hung for a sheep as a lamb, he thought. And like a truculent schoolboy he put his feet up on the table.

He expected Alex's reaction to be instantaneous, a sharp outburst. Instead, Alex sighed out the words. "Look," he began, "I know the place is full of rubbish furniture and that, but you don't have to make it worse. It's only ours for as long as we're renting it, after all. And I get the feeling you wouldn't put your feet up the table if it was ours."

Jamie remained stony faced.

"Anyway," Alex said. "I've put something on for your tea. That is if you're still hungry."

Shaking his head, he left the room.

Jamie slowly took his feet down from the table.

From bad to worse, he thought.

"I can't do anything right tonight."

His only hope now was that Dork and Mingy were leaving soon. Dork and Mingy?

"More like Madge and Raj."

~~*

After he heard the twins of evil leave the premises Jamie waited a respectful length of time before he made his move. Sniffing the air, he ignored the damp undertones that pervaded the flat and smelled food.

Stomach rumbling he crept up the hallway and into the kitchen.

Alex was at the bunker with his back to him.

The table was set, knife and fork at the ready.

Only one place setting—for me or for him?

Before he sat down, Jamie thrust his hands into his back pockets and tried to be as jovial as he could muster under the circumstances. "They're gone then?" he asked.

Alex didn't flinch, his back still turned to Jamie. "Aye," he sighed. "They're gone."

"Okay dokey, then," Jamie said bouncing up and down on his heels. He felt much happier now. Just him and Alex, alone in their own little home. And food. "So, what's for eating?" he asked.

"Your favorite," Alex said without turning around and clattering something down on a plate.

"Oh aye, and what's that?" Jamie asked sniffing at the aromas.

"Krap!"

Which brought Jamie's heels back to earth with a crash.

"Funny ha ha," he said and sat down at the table. "You're not eating then?" he asked.

"I ready have," Alex said. "Besides, I was feared to eat in front of you since you're always going on about me being fat, which I'm not. But here." He crashed down the plate in front of Jamie. "Enjoy."

"So, anything new on the brother and sister front?" Jamie asked as a way of making conversation.

"Thelma starts her new job tomorrow. That's about it." Alex said squeezing the suds out a cloth under the tap.

Jamie continued to eat.

"Mmmm. What is this anyway?" Jamie asked.

"Well, I wouldn't think it would take a brainiac to figure it out that it's no caviar and coleslaw," Alex said.

"Mince and tatties then?"

"And not out a tin either." Alex allowed himself a congratulatory tone at his culinary skills as he wiped down the bunker.

"I'll tell you one thing, though," Jamie said, shoveling the contents of his plate into his gob. "You know a way to a man's ark."

"And here I was thinking that you loved me for myself."

"Oh I do, I do. Don't get me wrong on that score." Jamie nodded vigorously as he sucked in a mouthful of mince with a slurp.

"Glad to hear it," Alex said. "At least you're not after my poverty status, then."

"This is braw. You'll have to give me the recipe."

Alex rolled his eyes. "Mince, tatties, boil them. I hope that's not too hard for the next time when you get the inkling to cook something for *me* for a change. And I don't mean out of a packet or a tin either."

"I promise, I will."

"Aye well, I'll believe it when I smell it. Let's just hope I don't barf in the process. But it's the thought that counts, I suppose."

"Mmm, yum," Jamie said, now finished. He leaned back and smiled. "You're a braw laddie that knows a way to a man's heart."

"You mean that there's no difference?"

"What?"

"Between your heart and your ark?"

"What are you talking about now?"

"Oh nothing," Alex said, picking up Jamie's plate.

He walked over to the sink and put it down.

"What's for afters?" Jamie asked.

Alex stood still for a moment.

"Well?" Jamie said.

"Jamie?"

"Alex?"

"You know when I said earlier that I would still be going away with you on holiday?"

A sense of doom began to descend over Jamie.

"Well ..."

"Well, what, Alex, friend."

Alex turned away from the sink and took a quick look at Jamie and away again. "I'm still going with you like."

"Phew," Jamie said with a great sense of relief. "And there was me thinking your evil twisted bra had got to you after all."

"Don't say that about him, Jamie. I don't like it."

"I'm sorry."

"I mean I know Derek can seem evil and twisted at times, but that's for me to say, okay? Not you. I mean I appreciate it when you jumped to my defense like, but I've known him all my life, remember, and he is my brother. More importantly, I know what he's like. I don't fall for it. And I hate to say it, but you acted just the way he wanted you to act. You fell for it. That's his kick."

Crestfallen, Jamie squirmed in his seat.

Alex sat down at the opposite side of the table. "Look, I know he's a sleekit get," he said "We all know he's a sleekit so and so, most of all me."

"I just don't like the way he twists you up like that," Jamie said. "I mean tonight for instance. I thought he was really going to try and stop you from going away with me."

"Listen, Jamie, my name's Craft no Daft. I knew what Derek was up to is soon as I clapped eyes on him. It's a kind of a game he likes to play I suppose. He likes to think he wins. He never does though. But it's just a game for all that."

"I feel stupid now," Jamie huffed.

Alex reached out and covered Jamie's hand with his. "Don't," he said. "For one thing what you did tonight means you care. Otherwise you wouldn't have done it, would you?"

"Oh Alex. I just don't like to see you hurt."

"Anyway, everything's all sorted now," Alex said letting go of his hand and leaning back.

"Sorted?" Jamie said. "What was needing sorted like?"

"Well, that's what I was trying to tell you," Alex said.

"Tell me what?"

"I told Thelma and Derek they could come with us."

"*What*!"

~~*

Bang, crash, wallop would be appropriate words to use, but Alex stood firm, or rather sat, and merely cringed with each.

"What do you mean they're going with us?" Jamie yelled before quickly holding up a hand (stop in the name of love). "No. Don't tell me. It's because you're mad. That's it. You're bonkers. And where was I in all of this? Eh? While you three witches were around the kitchen cauldron plotting against me?"

"It wasn't like that," Alex pleaded, cringing some more.

"Awe aye. And what was it like then? Eh? My God, and you've got a cheek to tell *me* to keep out of family business! Seems like I was completely chucked overboard on this one. Thanks very much, Eck. Now I really do know where I stand. Out in the cold."

"Jamie, don't be like that. They're my brother and sister."

Jamie paced around the floor, arms waving up and down like a madman. "I can't stand it," he said running his fingers through a luxurious number one crop. "I can't, I can't, I can't," he whined on like a banshee. "Oh my *God*! And you, *you*! You made me feel like an eejit for trying to stop that evil get of a brother of yours from hurting you. Aye, blood's thicker than water all right, laddie. That thick I must have been dense to even think about jumping into it to try and save you."

"Calm down, Jamie," Alex said. "It's only for five days."

Perry Mason meets Ironside. Jamie McFarlane—Judge, jury and prosecutor.

"You still don't get it, do you, eh?" Jamie said. "They're manipulating you, Eck. They'll never leave you alone unless you stand up to them."

"What would I want to stand up to them for? They're ma brother and sister."

"*Half* brother and sister."

"What's that got to do with it?"

Jamie turned on Alex, slammed his hands down on the table and looked at him right in the eyes. "*He's* a monster," he said. "*She's* an even bigger monster. That's what I mean. Can you not see that they're using you, Eck? They'll never let you go. What were you thinking?"

Jamie sprang back up and away before Alex had a chance to answer.

"What a nightmare," he went on. "All I wanted was for us to have a couple of days away for ourselves, Eck. Could you not see that?"

Alex's mouth clamped tight shut.

"No answer, Eck? Is that the only answer you have for me? None?"

Alex's eyes snapped closed when the kitchen door slammed. When he opened them again Jamie was nowhere to be seen.

He sat there for a moment not knowing what to do next. He thought this might happen. On that score, he knew he was fooling himself. He knew what Jamie's reaction would be.

He felt torn between two loyalties: family and Jamie. He thought he had struck a good compromise when he had agreed to Thelma and Derek's suggestion. They hadn't been abroad either for a holiday. It would be everyone all together.

Maybe he had been too soft hearted about it. But how could he refuse? How could he be as heartless as Jamie seemed to want him to be. How could he leave his own brother and sister behind?

He looked over at the old window with its rickety glass. Even that was quiet now. The kind of quiet where Alex was frightened to move in case it started an earthquake, or an avalanche.

He looked down at the empty table, at the chair, its varnish rubbed away where many others before them had sat, at where Jamie had only been too happy to sit and stuff his face with the meal Alex had made for him only minutes before. Then he looked at the door, maroon paint chipped, white showing through. It might well have been the door to a safe, ready to be blown off its hinges.

"Why can't I ever do anything right?"

~~*

Jamie sat in the living room in silence staring at the faded wallpaper again, feeling as lonely in a crowd as he had ever felt.

Nothing changes then.

The television was off, nothing but a blank square screen.

Alex stepped in and stood by the door. "Can I come in?" he asked.

His sorrowful tone made Jamie squirm with embarrassment. "It's your house," Jamie said. "You can do what you like in it."

"It's our house, Jamie," Alex corrected him. "Yours and mine."

"Same difference."

"So, can I come in?" Alex asked again.

Jamie's answer was noncommittal. "Of course you can come in, Eck. Who am I to stop you. And I wouldn't even if I could."

Alex smiled weakly.

"And don't look like such a scared wee lamb. I'm not going to bite you," Jamie said. "I should have asked you first, Jamie," Alex said. "I'm sorry. I was being stupid."

Jamie shook his head, pulling Alex close. "No you weren't, pal. If anybody was being daft it was me."

"How do you come to that conclusion?"

Jamie shrugged. "Don't know," he said. "Just feels right saying it. I think we all say things when we don't always know what we're saying."

A pall of silence fell as the pair sat side by side, saying nothing, listening to the silence, neither wishing to be the first to break their unspoken truce.

Jamie huffed.

"It's like a mortuary in here, it's that quiet," he said raising his hands and slapping them down on his legs.

"Aye, it's funny how quiet this place gets after the five o'clock rush," Alex said.

He seemed to think for a second before speaking again.

"I'll tell them they can't come with us," he said almost in a whisper.

Jamie's head snapped around, eyes looking at Alex in disbelief. There had been a flash of joy in his eyes, which quickly dimmed on realizing the argument had been won on quite different terms than those he had hoped for. It was a case of might over right, and it felt like a hollow victory for it.

"No, Alex, you don't have to do any such thing." Jamie sighed out his words. "Even if you tried I somehow think they would keep nipping at your good nature until they wore you down to a pile of shavings until you did agree. And that would be even worse."

Now it was Alex's turn to look in disbelief. "But you were right," he said. "At least I should I've asked you first. At least said something. It was your idea in the first place, you that organized the tickets and everything."

"And maybe it was just is well you didn't say anything to me after all. Otherwise I might have gone off my head at them instead, and told them stuff I would later hate myself for saying. In fact, I know I would have. But I'm getting used to the idea now. Sort of anyway."

"You make it sound like they were conspiring against you."

"I've no doubt about it, my man," Jamie sniffed. "Otherwise they'd have come bouncing through to tell me themselves about their sleekit intentions. But they just ran off and left it to you, as always."

"Come to think about it," Alex said, "they couldn't wait to get out the door once I'd said aye."

Jamie leaned forward and picked up his wallet of Scag. "Mind if I have a fag?" he said.

Alex shook his head. "No at all," he said. "I think I'll just go and make us a hot cup of coffee while you roll up your cig."

Alex stood up and walked across the room with lightness in his step. Jamie already had the tobacco pouch opened when he asked.

"Eh, who was the one that first suggested it anyway?" Jamie asked.

Alex stopped dead at the door.

"No, don't tell me," Jamie said. "They were probably in cahoots before they even got here. The whole thing planned out between them. And I don't want to get myself mad thinking about it."

Alex smiled, kept silent and nodded in agreement.

And when he had left the room, Jamie licked at his cigarette paper, tobacco perfectly deposited therein, and his eyes grew sleekit as an idea came to him.

One bad turn deserves another, he thought, flicking the tip of his tongue to the end of the paper.

"And they'll never know what hit them."

He leaned back into the cushions.

He placed the cigarette in his mouth, proud as a new father as his plan began to hatch in his mind, all in full glorious Technicolor, 3D, Sense-around Sound and wall-to-wall IMAX.

He flicked the match head with his thumb. The match burst into flame. He sucked the flame into the end of the cigarette, and flicked out the match.

He inhaled deeply. This is the life, he thought as he reached up and clamped the cigarette between his fingers, cool as any spaghetti western cowboy, and pulled the cigarette away.

Only it stuck to his lips and his fingers yanked of the burning tip instead, stinging him into action with an "eye-yah!"

"Ouch! Ouch! Ouch!" he cried with each successive nip clipping of fingers on the glowing end as it burnt him.

Heavy footsteps clomped nearer from down the hallway, and in blind panic Jamie mashed his foot down on the glowing cigarette end, trampling it into ash on the floorboards.

There were that many burn marks already there that another wouldn't make any difference, he surmised, throwing himself back, lighting up quickly again and relaxed with one arm thrown over the back of the sofa.

The door swung wide. Alex entered with two mugs of coffee in his hands.

He caught on right away.

"What's wrong?" he asked.

"Nothing wrong. What makes you ask?" Jamie said with a frown that corrugated his brow.

"The guilty look on your mug," Alex said.

"Speaking of mugs" Jamie said lurching forward, hands out. "Is one of them mine?"

"Of course one's yours. What do you take me for?"

"Cat's for?"

"Eh?"

"A posh way of saying cat's fur," Jamie said. "Like your gran's posh way of saying feesh instead of saying fish."

Now both were puzzled. And for the moment at least, each forgot what the other was about to say.

CHapter 5

A mongrel coughed early morning light at the window, scaring a curious pigeon from the sill as Derek wakened through his re-birthing nightmare before burying his head under a pillow when his sister's voice boomed through the door with her fist.

"Up!"

He hated even the thought of working.

Derek was good with wires and lecky, screwdrivers, plans, and solder. But other than that, his above average High Q usually found itself railroaded into scheming and conniving.

"Job centre," Thelma yelled. "Now! This morning!"

Now that Thelma had a new job it made things all that harder. The pressure was on. Job creation was lapping the shores of Derek's indolence like an acid. And Thelma had already been toppled from the safety of the beach, now the government was paying employers to take on rubbish staff.

One half-opened eye listened as she stomped back to her room and he sighed in resignation. Balance had to be restored. Either he had to work or his sister had to be stopped.

~~*

Thelma prized her bulk in front of the mirror and backcombed her Cherry Blossom hairdo until her face resembled a marshmallow poked into the middle of a giant black lacquered puffball fungus. After combing her eyebrows she bulletproofed the lot with spray on varnish, touched up her Slippy Lippy, and then rolled her cricket-bat-sting gob back and forth, *mmwuh mmwuh*.

"Yeah ... Perfect."

Finally she poked in her BA-stewardess-plutonium-blue contacts using eyelash curlers to yank her eyeballs open long enough for insertion. The left lens scooted to the back of her eyeball and she spent the next five minutes clawing it back to front with a scarlet talon. Exhausted, she looked at her bright red eyeballs stinging back. She squirted in instant whitener. Her eyeballs snapped to the size of raisins.

"Gawdstruth!"

She blinked, gawped, then flumped back and admired her sequel to the Modern Prometheus.

"That'll have to do," she said standing up. "New career, same old bloody town," she sighed, toggling her duffel coat with nervous fingers readying herself for her first day at yet another newsagent.

~~*

"You dial up the purchase the punter's wanting to make on the till, right?" Thelma's new boss explained. "Then you get them to stick their card into that wee thingy there, aye, there! But if they're *that* dense, you'll have to do it for them. And if they are that dense, you should be asking yourself what the hell they're doing with a card in the first place."

He drew in close, whispering. "You can tell how dense they are by how flat their heads are at the back. And by how far apart their eyes are." He gave Thelma a close look. She jerked back into her hairdo.

He sighed and went on. "Then you push that button there." He jabbed his howking finger at yet another electric contraption. "Then you key in that number there. Then you get the bubble-brained basket to put in its secret number into that wee thing there. Then you wait (forever) for the card to send its secret message to the Bank of Bangkok, or wherever the hell it sends it to. But whatever you do, for God's sake don't pull the card out before it's been confirmed at the other end. Otherwise the whole thing goes mental berzerk."

He stretched, hands on back, blubber gut hanging as he tried to straighten out his humph.

Impossible.

"Anyway," he went on, "the till then starts whirring and clicking like it's been taken over by a, by a … what-jimmy-call-it? God it's on the tip of my licker, a … a …"

"A hoogycompoofter?" Thelma offered.

"Aye, one of them. Anyway, then you take out the card and give it back to the sticky-fingered git of a customer. Just remember to make sure to tell the eejit to keep its Bostik paws where you can see them—high above its head. Then you give it a receipt. Got it?"

"Eh, I think so," Thelma said.

"Don't get it wrong!"

The boss turned his humph on her then whirled back.

"Oh, I nearly forgot," he said. "You have to get the thieving get's thumbprints as well."

"What do you do with them like?" Thelma asked. "Give them to the police or something?"

The boss's eyeballs disappeared as his blue lips stretched wide.

"No," he said. "We sell them on. But you don't have to concern yourself about that."

Thelma's jaw dropped wide as a basking shark's gob on the hunt.

"And remember," he said. "Always treat the customer with the disrespect it deserves. Don't smile. Don't say hello or good morning or any of that crap. They're all on the take."

He pointed a claw at the dark corners. "There are fifteen security cams in here," he explained. "And everything's been wired to the mains, even the crisps. So if you suspect anything, just jump on that big red button on the floor. But don't touch nothing metal, or you'll end up being crisped yourself.

Before she could think *run*, the boss turned back yet again, clacket cardy swinging.

"Oh, I nearly forgot," he said shuffling back.

"What now?"

"School bairns," he said eyes narrowing.

"What about them?"

"No more than one-and-a-half in the shop at a time."

"Eh? Don't you mean two at a time?" Thelma asked.

"No," the boss sniggered and a length of snot shot out of his nose. "It keeps them on their guard, you see."

Wheezing and coughing, snot swinging, he took a breath and sucked said snot back in too fast whence it whip-lashed itself to the side of his face.

I'm going to be sick. Thelma gripped at the counter.

"You see," the boss explained, dragging the goo away with his knuckles, "none of those wee gets ever wants to be the half bit of the equation, hee hee hee. So they don't *dare* touch nothing. But if they do, just remember that big fat red button down there."

"Are you having me on?" Thelma asked.

He ignored her. "There's an electrified length of razor-wire up there." Thelma's face snapped up to it. "Just make sure they all see it." He flicked a switch at the side of the till. Sparks zapped all over the wire. "Impressive, eh?" he leered.

He flicked off the switch. "Just do that every half-an-hour to keep the thieving gets on their guard. They'll get the message."

After all that the boss slithered off to the backroom for a cup of stewed tea and yellow-label biscuits.

~~*

Derek, lounging in front of his TV hero, Maury Povich, plopped his spoon into his instant pot noodle when the phone rang and answered it with his best posh "axe-scent."

"Heylow?" he said.

"It's my doofer," a woman said.

"Doofer, madam?" Derek said.

"Aye, doofer," she said. "It's not working."

"So," Derek said, "What's a doofer?"

"It's the a ..."

"Yes?" he prodded.

"It's my doot-doot machine," she said.

"Your doot-doot machine?"

"Aye."

"Sorry," Derek said, "but I don't know what a doot-doot machine is."

"It's the thing you go doot-doot with," she said exasperated.

"Oh, a thingway?"

"Aye!" She screamed down the phone.

"So," Derek said, "I've got a doofer, a doot-doot machine, *and* a thingway to deal with. Which one is it?"

There was a sharp intake of breath at the other end. "Are you stupid or something?" the woman yelled.

Derek ignored her uncalled-for remark and asked if, "It isn't maybe your thingymajiggery thing that's clonkurd?"

"You obviously don't know what you're talking about," she said. "I want to speak to the manager."

"He's out," Derek said, composing himself, "but if you want to hang on, and tell me about your jiggered doofery thing, I'll just get a pen."

"Okaaaay," she said slowly.

Derek put down the phone, took a slurp of his pot noodle and Bisto, and picked it up again.

"Okay, ready when you are," he informed her majesty.

"Right!" she blasted, "tell your boss to get somebody that knows what they're talking about."

"Anything about your doofer?" Derek asked.

"Aye!" she yelled. "You can tell him it doesn't work and I want another one, right?"

"We're clean out of doofers," Derek said. "Would a remote control do you instead?"

"Awe, get lost!" she said and the line went dead.

Derek carefully replaced the receiver and scribbled on his note pad.

"Another dissatisfied customer who'll never pester the boss again. And another fiver for me."

He picked up the phone and dialed.

~~*

After a week of it the strain was beginning to tell on Thelma. Fair kerfuffled she was, faffing with which button, which slot, which numbers, when to put the card in, when to yank it out.

And of course there was the inkpad.

"Thumb print," she said rasping her talons.

"What for?" a plooky faced punter asked clutching his special-offer yoo-hoo glue-in-a-bag.

"Just do it, will you?" Thelma said.

"What fur?"

"Cat's fur! Dug's fur!"

The punter rammed his thumb on the inkpad, then smudged it on the receipt. Thelma slipped the receipt into the till, slammed it shut, smiled, clacked her Bazooka Joe bubblegum, and bid him adieu with a "have a crap day!"

Hoods up, the punters would slither off. And more than once Thelma would learn of her new name when she pressed the release-button on the door.

"Fat *cow*!"

"I heard that!"

And they always managed to let go the bars before she had a chance to jump on that big red button at her feet.

But stress gave way to complacency and thus into boredom when Thelma would entertain herself.

Sparks flew and electric trickery arcs would zap lovely blue streamers hither and yonder to oohs and eye-yahs between the pot noodles and lucky bags as she flicked the magic switch.

ZzzaaAAAp! Phzz!

But then the enemy grew smart. There was a run on insulating yellow rubber gloves, a huge boon in sales. Then boom followed bust and sales dipped as low as Thelma's sharp learning curve grew high. But learn she did. And she also learned what a pain in the Channel Funnel the whole plastic card process was.

For a start it took ages.

"What's wrong with using dosh?" She glared at a poor old dear shrinking at the other side of the counter.

Silence.

"Because you've got none, is it?" Thelma said.

In went the card. The old dear took forever punching in her pin number as Thelma huffed and puffed.

"Come on, come on. We've not go till the *next* world war you know." She half-lurched over the counter.

Then came the wait for the thing to work. And the wait for the bank to register the transactions at the other end took longer and longer.

"God almighty! Modern *technology*?"

Thelma's eyes would dart an accusing glare at any customer who would *dare* cause her this grief. Her mouth would tighten. Her teeth would show. Just enough to let them know how furious she was at being kept away from her dreams of being the next Sarah Jessica Parker.

Then the machine itself had started to grind to a halt.

"God love us!" she would cry out.

She complained about it to the boss.

The boss told her to give the card machine a little tap.

It worked, for a while.

The tap with a finger progressed to a tap with a pen. But in the end Thelma didn't even bother waiting for the thing to work. She took up First Strike Option and bashed it with her fist instead.

"Come on for (thump)'s sake!"

Thump!

Thump! Thump! Thump!

"What's wrong with you using (thump)ing money?"

"This is doing my (thump)ing head in!"

"I know what I would like to do with you, yah load of (thump)ing greasers. I'd stick the lot of you all in (thump)ing (thump)ing Sing Sing. Yah load of (thump)ing, thieving (thump)ing, (thump)ing glue-sniffing gets! The electric chair's too (thump)ing good enough for you!"

Thumpthumpthumpthumpthump! Until the thing was left hanging off by its hinges.

Then there was the stocktaking; moldy stuff at the front. Good stuff at the back.

Thelma picked up a packet of Chocolate Digestives and peered at the sell-by date. Gasping, she then crunched her real imitation plastic Prada clodhoppers through cardboard boxes and stomped straight into the boss's hovel at the back.

His eyes screwed up through smoke belching from his cigarette end, he dropped the remote control and screwdriver he was holding onto a pile of the same by the phone on his desk.

"What is it now?" he sighed.

Thelma held up the moldy biscuits.

"These are a year out of date," she said.

The boss sighed and creaked up onto his feet, grabbed the biscuits from Thelma and called out "Follow me."

She followed him to the counter. He reached under it, found a hammer, swung it high and walloped the packet, then emptied the lot into a Tesco's carrier bag.

"Real baskets at Tesco's." He grinned handing the bag over to Thelma. "Bashed biscuits. Pensioner's Special *Offer*."

Thelma screwed up her face. "They stink," she said.

The boss grabbed a bottle of Febreeze off the shelf, squirted some into the bag, put the Febreeze back on the shelf then handed the bag back to Thelma.

"There," he said. "Now they won't know the difference."

"They'll get killed off eating them," Thelma said.

"Elma ..."

"Thelma."

"Whatever. What do you think the word *offer* means?"

"Eh?"

"It's a code word to them that's miserable with guilt for sponging their pensions off the state, them that can't afford to go all the way to Switzerland. We're doing the old dears a favor."

He whirled away and disappeared into the back office.

"I don't believe this," Thelma said and dumped the bag on the two-for-the-price-for-two shelf.

However, it was the rumors that were the last straw for her.

"She chucks her wet drawers in the pie-heater-upper-machine."

"Where's that (thump)ing hammer?"

And the big red button at her feet had been just too (bang)ing convenient.

She'd jumped on it.

"Hi-YAH!"

PHZZZZZZZZZZZZZZZZZZZZZZZZZZZZZZZZZZZZZZZZZZZZZZZZZZ
AP!

And some peeled wally old dear, in a moth-eaten rabbit fur Parka, sporting a blue rinse bubble cut that had been fashioned with Domestos and an old bit glass at the local borstal, transformed into an Afro-Caribbean in an instant.

The yellow-label ultra-cheapo-krapo-hydrogenated-to-hell-(even-pigs-wouldn't-eat-this-muck)-crisps in her wilting mitt, shrunk to the size of an atom in a flash.

"You're fired!" the boss yelled at Thelma as he poked the shouldering lump away from the live wires with a wet mop.

But by then Thelma was half out the door to the sound of sirens, giving a sigh of relief it was all over just as the ambulance whizzed past to the local takeaway.

~~*

"You nearly poked that mop through my ribs," Derek complained, pulling off the wig, scraping off the wrinkles and lippy as the boss counted out the fivers and tenners.

"Had to make it look convincing," the boss sniffed.

"Thank God it was me that done the wiring then," Derek said.

"Job well done, son."

"So, how long do you get paid for the social thinking Thelma's still working in the shop like?"

The boss tapped at the side of his nose.

"For as long as you can keep they punters off my humph about their duff tellies and remote controls," the boss said.

Derek smiled.

Evening light fell as a mongrel wagged its tail. Thelma patted its head and set down the bowl of Irish stew and dumplings for it to nosh on. She looked up at the third floor and watched a lone pigeon pecking peanuts that she had glued to her brother's windowsill. Smiling she walked back inside.

In the kitchen she emptied PAL into a pot and smothered it in Derek's favorite, Bisto, hoping one day he would take the hint get himself a job to pay for decent grub

CHaPTer 6

Thelma, talentless perhaps, at least tried, whilst her lazy, scheming, conniving brother Derek, talented to the hilt, did as little as possible as far as the work front was concerned.

At least Thelma tried her hand at all things. She felt skilled in nothing, but all was grist to the mill as far as she was concerned. For Thelma had big ambitions and the waters needed to be breaded with gold if she was going to stay afloat long enough to achieve them.

Working in the newsagents had been one attempt. But disaster as that had been she had stormed back to the Job Center and demanded something better.

They offered her the next best thing—a nursing home.

What could be easier, Thelma thought, striding through the doors confidently.

Everything, as she was about to find out.

In fact Thelma had waved her head in so many different directions for potential opportunity that she was in danger of slapping herself in the face with her own brain.

And still she marched proudly in through the doors of every opportunity, her head high, until her real talent was discovered.

"First things first," the nurse with epaulets the size of propellers told her on her first morning at the nursing home. "Sluice."

Thelma stuck her head in the door.

The nurse walked through, waving her arms up and down left and right as if she was giving signals to traffic, Thelma following.

"Bedpans, vomit bowls, catheter bags, urine bottles, commodes and (she slapped her hand on a machine) the bedpan masher—only two items at a time. Clear bags are for household waste. Orange bags are for contaminated waste: blood, feces, urine, body parts ..."

Thelma gulped. "Body parts?"

"Aye, anything that falls off unexpectedly. Toes, fingers, arms, legs ..."

"Oh my God!"

"... Heads."

The nurse turned to Thelma. "We don't get many of them though," she said. "Usually we get through a shift without anything too drastic happening. Anyway, there are the incontinence pads—white, blue, yellow, green, and the big purple ones are down there. Not used any of those in a long time. Net knickers, various colors, color coordinated depending on the size of the patient. Okay, wipes and well, blah blah blah. I'm sure you'll learn what's what soon enough."

Out of the sluice and into the office.

"Wear a different apron every time you go near a different patient. Always wear gloves and always wash your hands when you take the gloves off—always. Remember the emergency numbers for cardiac arrest and fire. Lives might depend on it."

Out of office into the corridor, Thelma's head was reeling by now.

"Fire extinguisher here, here and here," the nurse said turning to Thelma, almost decapitating her with an epaulet. "Red, black, blue—red equals water for paper fires, black equals carbon dioxide for electrical fires and blue equals powder for everything and anything. Emergency break-glass fire-point here and here and here."

Into ward.

"Buzzers!" the nurse said, fists on hips. "There's only one thing you have to remember about them."

"What's that?" Thelma asked.

"*Answer* them."

The nurse looked around.

The residents looked back.

Lots of smiling.

"Oh, nearly forgot," the nurse said. "Do not lift a resident. If he or she can't mobilize by him or herself, then we have lifting equipment to do the job."

"Cranes in other words," she whispered into Thelma's ear.

After that lot Thelma felt as if her head was stuffed by a taxidermist.

But off to work she went.

"Feed that one over there," the nurse with shot-putt balls for shoulders pointed.

Thelma's eyes slithered to the sides.

She spied the old woman propped up in bed, pillows like sandbags either side barricading her in place. And the first thing Thelma thought looking at her was: where's the pink fluffy angora bed jacket? The second was: she looks like she's got a tight mouth.

Thelma was right on the second score.

Nonetheless, Thelma stormed over to the breakfast trolley that looked like a pig's trough on wheels, and swiped a bowl of porridge from it.

Simple, Thelma thought as she planted her ample self down on the mattress.

The old woman sagged to the north wind.

Thelma reached out and pushed the old woman back up.

The old woman slithered to the side again.

Thelma tried rolling up her eyes in exasperation but her face got in the way.

Needing more room, Thelma decided.

She slammed the bowl of porridge down on the trolley table by the bed and pushed it out a bit.

The bedside trolley's wheels didn't turn.

This forced Thelma to stand up and to drag said trolley table a bit further away. The wheels still refused to turn but what did that matter? National Health Service after all. And as Thelma concentrated on yanking the trolley to the side, the old woman looked as if she were attached to it by an invisible string and keeled over to the side.

Seeing a disaster about to happen, Thelma threw herself between trolley and old woman, one hand on the trolley and the other on the old woman's thin shoulder. There was something Samson and Delia Smith about the scene.

She shoved the old woman.

The old woman's face tightened and shoved back.

Whereupon Thelma's ample thighs shoogled like the wattles of a chicken's gizzard.

"This was supposed to be an easy job," she said under her breath.

The old woman's smile tightened to the width of piano wire.

Thelma then had an inspiration borne out of desperation.

She maneuvered herself to the side, keeping her hand on the trolley, and jammed herself back down on the mattress and thrust her shoulder against the old woman's.

"AAAAAAAhhhh!" the old woman screamed. "Get your hands off my neck! AAAAAAAAAAAAAAAAAAAAAAAAAAAAHHH. I'm being murdered! HEEEEEEEEEEEEEEEEEEEEEEEEEEEEEELP! Jabba the Hut's killing me! Murder! Polis! AAAAAAAAAHHHH! Killer nurse!"

Thelma's blood ran cold.

No one had thought to tell Thelma that the old woman was a Star Wars fan. Yes times had finally grown into that generation.

Thelma looked around with desperate eyes.

Where was this Jabba the Hut character?

"Killer! *MURDERER*!" The other old women pointed and jabbing at the air in Thelma's direction.

"Who?" Thelma called out at them.

"You, yah fat cow!"

A foreboding of history repeating itself came over her.

And the old lady wasn't having it either. She might have been ninety-two, frail and with determined eyes, and a tight mouth, but this newcomer wasn't going to beat her.

Thelma remained on the edge of the bed.

It was her first mistake.

The bed sagged. Then a bit more.

The old lady slipped sideways off her pillows.

Thelma stood up, sorted the pillows, sandbagging the poor old bird back into place.

"Right," Thelma sighed.

She sat down again. The bed sagged even more (it hadn't recovered from its last assault).

The old lady tilted to the side again.

Thelma shouldered the old lady back up and maneuvered the plate of gruel she had in her grip, spooned a lump of slop out of it and waved it closer to the old lady's mouth.

The old lady forced her lips closed.

"Oh come on now." Thelma smiled. "It's good."

It looked like a bowl of sick.

The old woman clamped her gums shut.

Thelma waved the loaded spoon at the old lady's mouth.

Still the lips wouldn't budge.

"It's nice and tasty ... num, num, num, mmm." Thelma tried her best to entice the old dear.

"I'm not eating that muck," the old dear's gums parted enough to speak. "*You* eat it."

Thelma plonked the spoon back in the bowl of slop.

"She's not wanting it," she said to the nurse.

"Try harder then," the nurse fired back.

"I have!"

"She has to eat something," the nurse said. "The government says so, so get something down her neck."

"She's not hungry. She's not eating."

The nurse sighed, turned around.

"Help in the men's bay then," she said and stormed off.

Thelma teetered into the men's bay.

It stank of urine. Thelma wrinkled up her nose.

Not looking where she was going she stood on a plastic bag full of yellowish colored fluid.

An old man shot bolt upright in his bed and yelped.

Thelma stepped back in fright. Her heel punctured another bag on the floor.

Another old man cried out.

She spun around.

Tubes wrapped themselves around her legs. Ping, twang, phut. Catheters were pulled out hither and thither.

"You're fired," the nurse with the propeller epaulets screamed out the end of an accusing finger.

"Thank God for that."

Thelma was going to be a star. This was beneath her.

She hauled on her donkey jacket and raged off in a huff.

"What happened this time?" Derek said lowering his comic when Thelma stepped in the door.

"Don't even go there," she said storming past. She raised an arm when Derek opened his mouth to speak again.

"I said, don't."

That Saturday, Thelma would be scanning through the jobs ads and Derek scanning for ideas through the X-Men comic, until he couldn't stand Thelma's glares any longer and went through to the back room to tinker with the wheelchair.

And thought about ways he could soup up the engine.

For you see, in Derek's mind, why should anyone using one of these contraptions be resigned to a snail's pace. Surely there were frustrated wheelchair users out there who could do with a bit more octane.

Converting the thing to climb stairs was only the start.

Why not aim for the stars?

CHaPTer 7

Eight o' clock on Sunday morning, just over a week to go before the holiday away began, Jamie sat at the kitchen table with cotton wool stuffed in his ears. The cotton wool, however, hadn't been enough, so he had resorted to using headphones, big black headphones. But even cotton wool in the ears and headphones weren't enough, so he had to resort to tea towels folded into big fat squares and stuffed those in between the cotton wool and the headphones. It was the only way he could think of to get some peace and quiet from Alex's relentless DIY home improvements.

But it wasn't working.

Jamie tried ignoring the noise. That didn't work. He tried distraction therapy. He tried reading the papers at the table with the contraption clamped to his ears. The thumping and banging was only just dulled and no more.

Every thump at the wall had Jamie's head jerk lower and lower into his neck. Every *bang bang bang* had his face tighten and his grip on the paper become excruciatingly tighter still.

Bang bang bang went the hammers.

Zzzz. Zzzz. ZZZZZZZZZZZZ went the drilling into the wall and straight to his Jamie's teeth.

Baga-Banga-Banga-bangbangbang-zzzz-zzzz-zzzzzZZZZZZZZZZZ.

Then it all stopped.

The silence was unnerving.

But Jamie had been here before.

Like a periscope his eyeballs crawled over the top edge of his newspaper and scanned side to side with suspicion at the wall.

Still, there was silence. Then there was relief. He waited. Still silence. He began to relax. He took a breath. Then there was a burrrrrrruhuhuh-bruhuhuh-uh-uh-uh.

Banga!-Banga!-Banga!

"Awe for God's sake!"

Bang!

Wallop!

Crash!

"That *does* it!"

Jamie mashed up the Sunday Post and left it in a crumpled heap in the middle of the kitchen table. He stood up and ripped the headphones, cotton wool and tea towels from his lugs. He took a last determined drag of his cig and mashed it out on the old Mister Tiggy Winkle saucer Alex found in a junk shop convinced it was worth a fortune, an antique—a fake when Jamie spotted the Made in Pilton mark on its ark. He took one last slurp of tea, inhaled deeply until the loose plaster on the walls rattled, sucked in by the vacuum. Then he stormed out of the kitchen.

Thump thump thump went his feet along the hall to the bathroom door.

Without waiting, he shoved it in hard. It swung open on a surprised Alex, his eyes wide, a hammer in one hand, his fingers bandaged and plastered to the size of zucchinis on the other.

He stood with a mouth full of nails, the new bathroom cabinet he had been trying to fix to the wall above the sink lying face down on the floor in bits.

Jamie took one look at it and, forgetting what he was there for in the first place, shot a look at Alex.

"What did you do that for?" Jamie asked, pointing at the mess.

Alex tried blinking but his eyeballs kept shoving out of his head too far in surprise.

A preternatural calmness seemed to come over him as he reached up and calmly removed the nails from his gob one by one.

He sighed.

"Well, you see, Jamie. I tried using Blu Tack on the cabinet and chucking it at the wall hoping that it would just stick. But obviously I didn't put enough Blu Tack on it to make it stick for long."

The gap between Jamie's eyebrows and his chin shrunk. "Eh?"

Alex snapped. "What do you mean 'what did I do that for?'" he raged. "I didn't do it deliberately, you know."

He waved the hammer at the splinters of wood and glass that used to be the bathroom cabinet at his feet.

But Jamie wasn't having any of that nonsense.

"You're cracked," he said. "I don't know what you're on about but I know what you are doing, to me, and that's driving me mental with the racket. I can't even hear myself drink my tea it's that bad. It's supposed to be Sunday you know. And that means peace, quiet, papers, bacon rolls, a mug of Nambarrie."

Alex jaw dropped. "Awe, I see. It's all right for you to be sitting around on your fat ark reading comics while I do all the hard work, is it? Well, let me tell you something, laddie ..." he said, waving around the hammer in Jamie's direction.

Jamie lurched back.

Alex went on spitting words through tight teeth and gob stopper eyeballs.

"Watch out, Alex, or your teeth'll melt under the strain."

"Out!"

The bathroom door slammed in Jamie's face.

Shoulders pulled up tight, arms straight and fists down a raging Jamie stormed back into the kitchen and sat down.

Everything was quiet again, too quiet. Until he heard muffled footsteps at the other side of the door, Alex hurrying up and down, opening and closing cupboards.

Jamie knew what was coming next.

"No that, for God's sake. I can't take it. I can't I can't ..."

The *Hoover*!

And there it started. Vuuuum Vuh-vuh-vuh vuhvuhvuh VAA-UUUOOOO.

Clonk! Thud!

Jamie cringed as the floorboards were stripped of their skin by the wheels of the Vax that had gone square with age as Alex yanked it along by its trunk.

After ten minutes of eternity it stopped.

Silence for a bit.

The calm before the storm.

Then came the rumble of thunder as Alex's feet thumped closer and closer.

Jamie gripped the arms of the chair.

The kitchen door slammed wide.

Alex marched in, arms full.

"Geemeahand!" he shouted. "Now!"

Alex dumped rolls of wallpaper on the table.

"Eh?" was all Jamie could manage.

Alex stood up to his full height, which was hardly stratospheric.

"And will you quit saying that bloody annoying 'eh' every time I ask you to do anything?"

Jamie stood up.

"Help you do what?"

"Hang the wallpaper."

"It's Sunday. What do you mean 'hang the wallpaper?'"

Alex stood hand on one hip. "That wallpaper." He pointed. "We're going to hang it. *Now!*"

"Can we not just pay somebody to come in and hang it for us?"

"We've no *money!* What with frivolities like going on holiday. Or have you forgot?"

If you'd never bought the wallpaper in the first place we would have saved even more money. But saying that, Jamie realized in the nick of time, would probably have put too much tension in Alex's already over-stressed CK elastic. And the thought of high tension CK elastic going berzerk trapped inside an enclosed space was too much for Jamie to contemplate.

"But I've never hung wallpaper before," Jamie protested.

"Neither have I," Alex said. "But we can figure it out between ourselves. So, first things first."

Alex teetered on the top of the ladder and let the wallpaper drop to the floor. He looked down at Jamie. "Now you mark it where it stops at the skirting board."

Jamie hunkered down, drawing a line in pencil along the bottom of the paper.

"Right," Alex said holding onto the edge of paper and climbing down off the ladder. Jamie held onto the roll at the other end.

Both went back to the kitchen table where Alex laid down the roll and looked for the mark that Jamie had made. He hummed, scanning the line up and down. Using nail scissors, and the tip of his tongue nipped between his teeth, he cut a straight line along the pencil mark.

"There," he said, straightening up. "Now all we have to do is cut seven or eight lengths the same. Then after that start plastering paste on the backs of them and hang them up. Simple."

It took an age, but the boys got there, snipping paper and biting tongues in concentration until they had the required lengths cut.

That done, Alex stood up and both faced each other with self-satisfied smugs.

"See, Jamie," Alex beamed, "all it takes is a wee bit of thought and preparation and all the grief's taken out of the procedure. Watch and learn." He picked up the bucket of wallpaper glue and a two-inch brush and handed them to Jamie.

"Me?" Jamie yelped.

"Aye, you. Now get gluing," he said, "and I'll get hanging."

Jamie slopped the paste onto the wallpaper, remembering it was the back of the strips, not the front that required the paste.

"What's taking so bloody long?" Alex shouted from the bathroom.

"I'm here," Jamie burst in with the first strip of wallpaper folded over on itself, the paste slopping onto the floor.

"Right," Alex called down to him from the top of the ladder, "now gives one end of it up here."

Carefully, not wanting to tear the wet paper, Jamie let Alex take one end and let the sheet un-stick itself full length down the wall.

"Right, just smooth all the bubbles out of it and there … perfect. Kind of," Alex added when he saw that the paper was a wee bit too long. "We can cut it neater when it's drying a bit. It's just stretched a bit with the wet, that's all," he said. "Now you glue another length in. I'll wait up here."

Jamie was glad to get out of the room. It was as if he was scared of breaking something. Is it possible to break wet wallpaper? He didn't think so. But it surely felt like it could.

Another age went by.

"Come on, come on. I'm getting vertigo up here waiting," Alex called out.

Jamie rushed back in with another pasted sheet. It was a cinch.

Again he gave the paper to Alex. Again it slopped down the wall.

In full concentration, Alex, tongue poking out the side of his mouth, slithered the paper up matching the two strips of wallpaper side by side. Up a bit, up a wee bit more and a bit more.

No, they still didn't match.

Goggle-eyed in terror, Jamie watched the bottom of the strip climb higher and higher up the wall until it was a foot up above the skirting.

"Eh?"

"There!" Alex said, cutting him off and smoothing down the paper.

"Alex?"

"What?"

"I think there's something wrong."

Alex looked down through the clouds of Mount Olympus. "What's wrong?"

But Jamie didn't wait to answer and ran out of the room instead.

He hid in the kitchen.

And waited.

"Jamie! You stupid bloody ark!" came through the wall.

"I didn't do it. You told me!" Jamie shouted cowering in the corner.

Crash!

In went the kitchen door.

"Idiot!" Alex yelled.

"I only did what you told me to."

"You didn't match up the pattern."

"I didn't know."

"An idiot would have known."

"Well how come you didn't know then?" Jamie asked.

"Because I'm not an idiot!"

Head in his hands, Alex sat at the table with lengths of useless wallpaper all over it.

"Ruined," he said calming down.

Jamie made him a coffee.

"Can we no just buy more?"

"More?" Alex said. "It was the last that there was, of that pattern anyway. That was how it was so cheap."

Like the Beatrix Potter gen fake antique, Jamie thought.

"I was trying to save us money for this holiday of ours," Alex went on. "Now look what's happened. Disaster."

Just then Jamie had a brain wave.

"Could we not just cut the extra bits off the top then stick them on the bottom then?" he said.

Alex looked as if he had just been asked to eat something nutritious.

"Don't be such a ... mmmm."

"Hmm?"

"Well, better than nothing, I suppose," Alex sighed.

So off they went with renewed enthusiasm.

"Can't really see the joins," Jamie said encouragingly, plastering the top parts that Alex cut off each strip and sticking them down on the gaps at the bottom end.

Eventually finished they stood side by side and admired their handiwork.

A bit bubbly looking, Jamie thought, but didn't dare say anything that would antagonize Alex.

"Not bad, if you look at it through half-shut eyes that is," Alex said, cheeks pushing up to his eyebrows testing his theory.

He stepped back and shrugged. "Anyway," he said. "I'm knackered. Let's have a coffee."

Alex walked out.

Jamie was about to follow him when at the last second he turned back not quite sure about something.

Then he saw it.

"Alex?" he called out, cringing at the sound of his own voice.

"What is it?" Alex called back from the kitchen.

Jamie could hear him filling up the kettle.

Jamie's face scrunched up with a constipated gurn.

"Eh, the pattern on the wallpaper," he said.

"What about it?"

"I think it's upside-down."

Jamie's neck disappeared into his shoulders when he heard the kettle crash into the sink.

"You idiot!"

~~*

Jamie didn't know how to make it up to Alex.

"What do you want for your eighteenth birthday?" he asked. "It's only a couple of weeks away."

"Squash," Alex said, elbows on the table, fists on cheeks. The ones on his face.

Jamie cringed.

"You promised me months ago you would teach me how to play," Alex said.

Which Jamie had, only he had hoped Alex would have forgotten.

"Well?" Alex prompted.

"Oh, all right then."

Alex perked up. "When?"

"Whenever."

"You said that three months ago," Alex whined.

Jamie huffed out a breath and thumped back in his chair.

"A Saturday," he said. "Better on a Saturday."

Alex was already up and out of the room.

He came back with the calendar.

"Next Saturday then!"

"But your birthday's not until the Saturday after."

But Alex ignored him and in red ink he penned in the words SQUASH. "There. It's done."

Jamie smiled.

His heart sank.

One racket swapped for another.

CHaPTer 8

Later, Jamie slid forward in his armchair, bit the side of his tongue, stretched out his leg, extended his toes and wiggled them.

"Hey, look at that," he said. "I'm near enough losing my foot in your left ark it's that fat."

Poke, poke.

Alex was lying on the floor, flicking through the glossies when he jerked his hips forward away from the intrusion.

"Stop that," he said. "And I've no got two arks, left or right. Only one, right."

"Feels like a fat (poke) ark to me (jab, jab). You want to go on a diet, lad."

"I am on a diet. And I'm not fat!"

"Kind of diet?"

"A crash diet."

"Aye," Jamie said. "It looks like you've been in a crash right enough."

Alex spun around and jumped to his feet. "Quit it. I'm trying to concentrate!"

Later, with the night creeping in through the window, the pair sat in the living room with nothing more to look forward to than work in the morning. Something Jamie hated to think about at the best of times.

"Tell us one of your funny stories, Alex," he said.

Alex looked at him and raised an eyebrow. "I've already told you them all," he said, "Including the one about Thelma trying to dye her hair auburn."

"Can't remember you telling me that one, Eck."

"It turned out orange. Carpet-orange as well, if you know what I mean," Alex said. "God, she was mortified."

Jamie slumped down in the sofa. "Tell me some more, Eck."

Alex huffed, twiddled his thumbs.

"Tell me a real story," Jamie said. "One that's really happened."

"I've told you them all," Alex said. "I'll end up repeating myself."

Jamie egged him on. "You've never repeated any of them to me yet. Tell us some more concerning (that great lanky lazy skinny sponging blood sucking get and galoot of a half-brother of yours) Deek."

"And what do I get out of it for my troubles?" Alex asked, twiddling his thumbs faster.

Jamie jumped up and left the room, ran along the hallway to make Alex coffee, himself tea. And as he waited for the kettle to boil he raided his secret stash hidden under the sink just behind the OMO.

By the time he returned to the living room, Alex was already sitting in the armchair like a little Buddha, his fingers forked together in his lap, legs crossed at his ankles.

Everything now in place, coffee and tea, Jamie sat himself down himself on the sofa and opened the stash bag.

Alex didn't want to look too excited when he saw it so he took in a long slow breath of calm.

"Well," he began, "it was like this ..."

Jamie sat in rapture as he always did when Alex told him the tales of his older brother, Derek's, business ventures.

"This one woman was terrified of everything," Alex said, "anything with wings that is. Except for bees, bats and wasps, apparently."

"Moths?" Jamie asked hopefully, knowing how scared he was of them himself.

Alex shook his head. "Don't know about moths, but it was more birds this woman was feared of, apparently."

"All right," Jamie said with more than a little disappointment.

"I don't even know how Derek ever got her to think that he was the man for the job myself," Alex sighed. "But I suppose when folks are desperate, well ..."

Here Jamie nodded in agreement. Anything to get the story going. "So what happened?" he said.

Alex sighed sadly this time.

"Derek had had this big box made especially for the purpose, you see. Actually he had made it himself. Although Derek did say that he had had an accomplice to the Sheriff after he was arrested, an accomplice who had helped Derek build the thing. I think Derek only said he had an accomplice because he was hoping he would only get half the punishment if he could persuade everyone there was more than just him involved in it.

"However, from what I can make out, accomplice or not, Derek had made this big box out of bits of old cardboard, post office string and Sellotape. About the size of a telephone box this box was. Big enough and no more for this woman to stand up in. And the box had wheels on it that Derek had nicked from some bairn's guider. Anyway, Derek had this box tied to the back of this old banger of a car, then reversed the old banger up to this poor woman's front door."

Jamie nodded, mesmerized.

"So this woman then climbed into the box, as Derek had informed her to do on a previous consultation ... ."

"What consultation?"

"Awe, aye, nearly forgot," Alex said. "Derek had put this wee ad in the paper claiming that he was an expert at curing phobias. Anyway, this poor woman had read his ad because she was desperate to be cured of her phobia of birds. She'd never been out of her house for a hundred years or something like that because of—"

"The birds," Jamie cut in.

"Aye, the *birds*. So there was Derek and the box had been wheeled up to the woman's front door. The woman then climbed into it, whereupon Derek slammed the door shut on it and drove it off to the park. It was a quiet Monday morning. All the bairns were in school, folks at work, and it was an overcast sky, that kind of sky that feels like there's a safe door over your head just ready to fall down in flatten you, know what I mean, Jamie?"

Jamie nodded.

"Making sure there was nobody else about in the park, Derek then took these huge speakers out of the boot of the old banger, plonked them on the ground near the box, then went back to make sure all the car doors were locked. He then walked up to the box to make sure the woman was still inside it by giving it a kick. The women inside it squealed, confirming that she still was. And Derek had then shouted through the side of it, '*Get ready for the cure of a lifetime!*' I think he must've been watching too much Paul McKenna or something. But that's just my theory on the matter. Anyway, *then* it all happened."

Alex paused for effect, leaned forward and took a long slow sip of coffee.

"And?" Jamie encouraged him.

"Mind if I have a boiler?" Alex smiled over the arm of his chair at Jamie.

Jamie picked up the bag of boiled sweets from his secret stash and offered the already opened-in-preparation top to Alex.

Alex wove his fingers expertly into the bag.

"I think I'll have one of the strawberry ones this time," he said craning one out the bag between the tips of his fingers. "Ta," he said, popping a red one into his gob and clacking it against his teeth, which set Jamie's own teeth on edge hearing it.

But sometimes you just have to put up with things to get what you really want, he reasoned.

Alex gave the boiling a good suck before he went on.

"Aaaaand," Derek stood back a bit from the box with a bit string in his hand, a bit string that was attached to the top of the box. And then he said the magic word."

With bated breath Jamie asked, "What word?"

Alex looked at him in the eyes. And it was as if the lights in the room had suddenly dimmed around them, as a spotlight glowed on the pair in rapture.

"*Shazam*!" Alex said. "Then Derek yanked hard on the bit string. But the door on the box didn't just open, Jamie. All four sides of it did. Like the petals of a huge wilted flower they fell down to the ground, all at the same time, leaving this poor woman standing there, out in the open for the first time in a million years. And she was in *terror*."

"Oooh," Jamie said, wriggling down into the cushions. "What happened then?" he asked, popping boiler into his mouth.

"Derek then rushed over to switch on the speakers, full blast, a recording of birds squawking and screeching like they were on the attack! The woman went bonkers! She ran for cover, straight for the car. And there she was yanking and pulling at its doors ..."

"Which were locked, of course."

"Which were locked, you're right, Jamie. But then Derek started chucking wallpaper paste at the woman as well."

"Eh?"

"Aye," Alex said, settling back. "You heard me right. Wallpaper glue. Derek started scooping the stuff up out of this bucket and chucking it at her until she was drenched from head to foot in the stuff, as far as the court was told anyway."

"What did Derek do that to her for?"

"For to make the stuff stick. That's what for."

"What stuff?"

"Trill! Budgie seed. Derek shoveled it at the woman."

"What a creep."

"Of course every crow, starling, pigeon and sparrow then belted out of the trees thinking it was Christmas on a stick for them and went straight for the woman. Who by this time was a screaming loony with fright," Alex said with his arms shooting up in the air to the echo of the word *fright*.

He settled back.

"Derek's idea had been that this woman's phobia needed drastic measures for a cure to stick. And it wasn't just Trill he was shoveling at her either, but popcorn as well, that and a whole loaf of moldy Mother's Pride as well as the bags of budgie seed.

"I couldn't believe it myself as I sat cringing at the back of the court listening to it all. In the end I had had to close my eyes as well as my ears by that time."

"What happened to the woman?" Jamie asked.

"Derek told the court that she had tried to crawl under the car when the birds went on the attack. So to save her from herself, Derek had jumped in the car, drove off and left her there out in the open in the middle of the park. The last thing Derek claimed he saw, out the back window as he raced off, were all these birds burling around and going mental at the woman who had her hands stuck to her head, screaming as she ran after his car!"

"What a get!"

"That's what the Sheriff said."

"What happened to the woman?"

Alex, looking distant just shrugged.

"Nobody knows," he said. "She's still missing. Thing was it was the woman's husband that brought it all to a head."

"He told the polis?" Jamie said.

"No, he paid Derek a bonus. The husband had been trying to get rid of his wife for years apparently. He said that she was mental. That she had been driving *him* mental. So he had given Derek a fiver for a job well done. Pleased as punch Derek had then gone off and spent that fiver on crisps and juice. But it turned out that the fiver was a forgery. And that's how Derek ended up in court."

"Providence, Alex. Providence," Jamie said, waving a finger in the air.

"The Sheriff had also agreed that the woman was mental, but said that that wasn't the issue. It was the forged fiver that was the issue. But the be all and the end all of it is, Jamie, that that woman is still missing to this day, probably still running round the woods flapping her arms round her head trying to bat off the birds for all anybody know."

Both sat back with blank faces when Alex had finished his story, until ...

"You are going to teach me to play squash aren't you, Jamie?"

Jamie's mouth tightened.

"Jamie?"

"I said I would, right?"

CHaPTer 9

"I don't know how he got away with it all when I think about it, Jamie." Alex rubbed at his head. "Like Derek's constipation cure. He said it worked that fast that you would have to sit on the you-know-what-may as you drank it. Course there was the free net that came with it."

"Net?"

"Aye. Derek advertised it is a safety measure, that the net should be nailed to the ceiling above your head just in case."

"You took off?" Jamie said.

"Aye."

"What was in this constipation cure?"

"Raw cabbage, Brussels sprouts, grass cuttings, everything through an industrial blender. You were to drink it, but only if you were sitting on the you-know-what-may at the time."

Alex thought for a moment. "I think he means well, though, Jamie."

"If you say so," Jamie said.

"The slimming cure was the last of Derek's body malfunction cures though. Most people didn't believe it when they heard what it was. But some did though."

"What was that?"

"Tea," Alex said.

"Tea? How's drinking tea help you lose blubber?"

"What made it worse," Alex said, "was that there being a fat explosion at the moment in the modern world, folk were queuing up for miles around to give it a go. Desperate people, Jamie."

"But tea?"

"Well, they weren't to drink it," Alex said.

"I don't get you."

"They were to *eat* it," Alex explained. "One tablespoon four times a day, loose leaf PG tips. These women were buying it by the ton. Derek really did think he was helping them with their problems though. But problem was ..."

"It didn't work."

"No, it worked all right. It was just that they all ended up being sick all over the place."

Silence befell over the two as they sat there, Jamie lounging back on the sofa, Alex on the armchair.

"Tell me another one, Alex. And I definitely will teach you how to play squash."

Alex sighed, and huffed. There was no way around it. "Okay," he said. "One more.

"Gestalt Therapy, whatever that is. Derek had read about it. And there was these nurses, right, and the tension between them on the night shift was getting out of order. Appalling it was. So in goes Derek. He would cure them all, or so he had convinced them. But first he would have to see them at work. See where the problems was sort of thing.

"Anyway, there was three of them on the night shift, plus one from an agency kind of thing. Thus there was a fat one, a thin one and an in-between one, and that other one in a yellow uniform. She was the one from the agency.

"The fat one, the thin one and the in-between one all stormed in for the night shift. The one in yellow stood there terrified. She'd not worked in that hospital before and was scared already. Anyway, the other three ignored her and went in for the report. The day shift had already been waiting at the fire exit doors apparently for a quick getaway with their bags ready to do a runner as soon as they saw the night shift coming along the corridor. Anyway, the day shift belted off shouting that they'd left a note on the desk about what had been happening that day.

"First thing Derek noted was that all the buzzers were going off because these old folk wouldn't stop buzzing for attention, you see. Anyway the fat one then came out of the office and flicked a secret master switch."

"What happened then?" Jamie asked.

"All the buzzers were cancelled at the same time."

"What about the poor old ones needing help?"

Alex shrugged, as he was wont to do. "Pop psychology, the fat one informed Derek. 'If I can't hear the buzzers', she'd told him, 'then they must be all right.'"

"There were a few crashes and bumps after that, but the fat and the thin one, and the in-between one just pointed at the scared one in the yellow uniform, and then in the general direction of the noise and told her, 'That's what you're paid for.'"

"Away!" Jamie said shocked.

"After that was the drug round. And after giving all the old biddies double doses of everything, all the nurses went into the office. Except the one in yellow uniform. She wasn't allowed in there. She was to stay out in the ward in case any of the old biddies needed help.

"The one in yellow was mortified when the fat one gave her a torch and some comics, Buntys I think Derek had said. And she was told in no uncertain terms to sit at the end of this long creepy corridor all by herself.

"Anyway, back in the cozy comfy office, the fat, and the thin, and the in-between one prepared for the long night ahead.

"The fat one brought out her handy travel-size Ouija board and planchet. The thin one brought out her angel cards, and the in-between one brought out her tarot cards—an Alistair Crowley special extra creepy deck. Then out comes the pictures of their heroes, Yvette Fielding and Eric Pakora, or whatever his name is. That weird bloke from Most Haunted? Anyway, the lights went in the office went down and out comes their infra red cameras and EMF detectors, Pringles, coconut buns and chocolate cakes.

"I thought nurses didn't get paid that much to buy all that stuff."

"Aye, well, stranger things they say, Jamie."

"Who says?"

"They says."

"Who's they?"

"How should I know? I'm trying to tell you what happened, right?"

"Right, I'm listening."

With a deep sigh, Alex slumped back, and in a renewed reverie went on, eyes aglaze. "Of course then out went the lights completely and out came the incense candles."

At this point the sides of Alex's mouth pulled down, ghoulish like, his arms extending out in front of him, his fingers hanging limply, stirring them around in the air.

"Is anybody theeeeeere? Is anybody there?"

It didn't help when Jamie yelled, "Boo!"

Alex choked , spluttered and lurched forward, sparrow-beaked gob-wide, red faced and slavering.

"God, I nearly inhaled a whole boiler, yah tube!"

In fright, Jamie started thumping Alex on the back until the boiler shot out of his throat faster than a speeding bullet.

Arms waving him away and wheezing for a dying breath, Alex managed to screech out the words, "All right! All right! What are you trying to do? Kill me?"

A recalcitrant Jamie said, "I was just trying to add some atmosphere."

"By turning me into a ghost?"

"Sorry for trying to save your life!"

Alex settled back, the red in his face and the veins in his neck receding to normal levels. "Are you wanting to hear this or no?" he asked.

"Keep your paps on for God's sake."

Alex recomposed himself. "Aaaaaaaanyway," he went on. "The planchet plastic thing started moving around the

Ouija board and they all started accusing each other of shoving it. The ambience of the moment was lost, what with everybody yelling at each other, till the in-between one jumped up and told them all to ..."

"*SHARRAP*!" Jamie yelled and laughed.

"Will you stop doing that? And she didn't tell them to shut up. She told them all to calm down, which they did. And it was back to the Ouija board. *Is there anybody theeeeere.*"

"You've done that bit."

Face creased in consternation, Alex jumped his rear an inch off the seat and slammed back down. "Do you want to hear this or not?"

Jamie harrumphed and sat back, arms folded tight across his chest.

"Anyway," Alex went on, "the letters were spelt out by the planchet thing. M.y.k.i.l. J.a.k.s.i.n.

With a worried expression, Jamie asked, "My kill Jacks in?"

"Aye, now quit nipping my brain and listen."

Jamie folded his arms even tighter.

So these nurses started asking questions about all the other staff, evil stuff mind, and of course Derek was scribbling away like mad making his observations."

"I thought the lights were out. How could he see to write?"

Alex ignored him. "The next night Derek went back and told them all where they were going wrong. Instead of going stir crazy talking about each other behind each other's backs, and using Ouija boards and stuff to dig the dirt on each other, they were to say what they really felt about each other, face to face, instead."

"Interesting," Jamie commented, eyes rolling up as he popped a spangle into his gob. He crunched down on it hard. "So what was the outcome?" he asked.

"Well, instead of defusing the tension in the ward, it went opposite. Nuclear in fact. Near enough everybody wanted to kill each other by the end of the week. One nurse was even caught smuggling a grenade into the ward in her handbag. That's when it dawned on them what the real source of their problems were."

"Sleekit Deek?"

"How'd you guess? So it was another suing in court for him."

"Did the nurses get their money back?"

"That 'n more."

"Interest?"

"Damages from Derek for being an unqualified, unlicensed …"

"Ark?" Jamie said.

"… councilor."

"Did the nurses win?"

"Aye."

"How much?"

"Enough."

"Who paid for it?" Jamie asked, right eyebrow high.

Alex stood up quickly. "I'm away to make another coffee," he said "Want one?"

Jamie pushed what was left of the spangle into his cheek and looked up at him and sighed. "Why not?"

And as Alex picked up the mugs and left the room, Jamie slowly fumed away.

When will you ever learn? He thought shaking his head.

One thing Jamie did know, was that it was going to take a crowbar of a job to pry Alex's sponging siblings away from their ever-faithful little half-brother.

CHAPTER 10

Jamie's plan was to keep on Alex good side. To do that, he reasoned he would have to do more. Like more cooking, more shopping, more washing and cleaning the flat.

That was the way to win Alex over. Then Alex would dump those twins of evil.

Having managed to wangle a few hours off for the afternoon, he had rushed into a butcher's. Pointed to something hanging from a hook on the wall and asked, "What's that?"

The butcher told him.

"How'd you cook it?"

"You boil it till it's done," the butcher said.

That was a good enough answer. Alex would be pleased as punch. Wholesome food, just like he'd asked for.

Next came the grocers.

"What are they?" Jamie asked.

"Potatoes."

"And what about the orange things? What are they?"

"Carrots."

Okay. "I better take some onions as well," he said.

And after a few more items he decided that that was the meal for tonight taken care of.

Except the bus took an age to get him home. He jumped off the bus, barged through the crowds, his feet skidding along on the pavement, bashed open the main door to the flats above and bombed up the stairs. By the time he had made it to the third floor he thought he would need an oxygen tent.

The cigs could wait.

He threw the bags down in the hallway and rushed to the kitchen, pulled off his jacket and slung it across one of the chairs.

Right. First things first.

Washing machine, an old rusty thing that came with the flat.

He dragged it out from under the bunker.

Cheek to charge us rent for this old thing, he thought.

He hauled and yanked at it, convinced that it either had square wheels, no wheels, or that there was a hidden handbrake on it somewhere.

It would be a cinch once he got it started though, though. He'd seen Alex use it before.

Jamie plugged it in, unraveled the rubber hose at the back and rammed one end onto the tap. He opened one of the lids on top of the machine and looked inside. There was a big plastic twirly thing and big wooden tongs. He pulled out the tongs and filled the tub with water. He turned the dial on the machine to boil and hunted for the washing powder under the sink, found it and poured some in. Everything going to plan so far he felt pleased with himself. But how much washing powder was enough? He squinted at the instructions on the side of the box.

Who cares? "Men don't need instructions," he said and dumped in some more.

That should do it.

Everything would go to plan. The weather report last night had predicted sun. It had been right so far.

He pulled everything out of the wash-basket and dumped the lot into the top of the machine and mashed it down into the water with the big fat tongs like he was trying to kill a sea monster. After that he poked at a button on the machine. The twirly thing twirled side to side.

Sloosh sloosh sloosh it all went.

The steam coming out of the machine made him sweat. He rolled up his sleeves and dragged the back of his arm across his brow.

He bunged in more and more soap powder.

The twirly thing stopped after about fifteen minutes and Jamie dived in with the wooden tongs.

It was like fighting with an octopus with knots in its tendrils. He had to use both hands with the wooden tongs. He swayed back, teeth clamped tight, and tugged at the washing with all his might.

"Knew we should have an automatic, but no. Where the hell do twin tubs exist now but museums? 'Wait till we have a flat of our own,' Alex says. 'Wait till we've got enough dosh to buy a house of our own. Then we can have an automatic.' Damn blast it! What's wrong with this washing!"

A lump of clothing finally freed itself from the grey sludge and splodged out of the opening, steaming and wriggling from the end of the tongs as if it was radioactive, which Jamie sensibly kept at arm's length.

He plonked the lot into the other half of the machine.

It got stuck at the opening. He bashed the ends of the tongs down on the steaming mass of fabric pulverizing it down into the spin drier.

"Conditioner. I forgot the conditioner!"

Panic attack.

He raked around under the sink again, yanked out a bottle and poured the goo over the washing in the spinner.

"That should do it," he said.

He slammed down the lid, poked a button and stood back.

It began to spin.

The machine wobbled.

Then it banged its wheels up and down like it was having a tantrum and started to walk across the floor.

"I've overloaded it!"

Up went the lid. The spinner stopped. He lifted the clothes out and then dumped them back in. Slam went the lid again.

It was worse.

Then there was a bang.

Jamie jumped the height of himself as the plug exploded in the socket behind him.

"Oh God! What now?"

He looked at his watch. The clothes were still soaking. Then he had a brilliant idea.

A fuse for the plug? No, that was too simple. What he thought about was that big iron contraption thing in one of the hall cupboards that had been left by the previous owner before that get of a landlord had snatched it up for renting out with the flat.

He dashed out of the kitchen and into the hallway, skidded to a halt, yanked open the cupboard door and looked down at the thing at the back.

On his hunkers now, he grabbed for it and picked the great iron thing up off the floor. Staggering side to side his, legs buckled under the weight of it.

He swayed back through to the kitchen.

Right. What now?

"You screw it to the side of the sink."

He did.

He stood back and admired his handiwork and smiled.

"Now we're cooking with gas."

He looked at his watch. Sharp intake of breath.

"Look at the time!"

He forgot about the washing as he whizzed around yanking open cupboard doors grabbing for pots and pans, filling them with water and dumping them down on the cooker.

He grabbed for the bag from the butcher, emptied it end up and dumped the contents into the largest pot. It just fit and no more. He threw the carrots and potatoes into the sinks, scrubbed and peeled them and dumped them into another pot.

He stood back.

There, that's fixed.

He turned to the washing machine again and rammed his hand into the spinner.

"Ayah!" he screamed, yanking his hand back out.

It was still frazzling hot.

In he rammed the tongs like a mad dentist trying to extract teeth.

He pulled out a lump of clothes from the spinner and began to feed it through the twin rollers, all the while turning the crankshaft on the mangle.

The washing wilted through the other side and into the sink. The water being crushed out of it poured onto the floor.

"Hell! I should be shoving it through from the sink's side."

Except the crank handle would only go one way and not back.

There was nothing else for it but to squash the rest of it through.

He ran into the bathroom and grabbed the towels and dumped them on the puddle at the sink and swirled them around with his foot at the same time as he turned the crank on the mangle.

Leaving the now mangled-to-death washing in the sink, he picked up the towels from the floor.

He almost shoved them in through the mangle from the wrong side the same way as he had with the clothes.

Until he remembered and shoved them through from the sink's side. But to do that he would have to turn the mangle around, re-clamp the thing to the side of the sink, and start again.

Of course that meant that the washing in the sink ended up being re-soaked.

"Damn blast it! Idiot! Take the washing out of the sink and put it into the wash basket first."

He dumped everything in as everything else in his ideas was being dumped out. Everything was going wrong.

The pots started to boil over.

He rushed over and turned down the gas rings.

With that done he took a deep breath, calmly walked over and told himself that it would be all right.

He emptied the machine and shoved it back under the bunker. And with the gas on a low peep he grabbed the wash basket, the rope and the pegs and rushed out into the sunshine.

CHAPTER 11

"Last night I dreamt I was a pigeon again."

Not Manderley then, Alex thought, rolling up his eyes as he listened to Derek relating to a dream that he had had last night, Sunday night, a dream straight from Hitchcock by the sounds of it. But it wasn't *Rebecca*. And Alex just hoped this was going to be a short story.

The four-flight climb up the stairwell to the old house had been a long one; a climb loaded with memories. The vestibule door closing behind him as he had stepped in from the street had felt like it was shutting him in. Had it always been such a dark dingy place? The grime on the walls. The chipped paint. How long had it been since Mum had passed away? The place seemed to have gone downhill since Alex had last been there.

Christmas came to mind for some reason. Their last Christmas together, him with Thelma and Derek. The memory swept through him as he climbed, gripping on to banister like a weary old man, the wood cold and shiny, feeling the lumps cut out of it under his hand.

He stopped a few times and looked over the side, down to the darkness below. Then the memory of the tree had come back to him, the Christmas tree.

It had been huge, covered in decorations and red and green tinsel, baubles and lights. It had looked pretty as it had stood in the corner of the living room. But there was a sadness about it too. A living thing that had been cut down. And there it had stood with its branches out proud, like arms. Yet he couldn't stop thinking that it had been slowly dying.

A living thing made to look like a clown.

Alex shook his head at the thought of it now.

"I'm getting soft in my old age," he said, his head as he hauled himself up the last flight.

Each step up to the front door brought more memories, of how the needles from the branches had started to fall away.

"Dying."

Next he remembered how the brown of the branches had begun to show through, the greenness fading from them, the brown of its bones revealed, dead sticks. The tinsel had then started to sag lower as the days had gone by. And the baubles would mysteriously fall away one by one, the limbs of the tree growing too weak to hold onto them.

"Just a tree, Eck. It was only a tree," he had to remind himself.

Trapped by its own roots it hadn't been able to run away, cut down where it stood, then sold into slavery and turned into a clown.

The worst had been when it had been time to throw it out. Derek had pushed it out through the door. Alex's idea had been to carry it back down the four flights. But Derek had had other ideas. Making sure no one was at the bottom of the stairwell Derek had dropped it over the side.

The poor thing had landed on its stump, Alex remembered.

Leaning over the banister he had looked down at it, even in the darkness, he had seen how the last of its needles had been shaken off, saw the way it had stayed upright defiantly for a second or two before finally keeling over onto its side, finally out of its misery—dead.

Derek had laughed at the mess.

Alex had been mortified at what he had seen as the last act of indignity that they could have imposed on another living thing.

"It's just a bloody tree, Eck," Derek had said. "Get a grip."

After that Derek had simply turn tailed and walked back inside and left Alex to clear up the mess down below.

"Never again," Alex had whispered to himself as he had dragged the tree out into the street to lay it by the curbside. "Never again."

But he hadn't really been talking to himself, but to the tree. "I promise to you that, even although I know that you can't hear me, that I'll never let this happen again to another one like you for as long as I live."

And he had vowed then and there that he would never purchase a real tree ever again for Christmas.

Now he sat in the old family living room looking upon Derek who was lost in his own story of the nightmare he had suffered last night.

Alex was only half listening.

"I can feel a story coming on here," he sighed, hands in pockets.

"Well, I woke up and thought, what's wrong?" Derek went on ignoring his little brother.

"This was your dream?" Alex asked.

"My dream, aye. Anyway, I started moving my arms. Only it wasn't arms I had. It was *wings*!"

"Then what? Or should I not ask?" Alex yawned.

He looked at his watch. If this were going to take any longer Jamie would be wondering where he was.

"Well I was starving you see ..." Derek said.

"What's new?"

"And I needed my breakfast, you see."

"No I can't really," Alex said. "But go on."

"And all I could see was this bit popcorn on the ground."

"This is still your dream we're talking about here, or your guilty conscience?" Alex asked.

The sarcasm bypassed Derek.

"Aye, in my dream. So I went to pick up this bit popcorn with my hands. Only I couldn't get a hold of it, could I?"

"Because you had wings?"

"Aye, because I had wings. So then I thought, I'll have to use my feet."

"Your feet?" Alex said.

"Aye, my feet," Derek said as if his brother had asked the most stupid question in the world.

"Pigeons don't have feet."

Derek gritted his teeth at the intrusion. "My claws then! What does it matter?"

"Don't lose the head!"

"Anyway, as I was saying, wee brother of mine, I had to use my claws for *hands*. So, I nabbed the bit popcorn and then I tried to shove it in my gob. I was starving you see. It was the size of a football, mind you, that bit pope-corn was in comparison to me, being a pigeon that is. But the way I was feeling I was ready to crash it down my neck fast as I could because I was that starving."

"So you've said," Alex said standing up. "You don't mind if I have a cup of coffee, do you?"

Without waiting for an answer he made his way down to the scullery with Derek hurrying after, and almost tripping over his own feet in his haste to keep up.

Alex walked over to the kettle and filled it with water. And as he plugged it in, he asked, "So then what happened?"

Alex leaned back on the sink and folded his arms.

Derek seemed to have trouble recollecting his thoughts. "Well, I keeled over, didn't I?" he said suddenly.

"How come?"

"Have you ever watched a pigeon trying to use its foot to feed its beak *and* stand on one leg it the same time? It's no easy, Eck. And I'll tell you something for nothing, my eyes were like snooker balls on stalks with fright when I started to keel over. Anyway, the be all and the end all of it was that ..."

"Aye?" Alex asked, taking a quick look at the kettle, wishing it would hurry up.

"... I dropped it," Derek said.

By now Alex was searching though the overhead cupboard. "Dropped what?" he asked without looking around.

He reached up and grabbed the coffee jar.

Crap caff, he thought, wrinkling up his nose.

"My guts!" Derek yelped at the back of Alex's head. "The frigging bit popcorn, yah ark, what else? Are you listening to what I'm saying?"

"I'm listening I'm listening. I can't help but listen can I?" Alex said, giving him a sharp look. He unscrewed the lid on the jar. Green label cheap muck, he noted, taking a sniff at the granules.

"Well, pay attention then!" Derek said.

Alex slammed down the jar and turned to Derek. "All right!"

Derek, more relaxed now, went on. "So there I was cart wheeling along, trying to stay on my feet, claws, whatever, when I regained my balance. Then I started looking round for the bit popcorn again. But everything was looking all funny."

Alex turned around and started raking through the drawer for a spoon. "How's that?" he asked with as little interest as he could muster.

God this place is filthy since I've left the two of them to fend for themselves, he realized, and worse that there were no teaspoons to be had. He picked up a soupspoon instead and took a quick glance at Derek who was deep in concentration.

"Because my head kept jerking forward every time my feet moved," Derek said, eyes glazed over at the memory of his dream. He suddenly snapped to. "You know what I mean, don't you, Eck? You've seen pigeons walking, right?"

"I've never paid that much attention, I have to say," Alex lied as he picked up two mugs, sniffed at them, his nose about to retract into the back of his face in disgust. Turning on the tap he started to look around.

"Have you no washing up skoosh?" he asked.

Without waiting for an answer he hunkered down raking through the cupboard under the sink.

"There's more dust than cleaning stuff here," he said.

He grabbed for a red box, pulled it out and held it under the light.

"Oxydol?" he said. "This stuff belongs in a museum. I can't remember this stuff being here when I was here. When was the last time anybody looked under the sink?"

He shook the box.

"Solid," he said standing up.

He opened the flap of the box and peered inside. Dumping it down on the bunker, he searched through the cutlery drawer again.

"Eck, you're nipping my head," Derek whined impatiently. "Will you pay attention to what I'm saying?"

"I'm listening, I'm listening to your dead interesting nightmare," Alex said.

"Well, they do."

Alex found a rusty old knife and held it up. "What does?" he asked.

"Pigeon heads!" Derek yelped. "They jerk forward every time they take a step." Derek calmed himself with a deep breath before going on. "*Anyway*, I spotted this bit popcorn near the ark end of this wall in front of me. So I thought to myself, ah ha! And I went for it, gob wide …"

"Like something out of *The Birds*, you mean?" Alex quipped, stabbing the knife into the box. Satisfied that he had managed to loosen enough of the powder, he shoogled the contents over the mugs in the sink.

"… My eyes were like mini snooker balls, like practically out my head, my guts rabid for something to eat, when this sparrow nabbed it before I could get my beak on it! The get!"

"I don't suppose you've got any oven cleaner?" Alex asked.

It was a stab in the dark.

"Daft question, I know, since anything you two eat comes out of the chip shop these days. Neither of you would know what an oven was if you stuck your head in one."

But the meaning of what Alex said sailed over Derek's comprehension.

The silence was disconcerting.

Having rinsed the mugs, Alex looked over his shoulder with trepidation.

Derek was now sitting down on a deck chair, the only thing to sit on in the scullery after everything else had been sold off.

"So what did you do then?" Alex asked.

Derek thought for a bit, looking up at the ceiling as if trying to fathom his own thoughts from a deep dark distance.

"Well," he said. "I went for it, didn't I? I thought to myself, that wee fat get's no getting my breakfast."

Alex shoveled coffee granules into the mugs. "And?" he asked.

"So I cornered the wee bugger," Derek said. "I mean, Eck, that greedy wee fat get's beak was stretched to its limits with that bit popcorn, my bit popcorn mind you, in its gob. And I was determined to have it, wasn't I?"

Alex filled the mugs with hot water, sugar and milk, which of course he sniffed, but not too close. Satisfied that the milk was still a few days short of complete putrefaction, he asked, "What did you do then?"

He gave one of the mugs to Derek.

"Well, Eck, I thought to myself that I'll nab that wee fat greedy get and make it spit it out! Of course, I had forgotten that I had wings and not arms ..." Derek said leaning back.

"So no hands and no way to strangle the poor wee thing." Alex nodded sagely.

"Right," Derek said. "And no hands, either. So you can see how I was at a disadvantage there, can't you?"

"No I can't really, but no matter. What happened then?" Alex asked, looking over the lip of the mug as he sipped a mouthful of coffee.

With immediate effect he spun around and spat it out into the sink. Still retching, he asked, "What is this muck?"

"Bisto?" Derek stabbed at a guess when he tasted the contents of his own mug.

"Bisto?"

"Don't know," Derek mused, taking another satisfied gulp. "It's been there forever. Tastes all right to me though."

Alex chucked what was left of the contents of his mug into the sink.

"But it's got sugar and milk in it!" he said, turning on his brother, watching wide eyed in disbelief as Derek continued to sip.

But whatever he was drinking, it didn't put Derek off his stride, and he continued on with telling his story of the dream he had from the night before.

"But what I did do," Derek said, "was flap around it with my wings, and my feet grabbing at it."

He sighed whimsically.

"Your claws going for the teeny weenie wee sparrow?" Alex asked.

"Right! My claws was just nipping to get at it."

"Figures," Alex said, rolling up his eyes.

It had been at least three hours since afternoon break and it was killing him for a caffeine surge. He searched though the overhead cupboards again as Derek went on.

"So I jumped on the greedy wee fat get," Derek said.

Alex looked over his shoulder. "The sparrow?"

"I got my claws round its wee fat gizzard and started to choke the bugger. 'Gives it back,' I shouted. 'Gives it!' But *no*. It held on for dear life to that bit popcorn."

"Your bit popcorn," Alex reminded him.

He didn't find any coffee. What he did find were some tea bags.

"Have to do," he said plonking a bag into the mug. "But needs must," he huffed under his breath.

"Correct!" Derek shouted triumphantly.

Alex jumped at the forcefulness of his brother's emphatic call. Heart beating hard he rubbed at his chest.

Derek didn't seem to notice.

"So then I started jumping up and down on it," Derek said, calmer now that he had collected his thoughts, "with my claws tight round its thrapple, in case it tried to swallow the bit popcorn. But still the wee get wouldn't let go. You'd think it would, Eck, but it wouldn't. 'Gives it! Gives it! Gives it!' I shouted. And it was like a balloon, Eck, this wee fat get it was. 'Gives it back yah greedy wee fat gonk!' Boing! Boing! Boing! But no, the wee fat bugger wouldn't spit it out. So then, Eck, I bunched up the one claw that I had left ..."

"How many claws did you have all together like?" Alex asked, grimacing as he sipped at the lukewarm tea.

But Derek was too far-gone with his story to pay attention to the anomaly in his logic. "… And I rammed my foot down its gaping beak," he went on enthusiastically. "I was determined that there was no way that I was going to let that wee swine get my bit popcorn. But by this time the get had swallowed it."

"Your foot?" Alex sniffed.

"The bit popcorn, yah eejit!" Then in a more conciliatory tone, "Aye, well, and my foot as well by this time. But then, of course, the wee monster wouldn't let go of my foot either, would it? And I could hardly keep my balance by this time either, what with this sparrow's gob half way up my leg and that. Made it right difficult for me I can tell you, Eck. I kept threatening to fall over my own feet, claws, whatever, because of it."

"What a get, eh, that wee sparrow was?" Alex mused.

"Anyway, I kept shaking and shoogling my leg trying to get it off, but no. The get held on fast. I could almost feel my foot being digested in the wee fat psycho's guts."

Alex stood up. "A *psycho* sparrow?" he said walking out the door. "Who would believe it."

"Aye," Derek said, standing up, following Alex.

"So what did you do then, brother of mine?"

Derek shuffled up behind Alex, towering over him, eager to get his story heard. "Well my wings were flapping," he said. "And I was hopping around on one leg cause the sparrow's beak was half way up my other one, wasn't it? So this called for desperate measures, Eck."

"Like?" Alex asked, sitting down in the living room.

Derek hurried in and sat down opposite.

"Like I started clobbering it up in down on the pavement," he said. "Didn't I? What else could I do?"

"Clobbering what?"

"The sparrow on my foot! Are you dense or something, Eck?"

"How am I supposed to know what you're clobbering up and down?"

"Listen to what am saying, will you?" Derek pleaded.

"I am!"

"God save me from dense eejit wee bras."

"Get on with it."

"You've made me forget what I was saying now."

"This poor wee sparrow was eating a bit popcorn," Alex reminded him, "A bit popcorn, that could have been anybody's popcorn, and you, brother of mine, decided to ram your fist down this poor wee skinny sparrow's, starving-to-death-emaciated-neck just so you could get it back."

"Awe aye, that's right. The get. So there I was trying to shake it off my foot. But it wouldn't budge, Eck. So I tried flicking if off like. But it was like a sticky snotter that wouldn't let go. And you know something, Alex ..." Derek leaned forward. "I could swear that sparrow was smiling at me."

"Smiling? Oh aye."

"Aye, Eck. Smiling."

"With your fat fist in its teeny wee beak?"

"Aye, it was, Eck."

"Amazing."

"Because it was a psycho sparrow, Eck. Like it was the Lizzy Borden of the sparrow world."

"It was a poor starving wee bird, you mean."

"So was I!" Derek protested.

"Only about ten times the size of it, you mean. But we'll let that one pass, will we no?"

"Whose side are you on?"

"Awe get on with it, will you?"

"Anyway, is I was relating to you, you, my wee brother who's supposed to be on my side, the be all in end all of it was ..."

"You killed the poor wee thing, what with your fat foot stuck down its neck?"

"It wouldn't let go, Eck!"

"You mean it couldn't let go."

"What do you mean?"

"Och never mind!"

"What?"

"What did you do then, is what I'm asking you?"

"I clobbered it, didn't I?"

"Big surprise there then," Alex said.

"But I had to, Eck"

"Right."

"It really was smiling, though."

"Cause it was a psycho sparrow," Alex said with a grimace after taking a drink of his tea.

"It was smiling sleekit like."

"With your foot in its tiny starving wee mouth."

"Now you get it, Alex."

"God's truth! So what then?"

"I bashed it."

"Eh?"

"On the pavement. Whacked it up in down on it. It wouldn't let go of my foot would it? So it was its own fault. And I was desperate to get my foot back, wasn't I? Whack whack whack. Bang bang bang. But *noooooo*, it still held on."

"What a get, eh?"

"Right.

"Still smiling was it?"

"I don't know."

"What do you mean?"

"I mean something hit me at that point."

"What?"

"Some get seagull that must have been circling overhead spying on the proceedings."

"What was it doing to you?" Alex asked looking at his watch.

"The get was pecking at my head! God knows where it came from, but. But all I knew by this point was that I was under attack! Anyway, that's when I spotted this bit of a ping-pong ball. So I let this wee fat sparrow go in went for it. Well, I tried to let the sparrow go but it was still hanging on, it was that ruthless. So I had to kind of wobble over to the ping-pong ball, sparrow and all still on my foot."

"Ping-pong ball?"

"Half of one, aye. And all the while this big bully of a seagull was attacking me, Eck."

"So what did you do?" Alex sighed, rubbing at his forehead, trying to keep in the strain.

"Well, I had this brilliant idea. I took this bit ping-pong ball and shoved it over my head. What do you think of that then?"

"What?"

"The ping-pong ball. I wore it on my head like a crash helmet. Genius I thought."

"Imagine that," Alex said. "A pigeon with a crash helmet on its head."

"Great, eh?"

"If you say so. Anyway, what did you do then?" Alex said.

"I was blind. I couldn't see, could I?" Derek said. "The half bit ping pong ball was covering my eyes, you see. And all the while this big bully of a seagull was coming at me, and at me, and at me ..."

"I get this picture."

"So I took it off my head so as I could see again. Then I just flapped my arms like Billy-oh."

"As you do when your under attack from some big bully of a bird, a ten times bigger bird than you, one that's attacking you for no apparent reason, but for the fact that you're in the wrong place at the wrong time. And you're half starved to death like, an ..."

"Hold on, eh? It's me that's telling the story here."

"Awe aye, I forgot," Alex said face crumpling.

"Anyway, so I flapped my arms like right rapid ..."

"Your wings you mean."

"My arms, my wings, what difference does it make for God's sake?"

"Big difference if you were hanging over the edge of a cliff, I would have thought. But no matter. I'm only your stupid wee bra after all. But slaver on. I'm listening."

"I did something I'm ashamed to admit, Alex."

"Awe aye?"

"I kacked myself. I couldn't help it. It was automatic like. But you know what pigeons are like. It just shot out my ark."

"What about the poor wee sparrow?"

"Eh?"

"The one you were choking to death with your fat foot in its tiny wee per starving mouth?"

"What about it?" Derek asked.

"Awe, forget it. Right, you were flapping your wings."

"Aye I was. Well, then I just kind of went whoosh and that was it. I just pulled up my claws up and kept flapping my wings. And all the while the kack was shooting out me like a machine gun, Eck. I didn't know if that seagull was following me or not though by that time. But I was spinning all over the place way up in the air anyway. That was when that ping-pong ball fell off my head proper, which meant I could see again."

"Good news then?" Alex said.

"No really, because I was heading for this dirty great big building from nowhere. I thought am going to end up with a telescopic beak here."

"What happened?"

"I closed my eyes and I woke up before I hit it."

"Just in time then?"

"Just and no more."

"I take it your pants was packed it the back end when you woke up then," Alex said.

"What?"

"Never mind." Alex stood up. "Look I've got to go home," he said. "Jamie'll be wondering where I am."

There was something he still had to say, but so far he had managed to put it off.

He ran a finger along the mantelpiece.

"The place is covered in stoor, Derek. Do you and Thelma never clean this place?"

Derek shrugged, uninterested. "It doesn't seem to get any thicker the longer you leave it. Of course, if you was still here ..."

"Well, I'm no," Alex cut in, walking towards the door.

Strangely, he felt a pull, a pull that told him that he should stay, just for a little while anyway, just long enough to clean the place up a bit. He couldn't believe how much his brother and sister had let things go.

The windows were filthy, the carpet stank, and even the wallpaper looked like a coal-man had rubbed his hands all over it.

Why couldn't they just look after themselves?

Just stay then, he thought, for a little while, until the place looks decent enough.

Back to the nest. Trapped on the return visit. And then what? Would he ever manage to escape?

He turned to see Derek standing with a hopeful look on his face.

"I'm no coming back, Derek, so just forget it. You and Thelma should be looking after yourselves by now. I've got my own life to lead."

And he felt like a traitor for saying it.

The smile fell off Derek's face. He shrugged as if it didn't matter.

"And you should be in a steady job by now as well," Alex said.

"It's not my fault," Derek whined. "Nothing suits."

"Nothing suits? Nothing suits most folk in the end, Derek. But we still have to work."

"All my business ventures keep falling through, Alex."

"Look, you in Thelma both need to get your acts together. You both know that. I'm no here anymore to pick up after you."

Derek gave him a sharp look. "What do you mean?"

Alex was conciliatory. "I'm no coming back, Derek. You have to look after yourselves. And letting this place go to rack and ruin won't make me feel guilty enough to come back again either. So stop trying to play on my feelings."

"You've got right hard hearted since moving in with that one," Derek said.

"That one's got a name, and his name's Jamie. And no I haven't got more hard hearted, Derek. And anyway, you should be happy for me making my own why now in life. You're twenty-four Derek, it's about time you had a steady job."

"I'm no good it anything, Eck. I just wish I was. I just wish I could make it big and we could all be back together, like we used to be. Like the old days. You, me and Thelma. Just like the way we were when mum was still with us."

Alex turned away, closed his eyes and took a breath. He opened them again. Praying a few words under his breath he looked back, his hand gripping at the edge of the door, his eyes stinging. "Don't, Derek. Please don't.

Mum's gone now. And it's not like she just walked out the door one day and hasn't come back yet. She died a long time ago. So even if we all wanted to go back together like it was, we can't, Derek. We just can't."

Alex opened the door and looked back.

"I love you Derek," he said. "You know that, I love both you and Thelma. But the more I do for you the less you do for yourselves."

Derek stood there, looking sheepish. "We miss you being with us, Alex," he said.

Something seemed to rush up inside of Alex hearing his brother say it.

He sighed.

"No, Derek," he said. "No matter how badly you run your lives, I'm still not coming back."

He paused for a second, then. "So, eh, Jamie and me will be going away for a few days. It's not much of a holiday, Derek, and it means a lot to Jamie. So I don't need anything going wrong, okay?"

But all Derek could do was shake his head and slump back down on the sofa where he held his head in his hands.

"I know you try hard, Derek, but the time for playing around at life has to stop somewhere. For all of us."

Alex tried to sound as gentle as he could but no matter what words he chose to say the obvious, it still made him feel harsh.

"Have you and Thelma got things organized at your end," he said. "For the holiday?"

Derek slumped back in a sulk. "Aye," he said, Thelma's got all the numbers for the ferry, and the cabin next to your two's," he said. "Lucky they had hotel rooms either side yours as well."

"You're really going away us then?" Alex asked.

"Why wouldn't we?"

"Nothing." Alex shrugged.

He could feel his neck sink with disappointment that they, after all, really meant to go.

"Cheer up, Derek," he said.

"How can I?"

Alex put his hand in his pocket and walked over to him.

"Look, here," he said. "I'll give you a fiver. I can give you more later if you need it, but ..."

Derek looked up at his little brother standing there, holding out the worn blue note in his hand.

All he could do was slowly shake his head, reach out to his little brother and close his hand over Alex's.

"No, Eck," he said standing up beside him. "I owe you too much already."

Alex looked up at him. "You're my brother, Derek," he said. "You don't owe me anything."

"You keep it," Derek said. "You need it more than me and Thelma. We're just a bit skint getting the holiday thing together, that's all. And you're right, it's about time I started to get myself sorted out."

Alex sighed. "Are you sure?" he said. "You could buy something to cheer yourself up a bit."

Derek towered over his little brother. He reached out and closed Alex's fingers over the money.

"No, pal," he said. "You keep it. I'll be all right."

"Are you sure, Derek?" Alex asked.

"A course I'm sure. And all I know is that you're the best wee brother anybody could ever have wished for. The best I've ever had."

"Your only one, and only a half of one at that," Alex said.

Alex was startled when Derek gave him a hug.

"You're a great wee brother, Eck. Half one or no."

Now Alex felt worse. He didn't know what to think. And it was making it harder for him to leave.

Derek let him go and stood back, hands in pockets.

"You've always been there for us, Eck, that's the problem. Bailing me and Thelma out. You've always been hard working and never thinking about yourself. We're just selfish."

"Don't say anymore, Derek, or you'll have me greeting."

Derek smiled then laughed. He lurched forward and slapped his little brother on the back, almost knocking the air out of him.

"You go away home to your man," he said. "Just don't fall into the trap of doing everything for him like you did with me and Thelma, that's all I'm saying, Eck. We just don't want to see you get hurt, Alex."

Alex's face began to crumple.

"Awe, come on yah big wee softy. What are you crying for?"

Alex swallowed. "I just want everybody to be happy, Derek," he said, "that's all. And sometimes it's like everything just keeps going wrong. It's no fair sometimes."

Derek ssshed him in his ear.

Finally letting him go, Derek said, "Go on, your guy's waiting there with his pipe and slippers."

"Awe Derek sometimes you and Thelma just get me all confused and I don't know what to think half the time."

He wiped his hand under his nose.

"We do love you, Eck. No matter what it seems like sometimes, we do love you."

With that Derek saw him to the door.

Alex stepped out onto the darkness of the landing and took one last look at his brother as he stepped down the stairs.

"I love you, Derek," he said.

But when he looked back through the railings, the door was already closed.

CHAPTER 12

Alex knew there was something up as soon as he walked in the door. The place was like a sauna.

Should I or should I no? he wondered as he stood in the hallway. Left or right? Left to the kitchen where there was potential disaster in the waiting, or right to the living room where there was no kettle or decent coffee.

He only wished everything in life was that simple. Only two choices.

"Can only take one though," he sighed. Then again even with only two forks in a road there was always the chance he would keep taking the wrong ones.

"Que sera, sera, whichever way will it be?"

Left.

He went for the kitchen and peeked round the edge of the door.

No Jamie.

Must be here though because something is cooking, literally.

He stepped in and only glanced at the covered pots and pans bubbling away on the cooker as he filled up the kettle.

After he made himself a coffee he sat at the kitchen table and guzzled it down.

Jamie walked in. Hair plastered with wet, washing basket in hand, he crashed down on one of the chairs.

"You look a bit drookit," Alex said, raising an eyebrow.

He was still thinking about Derek and his story of the pigeon. Clicking and whirring in silence, his mind tried to fathom if there was a message in his story. Did it mean anything? Alex was beginning to think of himself as the tiny little sparrow. It sent shivers down his spine. Not about the fact that his own brother was dreaming of strangling him, but that Alex was seen as a wee fat greedy get.

"I'm sick of this," Jamie said, bringing Alex back to the room.

"Sick of what?"

Jamie blew out a well-aimed breath from a jutting lower lip and sent a nose drip flying. "Bloody rain," he said.

"Oi!" Alex said, slapping his hand over his coffee mug as the drip flew over. "We're in Kelly," he said. "What do you expect the weather to do?"

"I expect her on the telly to get the weather right, that's what," Jamie said. "*She* said it was supposed to be sunny today that weather woman Heather did."

Just then a beam of sunlight streamed in through the grime of the window and lit Jamie up like a downtrodden angel.

"I don't believe it!" he exclaimed, wiping the rain from his brow. "I put out the washing, it rains. I take it in, it *stops*."

He stood up swung the basket back under his arm and ran out.

"Awe well." Alex shrugged finishing off his coffee.

The kitchen suddenly dimmed. Alex looked over at the window and watched as storm clouds gathered. There was a bright flash of light, followed by thunder. He thought he could hear something like a loud *ouch*! from outside, but he put it down to imagination.

"Mmm," he mumbled to himself.

He looked around, stood up and went into the front room. When he came back, he was clutching a writing pad, envelope and pen. He sat down again at the table and began to scribble away, biting his tongue in concentration.

A few minutes later, Jamie burst back in through the door, wetter than the first time. He stood, wide eyed, panting, water pouring from the wash basket he was clutching.

"I'm going to kill her!" he said.

Oblivious, Alex kept on writing.

Jamie stomped over to the bunker and slammed down the washing basket.

"You're getting the floor wet," Alex said without looking up.

Jamie spun around. "What happened to you anyway?" he said. "You're late."

"I went to see Derek."

Jamie's face went from white to red to purple with rage. "That freeloading, back stabbing get? What did you go to see that for?"

"Cat's for," Alex said without looking up.

"What?"

"For trees," Alex said.

"What are you talking about?" Jamie asked.

"I'm talking about the fact that I had gone to see my brother, that's what. I don't need to go and see him for anything. No reason."

"I don't believe you," Jamie said, grabbing a towel.

He threw it over his head rubbing it at his hair and face. By the time he dragged it off sunlight was streaming through the window again. Bunching up the towel and twisting it, he then threw the towel into the washing basket with all the other drenched things. "I give up," he said, taking a deep breath. "Alex!"

Alex didn't flinch. "What is it now?" Alex huffed, scribbling away.

"We need a tumble drier," Jamie said sitting down.

"If it was our own house and not a rented one," Alex said, "I would agree, but until that time, no.

Jamie craned his neck. "So what are you writing then?" he asked, calmer now, intrigued.

Alex put his arm around the notepad, hiding the contents from Jamie. "Wait till I've finished it," he said.

Jamie sat back and sniffed. "Bloody weather," he said, looking out at a clear blue sky. "It's a conspiracy."

A few beats of perfect silence sailed by.

Jamie relaxed more.

"Finished!" Alex piped up.

Jamie jumped at Alex's sudden outburst. "Jesus, Eck. I nearly jumped the height of myself there."

Alex sat back, sighed, and began to read.

Dear Heather on the Weather,

I'm writing this on behalf of a friend cos he's a chookter and you wouldn't understand a word he writes, besides, he's driving me bonkers with his greeting and whinging about the problem. And the problem is this.

How come every time my man chucks his drawers onto the washing line, it buckets? And every time he takes them back down, it stops?

I wouldn't believe it myself either, but I saw it with my own eyes.

He stood at the front door with a pair of is barrage balloon specials—he's got a backend as big as Buckie after a bomb's hit it (he says he's no, but he's no got eyes in the back of his head, like I have, so what would he know?) Anyway he stood at the door and had a pair of his ginormous sized monikers hanging off his index finger and demonstrated this effect to me.

Guess what?

Monsoon!

He whipped them back indoors.

Guess what?

A drought!

Aye well, you might well be surprised.

He can't figure it out either, and my friend's at the end of his tether about it. It's that bad he's near murdering himself with grief. Me as well cos I'm the one who has to listen to his greeting and griping about it. It's got that bad that now he says he doesn't even bother washing his drawers first. (And believe me I'm gagging it that thought writing this). Now he just sticks them up on the line then skooshes fairy liquid it them, so when it rains, it gets them washed as well.

He says it's your fault. I say he's talking rubbish.

What do you think?

Ta for your attention.

Signed

Sick fed up

On the behalf of,

Jamie McFarlane

Flat 3/1,

Main Street,

Kelly.

P.S. Is it true what they said on the news about there being radioactive klinkers lying about Dalgety Bay beach? Cos there's no way we'll be going to a beach full of nuclear klinkers!

"Ha ha, dead funny," Jamie said, watching Alex smile and fold the note in half. "And I don't have a fat ark, that's you."

"Whatever," Alex said, still smiling, sliding the note into the envelope.

It was already addressed, Jamie saw.

"I'm sending it in," Alex said.

"You wouldn't know where to send it," Jamie said.

"Heather's Weather, BBC Scotland, Glasgow," Alex said, sealing the envelope.

Both sat facing each other.

It was a standoff.

"You wouldn't dare," Jamie said, narrowing his eyes.

"Who wouldn't?" Alex said, laying the envelope down.

Jamie glanced at it. "No you wouldn't," he said.

Alex waited a beat for effect, then: "Who wouldn't?"

Jamie mouth tightened into a thin lipped smile.

"You're doing a Deek," Alex said.

"I couldn't be that evil," Jamie said, his face softening, "And I know you'll no send that letter either."

Lifting the envelope off the table Alex held it up. "Try me," he said, cool as a spent nuclear clinker on a beach.

Jamie lurched, arm shooting out. "Gives it!" he said grasping.

Alex yanked it out of Jamie's reach.

He stood up. His chair clattered against the wall behind him.

Rushing around the side of the table, Jamie went for him, but Alex was too fast. Soon he was out the door and running down the hallway, Jamie in hot pursuit.

Alex took a quick look behind, yelped, pulled open the front door and ran out leaving it wide open, and ran along the landing, feet thumping, and ran down the stairs taking the steps two at a time.

Jamie stayed in close pursuit as Alex ran out into the street. Sidestepping surprised pedestrians, feet slithering on the wet pavement, Alex made it to the pillar-box at the corner. He stopped to catch his breath. With Jamie almost upon him he thrust his hand into the mouth of the letterbox.

Jamie skidded to a halt.

Hunched over, hands on knees, Jamie said, "You wouldn't dare, laddie."

"What's to stop me?"

Knowing he had the upper hand, Alex leaned in close to Jamie.

His fingers twitched on the envelope still inside the mouth of the box as bemused shoppers looked at them before making their way around the pair before moving on.

Alex tilted his head to the side.

"Tell you what," Alex said. "Cook me dinner and I'll no post it."

Jamie stood up straight. "What do you think I'm doing already? And anyway, what if I don't?"

"I drop this letter into its thrapple, and Heather gets to find out that it's your fault Scotland's weather's up the creak. Your fault, Jamie. Think about it."

"Mmm," Jamie murmured, forking his day old ark fluff between thumb and forefinger.

"I wouldn't have thought you would have had to think that much about it?" Alex said.

"Awe right. You win," Jamie said.

"Real cooking and no something out of a packet either," Alex said. "I'm talking real food. No that processed muck you're always thinking about feeding us when it's your turn for cooking. I use the word in a figurative sense, you understand."

"Awe come on, Eck. Now you're asking!"

"Well?" Alex prompted, eyebrows raised, smiling.

"All right, all right!" Jamie said. "I'll do it. Now give me that letter."

"Hmm. Okay, then," Alex said pulling his hand out of the pillar-box.

Until a woman slammed into his shoulder.

"Out the road, kid!" she said.

A startled Jamie watched as the woman sneered over her shoulder and moved off.

"What an ignoramus," he said.

He looked at Alex. He didn't like what he saw.

"What is it?" he asked.

"I've dropped it," Alex confessed.

~~*

"You don't think she'll take it to heart, do you?" Alex asked sounding morose as they entered the flat.

"I doubt it'll even get there," Jamie laughed. "Anyway, it doesn't even have a stamp on it."

Alex looked at him sorrowfully.

"Get a grip and sit on your ark," Jamie said.

Alex sat on the sofa. "I wished I hadn't done it now."

"God all mighty, Eck. What's wrong with you? Even if it does get there, what's going to happen?"

"That's what I'm feared of," he said curling over on himself.

"I'm more concerned about that woman bumping into you like that. Not even an apology from her. Anyway, it was the best laugh I've had in ages," Jamie said smiling.

Sitting beside Alex, he put an arm around Alex's shoulders.

"It's no just that daft letter, is it, Eck?"

Biting his lip, Alex looked at him. He shook his head with a fearful look in his eyes.

"Deek?" Jamie asked.

"Aye and no," Alex said, looking away. "I went round to see if he was still figuring on coming on holiday with us. I thought they might have forgot about it. But they haven't. They're that scatter brained about everything else, but this. I wished I had said no to them the first time,

Jamie. I know you had your heart set on just us two gone away by ourselves."

Just then Jamie pulled away his arm from Alex's shoulder, slapped his hands on his thighs and stood up.

"Like you say," Jamie said. "Spilt milk and all that. So, coffee? And dinner?"

Alex looked at him quizzically.

Jamie stood there, tongue thrust in cheek. He sniffed. "Strong? Stronger? Or thick as the crap round the neck of a bottle?" he said.

"Eh?"

"Your coffee?" Jamie said with a flourish as he zipped out the door and down the hallway before Alex could say anything else.

Letter forgotten, remembered with a shiver, then forgotten again, Alex wondered about Jamie's funny response to hearing that Thelma and Derek were still going on holiday with them.

"I can read you like a bairn's rattle in the dark," he said under his breath. "You're up to something."

And with that thought in mind, the letter and the wringing wet washing were forgotten.

CHAPTER 13

Later, in bed, Alex was having an after sex coffee when he asked Jamie, "What was it like?"

"What was what like?" Jamie said.

"The homes you were in?"

Jamie sighed.

"I don't know what to tell you, really. Nothing to compare it to." He shrugged. "What you don't have you don't miss. So they say."

"How come you weren't adopted then?"

"You're a right one for asking loaded questions, you are."

"Sorry."

"Don't be. It's just something I haven't thought about in a long time. A whole year in fact. But since you ask I wasn't the one who was doing all the picking and choosing. So I don't have an answer to that one. I never asked why either to tell you the truth. Maybe it was because I wasn't the bonniest baby going. No pictures of me were taken. With a physiognomy like mine I wouldn't think I would have won any prizes for cuteness. But I don't know why nobody wanted to adopt me. I was fostered for a bit a few times, but no adoption. There was nothing in my files anyway." He shrugged.

"Awe Jamie, all babies are bonnie."

"Well, I don't know why. Nobody picked me so it'll have to stay a mystery I'm afraid."

"Did you no ever get lonely?" Alex asked.

"What? Lonely? In they cracker palaces? With all the other kids? It was hard enough to get time to yourself. But you're right to ask. Because there's lonely and there's lonely, if you know what I mean. In fact there's plenty times you feel lonely, even in a crowd, Eck."

"Did you no ... ?"

"Did I no what?"

"You know."

"I'll tell you this, Eck lad, there's times all you want is to hold somebody and somebody to hold you, no matter who it is. And that feeling's even worse at night. It was always worse it night. You just want to feel as if you belong, Eck. You want to feel as if you belong to something, somebody, even if it's just for five minutes. That feeling means an awful lot, that sense of belonging, especially when you remember that you don't have a mum and dad. Worse that when you think that they didn't want you in the first place. So aye, you do need to feel as if you belong to somebody. So in answer to your question, Eck, I did sometimes. It's already bad enough that you're banged up in an institution for being born."

"What about the wardens?"

"They knew, I suppose. Must have caught a few of the lads at it. It's just a case of needing to hold on to somebody though, Eck. I never heard anything though, to tell you the truth, and I never asked."

"With about when you left though?"

"Well to tell you the truth you couldn't wait for your seventeenth birthday. That's when you're legally free. Actually it feels more like the state's obligation to you has ended and they can't wait to get rid of you. But it's different on the outside. You've lived your whole life in an institution, more than one, loads of them in some cases, banded about from place to place. And suddenly the walls in your world are blown down and it's out you go. You want to feel like a big man, all grown up, like, free to do what you want, except you're really the same wee scared bairn that was found on the doorstep. Huh! Doorstep if you were lucky. Some of the guys I heard were found in a plastic bag. That's how wanted they were. Thing is, scared as you are, you can't show it. They find you a place to stay and help you find a job, but they don't owe you a life, Eck. When you hit seventeen they've done their job, and that's that. And to tell you the truth, it feels like you've been kicked and the teeth for a second time—chucked out."

CHAPTER 14

A few days shy of his eighteenth birthday, and Alex was back at the local public library; his first visit in three years. And my how things seemed to have changed.

Even as he walked up to the desk for the first time in a long time, he was almost as scared as he had been back then. He noticed other things had changed too. The librarians looked younger for one.

Or maybe I'm getting old, Alex thought.

The other thing that changed was all the computer terminals, and the people sitting at them, typing away. Most of them making searches for books and journals.

The library was a lot noisier than he remembered.

Back then he had almost been too scared to breathe lest he catch a stern look from the head librarian.

But books weren't the things he was after today.

He waited in the queue. And when it came to his turn he put on his most confident face, even if he was shaking on the inside. Librarians, young or old, still held that fearful position of authority to Alex, and that somehow scared him no matter how many times he told himself he was being silly.

The young pretty librarian smiled down at him and he wondered if she was standing on a box behind the desk or if he himself had just stepped into a ditch.

Alex cleared his throat.

The words didn't come out right the first time and the librarian gave him a quizzical look.

"Computer?" he said apologetically.

She raised her eyebrows.

He thought for a second, went through all the words and phrases as he had practiced them walking along the road.

"I want to join up to the Internet."

Now she understood.

"Are you a member?" she asked.

Of what? Alex thought.

"The library, yes I am," he said in his best vernacular.

"So you want to set up a computer account then?" she asked, reaching under the desk and pulling out a pad.

Alex nodded.

"Can I have your card please?"

Alex fished his card out of his pocket and gave it to her.

"Do you have an email account with us already?"

Alex shook his head.

"Okay, we can do that for you. Terminal four is free," she said, scanning the barcode on his card with the red laser.

She handed him back his card.

He stood there.

She walked away.

"Miss?"

She turned around and smiled at him. "Yes?"

Looking sorry for himself, he said:

"I don't know what to do."

She had shown him how to set up an email address, how to use the search engines (Google! That's what Jamie used to look up stuff about him) and he was off.

At least he thought he would be except he felt handless, especially about using the keyboard, which he kept squinting down at to see where his fingers where going.

The main thing was that now that he needed was a new address, an address in cyberspace, and one no one else had access to.

All he had had to do in the end was to pick a name for himself.

But everything he tried came back as already in use.

Then he thought about their upcoming trip to Amsterdam.

A brainwave hit.

Eckandjamie.

Accepted.

Bingo!

"Yes!" he yelled thrusting his arms up in the air in triumph.

He quickly pulled them back down and shrunk into himself when old memories of the library came back at him like demons from the past.

No one said anything. No one even turned around to look at him.

For something so simple it sent a warm flush of success through Alex.

Then disappointment.

It had all been so simple and yet so hard. He wondered at his old school friends and how they must all have a computer at home, or one of those Xbox things.

Maybe one day he and Jamie would buy one, then he wondered what for.

The new address was the main thing, it was all he needed.

He scribbled it down before he forgot it, logged off and stood up.

He looked at the clock. He had managed to get away from work a half an hour early by working through his lunch hour. It had been a bad compromised, but he didn't want anyone suspecting what he had been up to. He didn't being secretive, but sometimes, well ...

Keep some things to yourself, Alex.

Why Gran?

Some folk will use your own words against you. They'll find ways to turn good into bad, love into hate. Keep some things to yourself and you have a fighting chance.

He stuffed the piece of paper with his new email address on it into his pocket, and walked out into the late afternoon sunlight. With any luck he would be home before Jamie had any inkling of what he was up to.

Tomorrow he would have to work through his lunch hour again.

CHAPTER 15

The next day, Alex trotted up the steps of the old Georgian building, not even taking time to look around. It had been a few weeks since he had been here, but he wasn't so scared now as he was back then, even if it did feet strange walking into this grand old building.

Two flights up and he was standing in front of the secretary's desk. A kindly face, she asked Alex if he had an appointment.

He told her that he had. He was a few minutes early though.

She tapped at the keys of her terminal as he told her his name.

Two minutes later and a smiling Mister Jamison was standing in his doorway, the same pinstripe suit and half moon spectacles beckoning Alex into his office.

"Please take a seat," Jamison said.

Alex did so and Jamison took up his position behind his desk.

Leaning back he asked Alex if everything was in order since the last time they had met.

Alex informed him that things were just dandy, which seemed to please Mister Jamison no end. To Alex it looked as if the old solicitor had even breathed a sigh of relief.

Things seemed to have switched around though. No longer did Alex feel as if he was under the behest of the solicitor. But then again, it was Alex who would be paying the solicitor, from the proceeds of his grandmother's will, and that changed things.

Leaning forward, elbows on his desk, Jamison looked over his spectacles at Alex.

"And what can I do for you this time?"

Alex straightened up in his seat. No need to doff his cap this time. He already had it in his pocket. "You said the last time I was here that if you could do anything for me then you would."

Jamison raised a finger and smiled. "That is if I can," he said laughing.

Alex laughed a little too and felt a bit silly because he didn't know what he was laughing for.

"So what is it you would like me to do for you?" Jamison asked.

Time is money, Alex thought.

Every minute was costing a fortune.

Don't waffle.

"I want you to find something for me?"

The solicitor raised his eyebrows. "Yes?"

"Only I wouldn't know where to start, where to look you see. That's why I'm asking you," Alex said.

"What is it you're looking for?"

"Well, it's no for me, exactly. And it is in a way. It's for somebody else."

"Any clues about what it is?"

Alex could feel himself squirming in his seat. When he had thought up the idea before it all sounded so simple, inside his own head that is. But now, on the verge of having to say it out loud, and to a stranger too, it all began to feel a bit mashed up.

Get to the point, Eck!

"I don't even know if it exists. That's what I'm trying to say, Mister Jamison. And that's left me a bit lost, if you get my drift."

Alex crinkled up his forehead as far as he could, trying to project what was still inside his head at the old man. That what words wouldn't form in his mouth would somehow magically zap between the two men and that the solicitor would second-guess what Alex didn't want to say out loud.

Jamison sat back and made a steeple out of his fingers under his chin, looking thoughtful.

"Any more clues to be had?" he asked, raising his eyebrows.

Alex leaned in closer to the desk, keeping his voice low. "There somebody I know, that, well ..."

"Yes?"

"I need you to find something out about him," Alex said.

"And what, pray tell, am to try and find out about this chap?"

"Something about his records?" Alex said.

Jameson's eyebrows shot up sharper than before. "I'm not a private detective," he said.

"Think that's what I need?" Alex sounded disappointed.

"That would depend on what it is you are looking for."

Alex fumbled in his pocket, pulled out a sheet of paper and unfolded it on the desk. "Here's his name," he said. "And where he lived, at least last place he did before I knew him that is. Thing is though I know that there's rules and regulations about finding things out about people. Know what I'm saying?"

"Not sure that I do," Mister Jamison said. "But since you know so much about this person, why not ask him?"

Alex bit his lip. "Thing is, you see, he doesn't know about this. But that's no my point. My point is the thing I'm looking for he doesn't think exists, you see, which is where I get stuck. And I'm no even sure of the legalities of it. No no, I don't mean it's illegal or anything, but I think it might not be easy for someone like me to just go in and start asking, see? Because they might say that I've no right to. Yes?"

He sat back and quickly shook his head.

"And I don't even know where to start."

He sat forward sharply.

"It's no that I'm trying to dig up dirt or anything," he said. "It's just something me and him both don't know exists."

"Why doesn't he try looking for himself?" Jamison asked.

"But how can he find something if he's convinced that that something doesn't exist?"

"And you know it does?"

Alex tightened his mouth and shook his head. "But it might, that's the point. And If I don't look, how will we know?"

"Okay," Jamison asked slowly. "Maybe you should just tell me exactly what it is you want me to try and do."

A shiver ran down Alex spine.

This was it.

No going back now.

And he told the old man exactly what he needed him to find.

CHaPTer 16

Jamie laid down two plates.

"Casserole," Jamie said beaming with pride. "Made it all myself. Just for you, special."

Jamie turned from the cooker, casserole pot in hand. Alex watched as steam wafted up from its innards. He smiled at Jamie and had second thought about making Jamie promise to cook him another meal, a real one.

"Mmmmm," Jamie said at his own creation as he ladled the lumpy gruel onto the plates.

Alex watched as whole carrots, whole tatties and whole lumps of other indescribable stuff slopped onto his plate. There were funny looking lumps of brown and pink meat mixed in with it as well—two-toned meat.

"Eat up," Jamie said, plonking himself down at the other side of the table. "You don't need to wait for me! I know you must be starving after a hard day at work."

Alex looked over at Jamie.

Jamie smiled over at Alex.

Alex smiled back as he reached out for his fork, then hesitated, as if he were about to get an electric shock from it.

He touched it with his finger.

No spark.

Good sign.

He picked up the fork then looked down on his plate.

There was something wrong with the gravy. No substance to it, as he would say, except he didn't to hurt Jamie's feelings so he didn't …

His fork hovered over the plate like a divining rod.

He looked up from the plate and over at Jamie again.

Jamie's smiling face looked as if it was pushing across the table at him.

The meat looked lumpy with stringy bits wiggling out of the sides.

There was no getting out of it.

Alex touched the stringy looking lumps with his fork. There were brownish lumps and pink looking lumps. What kind of meat comes in two different colors?

He touched it with the tines of his fork again, gulped then stabbed at a lump.

Jamie's eager face inched closer. Alex smiled and felt his throat close in defense as he lifted the meat with its stringy bits wobbling. He opened his mouth and carefully placed the lump inside.

"You'll never *guess* what you're eating!" Jamie yelled.

Alex dropped his fork, choked, lurched and gagged his craw wide over the plate.

He stood up, hand over mouth and rushed to the bathroom.

Crashing to his knees he started praying at the ceramic altar, his voice coming back at him from the depths of the toilet pan.

"Oh my God, oh my God!"

Jamie appeared behind him, plate in hand, shoveling the casserole into his gob.

"You've poisoned me!" Alex choked around his index finger poking at his throat.

"What's wrong way you?" Jamie slurped.

"What have you done to me?"

"Nothing!"

"You've killed me," Alex said, slumping to the side.

"What?"

"What is that stuff?"

"Rabbit!"

That did it.

Blooeh.

In between choking and gagging Alex managed a few strangled words.

"Awe God, I've eaten Bambi!"

"No, you've no," Jamie said him as he nibbled on a whole carrot. "Bambi was a deer, no a rabbit. Butcher's had deer as well, mind you. No heads on them though. They were hanging on hooks at the back of the shop though. I could see them. I could have bought one, but I didn't think I'd be able to fit it in the pot."

Blooeh.

Jamie helped a deliriously guilty Alex to the bedroom.

Alex lay down as Jamie patted at his hand. Alex felt like a killer, a murderous cannibal.

"Rabbit," he said. "I've eaten a rabbit."

And all he could see through his closed eyelids were tiny baby rabbits lopping though daisies in a field.

"Will I get the doctor for you?" Jamie asked sympathetically.

"Leave me alone," Alex said, his face buried in the pillow.

"For God's sake, Alex. They eat dogs in Japan."

Alex wailed. "What it you trying to do to me?" he cried out.

~~*

The next night Alex came home from work prepared.

Jamie was in the kitchen again.

"I'm vegetarian," Alex announced with a pious flourish.

Jamie looked over his shoulder.

"So what do I cook now?"

"Just veg for me from now on," Alex said sitting down at the table. "Nothing from any animal. Nowt. I've been reading some horrible stuff about what they're creating in they Frankenstein labs. God, the stuff they put in fast food, Jamie you wouldn't want to know. Chickens way four legs in three wings. It was enough to put anybody off eating animals for life. I'm no having any part of that cruelty."

Jamie smiled then turned away with a face that said *I'm sick of this palavering*.

He stirred at the pot boiling away on the cooker.

"Well all I've got," he said, "apart from *meat* is tatties on the go."

"That'll have to do then," Alex said, sitting back folding his arms across his chest.

He was a determined wee bugger when he had a mind to it.

"Okay, well if you say so."

Jamie spooned the mash onto a plate.

"And a wee bit gravy to go with it as well," Alex said looking down at the mountain of mash in front of him.

Jamie, Tea towel around the handle of the pot he was holding, his other gripping firmly at the ladle in his other, yelped, "I thought you said that you've decided to be a veg now."

"I am," Alex said.

"Then how can you have gravy?"

"How can I no?"

Jamie rolled up his eyes. "Where day you think gravy comes from, Alex?"

Alex's face crumpled up in concentration. The answer came to him quick as a flash.

"A packet!" he said.

Jamie rolled up his eyes, the steam from the tattie mash in the pot filling the room.

"And what do you think the stuff in the packet's made from?"

Alex bunched up his mouth, a deep V forming between his eyebrows.

"Well?" Jamie prodded.

"Packet stuff!" Alex blurted.

Jamie opened his mouth to say some more.

"Don't bother trying to blind me way science, either." Alex held up his hand.

Jamie slammed the pot back down on the cooker with a clang then ladled mince and tatties onto a plate for himself.

He'd had enough of this.

He sat opposite Alex and began to eat.

Alex looked at Jamie's plate, then at his own.

"Will you quit looking at me like that when I'm eating?" Jamie said.

Alex forked a mountain of plain tattie mash into his mouth. He grimaced as he tried to swallow the stuff. Half of it got stuck in his throat.

Jamie saw the pained look on Alex's face.

"What's wrong with you?" he asked.

Alex hand went up to his neck to help his thrapple push the tatties into his belly.

He gasped for air.

"It's a bit ..." Alex gulped. "... Dry."

"Welcome to the fun of being a veg," Jamie said tucking in.

"Well, if I can't have gravy I can have butter instead," Alex said, jumping to his feet making his way to the fridge.

But Jamie was even faster off the mark, balancing his plate of mince and tatties in one hand, fork up to his mouth in the other; as soon as Alex had pulled the door open on the fridge, Jamie slammed it shut again with a delft switch of his hip.

"Can't have butter either," he said.

Exasperated, Alex yelped. "How no!"

"Because butter comes from milk, Alex. And milk comes from coos. That's how no. So no gravy, no butter, no nothing."

Alex sulked back to his mountain of tatties at the table and slumped onto his chair.

Jamie followed, sat down himself and scooped up what was left of his dinner.

He sat back with a satisfied, "That was braw," rubbing at his belly. "Great gravy," he said. "Wonderful what they scientists come up with."

Alex stood up and walked over to the cupboard behind Jamie. He opened the door and took out the gravy packet. Tilting it up to the light he scanned with his eyes like slits at the teeny writing on the back of it.

"The writing's that wee I can hardly make out what it's made out of."

"Boiled rabbit's heads and lamb's hearts no doubt," Jamie said dumping his plate into the sink.

"That's no what it says here," Alex said. "Nothing but numbers way a big E in front of them."

With a sudden realization he looked up.

"There's no sign of any animals in this stuff," he said waving the packet at Jamie.

Jamie finished rolling up a cigarette and lit it.

"Who cares?" he said. "It tastes good.

"What of though?"

"Well," Jamie said, "if there's no animal stuff in it, you can have some on your tatties with a clear conscience then, can't you. So what's the problem?"

A sinking feeling came over Alex as he let his arm drop slowly, the packet still in his hand.

He turned back to the cupboard.

"Alex?"

Alex put the packet back on the shelf and closed the door slowly.

Sometimes there's a light at the end of the tunnel, he thought. And sometimes that light's a funny color.

"Eck, what's up with you, laddie?"

Alex turned around and shook his head.

"Nothing," he said.

As if he had been living in a fog all of his life, now it seemed to be lifting, and he could see further than he had ever been able to before.

"What have way been eating all these years, Jamie?"

CHAPTER 17

Jamie stood by the bunker, aiming a finger at the item lying thereon.

"And *don't touch that muffin*!" he warned Alex.

Alex's mouth tightened into a sealed O.

"I'm warning you!" Jamie went on, wagging his finger.

Jamie left the kitchen and went into the hallway. At the door he turned and took a last look. Alex sat with his back to him. Jamie smiled and left.

When he reached the front door he pulled it open, waited a second for effect, and then closed the door just hard enough to convince Alex that he had left.

Jamie counted to ten before creeping back up the hall to the kitchen door.

"Alex!"

"I never tushed it!" Alex spun around, cheeks bulging, face red, choking as he forced the chocolate mass down through it whole.

"I'm doing this for your own good," Jamie said taping the wires to Alex fingers. The others he taped to the spoon.

A disgruntled Alex sat at the table with wires, running from his fingers and the spoon, running to the transformer, which was plugged into the mains.

Jamie sniffed, pulled out his chair and sat opposite Alex. "Right," he said. "You're always bugging me about going on a diet, and of course you never do. So, this way, I'm helping you lose some weight for the holiday."

Alex didn't flinch. He looked down at the bowl, at the steamed chocolate sponge pudding, at the warm melted chocolate oozing out of it.

Jamie rolled up his sleeves ready for business, squinting down at the dials and then at Alex.

"Now," he said. "All you have to do is what you normally do, which is to shovel your gob full to bursting point. Then I push this big button on here." He pointed to the red button on top of the transformer. "And when I do that, you then get a shot of lecky in the gob."

"And what's that going to do for me like?" Alex asked before tightening his mouth shut.

"Put you off eating all that fattening rubbish you keep stuffing yourself with. You'll associate pain with eating then you'll no eat. Aversion therapy it's called."

And Jamie just couldn't wait to ram his thumb down on that button.

"Right," Jamie said. "Ready when you are."

Alex looked at the pudding then at Jamie. He picked up the spoon.

Jamie's finger hovered over the button. "Get ready for the cure of a lifetime," he said borrowing one of Derek's phrases.

Alex shoveled up a spoonful off steaming chocolate pudding and opened his mouth wide.

Jamie stared, heart thumping, finger twitching. He could hardly contain himself.

Alex pushed the pudding into his mouth.

Jamie closed his eyes and whammed his fist down on the button.

There was big flash and a yell of pain.

A chair was knocked over. Jamie opened his eyes and looked at the ceiling.

Wires still hanging off his fingers and the spoon, the bowl of pudding in his hands, Alex stood over Jamie.

"Whahhappened?" Jamie groaned.

"Deek tried that same trick in one of his many failed businesses," Alex said scooping up the pudding, really enjoying it as Jamie rolled around trying to pick himself up off the floor.

Jamie was still stunned. "But how come I got the shock and no you?"

"Because, you see, Jamie, I'm no that daft. And it helps when you've an A star in Higher Physics, like I've got. I just redirected the juice back up to the button and no down the wires to me. Simple really, when you know how."

"Yah sneaky bugger."

"I'd rather be sneaky than dead," Alex said walking away.

Tearing the wires from his fingers and placing the empty pudding bowl on the table, he reached into his jacket hanging over the back of the chair.

He pulled out a book.

Jamie staggered to his feet.

"This is what we need, Jamie."

"E for Additives." Jamie squinted at the label.

"Aye. So tomorrow, you and me are going down to the market together. I've learned a lot from this book. So should you. So from now on, no poisoning ourselves either."

He thrust the book into Jamie's still-twitching-from-the-shock fingers.

"Coffee or tea?" Alex said, filling the kettle at the sink.

CHAPTER 18

Supermarket D-day.

Alex sat at the kitchen table, demurely eating cornflakes. He'd showered and shaved and now watched Jamie go through his usual early morning palavering ritual. Darting in and out with a smile on his face as he picked up The Sun, his cigs and matches (the lighter had ran out), then back in again for his ginormous mug of Nambarrie with two tea bags still left in it—milk and four sugars—then back yet again for the ashtray.

And there Alex sat and fumed.

They would never get going at this rate.

He looked at his watch, then at the wall. How much longer was it going to take this time?

Jamie sat on the toilet, the air filled with smoke, his knees up, the sweat lashing off him with the strain of it, his teeth gritted and eyes clamped tight shut as he clung onto the side of the bath.

Right! "I'm no having it!" Alex said.

He pulled open the cupboard door under the sink for the solution. Grabbed a paper bag therein, blew into it, twisted the open-end shut, and exited the kitchen. He strode along the hallway, his fist high, and whammed the bag onto the bathroom door.

There followed by a barely muffled "Aaaaaaah!" from within.

Enough was enough.

A few minutes later, sitting at the kitchen table again, fingers drumming, Alex watched Jamie stagger in with legs buckling, declaring, "That was like giving birth to a giant hedgehog!"

The disgust on Alex's face apparent, never mind his voice, he said, "It's all that rubbish you eat. Now take a shower and be quick about it. I've been jumping to get out and do the shopping for hours."

~~*

"Right," Alex said. "You shove it, I'll fill it."

Alex marched in through the glass doors of the supermarket, which parted magically at his approach. It was still early in the morning, sun shining, just rained, and the air smelled fresh and clear.

This bolstered Alex in his determination to ignore all of the special offers on show in the supermarket, the glaring notices, which he now believed to be evil enticements to buy poor quality produce.

Not for him though as he brushed past and through them all as Jamie looked at each one in turn.

Alex grabbed a trolley and thrust it at Jamie. After that he pulled out his magnifying glass.

"Forewarned is forearmed, Jamie," he said, lifting the boxes and the packets in turn, magnifying glass up to one eye, the other closed as he scanned the small print. "Nobody's got a chance with this tactic," he said.

"What tactic?" Jamie asked leaning over the trolley.

"The writing's that wee you can hardly tell what's in this stuff," Alex said, waving about a box of dried noodles. He dumped it back on the shelf.

"But that tastes good, Eck," Jamie said.

"Aye, that it might, Jamie lad, but it's poisoning us with plutonium 'n stuff. No! We're no having it. Now mush!"

In went the fresh fruit and veg, the trolley wheels sagging under the weight of it all.

Jamie cringed at the thought of how much everything was going to cost.

Alex lifted and chucked everything into the trolley behind him, never looking back, aisle after aisle the same.

Then just before the checkout, Alex turned around, pleased as punch until he looked down into the trolley.

"What's all this green label rubbish?" he yelped at Jamie.

"It's the same stuff!" Jamie protested.

"What stuff?"

"Stuff, stuff stuff!"

Alex leaned over and looked down on the crisps, biscuits, grot noodles, all day breakfast in a can, chicken korma, hotdogs, chocolate muffins—five-percent-fat-free cocoa slops. Alex's hands thrust into the mound like grabbers on a mission. He held up both.

"Boil in the bag fish supper? Skoosh Joose? And what's this? Scotch salmon at a pound a kilo! Chemical minging radioactive farmed muck. I didn't put this in."

"What's wrong with it?"

"It's crap! There's nothing in here for me to eat."

"Aye there is. This," Jamie said holding up the crisp breads. "Low calorie cardboard."

"Cardboard?" Alex said. "I see. So you get to stuff your neck with the poisoning you want, but I've got to starve?"

"Crisp bread," Jamie beamed. "See, I'm looking after your figure. Better watch though. Before you know it you'll be fading away to an elephant."

"Don't get smart!"

"Well," Jamie said, "if you eat that stuff you were wanting, you'll get fat—"

"I'm no fat!"

"—er."

"I'm no is fat is you, anyway," Alex argued, forgetting what the plan had been in the first place. "And I'm no fat at all!"

"Truth hurts," Jamie said. "Even your clothes have got stretch marks on them. And you've been reading too much of that Gestapo woman, Fanny McGinormous-Teeth's books—You are What You Shove in Your Greedy

Fat Gob. If you don't watch out you'll end up looking like a big fat chocolate blamange."

"I've never eaten a blamange in my life."

"Then why do you look like an advert for one then?"

"Anyway, on this new diet, I never get hungry," Alex beamed.

Jamie's jaw dropped. "That's because you never stop eating long enough to get hungry."

Alex pushed Jamie out of the way and took control of the trolley. And so back they went, in reverse, aisle after aisle.

"I see I can't trust you with anything," Alex shouted over his shoulder.

And so all of it went back and to be replaced with what was supposed to be there in the first place.

After the checkout, arms breaking under the strain of shopping, Alex dumped the bags down when he spotted a set of scales.

He plopped a twenty pence piece in the slot and jumped on.

He would show Jamie.

"See, only nine-and-a-half stones," he said.

Jamie looked over Alex shoulder, checking that Alex wasn't lying.

"What about your other foot?" he said.

"Don't get smart," Alex said jumping off the scales and picking up the bags.

"Bit fat for you being only three foot two, do you no think, Eck?"

"Stop picking on me!" Alex said, storming at the glass doors. They didn't budge. "And I'm five foot eight, right!"

"When you're lying on your side."

"I'm taller than you," Alex said, shouldering the doors. They still wouldn't budge.

"I'm five foot ten," Jamie said, watching Alex struggle.

"Standing on a box, aye."

Alex turned and laid into the door with his back.

Jamie stood.

"Don't just stand there," Alex said. "Help me."

Jamie grabbed the bags off Alex and walked away.

"Maybe you should try using the doors with EXIT on the down here instead of trying to crash your way through the ones marked NO EXIT."

Later back at the flat, collapsing with the weight of the bags, Alex dumped himself down in the recovery position.

"Make us a cup of coffee, Jamie."

"We're going back out," Jamie said, standing up.

"I need a rest."

"You need the exercise, that's what you need."

"But I need a coffee."

Jamie grabbed Alex under the armpits and hauled him to his feet.

"Get up. We're going out for something you need for this holiday we're going on."

"Where are we going?"

"I'll tell you exactly where when we get there uptown. Now, get going."

CHaPTer 19

Shop windows glinted back golden sunlight. Saturday morning still and Alex and Jamie strolled along under seagulls squawking and wheeling around in the sky above, searching for a suitable head to use as a public inconvenience.

Alex veered towards McDonald's front door. Jamie grabbed him by the shoulders and veered him back onto the middle of the pavement.

"I need a coffee," Alex said. He made his way back to the McDonald's.

Jamie grabbed him by the back of his belt. "You don't need a coffee," Jamie said.

"Aye I do."

"We're just out the house," Jamie said.

"So what," Alex said, face crumpling in consternation.

"Anyway there's something you need for this holiday we're going on, so out." Jamie stood in front of Alex, took out a cigarette and lit it. He took a puff and blew out the smoke, belching grey blue clouds of it into the stratosphere as he said, "You're not going in there."

Alex looked at him. "Like you can smoke, but I can't have a coffee?" he barked.

"I'm addicted," Jamie explained. "I can't help myself." He took another beatific draw, oblivious to Alex protestations.

"Well, I'm addicted to coffee," Alex said.

"Have a cig, then," Jamie said, knowing full well Alex wouldn't take him up on the offer. And even if he did, Jamie wouldn't let him.

"I don't want a cig, because I don't smoke. I want a coffee," Alex said, making a dive for the McDonald's front door again.

Jamie jammed the cigarette between his tight lips, reached out for Alex, grabbed him, and pulled him round the corner into Fredrick Street.

"I'll buy you a coffee later," he said, holding Alex tight by the shoulders.

Alex wasn't sure if he was trying to pull himself away from the smoke billowing out Jamie's mouth or back towards the need for caffeine. A forced relaxation attempt saw him take a deep breath in through tight nostrils. He counted to ten. Made it to two and a half then said, in a demure tone, "I could just go in to McDode's for a minute, Jamie."

"No! And that's that. Right!" Jamie shook his head and took a last puff of his cigarette. He dropped it and stamped it out underfoot.

"Litter bug," Alex said. Jamie continued to grind down on the cigarette butt with his heel. "I think it's dead," Alex said.

Jamie looked at him and stood his ground. "There. It's out," he said. "Now we're even. Okay? I'll no have another cig until you have a coffee."

Alex couldn't work out if he's just been duped into a one sided deal. Suddenly he worked it out. "That's no fair. You've had a cig, but I've not had a coffee."

"A typical addict's answer," Jamie said. "It was half a cig I had, not a whole one."

"Well I only wanted half a coffee."

"Awe, for God's sake, will you quit griping?"

Before Alex could say anything else, Jamie gave him a sharp look. As always, the sharp V of eyebrows trying to meet in the middle of Alex's forehead started to cut down through his brow. Before it could cut Alex's head in twain completely, Jamie shouldered into Alex and pushed him up the incline of Fredrick Street.

"That's still no fair," Alex whined on.

Soon enough Jamie had pushed Alex to the front of Millet's camping shop. Alex, with his back to it, looked

Jamie in the face. But Jamie wasn't having any of it. Instead, he kept on pushing Alex up the ramp and into the shop, glancing over his shoulder at the camping equipment, tents, stoves, and sleeping bags.

Alex continued to protest. Jamie ignored him.

It's now or never, he told himself.

"Right," Jamie said, "we're here."

Alex looked confused, a face full of consternation, thrown off track. He'd been blind-sided. "What?" he asked looking around.

"In here," Jamie said, nodding over Alex's shoulder.

"What for?"

And before Alex had time to gather his bearings, Jamie had him by the shoulders again, spun him around and shoved at his back. Try as he might to back pedal on the shiny marble ramp leading up to the doors, the grips on Alex's heels were no match for Jamie's determined efforts.

The glass doors loomed ahead. Alex reached out and tried to push back. And as his hands slammed into the doors, Jamie gave him one last gargantuan push.

Alex only had time to shout, "Hey, watch it!" before the doors banged wide open and the treads on his shoes caught on the carpet, sending him flying into the interior. His fall was stymied when he crashed into a circular rail of quilted jackets and sweatshirts.

A young man turned from his duty of polishing down rails, smiled at them, then went on about his business after a nod and a "Good morning."

"Aye, right," Alex said after brushing himself down. Tight mouthed, he nodded back to the assistant. He turned to Jamie. "What are we doing in here?" Alex whispered.

Jamie blocked the exit to the safety of the outside world. "I'm helping you out with your compulsive behavior disordering," Jamie said, chest out, beaming from ear to ear. This was going to cost him a small fortune he had no doubt, but it was part of the same bait, if by a slightly different hook, to reel Alex away from the overbearing influence of his brother and sister and into Jamie's vision of the holiday.

He looked past Alex, still standing in front of the quilted jackets and sweatshirts on the rail. Only Alex looked sheepish—a fish out of his goldfish bowl.

Alex leaned in towards Jamie, speaking out the side of his mouth. "What behavior compulsive disorder?" he asked. He looked a little concerned that perhaps what Jamie had said held a modicum of truth in it. He craned in his head closer to Jamie, urging him for an answer, eyes wide, eyebrows up. "Mmm?"

Jamie looked at him. "You're whining, greeting, moaning, gripping, narking behavior!" Jamie elucidated with a huff. "Satisfied now?"

Alex pulled back, mouth wide as he took in a sharp breath, which sounded like a backward Ah! But before Alex could suck in another shocked, dignity-saving breath intake, Jamie grabbed him by the shoulders again and marched him down into the shop proper.

Stunned into silence, his legs not knowing which way to go, Alex found himself being barged through rack after rack of outdoor clothing. He shrugged his shoulders trying to free himself of Jamie's grip.

"Up!" Jamie said.

"What?"

Jamie's face dived in close to Alex's. "Up. The. Stairs." He grabbed Alex again and shoved.

Alex tripped on the first step and flew forward with a dull thump. He scrambled to his feet. "Watch the goods!"

On the upper floor, and suffering in what seemed like a rarefied atmosphere, Alex tried to compose himself, surveying the scene with bewilderment. He didn't like what he saw. His head cranked lower into his collar.

Alex looked around suspiciously. Everything seemed too quiet. He looked at tents, maps, thermal socks, compasses, backpacks.

"I'm going," he said.

"You're staying," Jamie said. Jamie pushed Alex backwards into the alcove at the back where row upon row of backpacks, of every conceivable shape and size hung, from hooks.

Alex looked over his shoulder at Jamie. "It's too quiet in here, Jamie," he said.

"It's soothing," Jamie replied.

"It's creepy."

"Whine, whine, whine." He stepped around Alex to the backpacks, looking at them, turning them from side to side. "Here," he said over his shoulder. "What do you think of this one?"

But Alex wasn't looking. Instead, he scanned from side to side, eyes like slits, taking in the unfamiliar, the weird surroundings, as if some wild beast was about to jump out and maul him.

"*ECK*!" Alex jumped. "What's wrong with you?" Jamie asked.

Composing himself, blood pressure sinking back to normal, skin pricking with his near death experience, Alex put a finger to his tight lips. "*Ssshhhh*!"

"What is it now?"

"It's too quiet in here. There's no even a suspicious-looking sales assistant to watch over us, taking our pictures, fingerprints, anything," Alex said. "No even one of those black limpet things stuck to the rafters spying on us."

He looked around again to make sure he had not been mistaken. "It's no right," Alex whispered. "It's weird no being treated like a potential burglar, a thief, a knocker, a killer—it's no right, Jamie, it's no right. Get me out of here. I can't stand it. It's creepy no being spied on."

"Pull yourself together, laddie," Jamie said.

"But it feels all wrong," Alex said. "Why are they no watching us?" He clutched Jamie's shoulder as he looked around for eyes hidden.

Jamie sighed and turned back to the backpack. "That's because the folk in here are trusting. And," he said looking over his shoulder, "the kind of folk that buy this kind of stuff aren't criminals. Anyway, it's not like I'm going to stuff one of these up my duke and knock it, is it? Now come over here."

But Alex didn't budge. It was as if he had been transported into a mysterious world where the floor was made of Velcro.

Unperturbed and taking advantage of the situation, knowing this might be Alex's last opportunity to see the light within the dark, Jamie reached out and took one of the backpacks from its hook on the wall. Carefully, as if stalking a wild animal, Jamie sidled around the back of Alex in gentle movements. First one arm and then the other, Jamie slipped the straps over Alex's arms, then up onto his shoulders.

"It's too quiet, Jamie, it's giving me the willies."

Mmmmnn, Jamie thought to himself. "We'll get to that later, laddie," he said.

The straps were now firmly in place over Alex's shoulders. Alex snapped to the situation in hand and suddenly came to out his reverie. "What's this?" he asked.

"How's that?" Jamie asked stepping back.

Alex's eyes recommenced their slithering from side to side as he kept a lookout out for the potential enemy, forgetting he had a backpack strapped to his shoulders. "Come on, Jamie. Let's get out of here now while we still can. Something's wrong with this place ..."

Jamie guided Alex along towards a full-length mirror.

"It's too quiet, it's too creepy ..." Alex dug in his heels.

Alex continued to talk to Jamie over his shoulder in forced, ever-increasing harsh whispers that verged on panic. Until fingers appeared in front of his face, between him and the mirror. "Jamie, something's wrong. Let's get out of here now before it's too ..."

Snap! Jamie clicked his fingers. Alex stopped talking, eyes wide before shrinking back down to a more reasonable diameter as he caught sight of his reflection. His jaw dropped.

"There now, laddie." Jamie's voice seemed to call to Alex from the end of a long dark tunnel.

Alex lifted one shoulder, then the other as he turned from side to side eyeing himself in the mirror.

He's hooked on his new image, Jamie thought, *line and sinker*.

His plan was working perfectly.

"I think it suits you very well," Jamie said.

Alex posed a wee bit more, his turns this way and that taking on a more exaggerated tone. "Don't know if the colors are me though," he said. "What do you think?"

Jamie leaned in over Alex's shoulder. They looked at each other in the mirror. "You can have any color you like, laddie. Just you name it."

~~*

Half an hour later and Jamie was wilting with exasperation as he clung to one of the pillars.

Alex darted into view, arms wide. "How about this one?" he asked excitedly.

"Aye," Jamie said, sounding bored.

Alex ignored him and strutted up and down in front of the mirror, turning from side to side, wearing a blue backpack with fluorescent green lightning flashes on the sides. He moved about quickly—shoulder left, shoulder right—swish, swish.

"Think this one's better than the last one?" he called out in a near screech of enjoyment.

"Alex, you could use that one for a sleeping bag the size of it," Jamie said. "Don't go overboard, will you?"

What he really wanted to say was, 'I can't see your ark'. But for now he kept his peace.

Almost.

"But the colors suit me," Alex protested.

"It's no about color," Jamie said. "It's about practicality. It's too big."

"But it feels comfortable."

"It's still empty!"

"Stop being so negative," Alex harrumphed.

Before Jamie could open his mouth to say anything else, Alex had zipped away, determined to try on yet another backpack. "Come on, Alex. We've been here for hours."

"Stop exaggerating," Alex called out as he rummaged through the racks, trying to find one he hadn't tried on yet. Suddenly he scooted back into view wearing a fluorescent yellow number.

He stopped and braced himself in front of Jamie, arms wide, all smiles. Jamie's face collapsed under the strain.

"What do you think of this one?" Alex asked.

"You look great," Jamie said.

"It's crap!" Alex said.

"So what are you wearing it for?"

"Because I wanted you to see the contrast between this one and the last one."

"Well, I've seen it," Jamie said.

"And?"

"And the last one looked better. Anything would look better than that."

"Cheers. You're a big help." Alex stomped off before Jamie had a chance to say anything else.

Jamie looked around at the racks. This was calling out for desperate measures. His sneaky plan was backfiring on him big time. He walked over to a rack full of dried food condiments deemed suitable for a trek to the North Pole and rifled through them whilst waiting for Alex to make up his bloody mind about choosing a suitable rucksack.

Alex zipped back, parading in yet another number, completely oblivious of anything else but himself in the mirror. "Just another few," he said. "Lots more goodies to get through before ..."

It appeared before his eyes. Jamie, not exactly creeping up on fashion boy, raised up the chalice. Suddenly Eck was in another place. Alex's eyes followed the little plastic cup as Jamie waved it slowly back and forth in front of his eyes.

"All you have to do is pull off the top and it heats up all by itself," Jamie said. Alex followed the cup with his eyes. "So," Jamie asked, "the blue number with the green lightening on the sides?" Alex reached up for the chalice floating in front of his mesmerized eyes. Jamie pulled it out of his reach. "I need an answer, Eck."

Alex was ready to agree to anything.

Jamie helped Alex take the ridiculously brightly colored backpack off and picked up the blue and green one. "This one it is, yes?"

Alex, eyes glued to the instant coffee that heated itself up with the weird chemical mix in its ark end, nodded.

Anything. Anything for a coffee.

CHAPTER 20

"I've got a surprise for you," Jamie said.

"A surprise?" Alex asked.

"Aye," Jamie said.

"What kind of surprise like?" Alex said, laying down the packing list he was scribbling out for the holiday, calculating how much he could stuff into his brand new blue and sparkly green ninety-five liter rucksack.

"A big surprise," Jamie said.

The last thing Alex needed. Predictable, yes, surprises, no.

"Don't look at me like that," Jamie said.

"Like what?"

"Like that," Jamie said.

"Well, what's the surprise then?"

"Eh ..."

"Well?"

Jamie bit his lip, trying to contain his excitement. "You'll have to come outside for it," he said.

Alex sighed, stood up and followed Jamie until three flights below, in a clatter of slapping footfalls echoing around the grimy stairwell walls, Jamie rushed ahead of Alex and held open the communal front door. Alex stepped out onto the street, keeping his eyes on Jamie, who had a silly looking grin on his face.

Walking up to the edge of the pavement, Jamie held his arm across his middle, clicked his heels together, bowed and extended his arm like a butler at the entrance to a banquet greeting a guest of honor.

"Well?" he said smiling at Alex. "What do you think?"

Alex looked out front, then up and down the street, then back to Jamie. Consternation mixed with confusion clouded his face. Jamie stood up tall, his smile beaming wider, pleased as punch. Alex frowned. "What do I think of what?" he asked.

The smile slipped on Jamie's face. "What do you mean 'of what'?" Jamie asked as if his surprise should be obvious.

"What's the surprise?"

"That's it!" Jamie said.

"What's it?" Alex asked.

"That!"

"What?"

"The car yah tube."

"Car?"

Alex looked at the heap of rusted metal by the nearside of the pavement. His jaw dropped so low it stretched the upper half of his face down so that it threatened to pull out his eyes with it.

He turned slowly to Jamie. "You're kidding, right?"

Now it was Jamie's turn to frown. He had wanted Alex to jump up and down in excitement, for Alex to rush up and hug him, to tell Jamie how wonderful he was. Instead, Alex looked like he had just been asked to swallow sludge.

"No, I'm no kidding," Jaime said. "I paid good dosh for that."

"You paid for it?!"

A thundercloud passed in front of Jamie's face as he strode passed Alex. "Don't sound so pleased, will you," he sniped.

"Does it go?" Alex snipped back.

"Of course it goes," Jamie said. "How'd you think it got here?"

"Jamie," Alex sighed, "I don't mean to put a damper on things, but we can't afford to buy stuff ..." he gulped looking at the art nouveau of rust holding the thing together and tried to put a positive spin on it, "... like that, like cars. Not just now anyway. Apart from the fact that we agreed to tell each other about big purchases. We did agree to that, didn't we?"

Jamie chose to ignore the words of prohibition reasoning. "I thought you'd be pleased," he said.

Alex watched the hurt in Jamie's movements. "Well, I am, but you've just ..."

"Just what?" Jamie shot a look at Alex.

"I mean, we've just got to watch what we're doing with the money. What about the holiday?"

"What money? We don't have any."

"That's what I mean."

Jamie knew he had just snared himself in his own trap and it showed. He knew it wouldn't make any difference which way he twisted and turned now without ripping his own logical counter argument to pieces.

Alex tried to sound more conciliatory. "You should have asked me," he said. "That's all."

Jamie turned away and found himself looking at what now looked more rust than gold. "It wouldn't have been a surprise if I had told you?" he said, trying to keep his voice steady.

Alex stepped closer to Jamie, who still had his back to him. "You're no understanding what I'm saying, Jamie," he said.

"Oh, I understand all right," Jamie said. Alex sighed and wanted to reach out, to touch Jamie's shoulder, to tell him it was all right. "But if we keep spending money like this then we'll never get out of that hovel upstairs and buy a place of our own now, will we?"

Jamie reached out to the rust bucket, stroking his fingers across a lump that fell off like orange-brown snow. Alex watched as Jamie rubbed his fingers together before wiping them onto the leg of his jeans. "I just thought it would be handy so you don't have to keep humping all they bags from the shops," Jamie said.

Alex looked at the back of Jamie's neck, at the short, clean-cut hairs.

"And maybe we could go out for a hurl into the countryside as well sometimes," Jamie said.

"I know what you're saying," Alex said softly. "And at least I know that you were thinking of me when you bought it." Jamie did a half turn and looked over his shoulder at Alex. "And looking at that," Alex said, "I wouldn't have to go in it very far to hurl up I think."

Jamie burst out laughing. Alex laughed at his own poor joke.

"Anyway," Alex said, "how much did it cost? An arm in a leg?"

Jamie turned around and faced Alex, shoulders back, bursting with pride. "No," he said. "That's just it. I got it for a knock-down bargain price."

"How much of a knock-down price would that be, Jamie lad?"

"You'll never *guess*," Jamie said, eyes opening wide on the last word.

"And I don't want to guess, either?" Alex beamed back, leaning in.

"Go on," Jamie teased. "Guess."

"But I just told you," Alex said shaking his head, his smile tightening. "I don't want to guess *anything*."

"I *dare* you."

Stony slabs piled up behind Alex's features. "No," he said through gritted teeth. "Now tell me."

Jamie stepped back, arms wide again. "Seventy-five smakeroonies!" he beamed.

Alex turned to him goggle eyed. "Seventy-five *quid*?" he asked.

Jamie mistook the look on Alex's face for pleasant surprise.

"For *that*?" Alex went on.

"Aye, see?" Jamie said. "I know what a bargain is when I see one."

Alex's mouth gawped. Over and over he repeated: seventy-five, seventy-five seventy …

He snapped out of it and looked at Jamie straight in the eyes. "What kind of car can you buy for seventy-five quid?"

Jamie turned on him. "Will you stop screeching?"

"Does it go?" Alex asked in the same disbelieving tone.

"Of course it goes," Jamie said indignantly. "How'd you think I got it here? I've already told you that." Alex didn't look convinced. Jamie spoke up again. "Tell you what," he said. "After our dinner tonight, I'll take you out for a hurl in it."

Alex looked at Jamie with an expression that could only be described as stunned. If anything, he looked as if he were about to hurl up onto the pavement there and then with the thought of getting into that death trap.

"It'll not be dark enough by that time," Alex said under his breath, looking around to see if anyone had been close enough to hear Jamie's suggestion. It was a case of shame by association.

"What?" Jamie asked leaning in closer.

"Awe, nothing," Alex said turning away. "Come on. The dinner won't be having it at this rate."

~~*

Alex ate very slowly, demurely; savoring each tiny morsel until it completely lost its flavor, until his stomach thought his throat was cut. Jamie stood towering over Alex from the back as Alex desperately tried to scoop up the last few crumbs from his plate. With his fork hovering a few millimeters from his mouth, Jamie snatched it from his hand.

"Hey," Alex protested. "I haven't finished yet."

"You have," Jamie said as the plate clattered into the sink. "You were just stretching it out."

Alex stuck the tines of his fork delicately into his mouth as Jamie stepped behind him. He had thought he was about to be left in peace in the kitchen, at the table, with enough breath left in him to wonder what his life might have turned out to be.

But Jamie had other plans and grabbed Alex's chair, yanking it back.

Alex choked on the tines of the fork, ready to throw a fit.

"Hey, watch what you're doing," he yelled, red-faced.

Jamie reached around and wrestled the fork out of Alex's clutch and slammed it on to the table with a whack.

"What's going on?" Alex yelled.

"This," Jamie said, grabbing Alex under the armpits and dragging him to his feet.

"We're going out in that car if it kills you," Jamie said.

Which was exactly what Alex was afraid of: dying of embarrassment, being seen by anyone as he climbed into that rust bucket crumbling by the side of the road down stairs.

Jamie pulled Alex out of the kitchen by the arm. Alex grabbed hold of the lintel. Jamie grabbed Alex by the wrist, turned and dug in his heels to yank at Alex with all his might. And after prying Alex off the doorway, they catapulted into the dark hallway.

"I can't go out without changing first," Alex yelled in a last ditch attempt at delaying tactics.

Jamie daren't let go of Alex's arm, though. "Right," he huffed, breathing heavily with the exertion.

Alex's heels skidded along the hallway as Jamie used centrifugal force to spin Alex into the bedroom.

"Quit shoving me," Alex said.

"Get dressed in what you're getting dressed in! Hurry up!"

Alex walked over to the wardrobe and pulled out his best shirt, tie, jacket and trousers. The last time he'd worn them was six months ago at his gran's funeral. This occasion had the same dreaded feeling about it.

"Hurry up," Jamie said.

"What's the rush?" Alex snapped.

Jamie looked at his watch, then out the window at the dying light outside. "I want us going out before it gets too dark," he said. "That's what the rush is on for, right?"

Alex carefully took each item of clothing from its hanger and laid them on the bed. "Give me five minutes," he said.

"You've got fifteen seconds," Jamie said, looking at the second hand on his watch.

Alex sighed, rolled up his eyes and smiled to himself, a smile that slowly changed to a grin. Until Jamie yanked at the waistband of his tracksuit bottoms.

"Hey!"

Jamie pulled Alex's t-shirt over his head.

"You're no fooling me," Jamie said, "with your delaying tactics. I know you too well."

Alex shuffled in a half spin, his tracksuit bottoms entangling his feet.

Jamie watched Alex's back end. "Nice CKs by the way."

"Get your mind out the gutter," Alex said.

"Just saying, that's all."

With a lot of pulling, stretching and twanging of stretchy fabric, Alex was eventually dressed up and ready to go.

"There," Jamie said, spinning Alex around to face him. "You look braw enough to shag."

Alex frowned and looked at Jamie with hard eyes. "I wore this to my gran's funeral."

~~*

Alex waited on the pavement while Jamie stepped off it and to the other side of the "new" car. Jamie took out the keys.

"Are you sure it goes?" Alex asked.

"Will you stop saying that," Jamie said.

Alex looked up and down the street, hoping no one was about to catch sight of him standing beside the rust bucket.

The shame of it.

He closed his eyes and whispered to himself, "Be feared, be very feared."

Until Jamie's voice snapped him back to the horror of it in hand. "Anyway," Jamie said. "There is something."

Alex cringed. He'd just known something like this was going to happen. He hadn't known what. But he'd known it was coming and it didn't feel good. "Awe, God! I knew it," he said.

Jamie gave him a hard look over the dented roof of the car. "Quit whining," he said. Jamie waited for a second, knowing that Alex wouldn't be able to contain himself for long.

"Well?" Alex huffed. "What is it, this something?"

Jamie bit his lip. "The petrol pump," he said

"What about it?" Alex asked.

"Nothing much," Jamie said. "It just needs a wee bit of a helping hand."

Alex's jaw dropped. He didn't know anything about petrol pumps. He knew even less about cars. What he did know was he had a good instinct for sussing out a pig in a poke when he saw one. And this one was flying out of the bag in front of his eyes.

Jamie pulled open the driver's door with an agonizing crunch of buckled metal that reminded Alex about the time Derek had made him bite into a lump of polystyrene as a bairn.

Before Alex could find the magic words that should have made it all disappear, something like "Shazam!" but in reality would have been "I'm out of here," Jamie was already inside and crawling over the seats to the glove compartment.

There was a lot of muffled cursing as he tried to pull its door open. Then Alex watched through the manky windows as Jamie crawled back out. Jamie stood up, head bopping up over the roof. He smiled at Alex.

Alex frowned. Here he was, dressed in all his funeral clobber, and now Jamie was looking at him in a way that said, "Don't ask."

Jamie held up a spanner, edging it up into view like an anorexic puppet. Alex folded his arms and tightened his mouth while Jamie walked around the back of the Beetle car. Jamie pushed the key into the lock of the boot and gave it a twist.

Nothing happened.

Alex raised an eyebrow and folded his arms. Jamie shook the key.

Still nothing happened.

With both hands now, he tried twisting the key in the lock and pulling up the lid of the boot at the same time.

Still nothing.

Alex tilted his head. Jamie stepped back and key hanging from the lock, raised his heel and rammed it at the back of the car.

The lid sprang up.

Pleased with himself, he rubbed his hands together, leaned over and stuck his head inside. The stink of petrol hit Alex hard. He took a step back, pulling a face.

"It reeks," he said.

Jamie ignored him, pulled his torso out of the boot and held up the spanner.

"Awe, aye," Alex said. "It's got one then?"

"Got a what?" Jamie said.

"An engine," Alex said.

"Of course it's got an engine," Jamie said. "What did you expect?"

"I expect for it to have its engine in the front of it, no the back of it. But no matter. What would you expect for a car you bought for seventy-five smackers?"

Jamie ignored him. "You have to come down here a minute," he said.

"I'm close enough," Alex said.

"Just get down here, on the road, in stand here next to me will you?"

Alex stepped off the edge of the pavement as if he had been asked to step onto molten lava.

"Right," Jamie said, wobbling the spanner up and down at the engine.

"What am I looking it first?" Alex asked. "Apart from a heap of rust."

"Funny hah hah," Jamie said. He waved the spanner at a little oblong lump of off-white plastic stuck in the corner by the side of the engine.

"See this thing here?" he asked Alex, who by now was peering suspiciously at the thing.

"Aye," Alex said. "What about it?"

"Well that's the petrol pump." Jamie tapped the spanner on it. Alex listened to the short but rhythmic tapping on what sounded like hollow plastic. "Well that thing there pumps the petrol from the tank into the engine there," Jamie said.

"Wow! You don't say. Right, well thanks for the lesson, see you," Alex said turning away. He set one foot on the edge of the pavement when a hand slapped on his shoulder and yanked him back.

Jamie, still with his clutch digging determinedly into Alex's shoulder, grinned up close and personal.

"That's the bit that needs a hand," he said.

He waited for Alex to say something. He didn't have to wait for long.

"I thought you said there was nothing wrong with this pit disaster?" Alex said.

"There isn't," Jamie said. "But like I said, it just needs a wee helping hand."

Alex pulled back. Jamie's clutch dug in deeper. "Hey, mind the shoulder," Alex said. Jamie let go and patted down the material. "This is my good clothes, you know," Alex reminded him.

"And I appreciate that, Alex lad. But there are things at hand that need to be explained to you first."

Alex brushed himself down. "Like?" he asked.

"Like the petrol pump," Jamie said. "Now listen to what I'm saying."

"Well hurry up then, or we'll be here all night."

Jamie huffed and tapped his foot. "If you don't calm down I'm no going to be telling you anything."

"Right, suits me. Bye."

A hand clamped back down on his shoulder again. Alex's soles spun around on the gritty pavement. Jamie leaned in to him, a bit angrier, but controlled in a tight-faced, smiley sort of way.

Alex pulled back his face. "Watch the suit!"

Jamie sucked in a deep breath. "Now listen out, laddie, we're going out for this hurl if it kills you!"

"Me? Why me? I don't even want to get into that death trap."

"Well, you are going in it, in that's that," Jamie said. "Now listen to me. The petrol pump—"

"Needs a hand," Alex cut in. "I heard you the first time."

"Right." Jamie stepped back. "Now we're getting somewhere."

He turned to the engine. The street-lights began to flicker on. Alex cringed. He might as well have had spotlights of shame shining down on him.

"All it needs is tapped," Jamie explained. "As in tap tap tap."

"Tapped?"

"Aye, tapped."

"What needs tapped?"

"The water supply. What do you think needs tapping? The petrol pump, what else?"

"What for? In stop shouting it me—I'm no deaf."

"Cat's for."

"Eh?"

"Awe, for crying out bloody loud. The petrol pump needs tapping. Now watch this," Jamie pointed the spanner at a little ivory-colored box thing in the corner again.

"That," said Jamie, "is the petrol pump."

Alex peered in, and then took a step back. "So you keep saying," he said. "What about it?"

"What about it is important. So listen to me. Watch and learn. The car goes all right, but it just needs a wee bit of a hand to get started. And that's where you and this thing," he said, tapping the blade on the petrol pump, "come in."

Alex stood, one leg buckled, arms folded, face squint, and watched. "Right," he said. "I'm listening."

Jamie gripped the spanner and aimed it at the petrol pump. "Now all you have to do is tap it, like this."

Tap, tap, tap.

"Eh?" Alex said, his arms dropping.

"It's a wee bit iffy, you see," Jamie explained, "but once you tap it, then the petrol gets to the engine. Tah dah!"

"So, let me get this straight," Alex said. "You start the engine and I have to stand in the back of the car tapping at that wee plastic box thing as you drive along. I just keep tapping till we get into town? You must think I came up the Clyde like a humph in a haversack!"

"Not all the way into town, yah tube. Just till the engine takes. Then you get in the car."

Alex thought about it for a moment, and then held out his hand. "Gives it then," he said.

Jamie beamed, slapped the spanner into Alex's open palm, and gave him a peck on the cheek. "Right," he said. "I'll jump in and start the engine. You get ready to tap."

"Right."

Jamie ran around the side and jumped in. Alex leaned forward, spanner handle hovering over the little plastic looking petrol pump, and waited. He screwed his face up at the stink of petrol fumes.

"Ready?" he heard Jamie call out.

"Aye."

"Eh?"

"Just start it, for God's sake," Alex snapped.

"Right, I'll just switch it on."

"Well, hurry up then."

There proceeded the evil sound of metal grinding on metal. Alex screwed up his eyes as exhaust fumes belched out the back end of the thing. He coughed and tapped at the petrol pump as Jamie revved the engine.

Eyes streaming and nearly vomiting, Alex tapped the spanner like a trip hammer at the petrol pump. "Hurry up!" he yelled out, clutching his throat. "God!"

And suddenly, like a magic trick, the petrol pump vanished, as did the whole car, in a grey black spume of engine muck. Doubled over, trying to catch his breath, Alex looked up just in time to see the Beetle vanish down the road.

After half an hour of waiting, Alex relented and finally climbed the three flights back up to the flat and waited.

And waited.

When he was done scrapping the Al Jolson impersonation off his face, he sat down at the table in the deathly quiet of the kitchen. Turning to the window he could see that it was fully dark outside now and so he sighed and waited some more.

One funeral was bad enough. Another ... ?

CHaPTer 21

Eleven o'clock and Alex was biting his fingernails up to his armpits.

What had happened to Jamie?

He thought about that old jalopy, the way it had zoomed off down the road in a cloud of fumes. By the time he had stopped choking to death on the exhaust and cleared some of the sting from his eyes, the car was gone.

Along with the one and only love of his life, Jamie.

What if he was lost? What it he'd had a crash?

The sight of blood and guts flashed into Alex's mind, Jamie's body half out the broken windscreen, white flesh, red blood, eyes staring wide.

Dead!

"Oh my God!" Alex stood up from the kitchen table and paced for the fiftieth time to the window. Leaning over the sink, he crammed his eyes up against the glass.

Why the hell did we have to pick a flat so high up from the street?

Because it was the only one we could afford, idiot.

Now look what had come of it?

Even the road down there was quiet, as it always was at this time of night. A car rolled by on the other side. Alex's heart leapt.

A Jaguar? Did Jamie buy a Jaguar for seventy-five quid? Alex couldn't remember. What Jamie had bought looked too blocky for a Jaguar.

He pulled back from the window.

Maybe I should go back down to the street. Can't see anything from up here. But if I do that then I won't hear if Jamie makes a phone call.

Or the hospital, or the police.

I'm going to throw up.

Don't be silly. Calm down, you eejit. Jamie's okay, he's okay …

It's been hours.

He's dead!

Stop it right now. Breathe deep. Count to ten, slowly. One …

I can't stand it! Maybe I should call the cops?

"For God's sake, what did you have to buy that heap of rust for? Yah ..."

There was a noise at the front door. Alex dived into the hallway, held his breath and listened. He could hear the sound of a key going into the lock. The door swung wide. A body staggered in, heavy footed.

"Jamie?"

No answer. Alex rushed right up to the door. "Jamie! Where the hell have you been?"

Sad-shouldered, weakening by the second, Jamie gave Alex a sorrowful look.

"What happened to your clothes?" Alex asked.

But all Jamie could manage was a weak shake of his head. "Oh, Alex," he whimpered. "You don't want to know, laddie."

"What happened to you?"

"It was terrible, terrible, Alex. I'm only glad you didn't have to go through what I did."

Hanging onto the lintel of the doorway, Jamie swung into the hallway as Alex reached behind him and closed the door quietly.

"I thought you had got yourself killed," Alex said. "God, Jamie, I was near beside myself with fear."

Alex noticed a carrier bag held tight in Jamie's hand.

Jamie took a step back, his footsteps faltering.

"What is it, Jamie? What's wrong?"

"Awe, Alex, help me, laddie, my legs is fainting under me. I don't think I'm going to make it," he said with a pained look in his eyes, batting his eyelids weakly.

"Are you hurt? What happened to you?"

"Help me through, Eck—" Jamie coughed, "—and I'll tell you all the gory details. But I'm about collapsing with exhaustion, laddie." He wheezed, eyes rolling up in his head.

"Here," Alex said, bolstered into action. "Put your arm around my shoulders. I'll help you. Just you take it easy."

"My hero," Jamie said, clutching onto Alex, hirpling through to the kitchen with Alex's help.

"Maybe you should have a lie down," Alex said. "Do you need a doctor?"

Jamie winced. "No laddie—" he coughed and wheezed. "—I'll be all right now that I'm at home and under your loving care." He smiled wanly. "And maybe a wee sip of hot sweet tea to get the strength back into my pins."

Gently, Alex let Jamie sink down onto one of the kitchen chairs. "Are you sure you're all right?"

Jamie nodded slowly and struggled to smile. Alex filled the kettle, plugged it in and switched it on. He turned to Jamie.

"So what happened?" he asked. "And where's the car?"

Jamie screwed up his face and looked away.

"Jamie?"

The sound of his name being called seemed to bring Jamie back to the present. "Oh, aye," he said wistfully, grimacing, "the car."

Alex sat down opposite, his arms folded. "Aye, the car. The bargain bucket special you bought from the scrapheap auction?"

Jamie sniffed. "Yes, the car."

Alex raised his eyebrows. Jamie caught that look. He rubbed at his forehead and groaned. Only Alex was well used to this same childish palaver from his older siblings.

"The car, Jamie," Alex said, leaning over the kitchen table. "The one you told me was a bargain at seventy-five smakeroonies?"

"Well ..."

"What?"

"I lost it."

Alex stood up so fast his chair fell over. "Whadoyihmeanyih*LOSTIT*!"

Jamie keeled backwards at the ferocity of the question. "Alex, lad, I'm no well."

"No well my foot. Where is it?"

"Your foot?"

"The *CAR*!"

"I told you."

"You've told me bugger all. And what's in the bag?"

Jamie took a deep breath, sat up and asked, "Am I getting that tea or no?"

"Car," Alex demanded, turning away and going to make the tea. "And keep it short," he called over his shoulder.

"Okay, since you want to know all the gruesome details."

"Everything," Alex snapped as he slammed the mugs down on the bunker.

"Okay, well, see when you were tapping at the petrol pump?"

"How could I forget?" Alex said. "How many sugars, one or two?"

"One."

"Go on."

"Since you ask," Jamie huffed.

"I am," Alex said, slamming a mug of tea down on the table in front of Jamie. Alex sat down opposite.

"Well, everything went all right," Jamie said, "for a bit anyway. But that was okay when it was on the straight and level, or when the car was going downhill. But that was the problem, you see? Going downhill was a cinch. Getting back up the other side was another matter."

Alex looked at him quizzically.

"The thing was," Jamie went on, "when it came to trying to drive up the other side of the hill, the engine conked out on me. So it ended up rolling back down again. Then when I got to the bottom of the hill, I could start the engine again—after about fifty goes that is. So up the hill I went and back down again. Up and down and up and down. I sat there for hours trying to get up that hill, but I was stuck.

"I sat there in the dark thinking I would never escape, Alex. And I really wanted this to be a special night for you, "Jamie coughed, "I really did, Eck. I even thought about trying to shove it up the hill myself, but the car was one of these auld numbers, made of concrete or something. There was no way I could shove it myself, Alex. I was too weak with exhaustion without having a cup of tea or nothing for so long."

"So you left it," Alex said, sounding more sympathetic now. "Well, it least you got back yourself." He reached out for Jamie's hand and gave it a squeeze.

Jamie smiled. "Thing was," he said, "I didn't quite just leave it. I was standing at the back of it having a cig, I hope you don't mind."

Alex shook his head. "You were stressed out," Alex said. "I can understand that. I went through a bucket of Rocket Fuel coffee myself wondering what had happened to you."

Jamie squeezed Alex's hand in return, smiled and went on. "As it happened, this geezer came walking past and like a Good Samaritan, he asked me if things were okay. Be all and end all was I told him the problem."

"What happened then?" Alex asked.

Jamie let go of Alex hand and sat back. "The geezer bought it off me."

"He bought it?"

"Aye, he said he could sell it for scrap. So I sold it to him for eighty-five quid."

And before Alex could shut his gaping gob, Jamie opened the bag. "I knew you would be disappointed," Jamie said, "at no going out in our new car so I bought you something in compensation. I know it's still a week to go before your birthday, Alex, but I bought you this. Mind you, by the time I found an Alldays that was open that late, there wasn't much to buy."

Taking the bottle out of the bag, he placed it on the table, reached into the bag again and pulled out a box and laid it down on the table.

"It's not a real birthday cake, Alex," Jamie said. "But it is a chocolate cake one, your favorite."

But Alex couldn't say anything for the lump in his throat.

Jamie stood up walked around the table and gave him a hug just as the clock struck twelve. "Happy eighteenth birthday when it comes to you, Alex. You're a right special laddie to me." He held on tight even as he felt Alex's shoulders begin to shake. "Come on, Alex," Jamie said.

"I feel rotten now, for everything I said before," Alex confessed.

"I don't."

"You don't?" Alex sniffed.

"No, because it tells me that you care, Eck. And that means an awful lot to a laddie like me after being in all the different homes, one after the other, year after year. To know that somebody really cares about what happens to me now. All I can say is, thanks for shouting at me because if I had meant nothing to you, laddie, I know you wouldn't have bothered."

"Awe, Jamie."

"And I got you this as well," Jamie said, pulling something else out of the bag. "Sorry I didn't have time to wrap it right," he said. "But when I saw it, I thought ... well, it just kind of said something to me about you. Anyway here."

And Alex watched as Jamie handed over the blue and pink paper bag.

"Happy birthday when it comes, Alex."

Alex felt the bag in his hand, heard the paper crinkle, and frowned. Slowly he reached inside and slid out his dark-blue present. "A notebook?" Alex asked, not really expecting an answer.

"Aye. Oh," Jamie said reaching into his jacket. "This as well to go with it." He held the pen out to Alex. "It's not an expensive one like," Jamie said, "but ..."

"Priceless," Alex whispered. He took the pen and opened the little notebook, looked at the lines on the paper, and felt the whole world calling out to him from the blank pages.

"What made you buy this for me, Jamie?" Alex sounded distant, still looking through the blank pages.

"Know this, Eck," Jamie said. "I really don't know myself. And yet, it seemed to mean something, like I was being guided to it. But maybe it's because of all those stories you keep telling me, and ..."

"Aye?"

"Och, I feel daft saying it," Jamie said. "But when I hear them, your stories, it's like I forget all about the bad stuff, and they stop me dwelling on the past. And maybe, if you were to write them down, then it could help somebody else. You make me laugh, Eck. And when you make me laugh it's like all that bad stuff disappears."

Alex excused himself, went through to the bathroom and blew his nose, still clutching at the notebook and pen. Sitting on the edge of the bath, he took the pen and wrote the date, time, address and started to write.

To whom it may concern ...

And after, he used half the loo roll to blow his nose he returned to his old self and walked back into the kitchen. The lights were out. He peeked around the side of the door.

The table was glowing—the chocolate cake ablaze with birthday candles.

Jamie sang out. "Happy birthday to you. A week early or no. Happy birthday, dear Alex. Happy birthday to yoooooooooooooo."

But Alex was already back in the bathroom, blowing his nose again on what was left of the toilet roll. Jamie looked around the edge of the door.

"The candles will melt if you don't blow them out and make a wish. Come on, Alex, you're supposed to be laughing."

Once he was back in the kitchen, Alex leaned over the table.

"Made a wish?" Jamie asked.

Alex nodded, closed his eyes, thought about Jamison the solicitor, and blew out the candles, then stood up to Jamie's clapping and cheering.

A few minutes later, Alex and Jamie were stuffing their faces with great lumps of chocolate cake. Alex groaned in pleasure loud enough for both of them at the taste. Still halfway through a slice he picked up the bottle. "This a good make, Buckfast?" he asked.

"Guy in the shop said it was."

"Better open it then and have us a drink, even if it is another week till it's legal for me to have alcohol."

After clinking their glasses together, Jamie remembered something. Digging into the bag again, he took out the CD. A look of shock came across his face when he looked at the cover. "Damn! I forgot to take the price off."

Turning his back to Alex, he picked and picked until the sticky label came away. He rolled it into a ball and handed the CD over to Alex.

One surprise after another. "Awe, Jamie, you shouldn't have."

"I hope you like it. I know that they're your favorites like," Jamie said.

"Pretenders, Greatest Hits," Alex said, reading the cover. "And they are my favorites," he said. "The old ones are better." Grabbing his glass, he stood up. "Come on," he said. "Let's put it on."

Without waiting for Jamie, Alex left the kitchen.

Jamie blew out a breath, took another slug of Buckfast. "2011 must have been a good year." He belched and went to find Alex.

By the time Jamie reached the living room, Alex was hunkered down in front of the music centre. Alex was muttering.

"What's up?" Jamie asked.

"The door on the CD player's stuck. The only modern thing that landlord rents out as part of the flat and it doesn't work. It's probably jammed up with dust since it's never used."

Jamie was filled with disappointment. "Oh well, never mind," he said.

Alex looked up at him. "No," he said, "I want to listen to my present."

"But the door thing's stuck?"

Alex smiled. "No for long," he said.

"Don't get you," Jamie said.

"I'll fix it."

"How?"

Alex gave him a serious look. "Get the fork," he said.

~~*

After twiggling the tines of the fork in the CD drawer, it sprang wide and soon thereafter Chrissie Hynde sang her heart out.

By the time it came to *Talk of the Town* and a few more glasses of Buckfast, Alex was on his feet in the middle of the floor giving it laldy.

He started singing along, screeching high and low, trying his best to outdo Ms Hynde on her take of her own song, until he eventually managed to drown her out completely.

He closed his eyes, reflecting on his own stage of fame.

Jamie cringed.

Alex opened his gob wide, bent double, then whooshed back up and screamed out the lyrics, finally obliterating even Chrissie's efforts.

Jamie stood up. "Alex, maybe we should call it a night," he said. "The neighbors. And we've got squash booked in the morning. You won't be fit to go."

But Alex wasn't listening to anything but the sound of his own voice as he screeched away into an invisible microphone. "I think the Buckfast's going to your head," Jamie warned.

"Minute, minute." Alex ducked around as if Jamie were trying to pull the stage curtain down on his performance.

"Alex, you're going bonkers. Now I know it's your birthday, but no for a week. You're singing too loud. Now stop before the neighbors call the polis."

But Alex was having nothing to do with it. He backed away from Jamie, his eyes closed. "Alex!"

"You're the talk of the tahawan."

Okay, Jamie thought when he remembered how it had worked for Doris Day when she was hysterical and how Tony Randal used a certain technique to bring her back to her senses. Jamie put down his glass, kept Alex in his sights, and said, "This is going to hurt me than it's going to hurt you."

He closed his eyes, counted to himself, and swung his hand through the air.

Crunch!

"Aaah!" Jamie sank to his knees. "My fuggin hand!" He clutched at is wrist. It was the nearest he could feel at his injury without actually further damaging his fingers. "Awe, my hand, my hand."

Alex was now in the middle of the living room floor, eyes still closed, singing louder than before.

Unfortunately for Jamie, when he had closed his eyes to take a swing at Alex for the Doris Day effect, Alex had ducked out of the way and Jamie had swung his hand straight into the edge of the open door instead.

On his knees and still clutching at his wrist, he glared at Alex.

"Yooove CHEYNGED!"

... Jamie gritted his teeth.

"*SHAARRRAAAAAP!*"

CHAPTER 22

Jamie sat up sharply. The back of his head shot off. The rest of him shot back down onto the pillow.

"Awe God, my head!" He dared open his eyes. The sun shone like a blowlamp through the blinds. "When did the light come back on?" he groaned.

The bedroom door opened. Someone was humming a tune. Jamie opened one eye to take a peek and watched Alex pull open the wardrobe door. The coat hangers clanged like Big Ben hitting concrete from a ten-foot drop.

"Do you have to make such a racket?" Jamie asked as he pulled a pillow over his head.

Alex slammed the wardrobe door. "Sore head?" he asked light as could be.

"Sore everything," Jamie said from inside a marshmallow.

"Eh?"

Jamie lifted the pillow high enough for his mouth to show and no more. "I'm dying," he wailed.

"You're late," Alex said. "Come on, get up."

"What time is it?"

Alex reached over and yanked away the pillow. "Time you were up."

Jamie pulled the quilt over his head. Alex grabbed the bottom of it and gave it a tug. Jamie held tight.

Alex yanked at it harder. "Get … *up*!"

Jamie lost his grip and Alex flew backwards, quilt in hand. Jamie curled up, shivering.

"We'll be late for the court," Alex said.

Jamie shot up. "What did a do?"

"Nothing, yet. Squash court, remember? You booked it for nine o' clock. My first lesson, you said. You would be teaching me, you said."

Jamie flopped back. "Cancel it."

"Come on or we'll be late."

"I can't. I'm no fit to play. My hand's sore."

"What's wrong with it like?"

"You broke it," Jamie said.

"Me?"

"Aye, you. You sat on it last night with your fat ark."

"Nothing to do with the fact that you clobbered it on the door when I ducked?" Alex said.

A sharp intake of breath from Jamie caught in the act of fibbing.

"Try it again," Alex said, "and there'll be more than a sore hand you'll have to deal with, kid."

"You were deranged, off your head with drink! Yah alcoholic!"

"I'm not the one with the sore head, right. So get on your feet, get in that shower, brush your mawkit gob, and get ready for teaching me to play *SQUASH*!"

Alex disappeared and Jamie dared open his eyes. Head sore, hand aching, gut churning, the taste in his mouth not worth thinking about, he vowed there and then that he was going to show this ungrateful little get how to play fair.

~~*

Now in recovery, and sick of waiting, Jamie barged into the bedroom and saw Alex's humph travel up and down along the far side of the bed.

"What's taking so long?" Jamie asked.

Alex's head popped up, red-faced with effort. "I can't find it," he said, blowing fluff off the end of his nose.

Jamie's face creased with questions. "Find what?" he snapped.

"My bat," Alex said, head diving down again to have another rummage under the bed.

Jamie stepped around the same side where Alex was hunkered over. "Bat?" he asked.

"Aye, my bat," Alex said.

"What kind of bat?" Jamie asked. "Vampire bat? Cricket bat? Baseball bat? Tennis bat?"

Alex came up for air, face covered in danders and fluff. "Squash bat," he said. "God, it's like Anniker's Midden under here," he said, peering into the depths of darkness. "I'll have to clean it out when we get back." He dived under again.

Jamie leaned over Alex's back. "There's no such thing is a squash bat," he said with a tight smile on his face.

Alex's head snapped up again for air and turned to the side. "And what," he said, "does you hit the ball with then, pray tell?"

Jamie looked him in the eye. "A racquet, Alex. You play squash with a squash racquet."

"Found it!" Alex said, holding up the racquet like Excalibur covered in dust and cobwebs.

"It's mawkit," he said, "but the strings are still intact though."

(Ping! Twang!)

Jamie looked at his watch. "Well, hurry up then," he said. "You should have had all of this sorted out before now. Organized like me."

Alex stood up. "I'll just give it a wee dust down first," he said, "then that's me." His knees cracked as he stood up straight. Hand on back, he stretched his spine. "God," he complained, "I don't know if my joints is in it though."

Jamie rolled up his eyes, and then tapped at the face of his watch. "We've got half an hour to get there. So hurry up."

Alex ignored him, instead inspecting the strings of his racquet. "It's never been used in years by looking at it. That's why it probably ended up in the jumble sale where I bought it."

Waiting until Jamie had left the room, Alex tested his technique by swishing his racquet through the air. He coughed, eyes streaming. "God, the stoor on it." He picked up his sports bag from the corner, stuffed to the gunnels with everything he thought he would need for a game, and strode confidently into the hallway.

Jamie was at the front door already holding it open. "Hurry up will you," he said.

"I'm here, I'm here."

~~*

Alex arrived at DeMarco's sports centre first, with his hood up and sporting ginormous sunglasses so that no one would recognize him, and with a bag big enough for a Kalashnikov on a hair trigger inside. The doors were just opening for the first of the day when he scurried along under the eaves, glancing this way and that to make sure no one was watching.

The street was still deserted.

He nipped inside. His bulging sports bag got trapped in the swing doors. That is until a helpful soul going by the name of Jamie helped him free it.

"What's the rush," Jamie asked.

"You were the one says we were going to be late," Alex said.

"Feared in case anyone sees you?" Jamie said as he handed over the fee for the squash court.

Alex took on an indignant look. "No, I'm no, right."

Jamie left it at that and they made their way up to the top floor. Puggled and dragging his bag up the last few steps by its straining straps, Alex slumped down on the last but one step.

"What does it have to be on the top floor for?" he whined.

"What does?" Jamie asked.

"The squash court," Alex said as if talking to a stupid kid.

"But it's no on the top floor," Jamie said.

Alex stood up too quickly, which nearly pulled him back down a flight of stairs with the loaded bag in hand.

"What?"

"The squash courts are on the bottom floor," Jamie said.

Alex's face crinkled and shrunk with rage down to the size of a hand grenade.

"Keep your paps on. I'm only kidding," Jamie said. "The courts are this way. Follow me, my son."

Alex stood for a second and wondered if he should leave right now or throw his bag down the stairs and defect with a "That's it."

Except he didn't.

Instead he pulled himself up straight, breathed deeply, and vowed he wouldn't be beaten. After all, once he was on that court there would be no going back, no matter how intimidating it felt.

~~*

Jamie changed into sensible attire: white T-shirt and shorts, as Alex continued to jump around the middle of the changing room swinging his racquet through the air.

"Right," Alex declared. "I'm ready."

Jamie finished tying his laces. Alex bounced around, sneakers squeaking, thudding around about as delicately as an iron butterfly, racquet cutting and slicing through the air.

Swish

Swoooooooosh

"Are you on something?" Jamie asked, tying a tight bow, looking up, frowning.

"I'm just trying out my moves for my first game," Alex said.

Swish

Swoooooooosh

"Don't tire yourself out before we get on the court," Jamie warned. "And hurry up in get the rest of your gear on. I'll go out and wait for you on court."

It was like walking into a cathedral, Alex noted: the high ceiling, the pews at the back of the courts, their glass fronts for all to see through.

He didn't like that. It would be like being on display. He was relieved to see that their court at least had no seats for anyone to sit and look on, just a wall.

Like a professional now and entirely at ease, Alex entered the slaughterhouse right.

~~*

Jamie stood leaning against the glass wall of the court, bouncing the ball on his racquet and wondering what was taking Alex so long to get ready when suddenly Alex appeared.

Don't say anything, Jamie thought to himself, walking to the middle of the court. But, no, he couldn't help himself.

"What's with the Stanley Mathew's shorts?" he asked.

"What?"

Jamie looked Alex up and down. At his baggy khaki shorts—a whole two inches above the ankle—at his lopsided white T shirt, at his gob bulging top and bottom with gum shields that must have once belonged to King Kong. He looked like Mick Jagger in a Botox nightmare. The lot topped off with antique motorcycle goggles that made Alex look cockeyed.

God save us. Jamie rolled up his eyes.

"What are you shtairin at?" Alex eyes bulged inside the goggles.

At least that was what Jamie thought Alex said.

"Nothing," Jamie sighed. "Nothing it all."

"Right," Alex said. "Litsh get on wish the game then."

Jamie took a practice swing of his racquet.

Alex dumped his bag down beside Jamie's with a clonk. Jamie gave him a quizzical look. Alex gave him a don't-you-dare look in return and Jamie decided to leave well alone.

Jamie opened the door in the glass wall. "After you," he said to Alex.

"Ashter you," Alex said back with a bulging gum-shields smile.

Jamie shook his head and waited. Alex relented and walked onto the court, the squeaking of his trainers echoing back at him from the walls.

"Right," Jamie said, taking a coin out of his pocket. "Heads I win, tails you lose."

"No, no," Alex said. "Headsh *you* loosh, tailsh I win."

"Okay," Jamie said, handing Alex the ball. "You serve first then."

"You dishint eeshin shuck the shoin."

"Just serve, will you," Jamie said.

Alex took the ball, looked around.

"What's wrong now?" Jamie asked.

"Welsh? Wersh shoosht I shtand?"

"There." Jamie pointed with his racquet to the red box painted at the back of the court. "You stand in that box, hit the ball to hit the wall, and that's us started."

Alex eyed Jamie suspiciously, shrugged, then stood in the box as he was instructed. Jamie crouched at the ready facing wall front. Alex hefted the ball into the air, squeezed his eyes shut and clobbered the air.

"I didn't even hit it," Alex protested.

"Do it again then, only this time, hit the thing."

Alex picked up the ball, walked back to the square, threw the ball into the air and walloped it. Arms over his head, racquet waving like an aerial, he dived into a crouch in the far corner—Duck and Cover.

Jamie stood up, hands on hips.

"Where's the ball?" Alex said after slobbering out his gum shields.

Jamie pointed with his racquet. "There," he said. "At your feet."

Alex stood up. "What is it," he asked, "a trick ball?"

Now it was Jamie's turn to look perplexed.

"Eh?"

"It didn't even hit the wall," Alex complained.

Alex kept muttering to himself as he hit the ball time after time. "It's no good, Jamie, there's something wrong with it."

"There's nothing wrong with it."

Alex picked up the ball again, sweating after so much effort trying to get it to hit the wall. "It must be made of putty or something. Here," he said to Jamie, handing him the ball. "You do it."

Shrugging his shoulders and standing in the red box again on his side, Jamie readied himself for the serve. Alex, however, danced and bounced around as if his legs were made out of springs, his racquet a blur—swoosh, swish.

Boing.

Boing.

Boing.

Jamie smashed the ball hard.

He looked around when there was no return serve and saw Alex cowering by the wall in the corner again, arms over his head.

"You can open your eyes now," Jamie said.

One eye open, Alex stood up. "What are you doing?" he raged, his eyes bulging towards the goggles' lenses.

"What do you mean, what am I doing?" Jamie said.

"You're not supposed to hit the ball *that* hard," Alex said.

"What?"

Alex picked up the ball, having now lost all of its energy after its fourth wall collision trajectory, and handed it back to Jamie. "Now," Alex warned Jamie. "Hit it the right way." He stomped back to the right hand side of the court and took up position.

"Ready?" Jamie asked.

"Aye." Alex crouched.

Nice ark. Jamie ogled Alex's rear straining through the shorts.

He hit the ball. Alex dived for it and walloped it back against the wall. Jamie, one hand on hip, racquet swinging in the other, easily returned the shots. One after the other, Alex jumped, dived, clomped and swung with ever increasing desperation at the ball.

Jamie sniffed and watched, thinking, *I could have a cig doing this*, as he gave perfect, effortless returns each time as Alex smashed himself into a pulp against the walls.

This time, Jamie hit the ball a little harder and it bounced back and sailed over Alex's head. Not to be beaten, Alex trundled backwards with ever-increasing squeaks of rubber soles and hit the ball back with a triumphant return.

Seeing his chance, Jamie rushed forward, hooked his racquet under the ball and tapped it. The ball barely hit the wall, but hit it did.

Jamie returned to the back of the court, beaming a smile, and said to Alex, "My point."

With utter disbelief, Alex yelled, "What the hell do you think you're *doing*!"

"WhatdoyoumeanwhatamIdoing?"

Alex strode up to Jamie. "I mean you can't do that," Alex said, pointing his racquet at the ball now a mere two inches from the wall.

"Do what?"

"Tap the ball like that."

"How else I'm I supposed to hit it then?"

"You're supposed to hit it hard enough for me to be able to hit it *back*," Alex explained.

Alex picked up the ball then slammed it into Jamie's fist. "Now play fair," he said, "or not at all." Head high he took up position behind the line and waited.

Jamie walked back to his box. "Right," Jamie said, "I've to hit the ball, but not that hard and no that soft."

"Aye," Alex said.

"Okay."

Jamie served.

Alex missed.

"I'll give you that one," Alex said in a gentlemanly way.

"And that."

"And that one as well."

After the umpteenth time missing the ball, Alex gave up counting altogether.

Jamie's strength grew from his ever-increasing wins.

Alex grew desperate, jumping in front of Jamie, almost decapitating him a few times in the process as he smashed his racquet at the ball.

Jamie didn't say anything—he was winning after all.

He was one point away from winning their first (and at this rate, their last)ever game together. He hit the ball. The ball hit the wall.

There was no return. Confused Jamie looked around. No Alex either.

Then he looked through the glass partition at the back of the court. Alex was standing at the other side, in the corridor, by his sports bag, racquet in one hand, can in the other.

"What's going on?" Jamie shouted.

Alex calmly pinged back the ring pull of the can, lifted the can to his mouth and glugged down the contents. He belched.

"Having some juice," he said.

"You can't just stop," Jamie said.

"I'm dying of thirst," Alex said, taking another drink from the can.

Jamie's hand near enough crushed through the rubber handgrip of his racquet. This was ungentlemanly conduct. But he wouldn't lose it, he wouldn't be beaten. He wouldn't, he wouldn't, he ...

Alex walked back onto the court, refreshed and not a hair out of place.

"Ready when you are," he said, nodding in Jamie's direction.

Jamie hit the ball. Alex made a perfect return. Jamie slammed it back. Alex returned it easily. Jamie missed the ball.

Alex's arms shot in the air. "The winner takes it all. Jamie missed the baaaaaalllll."

Head back, Alex kept his arms in the air, a beatific grin on his face as he took a lap of honor around the court. "Huh! Huh! Huh!"

Jamie said nothing as he picked up the ball.

Alex jumped like a pop up in front of Jamie's face. "We are the peep pill! Yah looser."

He strolled back to his side of the court, sniffed, and took up his position. He bounced around, racquet swinging triumphantly through the air—swish, swoosh—then he was down again, crouching at the ready like a constipated tennis pro.

Shaking his head, trying hard to ignore the distraction, Jamie reached back with his racquet.

"Minute, minute," Alex said jumping and bouncing around again. "I'm getting the hang of it now."

He crouched again. Jamie looked at his ark and saw a great big foot in his mind's eye kicking it.

Jamie swiped a perfect serve. But to his consternation, Alex won the point, and the next and the next. One point to go and Jamie was going to lose to this little fat amateur.

Alex made a desperate swing for the ball. One more point and he would win the game. Alex could see it now, the power and the glory.

"AAAAAAaaaaaaAAAAAAaaaaaHHHhhhhh!"   Jamie sprung up in front of Alex, his arms raised and yelled into Alex's face.

Alex collected himself and stood his ground. And being all very grown up he said, "No like being a loser, Jamie? That's sad."

"Well, you're always jumping in front of me!" Jamie said.

Very adult like now, or patronizing depending on who you were in the situation, Alex spoke slowly and calmly. "Jamie, son," Alex said, putting a fatherly arm around Jamie's shoulders, "there's only one point between us as to who wins the game. So, your serve and may the best man, me, win. I would wish you luck, but it's pointless."

Jamie smashed the ball. Alex smashed it back. Both collided into each other and did a mad search with their eyes for the ball. Whoever won this point was overall winner.

Both asked the same question at the same time.

"Where is it?"

Neither had heard it fall. They both shrugged and looked around. The ball was nowhere to be seen.

"Do dee do dee do dee." Jamie sang the theme from the Twilight Zone.

"I've found it," Alex said. Jamie followed Alex's eyes to the ceiling. There, jammed in the wire guard over the light, was the ball. "Providence," Alex said.

"Whatever," Jamie shrugged.

Alex put an arm over Jamie's shoulder. "I don't think it suits us to be competing with each other, Jamie, do you?"

"Maybe you're right, though I have to say that you put up a good game for a guy who's never played before."

"Let's go for a coffee," Alex said.

"And a cig," Jamie said.

"I'm glad it ended the way it did," Alex said. "I would never have forgiven myself for beating you."

"You beating me?"

"Aye, and I know that it would have hurt you that you lost to a born natural, like me," Alex said, swishing his racquet. "But don't blame yourself, Jamie. Life can be cruel sometimes.

Just then the ball dropped down, bounced and hit the wall.

"I win!" Jamie yelled. "Huh! Huh! Huh!"

"That's no fair!" Alex bawled after Jamie as he left the court triumphant.

CHAPTER 23

A week later, Friday morning, and it was Alex's real birthday. Jamie jumped out of bed, ran out of the bedroom and crashed into Alex in the hallway.

"I'm late for work," Alex shouted, running past him into the bathroom.

Jamie rushed to the front door. The postman always came early, but there was nothing lying at the door, no post. Perhaps Alex had already picked it up.

He ran into the living room. The mantelpiece was bare.

Jamie frowned. "They wouldn't have forgotten, would they, their own brother's birthday, his eighteenth?"

Just then he heard something being pushed through the letterbox. The posty must have been late after all. Elated, Jamie did an about turn and rushed back down the hallway. A pile of letters lay at the foot of the door.

He picked them up, flicking through the envelopes one after the other. "Bills, bills, more frigging bills."

No card. "The gets."

Still clutching the envelopes, he turned and looked at the bathroom door. He could hear Alex brushing his teeth.

There was still time. Rushing into the bedroom, Jamie dropped the pile of bills on the bed, hunched down and reached under it.

He pulled out the bag with Alex's present in it, one he had kept hidden for a week. Alex might have been a dust-bug, but he rarely looked under the bed. He'd already left his squash racquet to fossilize down there. Said it gave him creeps to look under it anyway. It was the perfect place for hiding things.

Jamie pulled the present, wrapped in shiny blue wrapping, and his birthday card to Alex out of the bag.

He took a quick look at the bedroom door. Time to put plan B into action. Jamie reached under the bed again and pulled out the paper bag.

Standing up, holding onto the present, the card, and the paper bag, he rushed into the kitchen. He would have to be quick. Alex's coffee was already standing at the edge of the table.

Jamie plonked down the present and placed the card, still in its envelope, next to it. All he had to do now was find a pen. He looked around frantically.

Living room! He was sure there was one on the mantelpiece.

Should have done this last night.

Still in his drawers and clutching at the paper bag, he stuck his head out the kitchen door, made sure Alex was still in the bathroom, then tip-toed down to the living room and grabbed a pen from the mantelpiece.

Hands shaking, he sat on the armchair, pulled the envelope out of the bag and took out the card. He looked at it, hoping that it would have been something Alex's sister, even his brother, if he had a heart, would have sent a brother for his first special birthday. It looked jolly enough.

Pulling the cap of the pen off with his teeth, card open on his closed knees, he sat, pen poised, wondering what the monsters would have written to their brother—half-brother, he reminded himself—for his all important eighteenth birthday.

It suddenly dawned on him that he had no idea what Thelma's handwriting was like. He didn't worry too much about Derek. Probably couldn't even write anyway.

He scribbled out a rushed "Happy Birthday, Alex. Love, Thelma and Derek" on the inside, stuffed the card back into its envelope on which he'd already stuck a stamp and stood up, hoping Alex wouldn't notice there was no postmark on it.

Near-naked and vulnerable, he made a mad dash back down the hallway, passing the bathroom door just as he heard it open. He thrust the birthday card under all the bills.

Alex entered the kitchen, combing his hair and looked at Jamie, standing tall and grinning in nothing but his skimpy nix.

"What's up with you?" Alex asked.

"Happy birthday!"

"Again?" Alex picked up his coffee.

"Your real one." Jamie leaned over and picked up the box from the table. "For you."

"You gave me all my presents last week."

"Aye, but I had got you this too."

Alex smiled. "Mind if I open it when I get back tonight? I'll be late for work."

Jamie looked disappointed.

"And it'll give me something to look forward to," Alex said, taking the present. He leaned over and gave Jamie a peck on the cheek.

"Thanks, pal," he said. Jamie acted shy.

"Oh," he said. "I near forgot. Here's your card."

"A card as well?"

"For your special birthday." He gave it to Alex who seemed to take an age just looking at the envelope. "Happy eighteenth, Alex," Jamie said quietly.

Alex opened it slowly and took out the card, opened it and read out the verse. "'Not just for a special boy. But a special friend too. Happy Eighteenth. Love Jamie. XXX.' Awe Jamie. This means a lot to me. You know that, don't you. Last time I had a card was from my gran ..."

"Oh, nearly forgot something else," Jamie cut in. "Looks like a card came through the post for you as well," he said digging through the pile of bills. He pulled out the envelope. "This one's addressed to you."

Alex took it, looked at it, then back at the envelope, a suspicious scowl creasing his face.

"Are you no going to open it?" Jamie asked.

"I'm just wondering, that's all."

Slowly he pulled the flap out, the sound of paper scraping on paper filling the air, reached in and slid out the card. He opened it, reading it in silence.

"Thel and Deek?" Alex said it more to himself.

"That who it's from?" Jamie said, all innocent.

"They must have got a guilty conscience," Alex said, "seeing as it's my one and only eighteenth birthday I'm ever going to have." A smile lit up his face. "Nice though," he said.

Walking around the back of Alex, Jamie gave him a big hug. He felt their warmth flowing from cheek to cheek.

"You should have just taken the day off, but I know what a conscientious wee lad you are ..."

"Man now," Alex said. "It's official."

"Both men now." Jamie gave him a final hug. "And off with you then and hurry back tonight."

With that, Jamie walked out the door into the bedroom to get dressed and ready for work.

~~*

With Jamie out of the kitchen, Alex reached out and touched the edge of the cards standing open on the table. He knew he should be happy. It was his eighteenth after all. But instead, something seemed to sink inside, a kind of sadness. His vision began to blur. What he wouldn't give if the cards had been from his mother and his gran instead, or even his father, whoever or wherever he was.

Then he felt bad, selfish and ungrateful. It was Jamie, Thelma and Derek who had remembered. His mother had died years ago now, his grandmother just over six months. And his dad? Well, Alex had never known the man anyway. His only regret on that point was that his mother would never tell Alex anything about the man. Then again, Alex realized, it was worse for Jamie. He had never known who his mother or father were. So why should Alex complain? Jamie never spoke about it.

Didn't mean it didn't hurt him though.

Alex shrugged, picked up his backpack from the hook in the hall and rubbed his eyes. And even for the secrets his mother had kept from him, and no matter that he would never hear his grandmother's stories again, or that his own father was the stranger he would never meet, Alex whispered something that he would only ever admit to himself: "You're still here, Alex. You've made it this far and more or less on your own."

He pulled the straps of his backpack over his shoulders, drew them tight, and opened the front door. He turned and took a quick look back at the cards and the present on the kitchen table and turned away before it was too late.

CHAPTER 24

"I'm stuffed," Alex said, sitting back and rubbing his belly. "Cheeseburgers and chips. Real cheese as well. You excelled yourself there, Jamie." He belched. "Oops," he laughed, hand coming up to cover his mouth.

Jamie smiled, stood up and picked up the plates and cutlery and dumped everything in the sink. He looked out the window, through the grime on the glass and at the endless rooftops stretching into the distance. The edge of the world came to mind.

Or the end.

Both eighteen.

He had rushed home after work, crashed through the front door, arms laden with the night's meal, and peered around looking to see if a second post had arrived.

Nothing.

He let out a sigh of relief. And disappointment for Alex's sake. It was a million-to-one chance, but there had always been the possibility that Thelma, even Derek, had suddenly developed a conscience and sent Alex a birthday card after all.

Selfish gets, he thought, rushing into the kitchen. And at the same time relieved that he wouldn't have to explain to Alex why there were two cards from the same people: a real one and Jamie's forgery.

A truck rolled by down below. The windowpane rattled as it always did and for a second, Jamie took fright thinking that Thelma was maybe rolling down the road in her new wheelchair stair-climber contraption.

But no, it was just a truck.

Still ...

They might have at least telephoned, wished their brother a happy birthday. But there was nothing.

Jamie filled the sink with hot water and left the dishes to soak. Drying his hands, he walked over to the fridge. It was time for the birthday drink.

He took out the bottle from the lower shelf on the fridge, closed it, then reached into the overhead cupboard and took out two tumblers. Big, thick, glass-bottomed clonkers refashioned from spent glass pilings when the Dounreay Power station had been decommissioned. *Made from gen. Plutonium glass* stamped on their arks—glow-in-the-dark specials.

He raked around the cutlery drawer, found the corkscrew and screwed it into the cork of the bottle. Alex watched, a satisfied look on his face. Jamie's smile back transmogrified into a grimace as he clamped the bottle between his knees and tried to yank out the cork.

The grimace turned to a constipated ache. Alex's eyebrows rose in expectation. Jamie tried to make it look easy.

What's wrong with this?

With a supreme effort the cork began to slide out the neck. At last it plonked out. He held up the cork impaled on the corkscrew, smiled as if it had been no effort at all, walked over to the table and filled the glasses.

The candle flame guttered in the saucer. Jamie put the bottle of Blue Nun beside it and gave Alex his glass. Holding out his, Jamie wished Alex happy birthday again.

The glasses clinked together.

~~*

Later, arms around one another as they sat watching *March of the Penguins* on DVD, Jamie kept one eye on the telephone, the other on the film.

Still nothing.

A paternal instinct he never knew he had stung up from somewhere deep inside of him when he watched a little baby penguin being kept warm and safe on its father's big webbed feet.

But there were still no calls from Thelma or Derek.

Having demolished crisps, nuts, birthday cake and ice cream, the pair fell asleep, heads leaning on one another.

~~*

Jamie jumped up in fright and looked all around. The room swam and Alex keeled over on the sofa, springs twanging when the support of Jamie's shoulder suddenly disappeared.

With groggy eyes, Jamie kept looking around, feeling lost.

The thumps came again.

Jamie's heart thumped harder than the thumping coming from down the hall.

"What the hell's that," Alex asked as he propped himself into an upright position and stretched his eyes wide. He glanced at the old clock on the mantelpiece. "Half eleven," he mumbled. "Who's at the door at this time of night?"

Jamie turned and looked at him as if not knowing what to do. "It's the door," he said.

"I know that," Alex said, waking up fully now.

"What'll I do?"

"Answer it would be a good idea." Alex yawned.

Jamie walked down the hallway. A floorboard creaked. He cringed and stopped at the door, listened, waited.

Nothing.

Must have gone away whoever it was. He started to walk away when the door shook in its frame.

"Who is it?" he called through the door.

"Alex?" came back the muffled reply.

Jamie's heart sank. He closed his eyes and counted to ten, hoped that it would all go away, that this was a nightmare. The worst nightmare he could imagine.

"Open up. I know you're in there?" It was Thelma.

Bang went the door again. Jamie reached up and undid the latch and opened the door a crack and peered through the gap. A fat eyeball looked back.

Then the door flew wide and Jamie jumped back, plastered in fear against the wall.

"Where's my wee brother?" Thelma shouted as she squeezed past.

Derek, the monster without horns, leered at Jamie peeling himself away from the wall. "We've come for the birthday boy," he said to Jamie, and then he was off following his larger-than-life sister.

"Bit late for that are you no?" Jamie said, closing the door.

Standing in the dark of the hallway, Jamie listened as Thelma and Derek shouted surprise and wished Alex a Happy Birthday. Jamie's heart sank.

They had made it then. Just in time.

It sank even further when he remembered something else. He hurried to the kitchen. With the voices in the background—Thelma's the loudest—Jamie stood looking at the kitchen table. The shiny blue wrapping paper from his present to Alex lay folded on one of the chairs. The little CD player with its tiny speakers and headphones lay on another.

The candle on the saucer was now nothing more than a waxy stump. No more a new thing, just a blackened spent thing. The bottle of wine, its cork pushed back into the neck, stood beside it. As did Alex's birthday cards, Jamie's one to Alex and the one Jamie had forged in Thelma and Derek's name.

Jamie blinked and sighed. *What'll I do now*?

And sometimes good things go bad, he thought.

He knew he should go through to the sitting room, be with Alex and his no neck monster half siblings. But he was shaking inside too much. The thought of his deception being found out in front of everyone was too much.

He walked over to the sink. The bubbles had gone. The plates and bowls lay beneath the water. He plunged his hands in, cleaning the crockery, running water from the tap over them. Like washing away sin, Jamie thought, twisting round, looking at the door, listening to the voices coming down the hall.

The thought of being found out.

Leave, run away, sneak down the stairs, don't come back.

Don't be stupid.

Face up to it. The humiliation.

Let nature take its course. Everyone will laugh about it.

Aye, right.

Doomed.

And each sound coming down from the sitting room made jump inside. It felt like he was waiting for the order for him to be to shot, standing, his back against the wall, waiting for the bullet.

He glanced over his shoulder, looked at the cards. It was too late now. No point in hiding them. Alex knew.

A banshee fluttered into the kitchen. The floor thundered under its Manolo Blahnik retreads. The thing whooshed up behind Jamie and squeezed the life out of him. Thelma planted a kiss on his cheek. Derek did the same.

Yuck!

"Thanks," Thelma said.

Jamie was taken aback.

"What for?" he asked.

Thelma studied him for a second, as if thinking. A gentle smile pushed through the blubber of her jowls before a seriousness came over her for a split second and a new Thelma seemed to break through.

"Just thanks," she said softly, then turned away to face Alex.

Jamie felt confused. Worse, the cards on the table were on full view.

Derek shot forward, grabbed Jamie and gave him a hug, then pulled back. "Me as well," Derek said.

"You as well what?" Jamie asked.

But all Derek did was shrug and turn away. After a little while, Thelma and Derek said their goodbyes and left. It wasn't even midnight yet.

Jamie turned back to the sink, hiding his face from Alex and said he would be back through in a minute once he had finished cleaning up the dishes.

~~*

Alex stood in the sitting room. Everything was quiet. The clock ticked. He reached down and picked up his present from Thelma, a second-hand *Lonely Planet Guide to Europe*. He picked up Derek's present, a half-priced CD of old tracks that Alex knew Derek loved.

It wasn't much. But it was more than he'd expected, which had been nothing, yet at the same time it was everything. He put them down again and reached down for the envelope. Derek and Thelma's birthday card to him. He picked it up, still unopened, and looked over at the living room door.

Feeling the weight of the orange envelope in his hand, the thickness of the card inside, he walked over to the sofa and sat down.

Jamie will be here in a minute, he thought.

Reaching for the edge of the cushion, the edge nearest the arm of the sofa, he pulled it to the side and slowly pushed the envelope from Thelma and Derek, still unopened, down the side as far as it would go.

Like a message in a bottle, maybe someday, somewhere, someone would find it.

Sometimes less is more, he thought, sitting back, happy.

And he waited.

~~*

Jamie looked around the side of the door like a scared kitten.

"All right, pal?" he asked quietly.

Alex nodded. "Knowing you're here I am, aye," he said.

Hands in pockets, Jamie stepped into the middle of the room. "It's getting late," he said.

Alex glanced at the clock. It was a minute before midnight. The day was almost gone. A day he would never see again. He stood up and walked over to Jamie.

Jamie bowed his head as if frightened to look at him in the eye. "Was it a good birthday?" Jamie asked.

"Aye," Alex said. "All the better that you spoke to me that first night and that you're still here."

Jamie smiled weakly. He felt embarrassed. "I wish it could have been better, though,'" he said, "for your special birthday."

Alex kissed Jamie on the cheek. "Jamie," he said. "It was the best eighteenth birthday I've ever had."

And the clock struck twelve.

CHAPTER 25

A few days later Jamie returned home from work to the sound of Euphoria.

With a worried look, he walked down the hall and into the kitchen. At first he thought it was lightening that was flashing. No? Well, perhaps it was strobe lights. But no, it wasn't that either.

It was sparks of static. The music was deafening and it was all going at the speed of light. He watched for a few seconds as Alex stood, iron in hand, scooting the blade of the thing up and down on the ironing board. On the bunker at his side was a steaming hot coffee. On the other, the kettle was boiling. It looked as if Alex was caught in a vicious cycle.

Jamie stepped closer.

Alex didn't notice. With iron in hand, he looked as if his arm was in another dimension, in a blur it was moving so fast.

Jamie picked up the coffee jar from the bunker and frowned. He'd feared this might happen. Jamie's worst nightmare had come true.

Rocket Fuel, the coffee jar read, caffeine with added guarana. High-octane, vicious stuff.

This was serious.

Alex slammed the iron up and down the board with one hand and slurped from his coffee mug from the other. His eyeballs bulged like peeled onions.

"Alex?" Jamie said.

But Alex was too far-gone to hear. The air was full of steam belching from the iron. The kitchen table was stacked high with a mountain of neatly folded T-shirts, jeans, trousers, underwear (all ironed), shirts and socks.

Sparks of static crackled between the iron and the ironing board. Alex's hair stood up as he created his very own Van Der Graph Generator.

"Alex, for God's sake," Jamie said. He would have physically tried to stop this laddie-on-a-mission but for fear of receiving a belt of lightening himself. "Alex, you're out of control!"

The Euphoria grew louder and faster.

"Busy busy, work, work, chop, chop, bang, bang, busy busy ..."

It was no good. Jamie would have to find a way to break the cycle—something that would act like a circuit breaker. Jamie reached out to touch Alex on the shoulder.

~~*

ZZZZZZZZzzzzzzaaaaaaP!

In a reflex arc faster than if he had inadvertently grabbed a hot poker, Jamie's arm flew back to the sound of "Oooyah bugger!" It was now obvious that Alex was surrounded by a force field of static electricity.

After taking a suck at his injured index finger to ease the pain, Jamie shouted, "What the hell are you doing?"

"The holiday, the holiday, get it ready for the holiday ..."

Jamie took a squint at the pile of neatly ironed clothes on the table again.

"We're only going away for four days," he said. "Not a gap century."

No response. Iron down, another T-shirt folded, another grabbed from the basket, iron back in hand. Slam molten plate of iron on item, wiggle wiggle of bum in time to wiggle wiggle of iron on crease of T-shirt.

Things were getting desperate. Even the windows were steamed up. Jamie needed something to push Alex away, to disconnect him.

A lump of wood (wood doesn't conduct electricity, does it?), came the brain wave.

Where to find a bit though? Could smash up one of the chairs and use one of its legs.

Don't be daft. Besides, that creepy get of a landlord would use any excuse to shove up the rent, again. Need something else.

A sudden brainwave.

Keeping a safe distance, Jamie did a limbo around the back of Alex, though the sight of his wiggling tight wee bum was a bit too much for a red-blooded laddie like Jamie to resist. Until he remembered what had happened to his finger when he had touched Alex.

It still stung.

Didn't want that to happen to anything else. He arched his arm around the back of Alex and nabbed the coffee mug from the bunker—a teaspoon was standing up in the middle of it the coffee was that thick.

Jamie sidled back and hid the mug behind himself, making sure he was at a safe distance. And waited.

But not for long.

Alex's hand whooshed out like a grabber, fingers like talons and folded in on themselves when they couldn't find the mug.

Jamie stood well back.

And it happened. As if a stream of electricity had shot up through his feet, Alex stood bolt upright, muscles and sinews tight, arms up and shook like the blazes.

"I'm in control. I'm in control." Alex's jaws jittered around the words.

Seeing his chance, Jamie lurched forward and switched the iron off at the wall, dragged away the ironing board, flicked a finger or two at Alex's ear just to be sure the charge had died down, then grabbed him by the shoulders and led him away to safety.

Before it was too late, Jamie emptied the offending, high-octane coffee down the sink and left the tap running to make sure there was no way it could come back.

Fifteen minutes later, lying in the dark, on the bed, Alex drew the cold wet cloth from his forehead and asked, "Wahappind?"

Jamie sat down on the side of the bed and replaced the wet cloth with a new one. Alex's eyes blinked, as if unseeing. "How are you feeling now?" Jamie soothed. "It's another four days before we go away, you know. And apart from that, you've ironed enough clothes to last a year."

"Jamie ..." Alex spoke weakly. "It was like a nightmare. I didn't know how to stop myself."

Jamie nodded knowingly. "See what happens?" Jamie said. "But I really didn't think you would go further than Nescafé. I really didn't, Eck."

Alex turned his head away, ashamed. "I'll never do it again," he sniffed.

Jamie nodded sagely. "I think it's about time this addiction of yours was brought under control." Alex turned and looked with fearful eyes at Jamie. "Aye," Jamie said, "I think we'll have to get you onto the decaff ..."

There was a sharp intake of breath from Alex. "No decaff!"

"... Tea bags."

Alex sat up sharp as a pin. "Tea?"

"Aye," Jamie said. "Tea. Decaffeinated tea."

Alex grabbed the cloth from his head. "I *hate* tea!"

"Tough bananas," Jamie said, launching himself to his feet.

In the kitchen, he surveyed the nightmare before him through a cloud of cigarette smoke as he puffed away. "I didn't realize that we had that much in clothes between us," he said. He tilted his head and squinted at the mountain-high piles of it on the table.

Something wasn't right. He poked an index finger at what looked like a burst weather balloon and picked the thing up.

"The dirty rotten ..." No wonder they were so nice on Alex's birthday.

"*Right*!"

~~*

Jamie stood on the landing in front of the twins of evil's abode.

Derek opened the door with a huff. He was obviously expecting it to be Thelma, that she had forgotten her key. Instead, a huge pair of weather balloon-sized bloomers hit him in the face. And the rest: a skip-load of his and Thelma's washing. By the time it stopped he was waist-high in the stuff.

"How could you?" Jamie yelled.

"How could I what?" Derek asked, unhooking a pair of his underpants from his ear.

"Get Alex to do both of your washing. No wonder you were so nice that night. Was that all you two had turned up for? Never mind 'Happy Birthday, Alex. But would you mind doing our washing in ironing for us like a good wee brother?'"

Derek opened his mouth to speak, but Jamie cut in before he had a chance. "You miserable pair of slobs. Gets like you make me sick!"

"Steady, wee man," Derek said, taking a step back.

"Leave him alone," Jamie said. "Leave us both alone!"

Jamie stormed off, running down the stairs before he lost it completely and ended up doing something he might later sit back and *really* enjoy going over the memory off endlessly.

But no, he had a plan already. He had swithered about putting it into action. But now his mind was made up.

The enemy had no redeeming features. That was obvious now. And he couldn't care less how much this was going to hurt them. They had asked for it in the way they continued to take advantage of Alex.

Well, Jamie had news for them.

"And now you are going to get it," he said, slamming the stairwell door.

CHAPTER 26

Alex stuffed the rucksacks with anything that came to hand. Jamie played the same game and took most things back out. They bickered with each other, fighting over what should go where and who should be carrying what.

In the end, Jamie pulled most of what he didn't need out of his rucksack and left Alex to put what he wanted into his. By comparison, Jamie's rucksack looked like a sad, deflated silver antique thing that had been retrieved from an Apollo moon mission.

Alex's, on the other hand, was bright shiny new and blue with lime-green lightning flashes down the sides and bursting at the seams. The list of essentials Alex had been writing and rewriting for a short holiday abroad since day one lay on the table, all ten pages of it.

Items were ticked off one after the other and new items added when Alex remembered what he had forgotten—everything except the bricks and plaster.

Alex went to the bedroom and came back with big thick clear plastic bags.

"What are they?" Jamie asked.

"Things for packing this lot in," Alex said.

He unzipped one of the squares and started stuffing clothes into it then went for the vacuum cleaner and dragged it by its square wheels into the kitchen. "This," he said to Jamie, "is a Space Bag. You stuff the clothes in and then you suck the air out of the Space Bag with the Hoover."

Alex demonstrated by jamming the nozzle onto the outlet of one of the bags and switched on the vacuum with a smile. Jamie looked on in amazement as all of Alex's clothes inside it turned into a big, square, multicolored crisp.

"Amazing," Jamie said.

"I got eight of them," Alex said, "four for you and four for me."

Alex slipped the crisp bag things into his rucksack. He beamed. Jamie frowned.

"What is it?" Alex asked, irritated.

"Well," Jamie said, "how are you going to carry the Hoover?"

"What are you talking about?" Alex said. "We'll not be taking the Hoover, you idiot."

Jamie stepped over to Alex's bright shiny new backpack, reached in and tugged at the crisp bag thing's outlet nozzle and pulled. And like a monster having gorged itself with too much, Alex's T-shirts, shirts and everything else spewed out of the top of the rucksack and fell like spent lava onto the kitchen floor.

"So," Jamie said, "how good are your lungs?"

"Blast," Alex said. "I never thought of that?"

So, out went the crisp bag things and in went the things the old fashioned way. The side pockets of his rucksack strained at the seams and Alex took to punching the contents deeper. "It won't fit!" he yelled in frustration.

"You don't need it anyway," Jamie said.

Bad move.

Alex's face grew purple with rage. "I do need it."

"What?"

"Everything," Alex said "I've got it all in my plan."

"How many pairs of socks do you need for God's sake?" Jamie said. "We're only gone for four days, remember?"

"Plus two on the boat," Alex reminded him.

Jamie stopped for a minute. "I never thought of that," he said grabbing the things he had discarded and stuffing them into his own rucksack again.

"See!" Alex said. "Right. Paperwork. Insurance, insurance. God, where did I put the insurance?"

"It's on the desk in the front room," Jamie said.

"Tickets, passports, dosh." Alex chanted the mantra as he dived into and out of each room in turn.

Jamie stood in the kitchen, his old rucksack dumped on a chair as he tightened the straps.

"Eck?" he called as Alex whooshed past for the fiftieth time.

"I'm busy," Alex snapped without stopping.

Jamie looked at his watch and frowned. "We'll be late. Come on," he said.

Alex popped his head through the doorway. "Have we forgotten anything?" he asked.

"Like?" Jamie said, unconcerned.

"Anything!" Alex snapped. "God, you're no help," he said, disappearing back into the hall.

Jamie looked at Alex's list again. "Six shirts, eight pairs of socks, eight pairs of jeans—two black pairs of 501s, two pairs of Lee Striders, two pairs of Lees and shampoo, razors, deodorant, after shave, ten pairs of drawers, six white T-shirts, six black T-shirts … What in hell's name do you need all this for?"

Alex turned on him, stabbing a look at Jamie as if he'd just asked the most indignant thing in the world. Ignoring him, Jamie hefted his on rucksack onto his shoulders.

"Alex, pal, we're only going away for a couple of days to Amsterdam. Not Outer Mongolia."

Alex folded the list and stuffed it into his pocket. "I can't help myself," he said. "I've never been abroad before. I keep thinking I've forgot something."

"Well, you're in good company," Jamie said. "I've never been abroad, either."

Alex made a dash out into the hall. He called back. "You get the razors and toothbrushes and stuff."

Jamie began to wonder if it was worth it after all. Still, all this busyness kept his mind off Plan B—Thelma and Derek.

Better not to think about it, he decided, and headed for the bathroom. He held up Alex's meticulous list and went down it until he came to *Bathroom Stuff*.

"Right, two toothbrushes, got them. Toothpaste. Right. Razors."

He pulled open the squint bathroom cabinet and took out the packet of razors. Should be enough for four day's worth. Or was it six? "Just take the lot."

His eyes fell on the old dusty bottle in the corner of the cabinet. Reaching out he picked it up and read the label. *Alex McMullen: Phenobarbitone.* In all the time he had known Alex, Jamie had only ever seen him have two seizures.

At first he had wondered what was going on. It was nothing drastic. Alex had just stopped mid-sentence and walked off in a daze then returned to normal the next time Jamie saw him. Alex hadn't told Jamie about this thing in the beginning. He only mentioned it when Jamie had asked. Jamie had been more intrigued than worried.

Alex didn't seem too happy about Jamie knowing, saying that it made it feel that he was admitting to a crime when he wasn't a criminal. When Jamie apologized for asking anything about it, Alex had relented.

"Absences," Alex told him. "Petit mal. A mild form of epilepsy."

"Epilepsy!"

Hearing Jamie say it like that had put a sad look on Alex's face. Even now Jamie cringed at how his outburst had affected him.

"It's all right though," Alex had said. "I understand."

And his smile had been one of resignation as he had stood up, turned around and started to walk away. But that time it was no petite mal at work. Jamie had lurched off his seat and caught up with him.

"Understand what?" he asked Alex.

"That you don't want to know me for it," Alex had said.

The reply had confused Jamie. What had just happened? They were just getting to know each other.

"Where do you get off feeling sorry for yourself?" Jamie had asked.

"Who says I'm feeling sorry for myself," Alex had shot back.

"Like hell you're no!"

"Don't talk to me like that."

"Well, stop being such a big bairn then," Jamie said.

"I'm no being a bairn."

"You are," Jamie had said. "I never said anything about it. It's not me that's walking away. It's you."

"Well some folk act like it's catching or something," Alex had said.

"And I'm perfect like?"

Alex hadn't known what to make of this.

"See," Jamie said, "one of my ears is higher than the other." He beamed, seemingly proud of his imperfections. "Of course, my conk doesn't do me any favors either," he said, turning his face to the side. "But I'm stuck with it, Alex. Nobody's perfect. Least of all me."

Just then Alex had laughed, blowing more bubbles into his iron brew than he could suck out (it was in the olden days when Alex had been trying to keep his caffeine intake under control).

At that point, all barriers had come down. And it was the first night they had spent together.

Jamie now held the little brown bottle in his hand, biting at his lip and wondering if he should ask Alex if he should take them along. Taking a closer look at the label, he saw that the expiry date had passed by a year, six months before they had first met in the Youth Club for sad arks—a last ditch Circus of Horrors of a place before real life took over.

Taking a quick look at the bathroom door, scared that Alex might burst through wondering what was taking him so long, Jamie stuffed the bottle into his pocket, picked up the razors, shaving foam, toothbrushes and paste, and walked back into the kitchen.

Alex was sitting on his rucksack that was now lying on its back on the floor. "Quick, give a hand," he said. "I can't get the frigging straps to click in."

Jamie rolled his eyes, knowing it was no use trying to tell Alex that he was taking too much, and so he sat on the rucksack alongside him. They bounced their backsides up and down on Alex's rucksack a few times while Alex bit at his tongue and managed to force the last clip into place.

A look of relief came across him. Until Jamie held up the things he had taken from the bathroom. "What about these?" he said.

"Awe, no!"

"Keep your drawers on," Jamie said. "I'll put them in my bag."

They stood up. Alex grabbed the list. "That's it then," he said.

"That's it then," Jamie agreed. "No going back now."

"Jamie!"

"What!"

"The tickets and insurance. I've left them on the coffee table in the living room."

"I'll get them," Jamie said. "You stay here."

As Jamie walked down the hall he pulled the door keys out of his pocket to make sure he had them. In the sitting room, he sat on the sofa, he put the keys on his lap, leaned forward and picked up the tickets and insurance papers from the coffee table and the endless copies that Alex had made of everything.

He grabbed for the keys in his lap. They were gone. Panicked now, he looked at the floor, even although he hadn't heard them fall.

Jamie got down and looked under the sofa. "Where the hell are they?"

He pulled up the cushions. Jamie still couldn't see the keys. He pushed his hand down the side by the arm and wiggled his fingers in the dust and fluff and God knew what else.

The keys were there all right and he breathed a sigh of relief. Hooking his fingers through the key ring, he slowly pulled them out. Something scratched at the side of his hand when he did. Jamie frowned.

He stuffed the keys safely into his pocket then pushed his hand back down the side of the sofa again. Whatever it was, he managed to grip it between his fingers and carefully pull it out into the open.

It was an envelope, an orange envelope. He flipped it over.

To Alex was written on the front.

Jamie sat and looked at it. He didn't need to open it to know that it must have been a birthday card from Thelma and Derek.

But why hide it?

Then it dawned on him.

"Awe, Eck," Jamie whispered to himself, realizing now that Alex must have known all along about Jamie's deception with the birthday card. And to save Jamie any embarrassment, Alex must have hidden the card down the side of the sofa that night.

Jamie found himself in a very quiet place all of a sudden. He asked questions, of himself, to anyone. But no replies came back. Alex had hidden the card for Jamie's sake, knowing that the one Jamie had said was from Thelma and Derek was a fake one.

Alex had known all along.

Slowly, he pushed the envelope, with its card still sealed inside, back down the side of the sofa where Alex had left it, and where Alex had meant it to stay. Replacing the cushions, he walked over to the door when something made him stop.

Half turning, he looked back into a sad looking, drab room, at the coffee table, the tiny television set, the old music centre, and saw Alex jumping around and singing into an invisible microphone, happy, oblivious.

He looked at that old lumpy sofa. Like a sad old man, he thought, now keeping a big secret. The card. But the old sofa was much more than a place that kept secrets to save faces. There were other memories it must have kept too. Alex and Jamie laughing, sometimes arguing, the stories Alex would tell Jamie to cheer him up. Alex and Jamie side-by-side, nodding off together in front of the television—feeling safe, feeling wanted by each other.

A lump came to Jamie's throat. He swallowed it down hard. And for whatever reason, that made him do so he looked at the old sofa now and said a silent thanks. A cloud passed the sun and the room dimmed as if a door had been shut on a light.

It wasn't Alex and Jamie's room any more.

But just a room.

In the kitchen, Alex was rinsing out mugs under the tap when Jamie walked up to him and gave him a hug.

Alex looked at him. "What was that for?"

"Nothing," Jamie said. "Just for being here."

Alex put the mugs on the draining board. "Well," he said. "If we're here for much longer, we'll never get away on this holiday."

Jamie smiled. The moment had passed, a secret was kept. "You're right," he said. "We better get going."

After yanking his arms through his denim jacket, Alex attempted to pick up his rucksack from the floor. "It's stuck!" he cried out.

"Eh?"

"It's stuck to the floor!"

Jamie walked over, his rucksack on his back. "You've put too much in it," he said. "That's what's wrong, yah galoot."

Alex put on his bad tempered look. "Well," he said, "it's too late now. You'll have to give me a hand to get it on my back."

Jamie blew out a breath. "Okay, then. You hunker down."

Alex got down like a sprinter waiting for the starter's pistol. Jamie grabbed the electric-blue straps of the rucksack and attempted a jerk and lift maneuver.

The veins bunched in his neck. Sweat matted his hair. "What have you got in here?"

With Alex still in the sprinter's position, Jamie squatted at the back of him. He had his knees wide and his arms clamped around the rucksack's circumference and his face squashed up against the lumpy front of it.

With an almighty effort, Jamie picked up Alex's rucksack, his eyes prepared to shoot out of his head and his neck strangled his words. "Quick, get your arms through the straps."

"Cinch," Alex said, pushing first left then right arm though the straps. Jamie held on tight as both of them lifted the rucksack, Jamie with his arms and Alex with his back. "Right, right. I'm all right now," Alex huffed. "I've got it."

Jamie still clung on. "You sure?"

"Aaaaaahhyuh. Lettttt goooooo."

"Here goes," Jamie said. He let go.

Alex crashed to his knees. Then flat on his face. "Damn!" His arms and legs stuck out the sides and made desperate swimming motions on the floor like a frog after a cowpat had landed on it.

A few minutes later Alex was staggering from side to side, knees buckling wide.

"I'll get there. I'll ... I'll ... Oh God! ... make ... it!"

Crunch!

Back on his knees again.

"I told you there was too much in it!" Jamie yelled. He sighed and looked at his watch. Thrusting out his lower lip, he let out a frustrated breath. "You better hurry up," he said.

"I can't get up," Alex moaned.

Reaching over, Jamie grabbed the back of Alex's rucksack and yanked it back as Alex's hands and feet scrambled for purchase at thin air. With a weak smile and corrugated brow, Alex looked at Jamie as if for approval.

"It looks like the Empire State Building on your humph," came Jamie's comment. "But it's too late to do anything about it now." Jamie did an about turn. "Right, my man. We're off," he said walking into the hallway.

With Jamie no longer able to see him, Alex grimaced at the weight on his shoulders, wondering how long it would before they snapped under the strain.

At first his legs kept up with the stress (as long as he was clutching at the wall). After a few more hirpling steps they buckled a bit more.

Jamie held open the front door. Alex smiled as if he was fine. He was anything but. He exited the hallway and entered the stairwell. He felt sick at the thought of having to keep his balance for the three flights to ground zero.

Alex stepped sideways like a crab as he gripped onto the banister for dear life.

Jamie shouted up to him. "Will you hurry up! We'll miss the bus to the station!"

At last Alex made it to the ground floor. They walked out into the street, albeit unsteadily, where Alex felt every passerby's eyes upon him.

He felt conspicuous, then stupid, then like an eejit. Alex wobbled over to the edge of the pavement, swinging at the curb as if it were the cliff edge to hell.

"Bus stop's this way," Jamie reminded him.

"Taxi!" Alex yelled.

"What are you doing?" Jamie asked with disbelief.

"There's no way I'm getting on a bus with all this clobber on my back in Kelty, in that's that."

So much for Jamie being put through the wrings for weeks of Alex's careful, down-to-the-molecular-level, budget planning.

A black cab pulled up. Alex pulled open the door before Jamie had a chance to protest. He stuck his head inside the cab, but his rucksack caught on the top of the doorway.

Jamie huffed, arms folded and watched as Alex struggled. But it wasn't long before his conscience was pricked and goaded him into action.

He pushed down on Alex's rucksack. Alex's legs buckled then gave up altogether as he fell flat on his face. His feet kicked out behind him through the open door. Jamie slipped his own rucksack off his back, threw it into the cab, then climbed over Alex.

"Train station," he told the driver.

"What about him?" the driver said.

"Just drive will you," Jamie said. Jamie reached down and dragged Alex into the cab. "And hurry," Jamie said to the driver. "We've a train to catch and two monsters to meet when we get there."

CHAPTER 27

Shirley walked down the grey worn steps in the early morning as sunlight cut around the edges of the door to her new world. All she had to do now was open it, stroll with pride into the open, under a sky full of wheeling seagulls, hail a cab and make her way to Newcastle Central.

She had been there before, many times before, but only ever in disguise. But her heart had sung out each time as she had wondered, planned. Each time a test run for the real thing.

Her final exit.

"Let me help you with that, love," the driver said, lifting her trunk into the back of the cab.

Voice trembling she thanked him and slipped into the back seat. *Don't look back*, she thought as she strapped herself in.

Opening her clutch bag, she found her compact mirror, her mobile looking glass, the sunlight hitting her eyes as she glared at her reflection. She felt wrong, looked all wrong. Too much mascara, too much eye shadow, too much everything.

"Going on holiday?" the driver asked her.

A lie came to her as she retrieved her lace hanky. *Another lie*, she thought. *Just one more to pile on top of all the others—what difference does it make now?*

Her throat squeezed on her word. "Yes".

She looked out the window, pretending to adjust her head square, hiding her face with her hand in case someone should look in at her too closely for it was the first time Shirley had been out in the daylight.

The streets looked too gray despite the sunlight. The buildings seemed to loom in, ready to fall over and crush her. Panic welled up inside as words screamed inside of her, go back, go back.

"No!"

The cab slowed suddenly and the driver turned his head to the side. "You all right, Love?" he asked.

Shirley pushed herself back in her seat. All she could hear in her head was 'go back, it's not too late'.

"Love?"

"I'm fine," she said, her voice shaking.

The cab sped up again. She looked at the men. She looked at the women. The young and the old. She looked at the shop fronts, their lurid colors of green and purple, yellow and orange, as Newcastle Central came into view.

Shirley had seen it a million times before when she had pretended to buy train tickets, and when her time came to be served, she had always left the queue at the last second. She had sat and drunk coffee while she had listened to trains coming and going, feeling the vibration of their wheels rumbling through the concrete under her feet.

She had listened to voices echoing off the walls and iron girders, announcing destinations and arrivals while she ate bagels and muffins before stepping outside with her empty suitcase to smoke a cigarette with waiting travelers. All the while she had been planning, but only ever when she had been in disguise.

The taxi stopped on the rank and the driver climbed out. Thinking he was about to lift her trunk out from the back, she was startled when the door opened for her.

"Thank you," she said to the driver as she stepped out onto the pavement.

"This weighs a ton." He smiled at her. "What have you got in here, a dead body?"

She felt her face flush. Had he guessed?

"No," she said. "I left all that behind."

The driver laughed then sighed. "Better get a trolley, love," he said. And before she could stop him, the driver was dragging her travel trunk into the station and lifting it onto a trolley.

"You're very kind," she said.

"Always for a lovely woman," he said.

Her hand shook as she paid him. She thanked him and waited until he left before looking up at the ornate hands of the station clock. She had an hour or so to wait yet and pushed the trolley over to the coffee stand.

The train station had always been a dead end when Shirley had come here before when she had no intention of taking a train.

But this time was different. She had intention. And there was no turning back now.

No longer in disguise, she was terrified now that someone might recognize her and kept reaching up to tug the sides of her head square, to have it closer to her face, trying to cover a little bit more each time.

She sat and sipped at her latte as announcements swirled around her and people swept by her with their bags and rucksacks, and for some reason, each and every one had her heartfelt thoughts. It was something she should have done years ago.

The clock hand ticked over another minute. Shirley opened her clutch bag and searched through for her papers. As a precaution, she had had them printed out from an internet café, black and white documents. The only thing she hadn't tested out was her passport.

She knew that it would cause trouble, but that was something that she would have to deal with when she came to it.

Her fingers traced over the envelope, her life written and ended with love on the short letter inside. She could feel her eyes stinging as she thought about the words she had written and rewritten at her tiny kitchen table last night.

As the percolator had bubbled away behind her, she had sat there knowing that she would never be coming back. She would never see her family again.

The letter was addressed to her mother, to the last address Shirley had known her to be living when she had last seen her eleven years ago. Seen, but never spoken to, she reminded herself. Stood and watched in the rain from a distance, for none of Shirley's family had wanted to know her by then.

They had already disowned her years before as if she had never existed.

Finishing her coffee she sat straight and buttoned up her powder blue Louis Vuitton coat. The game was at an end. The planning was over.

It was now time to leave forever.

As if by magic, the men and women parted as she pushed her trolley towards the red pillar-box at the corner. The letter hovered as she held it at the mouth of the box as the Tannoy announced another departure.

"Goodbye, Mum," she said under her breath. "Always love you forever."

And before her mascara could run, she dropped the letter into the box and strode out into the sun by the railway track.

CHAPTER 28

Jamie and Alex waited on the platform. Jamie left Alex with the bags and walked off, lit a cigarette, had a few puffs then bought a coffee for both of them. He considered buying a decaffeinated for Alex. The laddie's nerves were jangling enough. But he decided against it. Alex would have known within the first few gulps that he had been duped. Jamie even considered if it might have been wise to buy himself a coffee, since his nerves were in shreds with the thought of Thelma and Derek coming along anyway.

By the time he turned back from the coffee seller, there they were, Thelma all in black jammed into her wheelchair. Derek stood behind her in a great big rubber green hat, and Alex was smiling weakly over at Jamie.

Jamie's heart sank. But he had a plan, he reminded himself. He just hoped it would work. And if it did, that Alex would still speak to him afterwards.

"Thel, Deek." Jamie nodded his lackluster greeting at the pair. He handed over one of the coffees to Alex. Alex took the coffee with good grace, his smile growing weaker by the second.

"Where's ours," Thelma asked Jamie, her lips like big red rubber bands, her eyes glaring at Jamie over the top of her sunglasses.

"You weren't here," Alex countered before Jamie could say anything.

"We are now," Derek pointed out.

"And?" Jamie said, looking up at the timetable board.

It was 10:15. The train from Inverness to Edinburgh would be arriving in four minutes, if by any miracle Scot Rail was running on time.

"Got the tickets?" Thelma looked back and up at Derek.

"In my pocket," Derek sneered, more for Jamie's sake than Thelma's. They both knew that Jamie hated the thought of them all going on holiday together, and that suited them just fine.

The train arrived. Guards appeared and helped Thelma, bulk notwithstanding, onto the train with her wheelchair (even although there was nothing wrong with her legs) and her still wedged in it.

Alex and Jamie took their seats in the only smoking carriage. Derek and Thelma, as luck would have it, were in the non-smoking carriage at the other end of the train.

It was a blessed relief.

Alex said nothing as the train moved off. Jamie lit a cigarette and tried to keep calm. As the train rolled out of the station he went over in his head with the next stage in his plan.

"What's up," Alex asked.

Jamie snapped back. "Nothing! What makes you ask like?"

"You're too quiet."

"Just looking forward to our holiday," Jamie said. He took a last drag of his cigarette, crushed it out and settled back.

"How long before we get to Edinburg?" Alex asked.

Jamie shrugged "No long."

"And we change trains at Waverly?"

"Aye, we do," Jamie said. "Then from Waverly, to the ferry."

"To New Castle?"

"South Shields," Jamie corrected. "Not far from New Castle."

But his voice was shaking. It was a lie and he didn't like lying. Not to Alex, nor to anyone. But it was a little white lie—and only half a lie at that—but a lie all the same, a lie that someone as astute as Alex could pick up on very easily.

Alex's eyes narrowed, but he said nothing more.

When the train reached Waverley, the pair jumped off, Alex hauling his bag after him. No longer was he concerned that its newness would be compromised with the activity of travel. He looked relieved when Derek wheeled Thelma off the carriage down the way, clobbering its wheels down the steps like a baby elephant jammed into a pram.

They all made their way onto the station concourse. Thelma cranked up the juice on her electronic wheels as Derek staggered behind with the bags.

Jamie's heart was in his mouth. *Keep calm*, he thought to himself over and over. But it was like waking from a dream into a nightmare. He was sure everything would all go wrong. *Just don't act it. If Alex gets a whiff ...*

"You sure you're all right?" Alex asked.

"Course I am," Jamie said back a little too quickly.

Think, think, Jamie went over the plan in his head. Platform Two and Platform Eleven. Two trains, the one from Platform Eleven left first—in ten minutes.

Jamie's heart thumped in his chest. He gulped down hard, looking around, trying to hide his face from Alex. Thelma and Derek were catching up. Jamie's heart beat faster. The train was already on Platform Eleven: the one for Newcastle.

"This one," Jamie piped up, trying to sound confident.

Thelma looked at her ticket. Looked at the train. Leaned back and smiled up at Derek. Right train, right ticket. Same procedure.

Alex and Jamie made their way onto the smoking carriage. Derek pushed Thelma onto the non-smoking carriage down the way.

Jamie went first. He walked through the automatic door and scanned the empty seats side-to-side and said, "These two."

Alex frowned. "Where's the reservations?" he asked.

Jamie shrugged off his rucksack. "It doesn't matter," Jamie said. "We've got the whole carriage to ourselves."

Alex didn't question Jamie's logic, at least not verbally. He slipped off his rucksack. Jamie helped him jam it into the overhead rack. Then they sat down.

"How long before we take off?" Alex asked.

"No long," Jamie said, trying to keep cool. He sat twiddling his thumbs.

"It stinks in here," Alex said. "Maybe I should go and sit in the nonsmoking carriage with Derek and Thelma. He started to get up out of his seat.

"Alex!"

"What's the panic?" Alex said.

Jamie swallowed. "No panic."

Half out of his seat, Alex stopped. "It doesn't sound like it," he said. "What's wrong?"

"Eh ..."

"Well?"

"Alex?"

"Jamie?"

"I don't want to be left on my own," Jamie said.

"Well come with me and sit beside Derek and Thelma then," Alex said, stepping into the aisle.

"No!"

"What's wrong with you, Jamie?"

"Well ... If I sit down that end of the train I won't be able to smoke, will I?"

"And?"

"And, well, I bought you a coffee," Jamie said quickly.

"So?"

"So, you've had your fix and you can have another fix drinking another coffee here or down there. But I can only have my fix, here."

"God almighty, Jamie," Alex said sitting back down. "Get a grip."

Jamie didn't say anything else. He looked out the window at Platform Eleven, at the other side of the station.

"This is the place where Alfred Hitchcock filmed that scene in *The 39 Steps*," Alex said.

"Oh, aye," Jamie said biting his thumbnail as he continued to look at Platform Eleven.

"Don't over excite yourself, will you," Alex said.

But Jamie wasn't listening. He was just hoping that his plan pulled off.

And his plan was this: Thelma and Derek were on the right train. Alex and Jamie were not. The train Jamie had booked Alex and himself on was now standing on the opposite side of the station on Platform Eleven. And it was due to leave in five minutes.

Jamie was sweating. Less than five minutes to go.

It was now or never.

He squinted out the window and at the timetable board with all the train times. "Oh," he said.

"Oh?" Alex said. "What's 'oh?'"

"I think we're on the wrong train," Jamie said.

Alex jumped as if he'd just received an electric shock. "Wrong one?"

"We should be on that one over there," Jamie said. "Platform Eleven, no Two." Jamie looked at his watch. "We've got less than four minutes. Quick!"

Alex jumped up. "I'll have to run down in warn Thelma in Derek."

"No!" Jamie yelled.

"No?"

"No," Jamie said, "you'll get lost. I'll run down and tell them. You get our rucksacks out onto the platform." Alex looked confused. "Hurry up, Eck," Jamie said standing up. "We'll miss our train."

Jamie left Alex struggling with the rucksacks, glancing over his shoulder as he ran down the carriage to make sure that at least this part of his plan was working.

So far so good.

He nipped down through another few carriages, stopped short of the one before Thelma and Derek's, then jumped off the train. He looked down to his left. Alex was hunched over like something from Notre Dame as he hauled their rucksacks down the steps onto the platform. Jamie ran up and took his own rucksack off of Alex.

"Did you tell them?" Alex asked, puffing away.

"Aye," Jamie lied and hated himself for it.

Less than two minutes to go.

"They'll never make it," Alex said, running after Jamie to Platform Eleven.

"Trains are never on time anyway," Jamie called back over his shoulder.

Amazing what a little adrenaline can do for strength, he thought, seeing Alex struggle along with his overloaded rucksack, swerving keenly through the crowds.

Almost there and the train's engines were now powering into life. Jamie dived at the nearest open door. He threw his rucksack in, then himself. He turned back and looked out.

A guard blew a whistle.

Alex was struggling with his rucksack as he kept looking back over his shoulder.

The guard shouted. "*All aboard*!"

Alex tripped over his own feet and fell half back and half to the side and landed with a thud on the concourse onto his rucksack.

"Eck!"

"Jesus God!" Alex yelped, struggling like a helpless tortoise on its back.

Jamie jumped back out onto the platform. He grabbed Alex.

"They're on their way," Jamie yelled above the train's engines revving into life.

He dragged Alex to his feet. And over Alex's shoulder he saw that it was true. Thelma was on the platform in her wheelchair. Derek was beside her, bags jumping from side to side at his back, and both were racing towards them.

They must have been watching all along.

The guard's whistle blew again. Doors were slamming shut. It was all going wrong.

Dear God, Alex, forgive me for this.

Jamie grabbed Alex and threw him up the steps into the carriage. Then his rucksack. Jamie jumped in after him, crashing him into the opposite door just as the guard slammed the one he had just jumped in closed.

Alex pushed past him to the door. Jamie wrestled him to the floor. The train started to move with a shudder and a clunk. Alex wriggled free from under Jamie and made a dive for the door again.

"Eck!"

Alex stabbed a finger at the button. But the door wouldn't budge. He pulled down the window and stuck his head out, and for a second Jamie thought that Alex was about to take a nosedive onto the moving platform.

Jamie scrambled to his feet and pulled Alex back by the collar. Thelma, still on the platform, cranked up the gears on her wheelchair. At first it kept pace with the moving train, her face a picture of grim determination.

She disappeared behind a pillar.

"What happened?" Alex yelled.

"I think she's just found Platform Nine-and-Five-Eighths," Jamie said, breathing hard.

Alex pushed his head out the window again. "Where is she? *Thelma*!"

And just as the train was about to enter a tunnel, both watched as Thelma walked around the pillar, running to the end of the platform.

"*ASSASSIN*!" she yelled with her fist in the air. Derek stood behind his sister, his big green rubber hat wobbling, and doubled over laughing.

Jamie yanked Alex back inside the train just before he could be decapitated.

Silence followed.

Alex sat opposite Jamie but didn't look at him. When the trolley came along, Jamie bought two coffees and two bags of crisps and gave one of each to Alex. Alex didn't look at them, said nothing, and stared out the window. Jamie sighed, scratched his head and took the lid off his coffee.

"You betrayed them, Jamie," Alex said, still looking out the window. "They wanted this holiday as much as you do."

It's just me now, is it? thought Jamie taking a sip. *No longer we.*

He waited a beat before he said anything. "They've still got their holiday, Alex," he said. "There's nothing changed about that. It was our tickets that I got changed, that's all. They were even on the right train in the first place. And they've still got time to get back on it."

Alex looked at him. "Since when did you get so devious, Jamie?"

Jamie was about to tear open two sachets of sugar. He stopped and put them back down on the table. He swallowed. A wave of emotion suddenly swelled up inside him. "I never thought about it like that," he said, finding it hard to keep his voice steady. He looked at Alex in the eyes. "I honestly thought I was doing it for the good," he said. "I didn't do it to hurt anybody."

"And how do you think they'll survive without me being there?" Alex asked.

Jamie waited a few seconds before he spoke again. "I would have thought, Alex, that at their age that they would be old enough to look after themselves," he said in his defense, except it was making him feel worse. Everything was rusting before his eyes. Even the sky was overcast now. "I just thought ..."

"What, Jamie?"

"That it would be good for us to get away on our own for a bit, that's all," Jamie said. "I mean, we've never been abroad ourselves either, Alex. No me, no you, no them." Jamie shrugged weakly. "But you're right," he said. "I shouldn't have done it."

Feeling lost, Jamie pushed his coffee away, sighed and stood up. "Em," he said just for something to say. "I'm just away to the loo. We'll get off it the next station in go back to Waverly and meet up with Thelma and Derek later."

Riddled with guilt, he walked off down to the other end of the carriage and disappeared through the automatic doors.

~~*

Alex rubbed at his eyes. He didn't know what to think. Jamie was right, of course. And this would never have happened if he hadn't caved into Thelma and Derek in the first place that night.

Still, Jamie shouldn't have been so deceptive. Then again, would Alex have gone along with it?

Alex knew that the answer was no. He would have rather everyone had cancelled the whole thing and no one went away at all. No winners and no losers, either. A bad compromise. Something Alex realized that he had become an expert on over years. Nobody winning, nobody losing, nothing ever changing, growing roots of stubbornness.

And finding a wall had been built around you when you were too busy hiding from the reality that things change anyway, whether you like it or not, Alex. You end up behind a wall and find out that it was too late.

Alex thought he heard the tweet of a bird and looked around the carriage. But there was none to be seen. He pulled the lid off his coffee.

Deceptive Jamie might have been, but his heart was probably in the right place. Alex was still worried though. What would happen to Thelma and Derek? Then he thought that it would be good for them to look after themselves for a change.

Still, he had a twinge of guilt about it.

And Thelma. She's not changed. She's ten years older than me, for God's sake. Old enough to ... Forget it.

He took a deep breath, sighed, and looked up the carriage. Still no sign of Jamie.

~~*

Jamie was standing in the space between carriages when the door slid open and Alex walked in beside him.

"What are you standing out here for, yah galoot?" Alex asked.

"Because I feel rotten," Jamie said.

"What about?"

"About what I did."

The train jerked from side to side, the sound of steel on steel as the wheels raced over the tracks beneath them filled the silence. Alex looked around, out of the window, at the countryside whizzing by.

Maybe this is how it feels when you have to fly so fast the first time out of the nest, he thought. "Ever hear the story of the wee birdie in the tree?" Alex said.

Jamie glanced him and away again. "What birdie in what tree?" he said.

Sometimes you need a big kick to know what's good for you, Alex was about to say. "It never came back," Alex said.

Jamie looked at him for a second then back out the window again.

"Doesn't matter," Alex said with a sigh. "Come on back through. I'm feeling a bit lonely sitting in that reeking carriage all by myself."

The door slid wide. Alex walked back into the carriage. Jamie followed on behind.

"We can get off it the next station in then go back," he said.

Alex looked over his shoulder, the train swaying side to side. It made a sudden jerk. "No," Alex said shaking his head.

"No?"

"No," Alex said as he continued to walk to their seats. "We just keep going, Jamie."

Or nothing will ever change.

CHapTer 29

The train pulled into King's Cross fifteen minutes late, which was early for British rail.

"God's truth!" Jamie yelped as passengers crushed up behind him. "Quit shoving!" he called as he was flattened against the door.

The train hadn't even stopped yet. But no one listened. The train jerked to a halt. A hand shot past him. The door flew wide. Alex and Jamie were spat out onto the platform, slithering and sliding all over the ice rink, finished-and-polished-to-perfection, fake granite surface.

"Which way?" Alex asked, eyes wide, breathing hard.

"Same way everyone else's going," Jamie cried, tally-ho fashion, slinging the rucksack onto his shoulder a little too quickly. He swung with it, arms and legs akimbo, an out of control carrousel. His rucksack clonked into Alex and Alex ricocheted into a runaway-hopscotch, until he almost fell flat on his face.

"Hurry up," Alex said. "There's no time for dawdling." Alex righted himself as Jamie yanked him up by the armpits. Alex then ran off, rucksack flying side to side. Jamie followed suit.

"Where's the underground?" Jamie called out.

"Over there. I think," Alex pointed.

They both skidded to a halt. Neither had seen such a steep escalator before. Alex gulped. "I'm going to pass out."

Jamie gave him a shove. Alex closed his eyes and gripped for dear life onto the moving handrail as he felt the descent and the warm air rushed up from the depths of hell.

"Are we there yet?" he asked Jamie.

"Open your eyes," Jamie said.

White tiles faced them at the bottom. Commuters milled around. Everyone acted like robots. The tiles reminded Alex of a toilet, sparkly, clean and clinical.

Alex had a thing about clean toilets.

And there were barriers all over the place. "Where do we go now?" he asked.

Jamie stood in front of the plan of the underground, tilting his head from side to side. "Oh God, what line is it? Green, brown, yellow, blue?"

"What are we looking for?" Alex asked, trailing his eyeballs along the colored lines of the map.

"Where are we on it for a start?" Jamie asked.

"King's Cross, King's Cross," Alex mumbled. "Hah! Found it." He jabbed his finger on the board. "Now what?" he asked.

"We need to find Victoria Station," Jamie said.

"Victoria, Victoria … There!" Alex said.

"Where?"

"There, on the yellow line."

Jamie spun around trying to find a yellow line that would lead them to their destination. No good. "What line is it on?" Jamie asked. "What's it called?"

Alex squinted at the board again as commuters squeezed around them. "Piccadilly," he said. Jamie turned around, looking at the barriers. "So which one is that?" Alex asked.

"Over there," Jamie said, striding off.

Alex followed, rucksack high, but then stopped at the barrier next to Jamie. "What are you waiting for?" Alex asked.

Jamie turned to him and spoke through the side of his mouth. "I'm trying to figure out what I'm supposed to do way the ticket," Jamie said.

Alex looked at Jamie as if he were stupid and pointed to the slot. "You stick it in there," he said.

"The actress said to the bishop," Jamie said.

"Gives the ticket," Alex said. Jamie handed it over and Alex strode forward, put his ticket in the slot and walked up to the barrier. A crowd of impatient commuters swarmed behind him. The barrier wouldn't move.

The crowd bunched up tighter. Alex tried a shove at the barrier. Nothing budged. He shoved harder. The crowd muttered. Alex's head started to sink into his shoulders with embarrassment. He rammed forward in desperation.

Oowah! Oowah!

Hooters and alarms went off everywhere. Lights flashed.

"It won't open!" Alex called back at the crowd.

No one was interested and no one moved to let him back out either. He backed into them using his rucksack as a battering ram. That did it.

"It doesn't work," he said, waving the ticket in front of Jamie.

"I can see that," Jamie said.

"Duff ticket?" Alex said.

Jamie shrugged.

"Shouldn't be," he said. "We'll try that guy over there."

He walked towards one of the station personnel and flashed his ticket at the man. The man said okay and let him through. Jamie looked over his shoulder and smirked at Alex.

Once they'd both gotten through, they stood on the platform and waited. The train pulled up. Doors slid wide. But everyone else seemed to beat them at it getting on board. After everyone had crammed in, the train pulled off. Alex just hoped they would be in time for the train at Victoria leaving for Manningtree.

When the train stopped, bodies belched out the sides. Jamie and Alex ran along the platform.

"We're not going to make it," Alex said.

Jamie skidded to a halt in front of the timetable. Names and times flashed up then magically flickered away again. "Maningtree," he said pointing. "Platform Fourteen. This way. We've only got two minutes before it leaves," he yelled back at Alex.

He flew around the side of the barrier. A train was there. He just hoped it was the right one. Alex jumped up the steps. Jamie followed suit.

Out of breath, they found their seats and dumped themselves down. An hour passed before the train moved off.

"Is there a problem you have with times in places in tickets, Jamie?"

An hour and a half later they were the only two to disembark. At the other side of the track stood the ferry port.

"We're just early," Jamie said. "That's all." He looked at his watch. It was half past two. The ferry didn't leave until five.

"Two and a half hours early," Alex said. "All that rushing for nothing." He walked into the deserted ferry port inside. At least the escalator was running.

"Might as well make the most of it then and have a cup of strong coffee," he said.

Nothing changes, Jamie thought, following Alex to the upper floor.

"Awe, God, it's shut!"

Jamie suddenly felt bad. The quietness of the place didn't help either. "I'm sorry Eck," he said.

Alex turned on him. "What for?" he asked.

"Everything," Jamie said. He sat down at one of the tables.

"No your fault the place isn't open yet," Alex said.

Jamie shook his head, looking at the floor. "That's no what I meant, Eck."

Alex let his rucksack slip off his shoulders and thud to the ground. "What then?"

"Nothing's going right," Jamie said. He looked at Alex in the eyes. "If you want us to go home," he said, "I'll no blame you. I've got enough to get us back for the night."

Alex saw the sorrowful look in his eyes. "Jamie," he said softly, "we've only just got here."

"It's been a disaster from beginning to end so far," Jamie said.

"It's been an adventure, I'll give you that." He reached out and took hold of Jamie's hand. "Come on," he said. "I don't want to go back. And the shop will be open in half an hour. Twenty-five minutes now. I can wait that long for my fix. Come on, Jamie. Cheer up, lad. We're on holiday. Our first yin. You and me, alone it last."

"I still feel rotten about Thelma in Deek," Jamie said. "About what I did."

Alex sat back in his chair. "That pair of gonks! What's to feel sorry about them for? They're auld enough and ugly enough to look after themselves for a change. I reckon you did us all a favor. I'm no worried about them. Anyway, I know they'll be all right."

Jamie gave a weak smile. Alex brightened up. "We'll meet up at the hotel in Amsterdam anyway when way get there." Alex stretched and yawned.

"Eh."

"What, Jamie?"

"Well."

"Jamie?"

"I should've told you before," Jamie said.

"Told me what, Jamie?"

"We're no just going on different boats," Jamie said sheepishly.

"And?" Alex asked leaning closer.

"We're going to different places," Jamie said.

Alex closed his eyes. *Do not scream.* "Different hotels, then?" he asked calmly.

"Different countries," Jamie cringed.

"Jamie!" Alex jumped up and stormed off to the coffee shop.

"Where are they?" he said. "God almighty, how long does it take to boil a mug of water? Christ!" He grabbed the railings. "Hurry up!"

Jamie stood to the side, head bowed, hands in his pockets. At last the railings rattled upward. Alex ordered two coffees and paid for them. Jamie reached out for one.

"Awe, thanks, Eck," he said.

"They're both mine! Get your own!"

CHaPTer 30

After an eternity in glaciation, and coffee after coffee, Alex had begun to melt. He had huffed, refused to speak to Jamie, refused to make eye contact. He had checked his watch against the clock, huffed and guzzled yet more coffee.

The ferry port filled up with passengers.

Another coffee, then another, then ...

Ping!

"Mmm," Alex had said.

"Mmm?" Jamie had replied.

"Yes, Jamie, mmm."

"Okaaaaaay."

They checked in. The announcement finally came just as Alex exited the gents for the fiftieth time. He ran over and grabbed his rucksack.

"Run!" And they made it to a very long queue.

Through passport control and under eyes of suspicion, Alex wanted to shout, "Who are you looking it?"

He turned to Jamie. Saw him looking elsewhere. "What is it?" he asked.

"That woman over there," Jamie said.

"Her?"

"Aye, her."

Alex peered at the woman with a bouffant of blonde curls. "What about her?" he asked.

"Well ..." Jamie said, tilting in at Alex and raising his eyebrows, "either she's got a million blackheads or she shaves."

"Let's get going," Alex said hitching up his rucksack.

Neither saw when the mysterious was woman approached by two security guards and taken into a side room.

Alex and Jamie made their way up the long, windy and springy ramp towards the smell of diesel and then at last on board and up the carpeted stairway to level seven.

"Here we go, here we go, here we go," Jamie sang punching his fists into the air. "Here we go, here we go-oh!"

"Ma bloody legs are breaking," Alex said.

"I told you shouldn't have packed so much," Jamie said.

"I need everything," Alex said. "I'm high maintenance." He stuck a thumb under one of the straps and tried to pull it up. "God, I hope the hotel isn't far from the boat when we get there, wherever that is."

"Nah, five minutes or something," Jamie said.

"You might have bought another backpack for yourself, Jamie, like my one. A new one, I mean."

Jamie turned to him. "I couldn't afford a new one, Alex."

After I bought yours for you, he wanted to say, *never mind about what was supposed to be our car*, but held his tongue.

Alex shook his head, sighed, and humped his rucksack higher up his back. "I'll be on my knees again before we get to the cabin."

Jamie tightened his mouth, arched his eyebrows. "Here," he said. "I'll give you a hand." Moving around the back of Alex he reached under and lifted Alex's rucksack higher. "That better?" he said.

"Have to do," Alex said.

Jamie reached under again and tweaked Alex's cheeks. "Mmm, nice."

"Oi!"

"Sorry. Couldn't help myself," Jamie said, recomposing himself.

"Is that all you think about?" Alex said.

"Eh, well, hmm. Aye."

"Sex mad you are," Alex said.

"What's wrong with that?" Jamie said.

"Come on," Alex said, "before I collapse."

They walked along the narrow corridor, door after door on either side. It was like a maze of spongy carpets and dim lighting and yellow walls.

"It least it's above the water line," Jamie said. Alex kept walking. Jamie stopped dead. "It's this one here," he said.

Alex had trouble turning round his rucksack was so big. He came back and stood in front of the cabin door with Jamie.

Jamie poked the electronic card key thing into the slot of cabin number 773 and then jumped back, half-expecting it to explode.

"Are we going in," Alex said, "or will we just crash down in a heap of exhaustion out here?"

Jamie prodded the door open. He looked round the side then stepped in. He let the rucksack slip from his back and turned to Alex.

"What do you think?" Jamie asked.

Alex stepped in, eyes all over the place. "It's a bit pokey," he said.

"I don't know," Jamie said. "There's two beds, a table, a sofa—I think it's a sofa anyway."

"Is that what that is?" Alex said looking down at it.

Jamie pulled open a door. "Hey," he said. "And in look here, Eck. A shower and everything."

Alex took a squint inside. "Awe, aye. Hmm."

"What's wrong with you now?"

"Nothing's wrong," Alex said. "I'm happy enough."

"You don't sound it."

Alex shrugged. "It just doesn't look like on the telly."

"It's a ferry, Alex, not the QE2."

"But it'll do," Alex said.

Jamie rolled up his eyes. "Thank God for that then."

Alex walked back over to the little table and gripped it. "It's a bit shoogly," he sniffed.

Jamie tried the same thing, noting that the table was welded to the hull. It was as solid as concrete.

If you think that's shoogly, he thought, *wait until we get to sea*.

CHapter 31

Shirley sat in front of the young, handsome officers dressed in white short-sleeved shirts, black ties and trousers. Her feet were killing her.

The officers sat facing her as she clamped her newly-shaved knees together. Her miniskirt was a respectable length when she was standing up, but the Lycra had yawned and rode up high when she sat down until it was like she was wearing a micro skirt. And the Lycra was stretched to its limits over her thighs.

She took out her chunky cigarette lighter from her bag and lit her long, slim cigarette as the officers looked on.

"I'm sorry," one of them said, "but there is no smoking in the terminal."

Shirley pulled in the smoke and let it drift out of her mouth. *I am Lillie Marlene*, she thought over and over. "What are you going to do?" she said blinking her enormous black eyelashes at them seductively. "Arrest me for smoking?"

She crossed her legs.

And she wasn't wearing her y-fronts.

CHAPTER 32

The first thing they did was take a shower. Jamie had already had his and was now looking at his physiognomy in the mirror above the bolted-to-the-floor-in case-you-try-to-steal-it table. Alex was still in the en suite shower room-come-toilet-come-nasal-hair-pluck-outer-in-secret-room.

Still admiring himself in the mirror, Jamie watched as the door on the shower room opened behind him.

"Does my ark look big in this?" Alex asked, trying to break his neck looking over his shoulder and down at his own particular bothersome part of his anatomy.

Careful what you say now, Jamie thought.

Jamie looked in the mirror and over the reflection of his own shoulder. He needed to delay his answer. He needed time.

"Eh?" he said.

"Well?" Alex prompted.

Jamie's cheeks bunched up in a tight smile. His eyes stayed the same, sort of sad looking. "Ah ... well ..."

"Jamie!"

The dam burst. "Aye," Jamie's words burst out of him. "Ginormous." Slam went the door. "What have I said now?" he said turning around.

"Everything," came the muffled cry from behind the portcullis—fully drawn.

Jamie looked at the door. "Awe, for God's sake, Alex," he said. "Come on."

No answer. Jamie leaned into the door. "You've got a wee ark," he said. "A sexy wee ark."

Still nothing.

"Such a sexy a wee ark that every randy bugger around is wanting to screw it off you. Now come on!"

"No!"

"Suit yourself."

The door opened.

"So I've gone from a big fat ark to a no nothing ark then?" Alex said, standing in the doorway.

"You want to hold your gob shut sometimes, Alex McMullen," Jamie said, turning back to the mirror.

Ignoring him, Alex said, "So what is it? Big or what?"

"It's no big and it's no wee," Jamie said.

"And?" Alex asked.

Jamie sighed. "It's somewhere in between," he said.

"Just an ark then?" Alex asked.

"Aye, like mine," Jamie said. "Tight and sexy. Are you happy now?"

"Say it with feeling," Alex demanded.

"Come over here and I'll feel it for you then," Jamie said. "Or you can feel mine if you like."

Jamie leaned on the table and lifted up his T-shirt at the back. "See anything you fancy?"

"Don't start me, Jamie," Alex warned.

"You know you want to," Jamie said, swaying his hips from side to side. "Come on. I know you can't resist." Alex stepped closer. Jamie looked up into the mirror and smiled at Alex's reflection. "Come own, you dirty wee bugger."

"Hey!" Alex said. "Less of the wee."

"Come own then."

Jamie undid the button on the waistband of his jeans and started to slip them down until the mound of his backside began to show. "Come and get it," he said.

"Oh you, you ..."

"Aye?" Jamie asked.

"Step forward a bit," Alex said. "I don't know how big this thing's going to get."

Jamie's jeans dropped to his ankles. Alex let his do the same. He moved closer. Jamie looked over his shoulder. "You've got that look in your face, Alex. I know you can't resist."

Alex's underpants slipped down to his thighs. He reached out and started to pull down on the waistband of Jamie's and then stepped closer.

"Just shove it in," Jamie said.

Alex lunged.

"Damen und zu herren!"

Alex tripped over his jeans, which were wrapped around his ankles like a bolero. He fell with a thump to his knees.

Jamie grappled with his underpants, yanked them up into a castrating wedgy and leapt over Alex, who was still struggling to pull up his own underpants on the floor beside the lower bunk.

"Quick!" Jamie yelled, pulling the quilt over himself. "Pull up your drawers."

He pulled the quilt higher until only his eyes showed over the edge. Jamie watched Alex's feet snake and wriggle under the bottom half of the bunk.

"No in here yah twit," Jamie snapped.

Alex surfaced at the bottom end and looked up, "Kilroy was here" fashion. He looked around as he listened to the sound of the woman's voice that seemed to have emanated from nowhere.

"Where did she come from?" Jamie said, looking around but seeing no one except Alex at the other end of the bunk.

The voice spoke in Danish. The voice slipped into Dutch. It all sounded Greek to Alex and Jamie. Then the voice fell into a heavily accented English and spoke about ordering breakfast in next morning, about handing in reservations if you required tea or coffee to be delivered straight to the cabin.

"Oh, for God's sake!" Alex said, dropping the duvet down from his chin.

"Where is she?" Jamie said, wide-eyed.

"Up there," Alex said. "In the extractor."

Jamie looked up. "Where?" he asked.

"Up there!"

"Gives you a right creepy feeling," Jamie said. "But she's not saying anything now though. She gone?"

"She was never there in the first place," Alex said.

Jamie pulled down the quilt. "You sure?"

"Aye," Alex said with a sigh. "I'm sure."

Jamie smiled. "Still wanting a bit then?" he asked with a grin.

"I don't know now," Alex said. "They might have cameras or anything in here."

"Don't be daft," Jamie said. He lowered the quilt, sliding it down his bare chest, lower and lower still. "See anything you like, Eck?" he said.

CHAPTER 33

Later, they walked around up on decks, inside and out. Looked in glazed-eyed wonder at the shop, the watches, perfumes and after shaves, the rings, all so bright and silvery looking.

Alex looked agitated.

"What is it?" Jamie asked.

It's no good," Alex said. "I'm desperate for a coffee."

They found a machine. Alex looked at it. "It's in every language: Dutch, Spanish. Everything except English," Alex said.

Jamie hunkered down at the machine for a look himself. There were several silver tubes hanging down from the underside and buttons above each tube for coffee, milk, sugar and water.

"How do you work it?" Alex asked, peering at it.

"Well," Jamie said, "I think you put a Euro in this slot here, then you put one of those plastic cups from there under the tubes and press the buttons as you go. But ..."

"But what?" Alex asked from the side of his mouth, not wanting any of the other passengers to think he was thick. "I don't want to look stupid doing it."

Jamie looked in close again. "I think it says that you've only got fifteen seconds to do it all in before it cuts out. To stop more than one person using it at a time, I suppose."

Alex reached out and picked up one of the plastic cups at the side. Jamie shoved a Euro in the slot then yelled. "Go!"

All fingers and thumbs, Alex bashed at the buttons with one hand, the other scooting the cup under each of the tubes one after the other. Half the time everything missed going into the cup. In desperation, he rammed his thumb at the button over the tube for hot water. A teaspoonful skooshed out before the machine cut out.

Ping!

"No water?" Jamie asked, peering into the cup in Alex's hand.

"No coffee in it either," Alex said.

Not to be beaten, he tried it again and again.

"It's no good, Jamie. I can't do it myself. You'll have to give me a hand."

"Okay," Jamie shrugged. "You shove the money in it in I'll bash the buttons as you scoot the cup under each tube and fill the cup."

"Right," Alex frowned.

"Right," Jamie said. "Ready?"

Alex gripped at the cup, a Euro in the other hand poised at the slot. "Aye, I am now."

"Right," Jamie said. "GO!"

"Coffee! Milk! Sugar! *Water*!" Jamie cried out, bashing the buttons in turn.

"Ooyah! Ooyah! Ooyah!" Alex yelped.

"What is it?" Jamie asked.

"You burnt my hand with the hot water."

"Me?"

"Aye, you!"

Jamie rubbed at his forehead. "Eck, why no just buy yourself a coffee at the café?"

Alex stopped sucking at his hand for a second. "Because," he said close to Jamie's ear, "they don't speak English." His eyes widened as he nodded.

Jamie didn't get it. He pulled back with a squint look on his face, ready to unzip its grief all over the carpet. "What do they speak then?" he asked.

"Danish," Alex said. "We're on a Danish ferry-line, remember? You booked it. You should know."

"And what difference does that make?" Jamie said. "Just have to point to what you're wanting. I'm sure they'll get the drift."

"But what if they don't," Alex pleaded. "And don't look at me as if I'm an idiot."

In the end, Jamie walked off and did all the ordering in English. They even understood his version—Keltynite.

Alex sat at the table and waited.

Jamie stuffed his face with doughnuts, his mouth so full he had to gulp hard, forcing the dough down through his neck.

"God, there's no enough sugar on them." He protested. Still chewing away, he tore open little sachets and sprinkled more sugar on what was left of the doughnuts. He took another bite. "Yum," he said with relish. "That's better."

Alex sat opposite with a grim face.

Jamie spluttered. "What's wrong with you?"

"I'm starving," Alex said through gritted teeth.

"You're on a diet," Jamie reminded him.

"Who says?"

"You're fat ark says."

The V returned between Alex's eyebrows. "Am I no supposed to eat anything then?" he asked.

Jamie rolled up his eyes, leaned back and wiped his hand under his snout, sniffed, then thrust the same hand into his pocket. "Here. I got you this," he said, placing the item in front of Alex.

"Tomato juice? Is that all?"

Jamie put his hand in his other pocket and pulled out something else. "There," he said. "Now quit your griping."

"Tomato juice and an apple. Is that it?" Alex shouted in disbelief. "A Granny Smith's as well. I'll need a chisel just to bite into it."

Jamie poked the remains of a doughnut into his mouth, his cheeks bulging like a hamster. He reached over for Alex's coffee, grabbed it and gulped some down.

"Hey, that's mine," Alex said.

Jamie spluttered, swallowing. "I was choking. I had to."

"In that case, I'll have one of them, then," Alex said, reaching out for one of the sugar coated lumps of dough.

"Uh uh." Jamie smiled, waving a finger. "Remember your Milky Way-sized fat ark, Eck." Cheeks still bulging even as he chewed, Jamie drew what was left of the doughnuts closer to himself.

"And I don't have a fat ark," Alex said.

"You're deluding yourself, Eck."

Alex looked down at the apple and bottle of tomato juice. "I can't just have this."

"It's good for you."

"But I'm on holiday."

"And I'm in purgatory listening to you," Jamie said, chomping through dough and sugar.

Like a sprung trap, Alex reached out and grabbed one of the doughnuts.

"Oi!"

But Alex was already up and away, cramming the doughnut into his gob as he ran along the corridor, past the fruit machines, the portholes and the waves outside. Even before he could swallow anything his stomach was rumbling in anticipation.

He ran past the children's play area.

But Jamie was quick. His feet thumped closer behind Alex. Breathless, he grabbed Alex, spun him around, and with their feet and arms tangled, they fell to the deck.

For an awful moment Alex thought that Jamie might even try to gouge out what was still left of the doughnut he had managed to cram into his mouth. In desperation, Alex's stomach screaming 'gimme gimme gimme', he closed his eyes, stretched out his neck and thrust out his jaw until everything was nothing but taut sinews and muscles and gulped.

Gone.

Alex looked up at Jamie and laughed. But when he looked over Jamie's shoulder, the smile fell off his face.

A rather bemused purser looked down on them and seemed as if he was about to say, "Ooogil shproogil tattie noodle," or some such as the Danish folk (or "foowk" if you're posh) would say. Translation: "Not another boat load of eejits."

Alex tapped Jamie on the shoulder and nodded. "Eh, Jamie."

Jamie squirmed around and saw the purser standing in his neat uniform, white shirt, black tie and cap. He gave a quick, embarrassed smile, scrambled to his feet, reached down and dragged Alex to his.

"He's a bit simple." Jamie screwed up his nose in explanation. "No right in the head."

Upon hearing this, Alex's jaw hit Davie Jones' Locker, but before he could protest, he found himself being shoved, hauled, and thrust out the door, tripping over the bulkhead, and onto the outside deck.

The sea breeze hit them, but Alex was having none of it. "Simple?" he said.

"Got us out a tight corner, didn't it?" Jamie beamed, proud of himself.

"But me, simple?"

"What are you greeting for?" Jamie said, walking up to the rail. "That geezer could have had us deported."

"We're already at sea," Alex said. "There's nowhere to be deported to, yah gonk!"

"Look, Eck," Jamie said. "I'm older than you, remember. So that means that I know better."

"Only older by two months," Alex said. "And for all I know you could have been premature. So that doesn't count."

"Eh?" Jamie thought about it for a second. "If I was premature," he said, "then that would make me even older than you still."

Alex's face collapsed. A great gaping hole had been found in his argument. "Stop trying to blind me with science," he said, turning away and looking out at sea, the coastline fading in the distance as they sailed further away from home.

CHAPTER 34

To Alex it was like sitting on a slow roller coaster ride. The hull cut through the waves, going up and down gently, and sometimes a bit more up than down than he cared to think about. But he was getting used to it.

The sun was out, the sea spray refreshing, and there was something else. For the first time, he could see the horizon, flat, and without buildings, trees and hills being in the way. The earth really was round then, no walls, no limits.

Or did it have an edge after all, one that could never be reached?

The blue handrail was warm under the heat of the sun. Jamie stood beside him, both of them standing in silence. Passengers walked to and fro behind them and Jamie lit up a cigarette; a minor irritation to Alex now, who seemed lost in the simple wonder of it all.

The coastline had disappeared to be replaced by endless waves going on forever.

What it must have been like, he thought, *for those first explorers. And we're only on the North Sea.*

What of the Pacific, the Atlantic, the Adriatic? Places and times when they had no names, sailing off into the unknown. And those explorers knowing that they might have been sailing off the edge of the world and with the thought that they may never return.

And then Alex thought of those poor sailors who perhaps had had nothing to return to anyway.

Press-ganged men.

He thought of trade routes, new lands, exotic lands and peoples and a time when sea captains would use astrolabes to guide them, their discoveries of new species, of plants and animals, herbs and spices, clipper ships and tea, and new wondrous medicines. And from inside of him a sense of regret began to resurface, that he had never stayed on at school so that he could have gone on to university as he had always dreamed of doing.

But needs must. And needs came first. Families came first. Making a living and holding things together came first.

There was also a need and thirst for knowledge inside of Alex, however. A thirst he thought he had successfully extinguished until he realized how foolish that was. You quenched a thirst, he realized; you couldn't extinguish it.

And there it still burned, now realized all over again from deep inside and as alive as much as it ever was. Everything was coming back to him now: the books, the wonder, the need to know.

But needs must and it was too late now. There was no going back.

That didn't help him feel any better. For whatever it was that was still deep inside of him, it hadn't gone away. Life had merely pushed it aside and there it was waiting, waiting ... waiting.

"Oh God, Eck!" Jamie said through gritted teeth as he dropped his cigarette, crushing it out underfoot. "No now, Eck, please no now."

But Alex's fingers were like claws gripping onto the handrail. Jamie took a quick look around. No one seemed to notice, which was thankful, yet at the same time terrifying because that meant he would have to deal with this on his own and on unfamiliar territory. There was no one else who would understand, no one to lean on, to run to for help.

He tried prizing Alex's fingers off the handrail, but they were as tight as steel bands.

"Eck, laddie, come on pal. I'll do anything, promise anything, just no now, no now."

And it got worse. A wet patch appeared at the crotch of Alex's jeans.

"Awe, God!"

Then Alex's mouth started to open and close as his eyes stared blankly out to sea. But not a sound as he mouthed invisible words into the breeze.

Jamie took another furtive look around. The wet patch at the front of Alex's jeans grew to a flood.

"Awe, laddie, why'd you have to drink so much coffee?"

But Alex wasn't listening. Wasn't hearing anything now. One finger after another, Jamie finally managed to get Alex's hands from the rail.

"I'll just say you've spilt something on yourself if anybody asks," Jamie said, even though he knew that Alex couldn't hear him, knew that he was saying it more for his own benefit.

His legs like a zombie, aimless, Alex stumbled forward as Jamie guided him. Jamie had to get them both back to the cabin, only he couldn't remember where it was. There were so many decks, so many corridors. And they weren't even inside yet.

"Are you all right?" a woman asked Jamie.

The sound of her voice startled him. He gave her a quick look and at the same time wished that she would just go away. Alex's jeans were now soaked from crotch to ankles. His mouth kept gawping invisible words. And with Jamie's arm around his shoulder, Alex's feet lifted up and slammed down again as if he were a crazed marionette on strings.

The woman looked on sympathetically. Jamie shook his head.

"He's no well," he said, knowing that Alex would be mortified if he knew this woman was seeing him like this. "If I can just get him back to the cabin he should be all right in a bit. I think he's just got a bit over excited, that's all. It's our first holiday, you see."

"Should I call the ship's doctor?" she asked.

"Oh, no, no," Jamie said. "He'll be all right. He just needs to have a wee lie down, that's all."

The woman nodded as if she understood. But somehow, to Jamie, her knowing seemed to make it better and worse at the same time.

"Look," she said, "let me give you a hand with him." And before Jamie knew what was happening, she had put her arm over Alex's shoulder and was helping Jamie guide him inside.

"What's the cabin number?" she asked.

Still clutching onto Alex, Jamie fumbled for the key card in his back pocket. The woman looked at it.

"Deck seven," she said. "The one above this."

Most passengers were on deck, or in the cafés, or the restaurant, or shopping so the corridors were deserted, for which Jamie was grateful

A word began to whisper out of Alex's mouth, the same one over and over. "Baby, baby, baby ..."

"What's he saying?" the woman asked Jamie.

Jamie looked at her, a pained expression in his eyes. "Baby," Jamie explained. "He always says that when he's no being well."

The woman only gave a little smile of sympathy as if she understood and Jamie pushed the key card into the slot in the cabin door. There was a ting sound. Pushing the door wide and holding it open with one foot, Jamie guided Alex into the cabin and the woman let go of Alex's shoulders.

"Will you—he—be all right?" she asked from the corridor.

"Don't tell anybody, will you?" Jamie said, shaking his head. "He wouldn't forgive himself if he knew that anybody saw him like this, getting wet like that. It's just that he can't help it, sometimes. He doesn't know he's doing it."

The woman waited a beat before replying. "Not a soul," she smiled sympathetically.

Jamie smiled back at her. "Thanks," he said and closed the door.

CHAPTER 35

The shower cubicle was tiny, but Jamie eventually managed to pull Alex's wet jeans off him. More than once Alex lost balance and Jamie saved him from stumbling over and seriously injuring himself. Deciding that it would be better if he stayed with Alex, Jamie stripped himself and held onto Alex, the both of them under the shower. Reaching over, he grabbed the wet jeans and threw them down at his feet, letting the water run through them.

"What are you trying to say?" Jamie asked Alex, who was still in a daze. "I can't make out your words, pal." Jamie watched Alex's eyes and it was as if Alex was seeing into some far off place.

Alex spoke again. "... Baby ..."

Jamie could feel his own hurt rising. "Alex, I can hardly hear you," he said gently. "Come on, what is it? Why do you keep saying that?"

Alex looked Jamie in the eyes, then away again. "Baby ..."

"Awe, Alex, don't do this to me, please," Jamie said. "You're hurting me with how you're talking, laddie."

Alex was still in a daze when Jamie toweled him dry and put him to bed in the lower bunk.

~~*

Alex lay under the quilt, his face to the wall. "Did I pee myself?" he asked.

Jamie, sitting on the little sofa opposite was caught off-guard. "You're awake then," he said, trying to sound light.

"Jamie?"

"Aye?" Jamie said. He stood up.

"I asked you a question, Jamie."

Jamie breathed out silently. "I noticed," he said quietly.

"I'm in bed," Alex went on. "I've no clothes on and my hair's still wet, so I take it I've had a shower. Either that, or I fell over the side and the sea's made out owe Imperial Leather shower gel."

Jamie shook his head, knowing Alex couldn't see him.

"So?" Alex prompted.

Jamie bit his lip.

"And don't lie to me, because I'll know," Alex said, his face still to the wall.

Jamie looked around for something to do, anything, and couldn't find a thing. "Nobody saw you," he lied.

"So I *did* pee myself."

"Alex—"

"Jamie," Alex cut in. "Tell me."

Jamie rubbed at his nose. "It wasn't much, Eck," he said.

"So what did I need a shower for then?"

Jamie shrugged. "I just thought …" he said. "I don't know what I was thinking, Alex." He raked his fingers through his hair. "I thought it might wake you up a bit, that's all."

"What about my clothes?"

Jamie rubbed at his eyes. He was feeling the pressure. He shrugged again. He wanted out of the cabin, to be up on deck, in the sun, carefree, to watch the bow cutting through the waves. "I rinsed them out in the shower," he said.

His shoulders jerked back as if he'd been caught doing something wrong and there was nothing he could do about it. "I've hung them up," he said. "If they're no dry by the time we get to shore I'll put them in a bag. They'll dry at the hotel."

Alex didn't say anything.

"Alex?"

Still nothing.

"Are you all right?"

"Why did she do it, Jamie?"

Jamie found his eyes darting over to Alex's back, at his bare shoulder. He knew what Alex was talking about. But like always, he just didn't have an answer.

"I don't know, Alex. I just don't know why your mother did that to you. I wish I did, but I don't."

"My own mother," Alex said.

Jamie kept silent.

"My own mother," Alex went on, "suffocating her own bairn for attention for herself. I read it. I told you I had, didn't I, Jamie?"

Jamie was too frightened to speak, frightened that his voice would break. He swallowed, then said, "You did, Alex, aye."

"What did she do it for, Jamie? Why?"

But Jamie knew that Alex wasn't asking him for an answer. Because there wasn't one.

"I read my medical notes," Alex went on. "That was after I asked the doctor to look at them. But he wouldn't give them to me at first. I had to pay to see my own medical records for myself," Alex sniffed. "Munchausen by proxy she was suffering from, it said. It never mentioned anything about my suffering though. I didn't even know what it meant. It said she must have pinched my nose shut and put her hand over my mouth. Records showed that I had had umpteen admissions to Accident in Emergency with fits before they wondered why. Scan showed a scar own my brain ..."

"Awe, Alex, don't do this to yourself ..."

"What did she do it for, Jamie? Nobody will tell me. She was my own mother and I was only a wee bairn. That wee I couldn't even talk yet."

Jamie's eyes stung. He looked down on Alex, heard Alex's voice waiver, and watched his shoulders tremble. He had to swallow hard before he trusted himself to speak again. "Please, Alex. Don't greet, laddie."

He sat down on the edge of Alex's bunk and put his hand on the warmth of Alex neck, stroked at his hairline, soft as velvet.

"But I loved my mum, Jamie. And I still love her. I just don't understand what I did that would make her do that to me. I Just can't understand it."

"Come on, laddie," Jamie said. "Don't upset yourself anymore about it. Don't let her win."

"Jamie?" Alex sniffed.

"Aye, what is it, Alex?"

"Would you do me a favor?"

"What favor would that be, Alex?"

Alex sniffed, face still to the wall. "Cuddle me, Jamie. Please cuddle me. I get feared sometimes after a fit happens. I try no to be, but I can't help it."

Jamie slipped under the quilt, fully clothed, and held onto Alex.

"Jamie?"

"Aye, Alex," Jamie said softly. "What is it laddie?"

"Thanks."

A little while later Jamie woke up. "Eck? Do you want go back up own deck for a bit?" he asked.

Alex sniffed. "I don't want to go out," he said. "They'll all know."

"No, they'll no," Jamie said.

"I don't want to go out, Jamie. You go. I'll stay here for a bit."

Jamie sighed, blew out a breath, lifted his hand and laid it on Alex's shoulder. "I can't leave you on your own, laddie," he said. "No like this. Come on. You'll miss all the fun, our first trip at sea. Our first trip anywhere except uptown in Kelty. I wanted this to be special for you, Alex. Me and you, away together, on our own."

Alex didn't say anything.

"Tell you what, Eck," Jamie said. "Let's have a game of cards. We can have a game here in the cabin."

Alex kept with his face to the wall. "We don't have cards," he said.

"I could get some at the duty free shop or whatever they cry it," Jamie said.

"Am tired," Alex whispered.

Jamie smiled sadly. "You'll have to have something to eat, Alex, if nothing else," Jamie said.

"I'm no hungry, Jamie. I'm never hungry right after it happens."

Jamie felt as if he were treading water in a large ocean, knowing both of them were going to drown, trying to keep his chin above the waves, holding onto Alex, but feeling him sink under the surface, knowing that it was only a matter of time.

He slipped out from under the quilt and stood up. "I'll go up on deck in see what I can find anyway," he said.

Alex kept his face to the wall. As Jamie opened the cabin door he turned back and saw that Alex had pushed his face into the pillow, his shoulders shaking.

If only someone could tell Jamie what to do. But there were no wardens he could to turn to now.

Just then, a thought struck him. *What if I lost you, Alex? What would I do with myself then?*

The thought frightened him so much that he turned away. But knowing that Alex needed time to himself, Jamie stepped into the corridor and quietly closed the cabin door.

After a smoke on the upper deck, Jamie bought some sandwiches and coffees. He didn't bother buying a pack of cards from the shop. But there had been something that caught his eye. It wasn't expensive, and more of a symbol really, a symbol that would do until he could find something better.

Back inside the cabin again, he closed the door quietly. The boat swayed gently as he placed the coffee and sandwiches he had bought for Alex on the little table by the door.

Alex was laying on his side, still asleep, his mouth slightly open.

The weather had been glorious outside, the setting sun casting a golden road of light over the waves. In an hour or so it would be dark, and somehow it hurt him to know that Alex wouldn't see the sun as it sank beneath the waves on the horizon.

Jamie sat on the little sofa, Alex still sleeping, and as quietly as he could, he unlaced his boots, pulled them off and placed them next to Alex's shoes on the floor.

He looked at Alex, at his mouth still slightly open, and watched the gentle rise and fall of his chest. Seeing Alex, vulnerable in sleep as he was tugged somewhere deep inside of Jamie, somewhere he'd never known was there before.

Trying to push it out of his mind, he stood up and stepped over to the ladder. With the rungs digging into the soles of his feet though his socks, he climbed up onto the top bunk, rolled onto his back and put his arms behind his head and stared at the ceiling.

CHaPTer 36

Jamie was still on the top bunk, the ceiling only inches from his face when he heard Alex's voice calling out. "You're awake then," he said.

"I want us to have a baby, Jamie. I want a baby in I know we can't have one. It's not fair."

Hearing Alex beginning to upset himself all over again, Jamie climbed down the ladder. He reached into the bathroom, grabbed some tissues and sat on the bottom bunk. "Awe, Alex. Come here. Take this in blow your snout," Jamie said, giving Alex the tissues, "before you bubble all down my shoulder. Come on. Come here."

"I want us to have a baby, Jamie. I never told anyone before. But I can't help it."

"Well, you can have a bairn if you want if it's that important to you, Alex."

"I mean with you. And I know we can't. I know it, but I can't believe it somehow. It makes sense in it doesn't at the same time."

"You in me?" Jamie was taken aback.

"Aye, you and me."

"I don't know," Jamie said, "but with your ears in my conk, I wouldn't think that the poor bairn would have much going for it."

Alex sat up and blew his nose. Red eyed, he looked at Jamie. "What's wrong with my ears?" he asked.

"Nothing, Alex," Jamie said. "There's nothing wrong with your ears at all."

"And there's nothing wrong with your conk either, Jamie," Alex said.

Jamie smiled uncertainly at the compliment. "It would look like a cross between Dumbo and Concorde, our bairn would," Jamie laughed.

"Awe, don't say thaa-t!"

"But I tell you what, Alex," Jamie said in a more serious tone. "He would have your big brown eyes. Aye, lovely big brown eyes, just like yours."

"They're blue," Alex sniffed.

"What are?"

"My eyes," Alex said. "They're blue."

"Right," Jamie said. "I forgot."

"Forgot? What have you been looking it all these months?"

Jamie turned his face away. "What color is mine, then?"

"Yellow," Alex said.

"They are not," Jamie said. "Anyway, he would have great big blue eyes, just like yours."

"Awe, stop it," Alex said. "You'll have me greeting all night now." Alex sniffed before he went on. "I just wished we could though, you in me."

Jamie looked at Alex. "You'll have me greeting now," he said.

"Do you no feel it though, Jamie?"

Jamie nodded. "And I wished we could have a baby, Eck, but," he shrugged, "we can't."

"It's no fair," Alex said. "It's just no fair. I want us to have a baby, just you in me, Jamie, just you in me. And I know we can never have one."

"Och, Alex," Jamie said, pulling Alex close. "You're my baby. You'll always be my baby. And I'll tell you something else, Alex. That baby, if we ever did have one, would be the most loved baby in the world."

Alex and Jamie sat squashed up together in the bottom bunk. No one spoke as they held on to each other in the quiet, the ship sailing. But Jamie was talking, having a silent conversation inside his own head, wishing that he could dare himself to speak his words out loud. And every now and then, his hand or his fingers would betray his thoughts, drawing Alex to himself, a little closer each time as his thoughts tumbled over themselves

I'm feared, Eck. Though I might not show it, I'm feared. And I'm feared for a lot of different reasons, like me no being good enough for you. What I'm trying to say, Alex, is that since I met you I'm more feared now than I've ever been in my life. Feared of losing you, scared at the thought that we might never have met, might never have known each other but for the fact that we were in the right place at the right time.

I wasn't even going to go out that night. What would have happened if I had stayed at home?

You see, Alex, the real reason I'm so feared now, is that you're the closest thing to an angel on Earth that I've ever known.

CHAPTER 37

Jamie looked at his watch. It was after two in the morning. Alex stirred.

"Eck?"

Alex grumbled behind him. "What is it?"

The cabin door opened. Jamie stuck his head out into the corridor, looked left and right. The place was deserted. Alex stood behind him, not sure if this was a good thing.

"It's all right," Jamie said. "There's no one about." Jamie stepped into the corridor first and waited, bag in hand.

Alex stepped out after him like a scared rabbit. Jamie closed the cabin door quietly, turned and smiled at Alex, and beckoned him to follow. As they tiptoed along, the floor swayed gently under them in a dreamy kind of way, a gentle rise and fall as the ferry sailed the dark waves of the North Sea.

They reached the stairwell with its brightly polished banisters, the carpet thick and springy. The place was deserted, and except for the distant rumble of engines, it was silent.

Alex left Jamie to look at the plan of the ship on the wall next to the lifts. Each deck was a different color and he was having a hard time trying to figure out where they were. The London Underground had been bad enough. With several different levels to contend with it was difficult to tell where they were now.

Jamie's eyes scanned along the lines of the diagram.

"Level six, level six," he kept mumbling to himself. Then realized he didn't need to find where they were since there was a big red circle with *You Are Here* written on it telling him.

Now all he had to do was find out where he would be taking Alex.

Level six.

"Found it!" he said, then looked around in case his voice had been too loud.

He caught Alex looking out one of the windows into the blackness of the night. Jamie walked up behind him.

"Are you ready then?" he whispered. With a half smile Alex nodded. "It's just down the next flight," Jamie said.

"Okay." But Alex didn't sound too sure. This was a bit like sneaking out into the night when his mum hadn't been looking.

Gripping the brass handrail, the ship gently swaying side to side, they made their way down to deck six.

Okay, so now we're on the right deck, Jamie thought, looking around. *But where do we go? How do we get there*? It looked different in the daytime. But then, he didn't have much of a clue where everything was then either.

Ahead of them was the Duty Free shop, closed up now for the night. There were perfume bottles and expensive silver watches and toys in display cases set up against the glass.

"We go down this way," Jamie said, pointing to the corridor that went down past the Duty Free. Alex didn't say anything, just stood with his hands in his pockets.

It felt like a ghost ship. There was no sign of the crew either. The ship could be sailing itself.

They crept along to the end of the corridor leading into an auditorium. The wooden floor was dimly lit. The empty blue seats and tables were in darkness around the sides. The metal grills on the bar area had been pulled down and dim lights glinted off the bottles and glasses inside.

Jamie put his arm over Alex's shoulders and gave him a quick hug. "Just us then," he said. He took a quick look around to confirm what he had said.

He was shaking inside, but he didn't want Alex to know that so he let him go and walked away and stepped up onto the dance floor. Alex watched from the shadows at the sidelines, taking quick looks around.

Jamie waved his arm, beckoning Alex to join him. Alex slowly walked up the steps and under the dim lights over the dance floor beside Jamie. He was crouched down, rifling inside the bag he'd brought with him from their cabin.

He turned his head and looked up at Alex. "Come on," he whispered. "It's all right. Nobody's about. They're all sleeping."

But Alex still didn't look too sure. It wasn't that he didn't want to bump into anyone after what had happened up on deck when he had had a fit and peed himself yesterday's afternoon that was the problem now. It was the feeling that they shouldn't be here in the first place. Not at nearly two o' the clock in the morning anyway.

Hands in pockets, he stood behind Jamie, who was still hunkered on the floor. Looking over Jamie's shoulder, he watched Jamie place the portable CD player that he had bought for Alex's birthday onto the dance floor and the tiny little speakers to either side of it. Their power was only a couple of watts at best, but in the quiet it would be enough.

Jamie squinted at the controls and pressed play. Knees cracking, he stood up and turned to face Alex.

The walls of the ferry creaked. The floor under them tilted slightly. The music started, a little tinny sound from the tiny speakers.

"Come closer to me," Jamie said.

"Eh?"

Jamie reached out and took a hold of Alex, drawing him close as the music started to play. There was a barely audible intake of breath from the singer as the song began.

Suddenly, Alex hugged Jamie close as he recognized the song and looked at him. "I'm feared Jamie," he whispered. "I don't know what for, but I'm still feared."

"Don't be," Jamie said. "Come on. Put your head on my shoulder. That's it. We don't need to think of anything else but us. Just you in me. Nobody else."

And as they laid their heads on each other's shoulders, the warmth of each other's neck on their cheeks, they closed their eyes and drifted slowly around in a circle.

Jamie held onto Alex. Alex relaxed into Jamie as the song began: Chrissie Hynde—*Forever Young*.

"Hold tight, laddie," Jamie whispered into Alex's ear. "I'm as feared as you are. There's nobody here to see us, Alex. We're invisible to everyone except each other."

And Jamie laid his head on Alex's shoulder again.

"Awe Jamie," Alex said, "that's a nice song."

Jamie said nothing more as they continued to drift around the dance floor in slow circles, and as usual, neither knew who was leading who. Soon they were so close together, it was as if they were one, each predicting the slow fluid movements of the other, in perfect tune with each other.

CHAPTER 38

The woman with the blonde hair stopped short when she caught sight of the dance floor. She took a step back into the corridor, not wanting to be seen. At first she thought that perhaps it was a pair of lads up too late and too worse for drink to know when to go to bed.

From a dark corner she continued to watch their slow dance and heard the barely audible music. Sadness flooded through her, invading her heart, something from long ago, and something she had been denied for all of her life.

She looked away, knowing that what she was witnessing was something very private and thought of going back down the corridor the way she had come, back down by the side of the shop, closed for the night, with its glittery gems on display, its exquisite fragrances of Prada and Chanel sending out their secret, tantalizing messages to her. Perhaps she would sit alone, on the ledge of one of the windows and look out into the darkness with the deep rumble of the ship's engines beat deep below, a powerhouse of a heart helping her to escape.

Hiding in shadows was something she had been used to doing for all of her life. She had become so used to it, hiding, darting away from people, the human race, alone in her nightmare that she had begun to think of it as normal.

Would it ever end?

But instead of sitting down, she decided to take a walk outside on deck, to look into the dark, to feel the sea air, to listen to the bow of the ship as it cut through the waves, the foaming surf. But not to dream. She had been dreaming all her life of what it would be like. And just for once, she wanted for it all to be real, even if only for a split second, to find out that her life had not been in vain, that her dream had not always been something futile that would always be forever out of her reach.

Leaning over the rail, she watched the white waves racing by the side of the ship in the dark. White horses, her father would call them when she was little. And she would dream of riding off on them to a far off land, a magical land.

The breeze blew through her hair as she leaned over the railing, her heels on the verge of letting go their grip as the waves crashed against the hull far below, and in the distance she saw the flames, bright and orange, beacons, torches calling to her as the oil platform passed by.

She pressed herself closer to the railing, teetering over, for perhaps this was how her dream would end.

CHAPTER 39

"I don't know, Alex," Jamie said as they held on to each other, still moving slowly around the dance floor. "I sometimes think we're like monsters. Like nobody wants us. That's how I used to feel anyway. Now? I don't know. But I was thinking last night, while you were sleeping and ... Och, I don't know. I thought what would I do without my laddie. I mean that, Alex. I don't know what I'd do without you."

Jamie pulled Alex closer. "I mean it, Eck," he said. "I couldn't live if you weren't with me." He slipped his hand up to Alex's neck, to the side of his face. "My laddie," Jamie said. "Anyway," he said, pulling away. "There's something I've got to say."

"What?" Alex asked.

"Just a minute." Jamie slipped a hand into his pocket, dropped down onto one knee and looked up into Alex's eyes.

Alex looked down. "What are you doing, Jamie?"

Jamie pulled his hand out of his pocket and held the ring out to Alex. "It's not much," Jamie said. "I couldn't afford anything much like. You know what I'm like with money, but I saw this in the shop on board when you were sleeping in the cabin this afternoon, when you still weren't feeling so well, and ... and, well, when I saw it, Alex, it all made sense to me."

Jamie reached out and took hold of Alex's hand and tried to slip the ring on his finger. "Marry me, Alex," Jamie said.

"Awe, Jamie."

"Och, damn in blast it," Jamie said struggling with the ring. "It's too big!" His shoulders sagged. "I'll have to try and change it," he said. "I can never do anything right, Alex. I'm sorry. I wanted it to be perfect as well."

Alex took Jamie's hand in his, the ring loose on Alex's finger under both, and shook his head. "No, Jamie," Alex said. "The ring's not too big at all. It's your heart that's too big, bigger than both of ours put together."

"Och, I'm always getting it rang," Jamie said. "And I wanted this to come out right, too."

"No, Jamie," Alex said shaking his head again. "You don't always get it wrong."

"Thing is, Alex ..." Jamie said.

"Aye?"

"I love my laddie. I love you, Alex. Just don't ever leave me. I don't know what I would do with myself without you being beside me for the rest of my life."

CHapTer 40

"Mind if I join you?"

The voice startled Shirley. She hadn't heard any doors open or close. She hadn't heard any footsteps on the plastic netting covering the deck.

Just a voice, suddenly there.

At first, Shirley's hand had gripped onto the rail with a sudden desperation, as if she might lose control and throw herself overboard for being found out. Perhaps she should just walk away from this stranger in the night before it was too late.

But that would be too obvious.

Instead, she turned her head away from her as if looking at something in the distance, in the night. *Not my face*, Shirley thought. *Please don't look at my face.*

A face her family had known so well. A face they had rejected. And now here she was, anonymous, with a stranger standing beside her.

The sea breeze blew coolly at Shirley's silk dress.

So much make up. Why can't I get it right?

And how could a stranger ever understand Shirley any more than her family could?

"I can never sleep either on these trips," the woman said. "And being out here, alone, or not always alone, but when it's so quiet and peaceful, well, it's like nothing else matters."

Shirley still kept her face hidden, kept it into the breeze, pretended to herself that it was the coolness of air that was making her eyes water.

The voice sounded kind—too kind.

She heard the sound of a lighter grating on its flint and then the faint smell of cigarette smoke. Shirley had been looking out at sea, into the dark, watching the waves cut through by the iron of the ferry's hull. She was taken off-guard by the huskiness of the woman's voice, so close, so sudden.

"Nice, isn't it?" the woman said. "To stand here and get away from it all. You could almost believe that there was nothing out there, beyond the dark. No land, nothing."

The woman's words struck Shirley with their precision. It was exactly the way she felt, the way she wanted to feel, to be away from it all.

The woman was closer now. Shirley turned her head away a little more.

"You were the one who was stopped at passport control, weren't you?" the woman said.

Shirley nodded, the cool breeze fluttering the hairs of her blonde wig. "Yes," she said at last.

"They must have been looking for someone," the woman said matter-of-factly. "They must have thought you were a spy or something. Like Mata Hari."

"Margaretha Geertruida Zelle." Shirley barely whispered the words. "Dancer and secret agent. Double agent. Executed by the French in 1917."

"She took her name from Malay—*mata* for eye and *hari* for day," the woman said.

"I didn't know that," Shirley said.

"Just as well we're not heading for France then," the woman said.

Still clutching the coolness of the rail, Shirley turned slightly to the woman. "I don't know," Shirley sighed. "They didn't say anything to me about spies." She turned away again, thinking of the distance that must be between her and the place she had once called home. "I thought it was because of the way I dress," she said.

"I don't know," the woman said. "I think it looks very nice." Shirley turned her head and looked at the woman again. Before Shirley could say anything, the woman was offering her a cigarette. Without thinking, Shirley reached out and took one. "Jean," the woman said. "And yours?"

"Which one do you want?" Shirley said.

The woman lit Shirley's cigarette, then her own, drew in smoke and puffed it into the breeze. "Your real one," the woman said.

"It's ..."

"I mean, your *real* real name," the woman said.

Shirley thought about it, smiled, and said, "Shirley."

"Nice name," Jean said, leaning on the rail. "Had it long?"

"About twenty years," Shirley said. "Since I was seventeen. But I've never really dressed for the name until now. Not in public anyway."

"It suits you," Jean said. "Shirley. I like it."

Shirley smiled.

"Have you seen that Freddy Mercury video?" Jean asked.

"Which one?"

"The one with him in the leather mini skirt and bouffant?"

"*I Want to Break Free*," Shirley sang badly and laughed.

"That's the one," Jean said. "I thought it was the sexiest thing I ever saw. So did some of my girlfriends—at the time anyway. Seeing a man in a tight mini, a blouse and hair all done up like that."

Shirley felt herself frown. "Why sexy?" she asked.

Jean shrugged and took a long drag on her cigarette. "I don't know why. But why question it? A man who dresses as a woman? All I know is he—she—looked good."

Shirley thought about it for a moment before saying anything. "I've never heard of a woman saying that before. About a man in a woman's clothes being sexy, that is."

"Well," Jean said, facing Shirley, "you have now. I think I've made this journey a hundred and fifty times, and a hundred and fifty times, this is the best part for me." She spoke quietly, almost dreamily. "The nights, the calm of the waves, the way the ship moves gently. And then sometimes, you see those special people, people in the night."

Shirley felt her insides tightened at the sound of the 'special people.' It meant something different, funny, something amusing and safe from a distance, but something horrible close up. Something that shouldn't be there in the grand scheme of things. A monster trying to be invisible behind a veil, diffusing its image to soften the blow.

"Seems like we're not the only two who can't sleep," Jean said, turning around and looking through the oblong porthole over the way. "There are a couple of lads in there dancing together. God knows they look young. Young love. And you can't beat that now, can you? What I wouldn't give to go back to that time and live it all over again. And what I wouldn't give to stop myself remembering all the hell I would have to go through all over again if I did.

"I saw them this afternoon," Jean went on, turning back to the sea. "They were full of life, laughing. But one of them didn't look so well a little while later. He had to be helped back to their cabin. I thought at first that maybe he would need the ship's doctor, but he seems to have recovered now."

Shirley brushed a hair away from her eyes. "I ..." but the words were strangled before they could get them out of her throat.

"Sorry?" Jean asked.

Another waft of cigarette smoke sailed by into the night. "It's nice meeting you, Jean," Shirley finally managed to get her words out.

"Pleased to meet you too, Shirley," Jean said.

It was an invitation to turn around, or to run away from the inevitable pain. Slowly, Shirley turned her head and looked at Jean. "Yes, very pleased to meet you, too," she said.

But the woman called Jean did something very strange then. She smiled. "I like your dress," Jean said, smiling with approval. "Mind if I ask who made it. Jasper Conran, Gucci maybe? I'm in the dress business myself, but I don't recognize the cut."

Shirley caught her breath, reached up and touched her necklace. The woman hadn't run away once she had had a real look at Shirley's face. She hadn't reflected a look of horror back at Shirley.

"It fits you well, the dress," Jean said.

"I ... I made it myself."

Jean's mouth fell wide open. "You are kidding. Really?"

Shirley nodded, still not sure of herself—or of this woman's reaction to her.

"Are you in the design business? A designer? My God, that is one wonderful dress, and the fit ... I'm lost for words. Are you in the retail trade, because I could do with some of those for my line of business? I mean it. I am impressed," Jean enthused as she began to slowly circle Shirley. "It's a perfect fit. And you really made this—I mean designed it and everything?"

Shirley nodded her head uncertainly.

"From scratch?" Jean asked. "The whole works?"

"Yes ... from beginning to end," Shirley said. "I draw them in my spare time, then make my own patterns up and well, choose the material and ... somehow pin it and sew it all together."

"Can I?" Jean asked, reaching out.

"Well ... yes."

"Real silk?" Jean gasped. "Of course it is. You must have a lot of admirers. What do your friends say? What does anyone say?"

But Shirley could only smile sadly. She didn't really want to remind herself. She shook her head. "I wouldn't even have worn it on the trip, but I didn't think I would get another chance otherwise. So I thought I would take the chance to wear it now, in the middle of the night while no one was around." A perplexed look fell across Jean's face.

She took a step back. "Normally, after I'd made one," Shirley said, "I would wear it for a little while in the flat. But that's all. At home, never outside."

Jeans face softened. "You're hiding?"

But all Shirley could do was look at Jean, then away, saying nothing. Wasn't it obvious?

Suddenly Jean began to look around. "I wish they put more ashtrays out on deck," she said. "Oh, to hell with it," she said, flicking what was left of her cigarette over the side. "Ecology smollogy. One won't hurt. Not that I make a habit of it."

Shirley laughed.

"That was funny?" Jean laughed back.

"I don't know," Shirley said. "But maybe it's because someone likes one of my creations."

"There's more?" Jean said.

Taken aback, Shirley nodded vigorously, pressing herself backwards, arms out along the handrail behind her. "Sorry," Jean said, smiling, stepping back. "I didn't mean to startle you." Jean seemed to think for a second, then: "Did you have formal training in dress design, making? Anything like that?"

"No," Shirley said. And already there was warmth flowing through her.

"Nothing?" Jean asked. Shirley shook her head. "And no one else has seen this, or your others?"

"Uh-huh."

"My God, woman, you are a walking goldmine and you don't even know it! I go to London and scour for dresses, designs, something half decent that will fit my clients in all the right places, and all I can say is that this is the first time that I have ever seen something that fits so perfectly. I mean it is so *feminine*!"

Shirley felt goosebumps rise on her arms. She rubbed at them, not knowing if it was because of what Jean was saying, or because of the breeze. "It's getting a bit chilly," she said.

"Are you sleepy, tired?" Jean asked. "I mean, I know it's late and everything, and hell, half the time I'm only alive at night anyway, up all night filling orders or just trying to keep the business afloat, you know. Selling, I can do, but the books? Ugh! Well ... What I'm trying to say is, could we maybe go inside and talk a little more."

Shirley raised her eyebrows. "Yes ... why not?" she said.

"Great! There's one of those self-serve coffee machines by the reception. We could sit and talk there for a while. That is, if you don't mind."

"I think that would make me very happy, Jean," Shirley said. "Yes."

They walked along the deck towards one of the doors, Jean doing most of the talking, hooking her arm through Shirley's.

"Can I say something?" Shirley said.

"Yes, love?"

"I am a man," she said. "I mean, a real man, all the plumbing under all of this."

"Even better," Jean said, not letting up her stride.

"You don't mind?" Shirley asked.

"No, love, why would I mind? And it's incredibly sexy."

~~*

Jamie came back, holding his hands out and clutching the coffees. He placed one down carefully on the table in front of Alex, then sat next him in one of the seats in the shadows at the edge of the auditorium.

The swell of the waves came and went under them, up and down like a slow roller coaster and just as exhilarating. The windows were dark. But now and again a tiny orange flame glowed in the distance from an oil platform.

"We can just sit here for a bit," Jamie said as they sat leaning on each other in the second row with a view of the empty dance floor.

But Alex saw them all: passengers dancing, the entertainment acts in between, the lights, the smiles, the clapping and cheering, the families, the mums and dads, the children running around. Everyone together.

And suddenly, he was happy again. He reached out and put his arm over Jamie's shoulder and looked at him.

Neither said anything, just smiled into the darkness and listened to the silence, wishing for the ferry to keep on sailing forever, and for Alex to never let go of the silver ring that Jamie had placed on his finger.

CHAPTER 41

"A room with a view," Shirley said, looking out the porthole at the flames lighting up the night sky.

"Oil rig," Jean said, standing beside her. Shirley turned to her and smiled.

Jean handed her one of the drinks she had just poured. "Scotch?"

"And soda, but no ice, I'm afraid."

Shirley smiled again wrinkling up her nose. "Better without," she said.

"We have more in common than I thought," Jean said as she tapped her plastic cup to Shirley's. "Like to see some of my new designs?"

"Why my dear, of course I would," Shirley said.

Jean sat down on the small sofa and Shirley sat beside her. "It gets harder and harder to find anything decent these days," Jean said, taking the black folder from the table next to her. "They're either outrageous and covered in ostrich feathers or duller than dull. Nothing in between, if you know what I mean."

Shirley looked at the illustrations.

"And if there is anything decent, nothing fits in the right places," Jean said. "That's the problem. I would make them myself, but I'm no designer, and I'm no seamstress either. Even if I could find one, I doubt she would know what they were really for."

Shirley picked up the folder, turning the pages. "See what I mean?" Jean said, crossing her legs. "It's either dresses for the ugly sisters or some skinny bitch like Kate Moss. I sometimes wonder if I'm running a pantomime shop and fancy dress business rolled into one, which it is, but that's just a sideline really. Funnily enough, the customers seem to be more comfortable with it that way. The real stuff is in the back, what they really come in for.

But when I look at this lot," she said, nodding at the designs, "I'm surprised they buy anything."

"That's why I started making my own," Shirley said almost as a throwaway comment.

Jean refilled Shirley's glass. "What I really need is a designer," Jean said. "Someone who knows what's needed. Not something that looks more suited to a horror movie. But something real, elegant, womanly."

Shirley didn't say anything.

"Have you ever thought of going into business," Jean asked.

"Business?"

"Yes, business."

"I think it's everyone's dream to have their own business," Shirley said.

"How about partnership?"

Shirley raised her eyebrows. Jean sat down and faced her. "Look," she said, "there's no good me beating about the bush here, if you pardon the expression, but if I'm going to say it, I might as well say it now. We met. We might never meet again. And if we don't, then everything will be lost."

"Continue," Shirley said, taking a sip of whisky. It was her turn to cross her legs.

"I don't know what line of work you're in," Jean said. "I don't know where you are in life, either, or what your plans are. But I can guess from the way you're dressed that you're searching for something. But before you say anything else—" Jean raised her hand, "—what I am trying to say is, would you consider going into business with me. No, don't say anything yet. I have a business in Hamburg, not huge, not at the moment anyway. And I know there is a market out there. Sometimes I have customers coming in from all over Europe. But something isn't quite right. I need designs, real designs, and not some compromise off-the-peg numbers they could buy at M and S that don't fit them anyway. And I'm not asking for money. The business ticks over, just anyway. What I am asking for is something far more valuable. I need someone with a talent for design, who knows what she's doing, and with commitment. What do you say?"

Shirley was taken aback. "But we've only just met," she said. "We don't even know each other.

Jean reached out and placed a hand on Shirley's thigh. "I think we know each other enough already," she said.

CHAPTER 42

Jamie woke up to sunlight streaming through the porthole, thinking, *Where am I?*

Alex was already showered and dressed and moving about the cabin. "We've got another hour before we land," he said.

Jamie swung his legs over the side. "Dock, you mean."

"Whatever," Alex said, busying himself with his rucksack.

"I need a fag." Jamie yawned, climbing down from the top bunk then sitting on the lower.

And there he watched as Alex took out the small kettle, the cups, coffee and dried milk. Jamie blinked. "I was going to keep this for the hotel," Alex said, "but I don't want to have another fight with that machine upstairs.

"Well," Jamie sighed, "I'll still have to go up on deck for a smoke anyway."

Alex dropped two Nambarri tea bags into a little plastic cup.

"When did you get all that stuff?" Jamie asked.

"Needs must, Jamie."

"I'll still have to ..." He trailed off as Alex plugged a small black contraption into the electric razor socket and screwed in a little white tube. "What's that?" Jamie asked.

Alex poured water into the two little cups then spooned in powdered milk. He gave Jamie his tea. "That," Alex said, pointing to the little black contraption with the white tube sticking out of it, "is an electric cigarette."

Jamie nearly burnt his tongue on his tea. "What?"

Alex went over to the contraption, unscrewed the tube and screwed another white tube to it. "An E-fag," he said. He handed it to Jamie. "You suck that end and pure nicotine belches out. And none of the usual poisons that go with a real cigarette either."

Jamie sucked at it and choked. "Dear God!"

"And it doesn't leave a honk either," Alex said. "Or set off alarm bells in smoke detectors."

A green Jamie wheezed. "Is it legal?"

"It even glows orange it the end as well," Alex said. "Just like a real cigarette. So you can smoke it to your heart's content without the risk of being arrested."

And after fifteen minutes of smoking and choking and barfing his lungs down the super sucker toilet, Jamie finally managed to inhale without his face exploding. "I'll get the hang of it eventually," he squeaked.

"So you don't have to stand out in the bucketing rain just because you're an addict," Alex smiled at his own ingeniousness.

They were both dressed and showered by the time land came into view.

"They're still wringing," Alex complained, lifting his wet jeans off the showerhead.

An arm thrust in the open doorway, hand clutching a plastic bag. "Shove them in here," Jamie said. "They can dry off when we hang them up in the hotel."

Alex took the bag and made some yuck comments as he dropped his wet jeans into it and tied the top closed with a big knot. "I just hope it doesn't leak, that's all I'm saying," he said.

"You were a fair goer last night," Jamie said. "My ark is still sore. Just hope nobody notices me walking bandy legged."

"You complaining like?" Alex asked, stepping out of the shower cubicle.

Jamie grabbed the bag off him, dumped it into another and tighten it closed, dropped it into his own rucksack and stood up straight, grinning. "No, I'm no complaining," he said. "But I think I'll have to take some paracetamol for bum ache."

Alex laughed. "What time's it now?" he asked.

"Seven o'clock," Jamie said.

"Think the breakfast bar will be open?"

"Eating again!"

"Coffee," Alex said. "Might as well have one of their overpriced ones. I'll forgo my eating for now. Anyway, I want to go up own deck in see us getting into the harbor."

Alex saw the look on Jamie's face. "Don't worry," Alex said. "I'll be all right."

"Never said you wouldn't."

"Anyway," Alex said, "I took something for it last night." Jamie gave him a sharp look. Alex held up a little brown bottle. "I took one after you fell asleep," he said. "If for nothing else they helped me to clonk out." He yawned and stretched.

"I thought you didn't take them anymore," Jamie said, busying himself clicking the straps of his rucksack into place.

"I don't, no normally, no these days," Alex said. "But considering what happened yesterday to me up on deck, I would be irresponsible involving anybody else again in what's my problem."

"I thought you had left them it home," Jamie said.

"No, Jamie. I found them in your pocket. But for now, let's no go there. I know I shouldn't have been looking in your clothes, but I was praying you had had more sense than me and picked them up from the flat. I'm grateful to you, Jamie, because I know I'm no always great at knowing what I'm needing for my own good. I hope you forgive me for raking through your pockets, though."

Jamie walked up to Alex and gave him a peck on the cheek. "Let's just say I'm glad you did," he said.

Alex gave Jamie a guilty smile. "Come on, then," Alex perked up. "Let's fulfill our mutual addictions."

Jamie laughed, happy to see Alex smiling. "Coffee in cigarettes," Alex said.

"Coffee in electric cigarettes indoors," Jamie said.

After breakfast they rushed back to the cabin to finish packing. "Quick, we've only got half an hour!" Jamie yelled.

Rucksacks re-stuffed, they left the cabin again. Alex took one last look inside, the bunks, the shower room, the ladder, the little sofa and the table, the little radio and its dials on the back wall.

It all meant so much, though he didn't know why.

Passengers and mountains of multicolored luggage and smartly dressed uniformed staff speaking into walkie-talkies, converged on the upper deck. The passengers stumbled around, heavy bags in tow, chattering in different tongues.

German, mostly, as far as Alex could make out. Greek and Chinese as far as Jamie could fathom.

The crew, smartly dressed as ever in black and white, glided through the passengers as if guided by some mysterious force.

There was a child-like excitement in Jamie's belly. Dread in Alex's. A new exotic land awaited Jamie, the same way he felt about England. A fearful, out-there-place. As far as Alex was concerned, however, it was as scary as Kelty beach at midnight.

Suddenly, the doors opened and everyone began to shuffle forward in a crush, shoulder-to-shoulder, pushing their way through until they became enclosed inside a metal caterpillar for a ramp.

A faint smell of diesel filled the air. The crowd thinned out. Alex felt queasy with the way the ramp bounced around underfoot. Jamie beamed in delight, jaunting his way along. Not too fast though. He didn't want to leave Alex too far behind.

Alex huffed up with his rucksack. Jamie stopped and helped him with it, and Alex gave him a wan smile.

"You can dump your bag on that if you want," Jamie said to Alex, pointing to the conveyor belt running down the side.

It would be a short-term measure, but at least he could try and forget the next seventy miles they still had to go to get to Hamburg. Never mind the next seventy feet.

To Alex, everyone looked self-assured, as if they knew everything there was to know. To Jamie, the excitement was not in the full knowing.

The ramp steepened, and as it did so, Alex took a look out through the windows. His stomach lurched when he saw how high up they were. He kept his eyes on his rucksack rolling down the conveyor after that. Then he took one last glance out the windows, into the clear blue sky and sunlight.

The ferry looked a lot bigger than he remembered before they had first boarded it, and he wondered at how the thing managed to stay afloat. Yet there was something monstrous and magnificent about it at the same time. And he wondered if anyone else ever thought the same as he looked at the enormous letters *DFDS Seaways* emblazoned on the side of the hull.

Soon enough they were on terra firma, on the edge of the dock. Solid ground at last. Alex's heart lifted as he hitched up his rucksack again, the full weight of it nearly breaking his arms. Again Jamie helped. The padded straps still dug deeply into Alex's shoulders as it was hoisted it higher.

Out from under cover now, the full early morning sun beat down on them. A mild stinging covered the skin of their faces where it hit.

Something funny happened then. Alex turned slightly, looking round at the ferry. They were in a foreign country, yet it didn't feel that way.

Then he remembered the old history lessons from school. How could a place that felt so familiar have ever become such an enemy? And as the other passengers moved on by, their voices fading, accents nothing but a chatter of white noise, Alex realized he could have been anywhere back home.

He shook the strange feeling from his head.

"How are you, pal?" Jamie asked him with some concern.

A bit like a bird trying to fly with a broken wing, Alex wanted to say as he adjusted the straps of his rucksack.

"I'm all right," he said. "Don't worry so much about me. I'm fine. Honest."

Jamie didn't think Alex sounded like it, but he left it at that as they walked through what had once been Passport Control. Now it was nothing more than a long desk, redundant, running down the middle of a wooden enclosure.

There was something weird about walking into another land so freely. And there was something even stranger in that they had had to be checked before being allowed to leave their own, and yet not at all when crossing the border into another one.

Once outside, a mild breeze struck up, easing the sting of the sun on their arms and faces. Some passengers moved away, some stood around for the bus that would take them to the local railway station.

Soon enough, Alex and Jamie would be heading there too. But for now, Alex didn't want to be in such a rush to get going.

He stopped and rested. Jamie pulled back.

"What is it?" Jamie asked.

"It feels funny, that's all," Alex said, looking around.

For all the people who had been rushing to get off the ferry, few seemed to be standing around now, and there was a kind of vacuous silence approaching. Within a few minutes, everyone had dispersed, leaving Alex and Jamie on their own.

"Funny?" Jamie asked.

"Can't think of how to describe it," Alex confessed. "Maybe I just thought it would feel a lot more different."

"More foreign?"

"Aye," Alex piped up enthusiastically.

"Know what you mean," Jamie said, looking around at the deserted canals, the waiting tugs and small boats and barges, the key sides, the lochs. The name: Cuxhaven.

"Where's the rail station?" Alex asked suddenly.

Jamie shrugged. "No sure," Jamie said. "We'll have to look it the map again. It can't be that far, though. Maybe we should go back around the corner in wait for a bus to take us to it."

Alex blinked up at the sky. "Nah," he said. "The day's too good to be hanging about for buses. I have enough of them back home. Let's walk for a bit."

"What about your backpack?"

"What about it?" Alex asked.

"Looks over heavy to me. I don't want my laddie dropping dead from over exhaustion."

"Hey, I'm no a wimp, you know," Alex pointed out light heartedly.

"Never said you were."

"Let's get going then," Alex said, striding past. "Station can't be that far. Cuxhaven's only a wee bit of a place from what a read onboard."

Jamie noted that Alex's legs looked to be a little under strain, but shrugged and followed on.

"Christ how far away is this bloody station?" Alex whined.

"I told you we should have waited for the bus!"

"Don't go on it me. God, that's all I need." Alex slipped the rucksack from his shoulders, letting it crash to the ground. "And I'm dying for a coffee as well."

"Aye," Jamie said. "Must be a whole quarter hour since you last had one. Getting cranky with withdrawal are you?" he said before taking another drag on his cigarette.

Alex ignored him, stood up straight and rubbed at his shoulders. "Where is it?" he asked.

"Where's what?"

"The bloody station. Are you dense? We've been going round in circles for forty billion years."

"We only got off the boat fifteen minutes ago!"

Alex dumped himself down on his rucksack, slamming his backside down onto it. "Station! Where? Find it!" he yelled. "Look at your map. Damn heat. I'm boiling. It's like the Gobi Desert. I knew I should have stayed at home. It's a disaster. It's ..."

"Round the corner," Jamie said.

"How'd you know?" Alex said. "You haven't even looked it the map yet."

"Because," Jamie said, "I can see it from here, that's how."

CHAPTER 43

The train stopped at Hamburg. Alex and Jamie lurched to the right then the left as it came to a standstill. Alex was first to jump down onto the platform and look around. Everything looked the same, similar anyway, to any station back home.

But the signs were foreign. *(No. Really?)*

He stood still as commuters flowed around him. He adjusted his rucksack, cursing its weight under his breath as he picked at the straps. But it was no good. In the end it still looked squint, sagging to the left.

Jamie stepped onto the platform and looked around. He was a little more apprehensive than Alex perhaps, but there were things to be done. At least the clock looked the same as the ones back home, with big black hands. And they didn't run backward.

He breathed a sigh of relief for that.

As everyone was moving in the same direction, he decided to act smart, as if he knew what he was doing, and followed everyone else.

Alex glared at him. He was in a half-shut knife position, the strain of the rucksack on his back. Jamie raised an eyebrow and wanted to say, 'told you so'. But … this was a moment that called for delicacy.

Around the back of Alex once again, he cupped his hands under the bottom of the rucksack and hefted it upward. Until Alex stumbled forward and almost smashed his kisser onto concrete.

"What are you doing!" Alex yelped.

"Oops!"

Alex tut tutted and straightened himself up as best he could. Back killing him or no, he was determined to show he had the strength of his convictions for wanting a fridge-sized contraption on his back.

"Moving stairs," he said, cocking his head towards the escalator.

Without another word, and barely a pause in thought, Jamie headed off first. Inside, his guts were coiling in on themselves. Fear of the unknown.

Before alighting the escalator, he turned and looked back. Alex was right behind him.

"After you, know all," Alex said.

Jamie took the first step, gripped at the handrail and felt himself being wafted up to heaven covered in black metal struts and grimy glass.

Alex clumped one foot on the lower step then nearly cart wheeled backward to Cuxhaven. Another go and a firm grip, and bingo.

Gravity was so much denser on this moving platform on its way up than if Alex only stood still down below. The g-force pulled at the muscles in his face as if the wind had changed it so many times that it was now impossible for it to unravel itself back to its original state.

Jamie waited at the top with a look of kind concern on his face. Alex looked up at him through his lowered brow and breaking back and a deep-set glare.

As if in fear of a companion about to slither down the sides of the Eiger, Jamie reached out, grabbed Alex by the sleeve, and pulled him onto terra firma before Alex's feet were dragged into the steps on their way back down where he would have been reduced to lumps of mince as the escalator did its never-ending return trip.

Alex stood up straight and sniffed.

He sniffed again: Bacon, ham, bread, pastries, chips. His mouth slobbered at the omniscient aromas.

Suddenly, he found new strength. He straightened up. *Is that coffee I'm smelling*?

"God. What are we in?" he asked. "A food hall?"

The rucksack on his back might well have inflated itself with helium by that point, as Alex's tippy toes seemed to be incapable of touching the ground.

"God I'm starving," he said.

To Jamie, the place was more like a giant trap, one he was willing to go along with for now—anything that kept Alex distracted.

Shop fronts were well-filled with pastries and burgers, breads of every description, and cakes, the likes of which Alex had never seen, and which were proving a stronger magnet than his pig-iron will of resistance to food.

More than once Jamie had to pull Alex away and remind him that they didn't have much time to find their hotel, being late enough as it was. But Alex seemed to care not a whit, floating along as if on a sea of sugar and iced doughnuts freshly fried and sodden with jam.

"I need to eat!" he snapped as, once again, Jamie yanked at his arm.

"*After* we find the hotel!"

It was like moving through a baffle zone, buffeted from one side to the other by cakes, buns, pastries smothered in icing, gateaux of the darkest red raspberry jam and thick with cream too hard to resist. Alex was in a dreamland that he'd never been in before.

One last push from Jamie and Alex was under the awning outside the station. Distracted to the last, both stood stock-still, frozen in fear.

Oh!

My!

God!

They were surrounded by skinheads with grey hair and wearing black jerkins that had seen better days, with Rottweilers and Mastiffs and every other demon dog to be had. The skinheads stood, smoking and drinking. The smell of urine wafted up as dead cigarette ends—or as Alex might say, funny fag smoke.

The rucksack on Alex's back begin to keel to the left. Jamie could hear the old tin cups hanging from the ark end of his rucksack clonking in time with his quaking legs.

Alex spoke through the right side of his mouth at Jamie; Jamie through the tight-lipped left side of his own. Alex spoke first. "Whatdowedonow?" (Or as Alex really said it: Whoatdaywihdaynoo?)

"Don't move," came the short whispered reply from Jamie.

"I can't anyway."

"Do what it says in the guide books," Jamie said.

"What's that?"

"Don't look like a tourist?"

Alex's rucksack slipped further to the left. "Right," he said. Eyes like Clatuu from *The Day the Earth Stood Still*, they scanned to his left. "What now."

"Don't panic," Jamie said.

"I'm no," Alex said.

"Good lad," Jamie said.

"I'm going to kack myself," Alex said.

Jamie reached over, slipped a hand under Alex's rucksack, and just at the right point, nipped Alex bum. Alex jerked. His eyes widened as his cheeks clenched watertight.

"That better?" Jamie asked in all sincerity.

Alex didn't answer.

"Where's the map?" Jamie asked.

"In my pocket," Alex said.

"Get it out then."

"I thought you said we weren't to look like tourists," Alex said.

"We have to find where the hotel is."

Alex didn't move—daren't. So Jamie rifled through Alex's pockets for him.

"Found it," Jamie said a little too loudly.

A Rottweiler turned in Alex's direction. Alex gulped.

Jamie flicked open the map. "Thank God," Jamie said. "The hotel must be miles from this place." He mumbled to himself in his usual manner of concentration. "Steinberger tor ... Steinberger ..." He crumpled the map.

"What is it?" Alex asked. "Did you find it? Is it miles away from this God forsaken dump?"

But all Jamie could do was look blankly ahead, arm rising in the air, finger unfurling. "It's right over there."

Alex followed Jamie's finger, gulped loud enough for the Rottweiler to take another juicy look, push itself up from his haunches and come a sniffing. Tail wagging, it sniffed away at Alex's crotch, round the side and at Alex's juicy bum.

"I'm meat!" Alex stepped away in a delft move.

"Get a grip," Jamie said. "It's wagging its tail, yah wimp."

Alex shot a glance at him. "And what makes you so brave all of a sudden?" he asked.

Jamie didn't answer. Instead, he walked off out from under the awning, past the skinheads and their friendly soppy demon dogs, and into the early evening sun. He looked at his watch. Five fifteen p.m.

He would have looked over his shoulder, but his rucksack was in the way, so he did a sort of half-turn to see Alex following. When Alex had caught up, Jamie told him that the hotel was in Briemer Reihe, on the street opposite. The hotel was not far from there, just up a bit on the left. Hotel Mercure.

Just as Jamie was about to step across the road, Alex dragged him back. "It's illegal here," he said.

"Eh?"

"We'll have to cross over it the lights up there," Alex said, pointing and staggering off.

"What for?" Jamie called out after him, giving up and following.

"Because it's illegal to jay walk in Germany. Do you know nothing?"

It was the first chink in the armor that Alex would spring on Jamie. And perhaps not the last.

Even though the road was empty, not a bus, car, or tram in sight, pedestrians stood at the curb, and waited dutifully until the lights changed to the wee green man.

Once over the other side, Alex strode off in front of Jamie as if he were a native.

CHAPTER 44

Rucksacks wobbling from side to side, their knees at their best El Collapso bandy legit stance, the pair zipped around the corner and into the relative safety of Bremer Reihe, where the sense of relief was instantaneous.

"What's it called again?" Alex asked.

"Eh, Hotel Mercure," Jamie said.

Alex craned his neck left and right. "There it is." He pointed to a sign sticking out on their side of the road. His legs were on the verge of crunch.

Face to face with glass doors, they stood looking in. "Right," Alex commanded, "you first."

"Me?" Jamie screeched.

"You booked it. You can deal with it. Now in."

Alex slipped to the back of Jamie and gave him the Dutch courage shove through the doors that he needed. Jamie's foot caught on the step and he trip-hopped his way forward until his face nearly slammed onto the reception desk. He looked up at the guy behind it and smiled weakly.

"Guten tag," the man said.

Jamie straightened himself up and brushed himself down. "Eh, well, aye," he said.

"Get on with it," Alex said.

Jamie slapped at his pockets. "Eh, right. I've got it somewhere."

"Entschuldigung?" the receptionist asked.

Alex stood back, arms folded and glared.

"Well," Jamie began. "You see, we've got a room booked for the two of us. Eh, for foor nixts, like."

The receptionist said nothing and raised his eyebrows.

Jamie turned to Alex. "I don't think he knows what I'm on about, Eck."

"Neither would I outside own Kelty with that accent, yah tube."

"I don't know what to say, though."

In one delft move, Alex snatched the booking form from Jamie's mitt, shouldered him to the side, and slapped it down on the desk. "Mein dom freund, und mich, haben reservieren ein dopple zimmer fur fier nichte."

"Oh ja, aus Shottland?" the receptionist smiled.

"Ja, wir sind Schotte." Alex beamed, face up.

Jamie shrank by the second, eyes wide. He'd just dropped into the Outer Limits of incomprehension, everyone speaking in weird words.

"Ja," the grey-haired receptionist said, jabbing at his ledger. "Ich habe ihren reservieren heir." He pushed a form at Alex. "Unter shreiben Sie ihren name hier, bitte, und ihre addresse, mit ihren postlitzal, und telefonnummer, bitte."

Alex filled in the form as the receptionist picked up the keys from a hook on the back wall.

"Al ist in ordnung," the receptionist said. "Und hier ist ihren schlussel. Die zimmer nummer ist dreihundertzwolf, im dritten stock. Die fahrstuhl ist dort druben."

"Danke," Alex said, snatching up the keys and facing Jamie. "You look like you're about take give birth to a brick."

"You speak German," Jamie said incredulously, trotting after Alex.

"Aye, so?"

"You never told me."

"You never asked." Alex stopped in front of the lift and prodded at the button.

"Where'd you learn it?"

Alex huffed and turned to Jamie. "School, where else?"

"What else have you no told me?"

"I've only known you for six months and I've been alive for eighteen yonkers," Alex said. "How long have you got to listen?"

"Smart ark."

Alex sniffed snootily. "Correct, Jamie, correct."

The lift doors opened and the pair, like tired snails with their homes crumbling on their backs, trotted inside. The lift doors slid shut.

"What floor is the room own?" Jamie asked.

"Third," Alex said, "which in Germany means the second."

"Eh?"

"Ground floor's the first floor in Germany."

"Eh?"

Alex's shoulders sagged. "There's a lot you've got to learn about this place," he said. "Like no crossing the road unless you're at the crossing and other stuff."

"Hmmm."

Cross-browed, Alex turned to Jamie. "Jamie, you're beginning to sound like a straw sucker sitting on a dry-stone-dyke with hay sticking out your ears."

"Eh?"

The lift came to a halt. "Forget it," Alex said stepping out confidently. "Right," he said. "Door nummer zwolf."

"Eh?"

"Twelve."

"Twelve?" Jamie mumbled. "Zwolf?"

"Aye, zwolf," Alex said. "You're catching on."

The deep pile of the carpet made it feel as if they were traipsing over marshmallows.

"Plush, eh?" Jamie sounded amused.

"Better than what we've been used to so far anyway. The place must have coast a bomb," Alex said.

"It was worth it for my laddie," Jamie said with a cheesy grin.

"Eh, hang own there," Alex cut in. "I'm a victim of kidnapping here, unless you're forgetting, kiddo."

Jamie looked crushed. Somehow he had thought that his trickery had been left behind.

"I'm only kidding, yah eejit," Alex said.

Jamie brightened up a bit.

"Well, here it is," Alex said, pushing the key into the lock.

"Zwolf!" Jamie quipped.

The door swung wide. The pair glared in. "Hmmm," Alex said. "Not bad so far." He stepped inside.

"A double bed as well," Jamie said.

"Our bed." Alex let his rucksack slip from his shoulders. "God, it last."

Jamie did the same then walked over to the window. "Hmm, better view than back it home," he said looking out at the trees, ivies and creepers.

Alex walked up and stood beside Jamie. "Looks like a court yard," Alex said. "We must be back of the hotel."

He slipped an arm over Jamie's shoulders, turned and kissed him on the cheek. Jamie blushed.

~~*

"I still feel rotten about what I did to Thelma and Deek," Jamie said

"They'll survive," Alex said. "Anyway. I'm glad you brought me here."

"You mean that?"

"Aye, Jamie, I mean that," Alex said, turning back to the window.

Jamie slipped an arm round Alex waist. Alex went on. "We were all supposed to go to Germany when I was in third year it school," he said.

"What happened?"

"You had to pay something for the trip," Alex shrugged. "But my mum didn't have the money. Still. I did all the rest for the trip though. Learnt some of the lingo and that. I used to think about what it would have been like when I was lying in bed at night. It was to be a boat trip, too. A ferry. Then the day came when all the rest went away. I was heartbroken. But there was nothing for it. So, I just used to think what it must be like."

Jamie pulled him closer.

"Listen to me, feeling sorry for myself," Alex said.

"No, laddie. You're no feeling sorry for yourself. I know what it's like when you get yourself all worked up, looking forward to something, and then at the last minute it doesn't happen."

"I'm sorry, Jamie," Alex said "I wasn't thinking there. You must have had more disappointments than me considering the things you had to go through with all the homes you were in."

"Maybe we're even own that score," Jamie said. "But there's nothing to stop us now, is there? There's nobody with keys to our lives now. Just us."

Alex bowed his head. "I wanted to go on that trip so much, Jamie. And all I kept thinking about was how I could maybe make some money myself so that I could go. But, well, nothing but a dream. Didn't get there." He turned to Jamie. "Except now," he said. "Thanks, Jamie. You made my dream come true and you didn't even know."

Jamie explained that he had never been abroad either. Summer holidays were spent hiking in the highlands. It was all the homes could afford. Still, it had been fun, the camping, pitching the tents.

"Midges were murder though," he said. "And rain as well. We were drookit and miserable half the time, we were. But at least I got myself my Duke of Edinburg award."

Alex gazed out the window, at the trees and the ivies, everything green, alive, free.

"Alex?" Jamie said.

"Mmm?"

"Where are you, pal?"

Alex didn't answer for a second as he continued to gaze out the window.

"Alex?"

Alex took a breath. "I made friends with someone at school once. Well, a sort of friend," he said in a faraway sounding voice.

"Who was he?" Jamie asked.

"He was a she," Alex said, leaning on the windowsill, "and her name was Morag." Jamie's eyebrows shot up.

"Respite, they call it," Alex said. "Morag was disabled, you see, and her mother wasn't that well herself that summer. So Morag spent the first couple week's school holidays inside an institution. A carer from the home had taken her out for the day and that's how I first met her. After that, I used to go in everyday and take her out. A good laugh she was too, though it was hard shoving that wheelchair of hers at times. Spina bifida she had. We used to talk to each other about things, things we'd never dare tell anybody else, secrets: like what we wanted to happen when we grew up."

Jamie put a hand on his shoulder.

"I never did know what happened to her," Alex went on. "One day she just wasn't there anymore. It was as if she'd never existed in the first place and that was that. Out of sight." He turned from the window and looked at Jamie. "At least I knew I had a chance to make my dreams come true, Jamie."

Alex and Jamie held each other close as they looked down at the courtyard at the back of the hotel.

"Morag used to tell me all her dreams," Alex said. "About having a bairn, a house with a wee garden. But she never would. She knew that. No with the state she was in, anyway. At least she thought so. Then one day she admitted to me that, even if she did have a bairn, no that any guy would fancy she said, her being crippled like, she would be scared that they, the social workers, would take her bairn away from her. I didn't think they would, but she was convinced."

"What happened to her then?"

But all Alex did was shrug. "Like I said, Jamie, she disappeared. There one day, gone the next."

They stood in silence for a few moments longer before turning away from the window and exploring their room.

The pressure was off, the pressure was on. They zipped around the room, opening drawers, cupboards, peering inside, making comments like "mmm, it's not bad." And when it came to the little table in the corner in front of the window, from Alex it was "but shoogly, but it'll do."

Only something magical happened the moment he touched its wooden surface. Something so subtle he didn't even notice it until he had let go of its edge and start to turn away as Jamie went into the bathroom to explore its interior.

Alex turned back, reached out, and touched the table's surface. A nondescript thing it was, with chipped edges and a little wooden chair in front of it and the view out the window.

He saw himself sitting there, as an old man, content, his life almost over, but happy in memories, a pad of paper in front of him, his pen poised, the lines filled with his writing. Only it didn't seem to come to him as a dream, but something from the future yet felt, as if it was a memory.

"Shower and bath!"

Alex ripped his hand away from the table when he jumped at Jamie's words.

"What's up with you?" Jamie asked. "You look as if you've seen a ghost."

Alex didn't answer. Couldn't answer. Didn't know how to explain what he had felt just then when he had touched the cheap wooden desk. The thing was that he knew that ghosts came from the past, if even such things existed. But what Alex had felt, saw in his mind's eye, wasn't from the past, but from somewhere that hadn't happened yet. From someone's future. He just didn't know whose.

Soon they were out in the street, under the full early evening sunshine, clutching leaflets and maps.

"Better circle it on the map or we'll never find our way back," Jamie said, his old skills coming back.

They ate pom frits mit ketchup on the hoof and a hotdog or two on the way.

"Says here Hamburg's got more bridges than Amsterdam." Jamie tapped at the leaflet.

"But there are bridges and bridges," Alex commented. He could only imagine the delicate little hump-backed numbers in Amsterdam against these great, clod-hopping cast-iron things.

They visited the gigantorific harbor, and oo'd and aah'd at the colossal size of it all, at the museum ships, the paddle steamers, the Elbe River. Although, truth be told, the harbor was more a canal, seeing as the city was seventy kilometers inland. But it still looked like a harbor.

Then it was more hotdogs and chips smothered in ketchup.

"Couldn't be on a diet in this place could you, Jamie," Alex said, stuffing his face.

"No you anyway," Jamie said.

Then it was more cigarettes and coffee as pensioners on inline skates scooted past. Jamie nearly choked when he saw them.

And unlike in London, where there were barriers to fight through on the underground, none existed in Hamburg, no one to check their tickets either.

They stopped off at St Pauli, climbed the steps and entered the park, deserted except for the two of them. Everything was perfect as they sat in the sun at the little café.

A little tired. A little dazed. Peace, quiet. Safe.

Until the helicopters arrived.

CHAPTER 45

First one, then two, then four, until neither could hear the other talk as the helicopters zoomed overhead, then back again, hovering over their heads.

Their questions were lost in the racket of the copter blades. Copters and sirens.

Jamie and Alex left the park in a rush and headed back out to St Pauli where the traffic had come to a standstill. They headed down towards the river Elbe, past cars and buses standing in line and made their way to the harbor again. What they didn't see was the yellow police tape being strung from side to side behind them barring the way back out.

Unconcerned and with more curiosity than sense, they made their way to the paddle steamer pickup point.

Crowds had gathered, having been forced into such a small area. The helicopters continued to hover. Then the police moved in.

Hundreds of them.

"The only place on the planet where we can see that pigs really can fly," Jamie shouted above the din.

All in green, padded to hell, and in what looked like crash helmets, the police milled around the bemused crowds. It was only then that Jamie took a look back and saw the yellow police tapes strung across the road behind them.

"I think we're trapped," he said. But his words were lost under the hovering whirlybirds overhead.

Alex stretched his neck. "Can't see a damn thing," he yelled.

Excitement mixed with dread in the pit of Jamie's stomach and he wished he hadn't eaten so much.

Without further ado, Alex squeezed through the crowd to get a better view of what was going on. Jamie followed, hand on Alex's shoulder in case they lost sight of each other.

A green truck like thing pulled up. Jamie gulped when he looked at the top of the thing as it came to a standstill: Water cannons!

"Eck!"

But Alex wasn't listening, or he couldn't or wouldn't listen.

"Eck!"

"What!"

"They're riot police!"

Alex looked around. "Riot police?"

"Aye, look, over there." Jamie pointed excitedly at the water cannons jutting out from the top of the truck.

"But it's nothing but us and hundreds of pensioners waiting to get on the paddle steamers," Alex yelled.

"What's that got to do with anything?" Jamie screamed back. "Maybe they're all terrorists or something."

But Alex didn't answer and instead made his way further down until they were at the waterfront. The crowds had thinned; the police stood around, smiling.

"I don't get it," Jamie said.

"Hey, this is exciting," Alex replied.

"Exciting?" Jamie screeched in terror.

"Come on," Alex said. "We'll go this way."

And off Alex marched, through what was left of the crowd, through the police who seemed more interested in just standing around doing nothing. No one stopped Alex or Jamie from going forward. It was going back the way they came that was the problem.

After a little while, Alex dumped himself down on the waterfront wall, legs swinging.

"Wonder what's going on?" he said more to himself.

"I don't know," Jamie said. "But it's weird."

"Keep your drawers on," Alex said. "It's not like we're being attacked, is it? Must be something though."

A helicopter zoomed over their heads and over the Elbe River into the distance.

"Can say that again," Jamie said, dumping himself on the wall beside Alex.

Alex looked at the map, turned it this way and that. "We're here." Jamie jabbed at the map.

"All, right. So, if we go this way ..."Alex said.

"We can't," Jamie said. "They've blocked off the road. We're stuck."

Alex sniffed, peered closer at the map. "We'll go this way then," he said.

"Where?" Jamie asked.

"Up there. To the Fischmarkt." Alex folded the map, handed it to Jamie, and jumped off the wall. "Come on," he said. "This way."

Jamie stuffed the map into his back pocket, jumped off the wall and followed Alex. Every hundred yards Jamie looked back to find that more police tape was blocking their way back.

It grew quieter the further they walked, too quiet for Jamie. He could even hear the grit crunching under their feet as they made their way up the steps and into ...

The Hood.

Only then did Alex slam to a halt.

But it was too late. More police tape appeared behind them from out of nowhere. One of the policemen, dressed in riot gear of green and black armor, and who strangely reminded Jamie of RoboCop, beamed a brilliant white smile down at him.

Jamie gulped.

Not looking where he was going, he crashed into the back of Alex.

"What's wrong? What have you stopped for?" Jamie whispered into Alex's ear. Jamie kept one of his eyes on RoboCop, who was standing at ease a few yards away whilst his other eye went berzerk with fear.

Alex finally came to his senses. "I'm no going in there."

"I think we'll have to," Jamie said.

Alex turned and took a few steps back. But RoboCop wasn't having anything to do with it. He smiled wider, flashing whiter teeth, and shook his head slowly side.

"I think he's trying to tell us something," Jamie said.

They turned around slowly to ...

The Hood.

Scaffolding, rusted, green netting hanging and ripped, paving that was dusty and smashed.

"Oh God!" Alex said.

"Where's this Fish Market place then?" Jamie asked.

"Through there, I think." Alex pointed.

"It would have to be."

Each step was deliberate, well thought out, and ever forward.

Punks in black jerkins appeared out of nowhere, standing around nonchalantly. Rottweilers sat at their feet. Skinheads in green jerkins did the same. Some of them hung out of the derelict buildings. No one said anything. Everything was turning preternaturally quiet.

"Don't say anything," Alex whispered at Jamie from the side of his mouth.

"No intention to," Jamie replied. *Murder country*, he thought to himself.

Alex caught sight of a younger and older skinhead standing side by side, an Alsatian at their feet. The younger skinhead winked at Alex.

"Cheeky bugger," Alex said.

"Eh?" Jamie asked catching up.

"Eh, nothing," Alex said, looking back at the young, handsome skinhead, who winked again and smiled.

"Hmm," Alex let slip.

"What are you hmmming at?" Jamie asked.

"Awe, nothing," Alex replied with a renewed spring in his step.

He looked back again over his shoulder. The young skinhead waved.

Jamie bashed Alex on the shoulder. "Hey, what's going on?"

Laughter behind them.

"Nothing wrong with a bit of window shopping," Alex said.

"There is when I'm here," Jamie snapped.

Alex slung his arm over Jamie's shoulder. Reaching down Alex's back Jamie squeezed at his left ark cheek, looked over his shoulder, and stuck his tongue out at the older and younger skinheads.

More laughter followed.

Getting to the other side of the area was like stepping out of a pressure cooker. Jamie sat on the steps; Alex joined him.

Jamie lit up a cigarette. "Now what?" he asked puffing away. "I'm knackered."

The Fischmarkt stood before them, a desolate red brick building in a deserted neighborhood.

"We go back, shower, shave ..." Alex said.

"Shag?" Jamie asked hopefully.

"... Take a nap then go out. We just have to find a safe way back, that's all."

They stood up, they walked, and Jamie flicked away his cigarette end.

"*Halt!*"

"Act daft," Alex said to Jamie.

"Eh?"

"Act like an eejit," Alex said. "Say *me no understand* or something."

The cop stood like a giant before them. "Was ist Ihren namen?" he asked.

"My name?" Jamie said, turning to Alex.

"Aye, just no your real one," Alex said, smiling at the cop.

"Ihr name?" the cop insisted.

"Eh," Jamie stumbled for words. "Brad Cruise." Alex shot him a look.

"Und Sie," the cop asked Alex as he scribbled in his notebook. "Was ist Ihr name?"

And so Alex blurted out the first name that came into his head. "Tom Pitt!" Jamie laughed. "I couldn't think!" Alex said mortified.

"You're right there. Tom Pitt! Hah!"

"You had me kerfuffled," Alex said. "I don't know what I was thinking."

As it was, the cop let them pass. Obviously they weren't on the most wanted list. And all Jamie could do was double up with laughter as they made their way back. "Tom Pitt!"

"*Sharrap*!"

Once back at the hotel, Alex switched on the television. "Das fernsehen," as he informed Jamie.

Everything was in German, but even Jamie could see what the big story in Hamburg was that day. "All the police in riot gear to move on a couple of squatters and caravans?" Jamie sighed.

"Aye, Jamie," Alex said. "Travelers. Just travelers."

CHAPTER 46

"I think we should just stick to the neighborhood round the hotel when we go out tonight," Alex said, sitting at the desk, the little lamp shining down on the map as he peered in close.

Even so, every now and again he would find his eyes looking out of the window, drawn out to the trees, to the backs of the houses beyond them with their lights flashing on, windows lighting up, shining pale-yellow, then looking up over the rooftops, at the darkening sky. And for the first time, thinking to himself about how different it felt after all to what it felt like back home.

Jamie stepped out of the bathroom rubbing a towel at his hair. "What was that?" he asked.

Alex snapped out of his reverie. "Was just saying I think it would be better if we stuck to the local places," Alex said, twisting round in the chair. "Safer. In case we get lost."

Jamie looked into the mirror above the wash basin, thrusting out his chin. He looked at Alex in the reflection, seeing him sitting there, gazing out the window. "What are you thinking about," he asked.

Alex reacted as if he had just had his ear pinged. "Nothing," he said, quickly folding the map.

Jamie let it go.

They stepped out of the hotel and into the street, quieter now that it was dark. The air was warm.

"Which way?" Jamie asked.

"Eh," Alex started, lifting his right hand, then his left, then right again. "This way," he said.

They walked along, feeling at ease, feeling safe, even as shadows emerged out of doorways then slipped back in again at their passing.

"Who are they, you think?" Jamie asked, leaning into Alex.

"I don't even want to think about that. Here!" Alex said, stopping suddenly.

Jamie stood at Alex's side. Both looked down at the basement. "A bar, you think?" Jamie said in the quiet.

"What else could it be?" Alex answered. "There's only one way to find out."

"You first then," Jamie said.

"Typical," Alex said, his legs quaking as he took the first few steps down. He pushed open the door slowly when he reached the bottom and held it open for Jamie.

"Is it all right to go in?" Jamie asked. "What's it like?"

A hand shot out and garroted Jamie by the collar and yanked him inside. "Take a look for yourself," Alex said, letting go of Jamie's collar and then walking up to the bar and sitting down on a stool.

Jamie caught up and did the same. "Thanks for that, Alex," Jamie said. "I really needed to be embarrassed out of my skull like that."

Alex sniffed. "Don't mention it," he said.

Jamie looked at the bare light bulb hanging by a wire from the ceiling. Then at the few other patrons—no one under a hundred years old, he noted, peering through a cloud of imitation Joop he'd splashed on earlier.

He'd asked Alex what he thought about his aftershave, to which Alex had said, "It's clearing out my sinuses right enough."

Jamie turned to him now. "What are they all looking it us for?" Jamie asked.

"We're strangers," Alex said.

The barmaid walked up to them. "Guten abend meinen Herren. Was darf ist sein?"

"Eh?" Jamie quipped at Alex.

Alex ignored him. "Abend, eh, aye, meine Frau."

"Freut mich." She nodded.

"Eh, aye, you too," Alex said. He turned to Jamie. "What do you want to drink?"

"Eh," Jamie helpfully said.

"They've no got 'Eh'," Alex said. He gave up and turned to the barmaid. "Two, I mean ... Zwo fleischen Bieren, eh, bitte. Aye, zwo bieren."

"Zusammen?" she asked.

"Yeah, aye, together, zusammen," Alex said.

"Welches bier, mein herr?"

Alex was now ready to unravel in a kerfuffle. "Awe, God, Jamie?"

"What?"

"What do you want to drink?"

"Beer!"

"A know that!" Alex growled through gritted teeth. "What kind-duh?"

"*Tennents*!"

"Awe God, save us," Alex sighed. He looked over at the squint fridge behind die Frau and said to her, "Hof, bitte."

"Genau!" she said.

Bottles opened and plonked down on beer mats in front of them, die Frau took a pen out from behind her ear and marked the mats. After that she walked back down to the other end of the bar to talk to her regulars.

Jamie's eyes slitted suspiciously. "Are these free or something?" he said, looking at the two bottles on the bar, then at Alex.

"No, we pay for everything at the end, when we're leaving," Alex said. He picked up his bottle and took a slug. "God! This stuff's strong."

Jamie agreed. After another bottle, Alex needed to go to the loo. They both looked around for it.

"There in the corner, I think," Jamie pointed.

Alex slipped off his stool and toddled off.

Open door, bare light bulb hanging from a strangled wire, sharp intake of breath, instant gag reflex. Splish splash sploosh as feet do an about turn.

Jamie was still sitting at the bar when he heard the footsteps thumping closer. He turned and saw it was only Alex. His heart trip-hammered back to nearer normal.

"What is it?" Jamie asked.

"I'm no going in there," Alex said.

"What's wrong now?"

"It's minging," Alex said, sitting down.

"What's minging?"

"In there," Alex jerked his head to the side.

"What's wrong?"

"It's like a sewer in there," Alex said.

"It is a sewer!"

"It's supposed to be a bog," Alex said.

"What's the difference?"

"Nothing to you obviously, yah pig!" Alex picked up his bottle and glugged it back. He belched then threw some Euros onto the bar top. "We're going," he said slamming the bottle down. Everyone looked down from the other end of the bar at them.

Alex stood up, yanked Jamie's stool out from under him, and said the magic words. "Come on."

Jamie's teeth nearly snapped on the neck of the bottle. "Hey! Watch it!" Jamie said. "You nearly poked my epiglottis into reverse there."

"I don't care. *Oot*!"

CHAPTER 47

Pink and blue bendy neon lights in the window. Nothing else was to be seen.

"Do we go in or what?" Jamie asked.

Alex shrugged. "It can't be any worse than that other place," Alex said.

"After you then, Eck."

"Right," Alex said. "Here goes."

And so on down the steps to below street level again, every footfall taken as if they were negotiating a field of landmines. They came to the door.

"Open it then," Jamie said helpfully.

Alex turned to him, Jamie's face lit up in the pink overspill of neon light. "I'm no sure," Alex said in a whisper.

Jamie gave him a shove and Alex bashed his way through the doors. Jamie followed up quickly and the door swung shut behind him. Airtight and inside they straightened themselves up.

Bleach blonde everywhere. Crash helmet hairdos.

"It's all women," Jamie whispered.

"I can see that, yah gonk," Alex said.

A bleach blonde at the bar sat with her back to them, sipping from a tall glass of fluorescent blue liquid. Alex blinked a few times. If nothing else, the place was very colorful. Sherbet-yellow, lime-green, Day-Glo pink—all the patrons dressed in chiffon ball gowns.

"There's no men," Jamie said.

Alex strode up to the bar, ignoring him, plonked himself down and waited to be served. Sheepishly Jamie drew up a stool and sat beside him.

"What's this place called anyway?" he asked under his breath.

"*Titanic* it says up there," Alex pointed to the sign at the back of the Gantry.

"Titanic?"

"Aye, as in the boat."

"The one that sunk?" Jamie asked. "And what's with every woman in here looking like that old singer Dusty Springfield about?"

"That one over there doesn't," Alex nodded. All in leather, neck to foot, a slim dark haired woman nursed her drink.

A peroxide blonde number in a sea-anemone-eyeball-frazzling-purple ball gown flounced up from the other end of the bar to them.

"Uh oh," Alex said.

"What?"

The barmaid with the peroxide hairdo beamed a set of perfect white teeth through her beard and moustache.

"It's a *bloke*!" Alex said.

"They're in *draaaaaaaguh*!" Jamie said. "I'm leaving."

Alex reached out, grabbed Jamie by the shoulder and rammed him back down onto his stool. "Sit down!"

"Guten abend meinen herren," the blonde beauty said.

"Guten abend meine Frau," Alex greeted her in his politest voice.

"Was morchten Sie?" she asked.

Alex turned to Jamie and asked though a tight smile, eyebrows raised. "What are you having mein freund?"

"Out of here," Jamie said.

Alex turned back to the barmaid. "Zwei flaschen bier, bitte," he said.

And off the barmaid clopped to the refrigerated unit at the other end of the bar, which exploded in cerise pink light as soon as she opened it.

"Right!" Jamie piped up. "Run!"

"Sit on your ark!"

Jamie slammed back down.

Another drag queen punched in numbers at the jukebox and out strained the words of the legendary Dusty.

Everyone joined in.

The barmaid returned, winked at Jamie and placed the two cold bottles of Hof in front of them and went off back down to her friends at the other end.

Everyone joined in a chorus or two with Dusty.

"We're no staying here are we?" Jamie asked.

"Get a grip. Relax."

The dark haired woman leaned into the crowd, listening intently, nodded, then walked away from the bar and stepped up onto the little stage at the back. Everyone clapped politely and Alex looked on in fascination. There was something very familiar-looking about this woman. He just couldn't place his finger on what though. He bit his lip in concentration as someone else tapped at more buttons on the jukebox and another song began.

The dark haired beauty took hold of the microphone and began to sing.

"I know that song," Jamie said.

"You should," Alex said. "It's on that CD you bought me for my birthday."

"Pretenders?"

"Shhh! I'm trying to listen," Alex said, leaning on the bar. It's that song about Mother Earth."

"Awe right. Saw-*ray*. Gosh!" Jamie said, Muppet eyeballs popping. "Could-ah fooled me."

But Alex was lost in the sentiment of it all as the woman sang on, seemingly lost in her own little world.

Alex leaned back and spoke to Jamie. "Shisnobad. For an amateur like." The song ended and the woman bowed her appreciation. "Even looks a bit like her," Alex went on.

"Who?"

"Chrissie Hynde."

"Awe, right."

"Mind you, I could sing better myself," Alex said.

"Aye?"

"Aye."

"I dare you," Jamie said.

"Dare me to do what?"

"Get up there and sing," Jamie said.

"Hmm."

"Go on," Jamie bumped his shoulder into Alex's. "I know you're *dying* to."

"Sing what?"

Jamie jumped up off his stool. "Come on over here to the jukey and see."

Alex followed Jamie as every over-makeup-troweled eye looked on. He looked at the list of songs the jukebox had.

Excitedly, Jamie tapped at the glass. "There," he said, "your favorite one."

"What one?"

Alex climbed onto the stage to polite applause. And when the limelight glared upon him like a starter's pistol, Alex screeched and wailed through Talk of the Town.

"You've CHEEEEYNged … in this wuh-huh-huh-huh-urld. You've cheynged …"

Jamie clapped his hands to his ears. "God almighty!"

The crowd stomped and cheered their appreciation at Alex. Alex took his bows. More claps and cheers. Even the dark-haired beauty raised her glass to him.

Alex floated down the steps, basking in his glory, passed by the Chrissie Hynde lookalike and said to her, "That's how it's *really* done."

The lookalike laughed politely and Alex sat back down next to Jamie. Drinks appeared out of nowhere fast.

"See what talent does for you, Jamie?"

"Watch it or you'll need a crowbar to get your ark out the door," Jamie said.

Alex ignored him, turned and nodded appreciatively to the onlookers. The crowd grew quiet and Jamie pecked Alex on the cheek.

"Ooh la la," one of the drag queens said.

And as Alex and Jamie stood up to leave, everyone clapped and Alex took more than a few bows.

"Come on, while the gong's good," Jamie said.

As they backed their way out the doors a man and a woman pushed in. Everyone collided. Jamie looked up. The man was a woman and the woman was a man. Before he could say anything Alex was already running up the steps and into the balmy still air of the night.

~~*

Jean handed Shirley a tall glass filled with blue.

"What's up?" she asked Shirley.

"That pair we bumped into," Shirley said, looking at the door and back.

"Strangers," Jean said. "No one comes in here without a good reason otherwise."

"No," Shirley said, taking a sip from her glass. "I'm sure I recognized them. They were the two lads from the ferry. The love birds on the dance floor. I'm certain."

"My God!" Jean said. "I think you're right."

CHAPTER 48

Early next morning, in a tangle of arms and legs, Alex wondered where he was.

Jamie rolling over in bed beside him and pulled the pillow over his face, muffling the sound of his words. "Awe God, my head."

Alex dragged himself out from under the quilt. And like a snail waking from hibernation, he got himself onto his feet with his eyes half-shut, and unfurled his arms out in front of him like wilted antennae. Staggering a few steps he clonked into the wall twice before instinctively deciding it was better to feel his way along, via a kind of inbuilt streetwise brail, the skirting board instead, until he finally found out where the bathroom door actually was. Then clawing his way back upright he finally made it into the cubicle where he managed to take a shower without actually drowning himself whilst still standing up.

Thus brought back to life with the elixir of youth that had never left anyway, he approached a snoring Jamie and prodded him in the ribs. "Get up in take a shower," he said. "You're minging"

"In a minute," Jamie groaned.

Alex dragged the covers off Jamie's body."

"What are you on?" Jamie said.

"Get up," Alex said. "We'll miss breakfast."

With that, eyes half-shut, Jamie staggered into the bathroom and shut the door. Ablutions time.

And now that Jamie was safely out of sight, Alex sat at the desk by the window and opened the drawer. Dressed only in shorts, he looked out into the clear morning, thought for a minute and wondered at what he was doing.

He looked down into the open drawer, at the notebook Jamie had given him for his birthday, took it out and placed it on top of the desk. He opened it and picked up the pen as he heard Jamie turn on the shower.

Leaning forward in concentration, not sure of what he was doing, Alex began to write:

Invisible Monsters, Jamie and Alex...

"It's no bad," he mumbled, hunched over the page. "Could be better. But it'll do for now."

And before he knew what he was doing, he was scribbling faster and faster, line after line, and like trickles of water flowing over the lip of an overfull jug of spring water, he wrote each drop, every word, as they poured out of him.

Somehow, it all felt so natural; nothing forced, just on and on, writing about how he and Jamie came to be where they were as he scribbled the words at a furious pace, somehow not wanting Jamie to catch him in the act of writing. It wasn't that he was ashamed of what he was doing. But he didn't want any questions about what he was writing. He didn't want anything to impede what he felt was a natural outflow of emotions, feelings, thoughts and wonders.

After three pages, he closed the cover, snapped the clasp into place, and put the notebook back inside the drawer just as Jamie appeared in the bathroom doorway fresh as a daisy, fighting the aftereffects of Round Up.

His hair was sticking up at the back of his head.

"Shaved?" Alex asked.

"And everything else," Jamie said. "God, I'm knackered. But I'll survive."

They dressed in a rush, gathered up maps and leaflets and money and rushed down the stairs into the breakfast room. There were only a few other patrons there. The windows were open and a cool fresh breeze blew through the blinds.

Alex didn't want much. Just a croissant, butter, eggs, bacon, bratwurst, "Aye, two, I mean zwo, bitte," jam, orange juice, Cornflakes and a roll. "Oh, und café, bitte."

"Just something to keep me gone for a wee bit," he said, turning to Jamie

Jamie had Cornflakes and a cigarette.

And to the strains of Jamie saying, "I don't know how you're no a wee fat get after eating all that," they trotted out into the early morning sunlight.

"Where first?" Alex asked.

"Harbor," Jamie said. "Where else?"

They visited the San Paulo, a permanently docked liner and oo'd at the plush interior. They hired inline roller-skates. Jamie whizzed along as if he had been born wearing them. Alex clomped along on his ankles. Then it was off to the Rathaus.

"For rats?" Jamie enquired.

"Town hall," Alex explained.

There they sat and drank coffee and ate some more as a band played, with the players dressed in traditional German clobber, belting out an oompah oompah number.

Before long they found themselves under the quiet canopy of leaves as they walked through trees, the sunlight all but blocked out, but the air still warm.

Alex stopped before a stone sculpture covered in patches of green algae. Jamie caught up. There seemed to be something sacred about this place.

"What is it?" Jamie asked.

"War memorial," Alex said flatly.

After that, Jamie didn't want to know any more. War was something involving others in far off places in far off times. Something you watched in old black and white films. Not this, not up close and personal.

"It was bad, Jamie, really bad," Alex said, looking up at the memorial.

Jamie saw a faraway look in Alex's eyes. "We bombed everything flat," Alex said. "The Brits did. The whole harbor. Fire storms. More people died of suffocation than anything else. All the air was burned away by the flames, it was that bad. And that caused hurricanes that destroyed everything else. Why do men do it, Jamie? Why?"

"But we didn't start it, Eck," Jamie said quietly.

"Aye, we did," Alex said. "We declared war on Germany. It wasn't them that declared war on us."

"I didn't mean that, Eck. But they did invade Poland, remember?"

And as he said this, Alex shook his head. "A few guys make a decision," Alex said, "and then they get everyone else to kill each other. But these folk—" he pointed at the memorial, "—they weren't even soldiers, Jamie. Just dock workers and their families. Not even a gun between them. Awful."

Alex crouched and plucked a lone daisy from the earth and walked up to the base of the memorial.

"It's not much I know ..." he said as he laid the little yellow flower against the neglected stonework and turned to Jamie. "Never again," Alex said walking away. "Never again."

CHAPTER 49

That night they decided on new territory. They passed by the bars they had visited the night before, although Jamie had to grab at Alex's arm when they closed in on Der Titanic.

"Just one drink," Alex protested.

"No! You'll be up on that stage again. I'm no having it."

And so on they went.

Hookers emerged out of the shadows and the police moved in. Everyone smiled, including the police, Alex noted, and everyone was on first name terms.

They rounded the corner. An older woman emerged from the depths of a darkened doorway and smiled at them. They passed by. Rounding the corner, the street opened up. They were light on foot and smiled a lot.

They came to a stop at the corner. The street was dark and not another soul was around. There were noises coming from within. The clinking of glasses—or was it breaking glass? There was laughter and shouting.

"Sounds lively enough," Alex said to Jamie.

"What'll we do then?" Jamie asked.

"One," Alex said.

"Two," Jamie said.

"GO!"

And straight through the doors they crashed and right into Muscat and Astrakhan, blonde hair and wide open Kolosolashez (because I'm worth it) fluttering under ruby, green and purple lasers ricocheting off silver and gold cigarette holders, a dartboard full of bullet holes that a woman was chucking darts the size of javelins at while two other women arm wrestled in karate outfits as yet another smashed her bare nut through a stack of reinforced breezeblocks while being cheered on by a couple in skimpy white Wimbledon outfits (Martini and Billy Has

Been) brandishing tennis racquets covered in twinkly fairy lights with Katherine Hepburn behind them, cigarette in one hand, golf club swinging through the air in the other as her other half—who was also female—a skinny version of David Beckham (no Posh in tow) bounced a medicine ball in the air with her head. They all were female.

It was fantasy night in the all-woman bar.

"I'm leaving." Jamie spun around.

Alex grabbed his collar. Jamie croaked. "We're in now," Alex said. "So come on."

He squeezed through biceps where there was hardly enough room to squeeze a bus ticket to get to the bar. But the crowd was too thick for them to make it all the way.

A blonde beauty with elastic red lips peered down at him. "Platz?" she asked, poking her cigarette holder into the stratosphere.

Alex wasn't sure. "Platz?"

"Ausländerin!" die frau hollered at the crowd.

Silence. Faces pushed in.

"Und Jungen," she leered in close. "Ich glaube. So ..." She sprang back up.

Jamie cringed behind Alex.

The woman swept her arms wide, fake fur bristling with static, her smile sinking back into dough ball cheeks as she pushed the others aside to make room for Alex. "Meine Herren, freut mich."

Alex plonked himself down and asked Jamie what he wanted to drink, though by the looks of it, there was nothing weaker than petrol and creosote cocktails on offer.

But Jamie was too busy trying to find the escape route to listen.

"Jamie!"

"What?"

"What do you ... Never mind." Alex ordered a coke for both of them.

Jamie smiled weakly up at die ginormous frau and cowered beside Alex. "They're all women, Eck," he said into Alex ear. "I mean real women this time."

"I'm no daft, Jamie," Alex squeezed out the side of his mouth. "Just act natch."

Die frau slammed her elbow down on the bar in front of Alex, flexing her grippers so he could see the cords of steel working in her arm.

"Woher kommen Sie?" Her knuckles crunched.

"Eh, Scotland," Alex eyebrows went up as if he didn't believe it himself.

"Sie sind Schottish!" die frau called out to the crowd again. "Mmmm. Und ich bin Harry Potter's schwester ... " She grinned sucking at her foot-long cigarette holder. "... Pansy. Und Sie?"

"Pansy Potter?" Jamie said to Alex.

"Well, Pansy," Alex said to her. "Ich bin Alex, und dies ist mein man, Jamie."

Die frau behind the bar popped the caps off the bottles with her thumbnails. The caps spun through the air. Another frau caught one of them in her gob, chewed it, swallowed and grinned at Jamie.

Help.

Jamie stood up.

A hand slammed down on his shoulder. "Sitzen."

"Alles ist in ordnung," Pansy said. "Sie sind schwule. Ich denk."

Faces crammed in again to make sure, eyeballs examining the pair. Everyone started talking to each other again.

Alex sipped at his coke demurely. Jamie could hardly swallow. "I think we should go, Eck," he said.

"They're bored with us now," Alex said. "We might is well stay and finish our drinks. How were we to know anyway? Besides, we're harmless. They'll no bother with us if we just sit here."

A fistful of mega-tungsten darts appeared in front of Jamie's eyeballs.

"Spiel?"

"Eh?"

"Play, Jamie," Alex said. "Or we'll never get out …"

"Thanks, Eck."

"… with our heads still on our necks."

Jamie near fainted away.

"Be a man," Alex encouraged Jamie, spreading wide all over the stool beside him like a jellyfish, nothing but great big flat eyeballs looking back up at him. "I think that one over there's taking a chainsaw out of her handbag," Alex said. "So you better hurry up."

Jamie slithered off the stool to make a getaway until a frau's arms jammed under his armpits and picked him up. With his feet spinning through the air, Jamie was dumped in front of the crater laden dartboard.

Alex smiled and waved at him from the sidelines.

Der, das, dem, des, den, die (six words for *the* in German) frau flicked back her mane—and nearly took out her volgen's (bird's) eye as she was standing hinterland behind—and dumped a set of tungsten darts into Jamie wilting mitt.

His arm dropped with the weight of them.

"Just chuck them at the right bits on the dart board and we'll be out of here in one bit," Alex yelled, grinning.

And as dart after dart tried to find a bit of the board that was still there, that hadn't already been nuked to oblivion, Alex stood on his stool and cheered Jamie on.

Die frau turned her back to the board and flung her darts over her head and hit a bull's-eye.

"You can do better, Jamie! Go Jamie, go Jamie, go go go!"

"Du?" his opponent asked.

"Do what?" Alex asked her.

Hands gripped and lifted him onto the bar top.

"Hey, watch the goods," Alex said.

"Mass oder ein gross?" die frau behind the bar said, poking her cigarette out in the ashtray.

"What?" Alex asked.

"We won!" Jamie yelled above the crowd.

The bar woman held up gallon mugs.

"Fur Sie und der freund." Die frau smiled at Alex. "Die champions!"

"Jamie?" Alex called from the top of the gantry over the crowd.

"We won, Eck," Jamie said over and over and he pushed his way through to Alex. "We won!" Jamie then flew up into the air as he was lifted onto the bar top to stand alongside Alex.

"No," Alex said. "We didn't win."

"What do you mean?" Jamie said.

Alex gave him a hug. "You won all on your own, Jamie," he said.

Everyone cheered. They were heroes. Jumping down from the bar, their photographs were taken.

And as Alex waved in the glory of it all, Jamie dragged him closer to the exit. "Time to go, Eck. "Come on before we outstay our welcome."

A tall, willowy figure turned in their direction.

"Helena, trink?"

"Nein danke," she said. "Ich arbeit zu morgen."

"Okay," the woman behind her said. "Was ist es?"

"Ich verstehe nicht. Nothing," Helena said. "Nothing at all."

Alex and Jamie disappeared out the door.

"You're talking strange again, Helena," her friend said.

Helena sighed and shook her head. "I am tired," she said, "that is all. It is nothing."

"The boys?" the woman asked her.

The doors swung closed. "I don't know, Margot," Helena said. "Just something."

"They were quite entertaining."

"Innocent," Helena said.

"Perhaps."

"Nein," Helena said turning to her. "Real innocents, and that scares me."

"Maybe you should stick to Deutsche when you talk."

"Practisch," Helena said, pecking her on the cheek. "Und ich habe zu hause." She made for the door.

"There is something wrong with your heart, Helena," the woman called out after her.

"Ja?"

"Ja, es ist zu gross."

~~*

"There's no windows," Jamie commented.

"There's a door, though." Alex said turning to him.

"A big black door."

They stepped from foot to foot as if it was freezing, only the air was warm.

"Will we go in or no?" Alex squinted at Jamie.

Jamie shrugged.

"Don't know if I trust a place with no a window in it," Alex said. "It doesn't even have a name on it anywhere. Might not even be a bar."

"Only one way to find out then," Jamie said.

Alex trotted up the steps and disappeared inside like a bridegroom reeled up to the alter on a fishhook. Jamie sighed and followed and found himself plunged into darkness so treacle thick that he stuck his arms out in front of him like a mad Dalek.

Crunch!

"Help, mah boab! Steps and no lights," he moaned.

A helpful hand reached through the dark, grabbed his arm and dragged him back onto his feet. "Mind the step," Alex said.

"Gee, thanks. And I still can't see anything."

They felt their way around a pillar and there it was: a big bar, and not a barman or a barmaid, or anyone else in sight.

"Deserted," Alex said.

"At least there's light at this bit."

"Where is everybody?"

Suddenly, a lean older man—he must have been all of thirty—sporting a beard and a leather waistcoat over a naked, if crackled, torso, emerged from the back of the gantry.

This time it was Jamie who spoke first, ordering two beers in his best faltering German.

"I'm impressed," Alex said.

"So you should be. I've been practicing it all night in my head."

The barman laid two cold beers on the counter.

"Well, at least he understood what it was you were saying for," Alex said.

After another beer the place began to fill up with an assortment of bearded and mustached characters, some older than others. Black leather being the name of the game.

Alex looked around the milling crowd then caught sight of the sign in the far corner. He pronounced the letters as they were written.

S-L-U-T?

"Now I know what it's called," he said.

"What?"

"This place. It's called Slut Bar."

"Aye?" Jamie said looking around.

"I think we'd better be going," Alex said.

"I quite like it here," Jamie said, relaxing, leaning back against the wall.

"You would," Alex snapped. "Now drink up."

"We've just got here!" Jamie said.

"We've been here long enough. Now let's get going. Now!"

"Okay, so what now?" Jamie said, catching up with Alex as he trotted along the street.

"Anywhere but there."

"I thought it was quite good."

"Aye, right."

They crossed the road and saw a crowd entering a doorway stage left.

"We'll try in there," Alex said.

"Whatever," Jamie said. "You're the boss."

The heat hit them as soon as they pushed their way in through the doors of Tom's Cabin. Alex took the first tentative steps down into the subterranean bar below. The thumping rhythm of the music came up to meet them. Jamie nearly lost his footing on the metal steps, wet with condensation—or was it sweat?

"It's like a jungle heat in here," he said.

But already Alex was down in the crowd and pushing himself through to the bar.

"Christ, can hardly move. The place is mobbed," Jamie called out.

"What?" Alex yelled back.

"I said … never mind."

Alex handed him a beer. Suddenly the music and lights died. Silence.

"Power cut?" Alex asked too loudly.

The crashing wail of guitars burst through the speakers. The stage lit up in red. Alex and Jamie stepped back and sucked in a sharp breath.

"Get me out of here," Alex said, eyes wide, molars glued shut.

Glistening muscles, leather vest, shaved head, dark wrap around glasses, drooping moustache, leather chaps and a great big bulging jockstrap.

Oh.

My.

God!

Alex almost swallowed his bottle of Beck's whole.

"Jesus Christ!" was Jamie's response as The Terminator burst into an Alice Cooper number.

"*Poyyysaaaaahnnnnnh*! Your *poyyyyysaaaaannnuh burning* through my *vayeeayeaaneszzuh*!"

Alex and Jamie clutched onto each other in terror. The song ended. The place plunged back into darkness. The crowd stomped its feet in approval.

"What is this place?"

Maybe it was the heat. Maybe they were stunned. And maybe it was because the beer had let them slide into a mellowed mood, but they soon relaxed and started dancing around to the music.

"Go on yourself, laddie," Alex yelped at Jamie's gyrations.

Alex himself went through everything he thought he knew. The chuggy pull, the mashed tattie, the sloshed. Jamie reached into his pocket as he danced and swallowed something down.

"What's that?" Alex asked jumping up and down.

Jamie dropped the little purple one into Alex hand. Alex gulped it down whole.

Thereafter he was in danger of overheating. The place oozed sweat, muscle, facial hair and jockstraps.

Jamie and Alex danced their best in pneumatic fashion. Alex's head almost unglued from his shoulders with the force.

"I can't stop I can't STOP!" he called, bouncing up and down on an invisible pogo stick.

One muscled number, in nothing more than a bulging jockstrap, wrap around Ray Bans, and with a hairy ark danced around with Alex.

Alex's head boing boing boing-ed all over the place. Jamie saw what was going on and bumped the muscle man out of the way.

Everyone stomped and clapped along to Alex's frantic rhythm. He shook as if he was being electrocuted from the feet up. Wolf whistles filled the air as he ripped off his T-shirt.

More muscle men surrounded him.

"That's it!" Jamie yelled. He'd seen enough. He burst through and dragged Alex off the dance floor. "Eck!"

"I can't stop, I can't stop," Alex's head vibrated as he bounced up and down. "It must have been that pill you gave me!"

"What pill?" Jamie asked.

"That purple pill."

Jamie reached into his pocket and held up the little tube. "One of these you mean?"

Head still jerking with the strong compulsion to rip off rest of his keks and be adored, Alex peered in close. He stopped dead.

"A *Parma Violet*?"

"What did you think it was?" Jamie asked.

"I was going berzerk because of a Parma Violet?"

But all Jamie could do was sigh. "I don't think you need any pills to go berzerk after what I just saw."

Jamie expected the full onslaught of Alex wrath. But Alex only laughed and doubled over, hysterical.

Alex and Jamie demonstrated to the crowd new dance moves. Curious looks and nods of baldheads and droopy moustaches notwithstanding, one onlooker asked. "Was ist das sloshed?"

"Die slosh!" Alex said "Here, Jamie, come here." He grabbed Jamie away from the other side of the crowd.

"What are we doing?" Jamie said.

"Showing them how to dance," Alex said. "The right way."

Dance what? was Jamie's last unasked question. But he just followed what Alex was doing and soon they were in rhythm tanzen.

There were quizzical looks from the crowds, glistening flesh, sweat, and a few hairy knuckle draggers—gorillas.

They smiled and then grinned. "Neue tanzen auf Gross Britanien!" one called out.

"Schottland! If you don't mind," Alex called back without losing his step.

"Schottern?"

"Aye!" Jamie called out, surprising himself with new his grip of the lingo.

"Oh, ja! Kilts! Mmmm. Und, och aye das noo!"

"Lang may yer bum leak!" Jamie called out, sloshing around now that he was getting right into it.

"Und es ist 'Och aye the noo,'" Alex corrected. "No, jetz dee noo.'" Then to Jamie, "Bloody foreigners."

But it didn't matter by then that even the Vin Diesel look-a-likes were sloshing around to the new tanze from "Schottland!"

They stood next to the DJ. Alex looked over the consol, then leaned in, asking the DJ something. The DJ nodded, then smiled. "Of course," he said.

"Of course, what?" Jamie said to Alex.

"Finish up you drink," Alex said. He nodded at the DJ who gave the thumbs up.

The music stopped. Alex grabbed Jamie by the wrist and dragged him up the steps onto the stage.

"Oh, God, Alex, what are you doing."

"What we're doing, Jamie. Karaoke."

The spotlight him them. Jamie shoogled inside as they faced the crowd.

"You know this one," Alex said.

"What one?"

"The song." Jamie turned to run.

Alex grabbed his collar and dragged him back, center stage. He gave another thumbs up to the DJ.

"The Arches," Alex said to Jamie. "You know this one."

"I don't want to know it now."

"Sugar Sugar," Alex said to him. "Ready?"

"No ..."

Pitch perfect, and into the microphone, Alex sang to Jamie. "... You are my candy boy ..."

As leather-strapped, bulging biceps swayed together in unison and joined in the chorus with Jamie and Alex.

"... *honey honey, sugar sugar* ..."

CHAPTER 50

Johan couldn't sleep, which wasn't unusual. Working nights for over a year now had that affect on him. Night had turned into day. And no matter how much he tried he couldn't fight his way back into a normal routine on his time off. In the end it had been easier to give in. He would only have to go through the same thing again when he went back to work at Tom's Cabin bar tomorrow night anyway.

He glanced up at the clock, then at his watch to confirm it really was half past two in the morning. He lay down his book, stretched his legs, stood up, grabbed his keys and mobile, and called out for Sam, his faithful black German Shepherd. Tail wagging, Sam followed his master out the front door and down the steps. He would walk around the neighborhood for fifteen minutes, maybe half-an-hour, Johan thought. After that, it was bed.

Johan pulled his mobile out of his pocket and checked for any messages he might still have.

Nothing since last night, when Klaus had asked him if he was coming out to Tom's for a drink. Looking at the message now he wondered if Klaus was still there. He shrugged and slipped the mobile back in his pocket.

The street was quiet, but Johan knew that appearances were deceptive. A few months back, rival gangs of skinheads had invaded the area and begun prowling around. Nothing much happened except for some minor skirmishes, but Johan knew it was still a place to keep your wits about you, especially at night.

Sam, trotting a few meters behind him, happily stopping now and again to sniff at doorways and lampposts. Johan stepped over the road, the street leading down to Tom's Cabin on his left. He took a quick glance, saw a couple of guys walking, arms over each other's shoulders, looked away and moved on.

Neither of them was tall enough to be Klaus.

Just as he stepped around the corner his mobile rang. In the quiet it sounded too loud. Johan quickly reached into his pocket and took it out and answered it.

A text was waiting. The blue screen glowed.

Klaus was still at Tom's after all.

~~*

"God, that was a night to remember," Alex said, reaching out and putting his arm over Jamie's shoulder. "Nothing like this in Kelty."

"Right there," Jamie said, pulling Alex close, smiling at him. The street was dark, quiet, warmth in the air. "Glad you came now?" Jamie asked.

Alex didn't say anything for a second as they walked side by side down the street. "Aye, I think you did me good there, Jamie son. Near had a heart attack though when I caught sight of that guy, then him singing Alice Cooper."

"I could see by the look on your face," Jamie said. "I was a bit feared myself, to tell the truth."

Alex laughed. "You're right there. Yours wasn't much better, either."

They kept walking, feeling as if time had slowed down. Then Alex caught sight of a shadow moving left to right. The skin on the back of his neck prickled.

"You're shivering," Jamie said.

"Just that guy up there," Alex said. "But he's gone now."

"One man in his dog?"

They both watched as a large black dog trotted after the shadow. Suddenly Alex stopped dead.

At first Jamie didn't know what was going on. He spun around and faced Alex. "What is it?" he asked.

Alex looked past him, at the doorways left and right. Something moved. His first thought was to walk back to the safety of the bar.

At the sounds of feet scraping on the pavement behind him, Jamie turned and looked to where Alex's eyes were fixed. He took a step back and stood side by side with Alex.

A shadow darted out from a doorway to their right. The next thing Alex knew, Jamie was spinning around, arms flailing as he was dragged to the ground. There were muffled thumps as fists and feet punched and kicked at him.

Jamie curled up into a ball, throwing his arms over his head defensively. Alex yelled out and dived in, trying to pull the men off Jamie. A fist flew at his face and sent him flying. Tripping backwards, Alex lost his footing and slammed into the wall.

Someone grabbed him, yelling. Hands pulled him this way and that as fists punched at his belly, his face, until he keeled forward, legs buckling. On his hands and knees, winded, Alex tried to look up. He couldn't pull any air into his lungs. He wanted to be sick.

His guts churned. Mouth agape, he was about to lose everything from his stomach on the pavement when a Doc Martin met his gaze full on.

And the world turned black.

~~*

Johan stopped when he heard the yell.

Someone in pain?

There was another yell. He moved back quickly to the street leading down to Tom's. Maybe the guys he'd seen had gotten themselves into a fight.

He took a look round the side of the building. There weren't just two men now, but a group of them. Six altogether, if that included the two he'd seen a moment earlier.

And no one was shaking hands.

Sam came up behind Johan, wagging his tail. But even he could sense trouble now and his tail lowered.

Two of the guys were on the ground and another two were on each of them.

Skinheads.

Johan called for Sam. Without need for another command, Sam ran at the skinheads. One of the skinheads looked up and called out to the others.

The guy on the ground being beaten to a pulp raised his head. One of the skinheads, a fat guy, turned and swung his boot. Johan had never seen such a sickening jerk of a person's head as the boot hit home. The guy flew sideways, blood flying through the air.

Sam was running at the skinheads now. One of the others called out and they all ran. But the only way out of the street was towards Johan.

They came running with, Sam in pursuit. It would have been funny at any other time, watching one of the skinheads jumping up, his heels jerking in the air as he tried to get away from a big, powerful dog like Sam.

Reaching for his mobile, Johan switched it on, raised the lens to his eye and snapped off some video.

The fat skinhead lagged behind the other three. Sam caught up with him, leaping high, his jaws wide. The fat skinhead yelped as Sam sank his teeth in, biting him on his even fatter backside. Sam hung on, growling hard.

The other skinheads ran past Johan and spat in his direction. Johan jumped back.

When he looked back down the street, Sam had lost his grip on the fat guy, who was now running, his legs bounding up in front faster than his belly.

Sam followed in pursuit. Johan called out to him, and he stopped, his claws scraping on the road. Looking down the street again, Johan saw two bodies lying on the ground: one in a doorway, the other on the pavement. He was on his side, not moving.

Hands shaking, Johan called the police. Then dialed in a text.

Johan just hoped he wasn't too late.

~~*

Something flat pressed against the side of Jamie's face—something cold, hard and gritty. His mouth felt like it was full of slime, tasted funny. He groaned at the pain in his arms and legs, his chest and head. When he tried to open his eyes, the left one wouldn't work. Propping himself up on his hands he tried to look around.

Where was Alex?

Jamie called out Alex's name, but it came out in no more than a gurgling whisper with his mouth so full of blood. "Alex?" he groaned.

He spat the foul taste out of his mouth. Something dark splattered on the pavement. "Alex!" Jamie staggered to his feet, lost his balance and crashed backwards into the door behind him. "Alex!" he called out again.

But there was no answer.

Gripping the wall, he peered around the side of the doorway. When he stepped out into the open he saw a dark shadow lying on the pavement.

He felt sick.

Jamie's voice grew small as he called out Alex's name again, as a question, as if he didn't want it to be him.

Every bone in Jamie's body ached. With his left eye still not working and his right thudding in pain, Jamie dropped to his knees as he watched a dark pool forming around the head of the body.

A silent rage built up inside of him, coming from a place he'd never known before. And without thinking, he scooped his arms under the limp body and tried to lift it up. He almost fell over and cursed himself for being so weak and he scraped his hands under the body again.

Alex's head lolled to the side and blood streamed out of his nose and mouth. The sight of it made Jamie catch his breath. His eyes were closed, as if he were sleeping, his mouth open wide.

Gritting his teeth, Jamie pushed down the lump in his throat and rolled Alex back into his arms. He forced himself up onto his feet, his legs threatening to collapse, until he had Alex's limp body off the ground.

Tears blurred most of the vision Jamie had left, but he could still see the blood pouring out of Alex's mouth, splashing down on the pavement in a sickeningly thick way, and so dark looking. Swaying now, Jamie staggered forward, Alex's body a dead weight in his arms as he stumbled a few feet onto the deserted road.

Everything was deathly quiet, but one word, *Alex*, kept going through Jamie's mind as he stumbled on, not knowing if his next foot fall would hit the ground, that he wouldn't misstep, trip and fall over himself, if his strength would leave him, or it he would drop Alex before he could carry him home to sleep. Alex always needed to sleep when he wasn't well

"... I'll get you back home, Eck ... I'll ..."

Then one word over and over came into Jamie's head: Angel ... angel ... angel ...

And as his breath was pulled out of him, the weight of Alex's body dragging Jamie down further, the words slipped between his bloodied lips, a strangled cry. "You've killed an angel ... What did he do to you? What did my laddie ever do to you? ... You don't know what you've done."

Jamie looked down at the dense form in his arms, his vision blurred with tears and blood as he stumbled off the pavement, lost his balance and went down on one knee.

Alex's lifeless body swung in his arms, but Jamie gripped on tight, swaying, and praying for more strength.

Somehow he managed to push himself back onto his feet and staggered down the middle of the road, where, in a daze, the blood draining from his head, Jamie no more saw the shadows rushing at him than he had when they appeared the first time, and feared that the monsters were back.

But all he could do was keep on going for as long as he could. With Alex's body in his arms, Jamie mumbled through his swollen mouth to Alex. "They broke your wings before you even had a chance to fly."

~~*

Klaus was saying his goodbyes when he felt the vibration of his mobile in his pocket. It was a message he'd hoped he would never receive.

He looked around at the others. A few of them were looking at their mobiles too, then at each other, as if they couldn't believe it. Then, as one, they all rushed at the steps and slammed the door wide on the outside world.

~~*

Johan and Sam were the first to arrive.

The young man carrying the body wouldn't stop. Johan talked to him gently, but the young man didn't seem able to see or hear and kept staggering on.

"I have to get him home," the young man said. "I have to get Alex home ..."

Johan laid a hand on the young man's shoulder in an effort to try and make him stop. He looked up at Johan, one eye a bloody mess, the other full of tears, uncomprehending. He was saying something, a harsh whisper, the same words over and over.

"Langsame," Johan said, but the boy didn't seem to understand. The body in his arms dripped blood. "Bitte?" Johan said.

But the boy just looked up at him, his face screwed up with emotion. "I'm sorry, Mister, but I don't understand what you're saying." And the boy's legs kept going.

There was the sound of running feet again. Johan still had his hand on the boy's shoulder when he saw them rushing towards them. The boy dropped to his knees, exhausted, weak, huddling over the broken body in his arms, letting it slip to the road.

"Er ist Schotten," someone said.

"Kein Deutscher?"

Klaus went down on one knee, speaking to the boy. "What happened?" he asked in English.

The boy looked up at him slowly. At first he didn't seem to understand, but then the words came out of him in a strangled cry. "They killed my laddie."

"Was sprechen ist er?" Johan asked Klaus. "What is he saying?

Klaus shook his head at Johan as if it didn't matter. He hadn't understood most of what the boy had said himself, except for one word: Killed.

He asked Johan if he had called an ambulance. Johan told him that he had.

"It will take too long. Here," Klaus said, holding out his keys to him. "Get my car for me will you? It's in the usual place. I will drive them there myself."

Johan took the keys and ran off down the road followed by Sam. Others milled around, looking on, talking to each other. Some talked into mobiles, and except for the place and the time, it might have seemed as if any of them were in a business meeting.

The roar of motorbikes came around the corner until the street seemed to be full of them. A few other stragglers arrived, younger and older men in jerkins, black dogs in tow. Each of them talked to one another. Some moved off quickly, still speaking into their phones.

Klaus reached out and touched the unconscious boy—Alex's—neck. He could feel a pulse, rapid and growing weaker. He looked around at the others and asked if any of them had a torch, something with a light.

One of the men from the bar, still talking into his mobile, reached into his pocket and threw a set of car keys at him. With a perfect swipe through the air, Klaus caught hold of them. He pinched the keying between his fingers and it lit up.

Perfect.

Hunching over, he gently pulled open an eyelid on the unconscious boy lying on the road and aimed the thin beam of light at it. The boy's pupil narrowed, but it was too slow, sluggish.

No matter how many times he had seen this before, it still had the same effect on him. Heart beating faster now, Klaus gently pulled open the eyelid on the boy's damaged eye. His fingers slipped on the blood. Wiping them on his jeans, he tried again, holding the beam close. The pupil in the left eye was wide. But no matter how many times he flashed the light at it, it refused to narrow like it should have.

This was bad news.

Some of the men who had run out of the bar when they had received the text walked over to the other guys, who were still on motor bikes, all talking, all pointing, all jabbering away to each other. Some of them jumped onto the backs of bikes, riding pillion, and drove off.

The young man who had carried the other sat as if in a daze, looking down. Klaus looked at him, wishing he could say something to make him feel better.

"His pulse is very weak," Klaus said to him. The boy looked startled for a second. "I'll take him to hospital myself," Klaus said. "It will be quicker."

A car pulled up. Engine still running, Johan stepped out of the driver's seat.

"Help me get him into the back," Klaus said to him. Klaus caught the look on the other boy's face. "No," Klaus said to him, shaking his head, "he has not been killed. But we must get him to hospital quickly."

And that was as far as he dared to speak for the moment.

With Johan's help, Klaus gently lifted the boy's unconscious body and laid him down on the back seat. The other boy climbed in the back on the opposite side. Klaus told Johan to drive. He had calls to make on the way.

When he climbed into the passenger seat, he looked back and told the young man to hold his friend's head as steady as he could. It was important that it didn't move around too much, or better still, at all.

~~*

Johan drove as fast as he dared without breaking the speed limit. The roads were quiet and so the journey to the hospital wouldn't take too long.

Klaus sat with Sam half in his lap, half at his feet while he talked into his mobile, giving instructions.

Everything was happening so quickly, as if a nightmare had suddenly sped up.

Jamie listened to the guy talking in a gibberish version of German as he held Alex's head still, fearful that any sudden movements would him do more harm.

Suddenly, everything looked too bright as the car swung into the hospital grounds. A trolley rolled out of the swinging doors, a nurse on either side pushing it along as the car pulled up.

Klaus jumped out and said something and the nurses rolled the trolley to the other side. The door was opened and Jamie was helped out. While he stood there, the nurses and Klaus somehow managed to slide Alex out and then lift him onto the trolley and rushed him inside.

Under the fluorescent lights Alex's injuries looked like a nightmare. His face was covered in blood, the flesh swollen on his jaw and forehead, so swollen that under all the blood he looked like an old man.

Klaus barked out orders at the medical staff, words that Jamie couldn't understand. Doctors came running. Jamie was taken inside by a nurse. Everyone seemed to be running around.

A young female doctor, white coat flapping, rushed up and took a look at Alex's eyes. She said something to Klaus that Jamie couldn't understand.

"Sind Sie ihr bruder?" the doctor called out. At first Jamie didn't know who she was speaking to.

"Nein! Er ist scwhule bruder." Jamie heard Klaus say.

"Okay okay," the doctor said. "Theater acht!"

And with that, Jamie watched as the trolley was wheeled away down the corridor, and suddenly Jamie was standing there in the bright corridor, alone, everything fallen quiet.

Someone came up behind him and urged him to sit in a wheelchair. Without thinking, he dropped down into it, hung his head forward and cried.

"You are the victim's next of kin, yes, no?" the nurse asked him in faltering English as she dabbed at Jamie's swollen eye.

Just then, the screens pulled wide and Klaus appeared. "Doktor Braun?" the nurse said on seeing him standing there.

Klaus acknowledged her greeting with a nod. "Wie ist er?" he asked, nodding at Jamie lying on the couch. But the nurse only shrugged as she dabbed at Jamie's eye.

"Gibt es mir eine moment," Klaus said to her.

The nurse stopped what she was doing and walked out, closing the screens behind her. Klaus drew up a chair and sat near the couch Jamie. One eye still swollen closed, Jamie turned to him. He sniffed as if he wanted to cry.

"How is Alex?" Jamie whispered the question, fearing the answer.

Klaus looked at him sympathetically. "How long have you two been together?"

"Six months." Jamie sounded almost apologetic when he said it.

"Alex is in theatre at the moment," Klaus said. "Being prepared."

Jamie sat up, grimacing in pain.

"Easy," Klaus said, placing a hand on Jamie's shoulder and easing him back down.

"What's wrong?" Jamie said.

"Alex is hemorrhaging badly," Klaus said. "Bleeding in his brain. We have to operate. We have to relieve the pressure."

Jamie closed his eyes, a tear welling up as he listened. The thought of Alex's brain being operated on made him feel sick and sad at the same time. "He's going to die," he said. "Is Alex going to die?"

Klaus reached out and took hold of Jamie's hand. But there was nothing else that he could say, only give Jamie's hand a gentle squeeze.

"Is he going to die, please tell me?" Jamie asked, his voice breaking.

Klaus only shook his head. "I'm sorry," he said. "I just don't know."

CHAPTER 51

Alex remained unconscious. Tests showed his intracranial pressure was rising, his systemic pressure falling. His right pupil remained fixed and dilated, his left responded to light, but it was still slow. An emergency CT scan showed internal bleeding inside his skull was putting pressure on the occipital lobe at the back of Alex's brain. If left, the bleeding would continue until the pressure became so great that the soft tissue would be forced down into his spine—a process known as conning.

Rushed to theatre, head shaved, co-ordinates mapped out, the surgeon drilled a hole through the back of Alex's skull, releasing the blood, and thus releasing the pressure. After two hours, Alex was wheeled into Intensive Care where he would be kept under anesthesia to prevent him moving, even if he were capable of waking, thus preventing the possibility of further bleeding.

A tube attached to a ventilation machine was forcing air into Alex's lungs, doing his breathing for him. He was catheterized and his veins punctured and drip-fed with fluid. A central venous pressure line was inserted through his subclavian vein and a syringe driver pumped anesthesia directly into his brain.

X-rays were taken of Jamie's skull, the normal procedure for anyone who had lost consciousness after trauma. There were no fractures, no bleeding inside his skull. And so now he sat in the corridor and waited, his right eye closed, blackened and bruised, a cut above his brow sutured together, another, smaller one closed with steri-strips. The overhead strip lights hurt his right eye and so he closed them both, leaned forward in the little plastic bucket seat and tried not to think.

Emotions welled up inside him. A tear would try to escape as if attempting to alleviate the pressure pushing up inside of him. When this happened, Jamie's lips would tremble, his mouth open a little as a silent scream escape.

He heard soft footsteps approaching him from down the long corridor and he dared open his one good eye that he could see through. In perfect English, the nurse assigned with language co-ordination duty sat beside Jamie and explained, as best she could, what had happened to Alex.

She told Jamie a lot and nothing at the same time, for he was incapable of really understanding what was wrong. Alex may or may not wake up, the nurse said, he may or may not regain consciousness, he may or may not be permanently brain damaged. He may or may not live. It was like one door after another opening with hope only to slam shut in his face in the next breath, each door blocking his way further and further from Alex.

Until the nurse took him to a real door in another part of the hospital. It opened quietly into a dimly lit room and Jamie saw the tiny, insignificant body lying there, in cruciform, arms out to the sides, the veins, arms and fingers hooked up to tubes and machinery. A tube had been forced down Alex's throat. The rest of the tube hung from the side of Alex's limp mouth. Bandages were wrapped mummy-like around Alex's shaven skull. His eyes were closed, his left bruised and swollen.

At first Jamie couldn't recognize who it was, although he knew. And then it hit him full on in his stomach and through every inch of him.

Quietly, Jamie approached the space-age looking bed and equipment, the syringes and wires, the blood pressure cuff, the wires attached to the pads stuck to Alex's bare chest. A white sheet, neat, too neat and too white, had been pulled up to just under Alex navel.

As if waiting for approval from the attending nurse, Jamie stood at the foot of the bed watching, willing her to give him permission, to acknowledge that Jamie was even there. He felt frightened, awkward, as if he was in the way somehow, that even if he should breathe too deeply that somehow that would make things go wrong.

And so Jamie stood and waited, until the nurse finally looked up from the machines, the paperwork, nodded and smiled at him in a way that at least let him know that he was there in the same room.

Machines blipped glowing lines.

Alex remained still, unconscious, dreaming maybe, maybe not, lost inside a world inside his own damaged imagination, who knew.

Without a word the nurse walked up to somewhere behind Jamie, picked up a small plastic chair from the back of the room, a chair like the ones in the corridor, and placed it near the bed at the left-hand side. After that, she went back to the machines, read the figures, scribbled numbers and readings.

Jamie remained standing, feeling as if he were still in the way somehow, feeling apologetic, ready to run but glued to the spot. Wouldn't someone talk to him? Tell him what to do?

At that thought, the nurse looked at Jamie again, gave a little smile and nodded in the direction of the little blue chair at the other side of the bed.

Jamie crept over to it quietly and sat down. He wanted to reach out, to touch the fragile figure but daren't, as if by doing so he would break something, kill something, put Alex in danger.

But instinct and emotion punched through Jamie and won. And so he leaned forward and reached out, his one good eye flicking up at the nurse who so far hadn't told him to stop what he was doing, and touched the only thing of Alex that hadn't been attached to machinery: his right hand.

And as soon as he felt the warmth of Alex's skin, Jamie closed his fingers around it. But there was no similar response from Alex. His fingers remained limp. And at that point, the worst of two possible worlds surrounded Jamie.

Alex was so near, but so far away, lost in his own world, ignoring Jamie, incapable of even knowing of Jamie's existence.

It proved too much, and so in silence, the tears flowed from Jamie's eyes, the left thumping and aching, stinging through the swelling and bruised flesh as Jamie held on tighter to Alex's unresponsive hand. Jamie's shoulders hunched over, shaking with emotion, his whispered words speeding up until they escaped in a hurried rush as he rocked forward and back and lifted Alex's lifeless hand to his lips, trying to seal off the words that Jamie didn't want to hear himself say.

"Don't die, Alex," he said. "Please don't leave me alone."

Twelve hours later, Jamie returned to the hotel, sheepishly slinking past the reception desk and the receptionist, feeling as he were a criminal. He needn't have, for the police had already been in touch with the staff, checking details, explaining.

But the dried blood looked worse in the cruel light of the early afternoon, the rips in his T-shirt, the bruised and scrapped flesh of his hands, his arms and face, and made Jamie feel like a monster. For if it hadn't been for his meeting Alex in the first place, if it hadn't been for bringing Alex here, he thought, then Alex would never have been put in so much danger.

And so Jamie was grateful when he entered the lift to shut his guilt off from the world. Once inside their room, he closed the door quietly behind him, stood for a second and wondered at what he needed to do. Insurance papers for one, a shower, and change of clothes to feel and look half-decent. Things to take back to the hospital. Things for Alex.

He walked up to the window and looked out at the trees, at the birds flying from branch to branch, twittering. He looked at the ivies, at windows in the distance, the sun beating down.

All quiet, too quiet.

After a shower ,he sat on the edge of their bed, already made, and clutched at the things he thought Alex would need.

Remorse flooded through Jamie, self-hatred and recrimination. If only he hadn't forced Alex into it. If only he had listened to Alex and they had stayed at home. If only they had stayed and remained in the same bickering world with Thelma and Derek constantly pecking at their door like vultures too impatient to wait.

If only he had never met Alex then this would never have happened.

"If only it wasn't for me insisting on bringing you here," he said, burying his face into the little bag he had filled with Alex's toiletries, for Alex had always been particular about his appearance.

And now Jamie realized what it was really like to be a stranger in another land, far away from home, the homes he had grown up as a stranger in. Only there were no wardens to turn to now. No one to listen to him, to advise him, to tell him what to do.

"Alex, I'm so sorry."

CHaPTer 52

The story appeared in the papers. Get well cards flooded into the hospital, enquiries poured in from strangers and reporters for the latest updates to the hospital administrator's PR department. Flowers appeared from well-wishers, until the nurses began to complain gently to Jamie that there wasn't enough space left in the room. But then Jamie didn't know who they were from anyway, only people who had read the story, seen the news.

Days turned into a week, and every few hours the nurses would ask Jamie to leave the room so that they could change Alex's position in bed to make sure that there was no pressure on any one area for too long, that it helped with Alex's circulation. And sometimes, when Jamie re-entered the room, there would be the trace of a foul odor he didn't want to think about.

The insurance paid for the medical treatment and the room at the hotel. But night after night, Jamie would sleep at the hospital in the chair at the side of Alex's bed. He would be awakened every few hours asked to leave again while the nurses attended to Alex.

Until one night, Jamie said he wanted to stay and help Alex himself. The nurses looked at each other and shrugged.

But when the crisp white sheet was pulled down off of Alex's body, Jamie had had to swallow down on the shock he felt. Not only had Alex lost weight, he was also wearing what looked like a nappy. Now he knew where that foul odor came from.

Emotions welled up inside Jamie, but he stamped them back down, determined to help. The nurse took sympathy on Jamie. But no, he would stay.

And Alex, like a new born baby without control of his bodily functions, was cleaned and washed. Jamie gagged until he pushed down that reflex and learned how to place Alex's arms and legs in the correct position. How to place pillows at Alex's back and between his knees, let Alex's arms draped over others.

And all the while, Alex would simply flop from side to side, lifeless.

One day, whilst cleaning out Alex's mouth with a tiny pink sponge on a stick dipped in mouthwash, an act that was second nature to Jamie now, the nurse told Jamie that he would make a good nurse himself. Jamie almost allowed himself to beam with pride until he realized the seriousness of Alex's condition.

It wasn't long before Jamie started learning a few words in German, and with Jamie's help, the nurses brushed up on their English at the same time.

Though he would tell them things that he shouldn't have. Yes, "Lang may your lumb reek," was a famous Scottish saying, he would tell them, not knowing what it meant himself.

Visitors came and went, great big hairy men clutching presents, teddy bears, young skinheads and their friends who had been at Tom's cabin that night, guys who had been in leather but now visited Alex in their suits, and a man and a woman who were really the other way around.

Jamie recognized the one from the ferry. Her name was Jean, and the woman who accompanied her, Jamie learned, was called Shirley, a woman who dressed herself in a power suit, businesswoman way. Anything he needed, Jean and Shirley said, all Jamie had to do was ask.

But all Jamie wanted was for Alex to wake up, to sit and say, "What's going on?"

After a few weeks, the money from the insurance company began to dwindle. It was just enough to pay for the hotel room, which Jamie hardly ever saw.

And so one day, a nurse told Jamie that there was a bulletin board full of job vacancies. Jamie applied for a job as a domestic.

He slept by Alex's bed each night and worked his way around the wards during the day, mopping floors, being cheeky to everyone and scrubbing toilets. Each night he would shower and return to Alex's side, and whisper and talk and reminisce. And each night he would fall asleep holding onto Alex's hand, hoping that Alex would wrap his fingers around his.

"How's my laddie doing?" he would call out to the attending nurse.

"The nurse would smile, shrug. "No change."

No change.

Nothing changed.

Nothing got worse and nothing got better.

After three weeks of the same no change, Jamie placed the earphones in Alex's ears, laid the CD player on his pillow and pressed play.

"One of Alex's favorites," Jamie said to the nurse.

"His?" the nurse asked, perplexed at this new found complicated language structure.

"Favorites, aye. Alex used to sing it, he did. He was good as well. Pretenders he used to sing—*Stand by Me*."

And so slowly the weeks passed on by.

CHAPTER 53

Gran's house hadn't changed after all.

Alex looked around at it now. And as he did so, the house vanished and Alex found himself standing outside, on the greenest grass he had ever seen under a sky so clear and blue it took his breath away.

"Alex?"

Alex turned to the voice, the sound of it giving a golden glow to his heart. "Gran?" Alex said.

She stood before him, smiling, not speaking, her arms protectively holding the little bundle close to her chest.

"Awe, Gran," was all Alex could say as he took the little body into his own arms, felt the weight of it, saw the smile and the china-blue eyes. Alex's tears streamed down his face as he smiled in closer.

"Bonnie baby. Wee mite." And he clutched the baby close to him, felt the bind that ties, the once denied now in his arms.

But after a little while, his grandmother held out her arms to him. Only Alex didn't want to let go of the baby. It would be too painful to let go.

But you must, he felt, though he never heard her gentle command. "But why Gran, why?"

And without moving her lips, without even words forming, Alex knew why. And it broke his heart, until it came to him in a sudden rush.

"I can stay, Gran? I can stay and keep the baby with me."

But all his grandmother could do was gently take the baby from his arms. It wasn't to be. And this was the reason why ...

As she held the baby close, protectively, she said, smiling, "We love you, Alex."

Something stung at Alex left hand then. He pulled it back with a violent jerk and slammed it into another pain deep inside his chest, then another and another.

"Yours and Jamie's baby," she said. "There's no need for him to be born on Earth and returned to Heaven." Alex looked up her as she spoke again. "Because, you see, Alex ..." she smiled at him. "He's already perfect."

~~*

"Alex!"

The nurses pushed a hysterical Jamie out of the room even as the electricity slammed though Alex's body. Jamie clutched at the doorframe, his fingers almost breaking, as he was forced bodily out into the corridor.

"No, Alex!" he yelled.

~~*

"You must leave, Alex. You must go back," his grandmother said.

And Alex fell to his knees at the pains inside him, the emotional, the physical. "The baby, Gran let me stay with my baby."

She looked down on her grandson with pity and love in her eyes, then at the baby in her arms. "Do you really want to stay, Alex?" she asked.

Alex pushed himself to his feet, his steps faltering, and held out his arms to her, to the baby, until a pain ripped through his heart and forced his eyes closed and his world to go black.

CHAPTER 54

His heart started to beat again, but it had been a struggle. There were several mild burns on Alex's chest where the paddles had shocked his heart back to life.

On the second day after Alex's cardiac arrest, Jamie made his way back from his work as a domestic from another ward in the hospital. Only now, knowing how fragile hope could be, he moved around in a cloud of fear where anything might happen.

He was stopped by one of the nurses before he could get into the room. "Awake!" he yelped when he heard her.

"Yes," she said. "About half an hour ago. We've been trying to find you all over the place."

"I've got to see him," Jamie said. But the nurse laid a firm hand on his shoulder. "What's wrong?" Jamie asked.

Jamie slowly pushed open the door. Alex was sitting up on the edge of the bed with his back to him. Half-crouching, half-smiling, Jamie wanted to rush over and hold onto him.

Only something was stopping him. "Eck?" No response. "Eck, it's me."

But the words that came from Alex's mouth came slowly, gravely, filled with emotion, the kind of emotion Jamie didn't expect. "I know who *you* are," Alex said.

"Eck, laddie."

Alex's head shot round in Jamie's direction. "Don't you come near me," he said.

"Alex, what is it? It's me, it's ..."

"I *hate* you!"

"Alex, lad."

"Get away from me."

Stunned now, all Jamie could do was stand still, frozen in shock at the end of Alex's bed.

Alex stood up slowly, limping round on his right leg to face Jamie. "You *bastard*!"

"Alex?"

"What have you done to me? Get out of here. You hear me? You get the hell away. I hate you. I hate you like I've never hated anything in my life. Bastard. *Scum*!"

Something flew up through the air and hit the side of Jamie's face.

"Jesus!" Jamie yelped, clutching where he had been hit.

Two nurses flew into the room and grabbed at Alex's arms before he could do even more damage.

"What's wrong with him?" Jamie said, the life suddenly drawn out of him.

The doctor explained that sometimes personality changes could take place after head injuries. Placid personalities could sometimes turn into raging monsters. Some even resented being brought back out of a coma. No one knew why really. The obvious answer was that brain damage could explain it, most often it couldn't.

"Will Alex get better?" Jamie asked.

The doctor could only shrug. The bad news was that sometimes, head injury victims didn't. The doctor's advice to Jamie was that he should stay away for a few days. Let things settle. Keep calling on the phone, at least that way Alex would know that Jamie is still there, concerned for Alex, caring.

The rest?

Only time would tell.

~~*

Jamie stopped going into work. There was no point any longer. And so he would sit in that little hotel room, resenting its cold walls, walls that seemed to close in by a foot every day.

His money ran even lower and he was eating less and less. He wasn't ever hungry enough anymore.

So he smoked and drank coffee, slept fitfully and little, and cried himself to sleep every night. He called the hospital three or four times a day. Physically, apart from a slight limp, Alex was fit and healthy, they said.

Nothing else had changed. No, Alex still wasn't accepting visitors.

After a week, Alex had withdrawn his permission for any medical details to be given to anyone. All that Jamie could be told was that Alex was still an inpatient. No, Jamie couldn't be informed of when Alex might be discharged. That right to know had also been denied.

The sun shone during the day, but the days grew duller, grittier somehow. And Jamie saw less and less of them. Nights brought the self-recriminations that only nights could muster for the lonely.

After ten days and the deepest of sleeps that Jamie had had in a long time, he had woken, climbed out of bed and taken a shower.

It was all so obvious now what he had to do, as it should have been all along.

Jamie stared at his gaunt face in the bathroom mirror. Exhaustion had aged him. He felt ugly. Every imperfection stood out so plainly now.

He had been to this place before. Every time he had been up for adoption. Elation had coursed through his veins that a family, a new mum and dad, had wanted him. And so he would be on his best behavior. Then, at the last minute, everything would change.

But there was always the chance of other times, they would say. And each time it was the same. He had aged then too, and then refused to smile for fear of his happiness being slapped away again.

Jamie walked back into the room, looked around at the bed, the table by the window. It was more a cell than a room now.

There would be calls to make, of course. Jamie was responsible enough and grown up enough to do that at least. Things would need to be folded, neatly folded and accounted for. He had heard the saying before. Jamie had repeated it himself sometimes. He wondered what age he would need to be before it rang true.

No fool like an old fool.

He had had ideas above his station, Jamie told himself. And this was his payback. After all, if he hadn't brought Alex here then this would never have happened.

Even pain ceased to hurt any more. Just another feeling, something in the distance, out there, far away, out of reach, out of sight. Ritual would pull him through.

He opened the wardrobe doors and drawers and took careful inventory. He laid out neat piles of clothes, two of them, side by side, neither touching. He laid another pile that needed to be taken to the laundry.

It was something to do.

And if a tear should threaten to sting through and blur the way ahead, Jamie would take a deep breath, light up another cigarette and wait for it to pass.

It was easy really when you know how, he thought. And so he neatly folded Alex shirts and T-shirts just the way he knew Alex liked them to be. He rolled up Alex's socks into pairs and then folded his underwear and his jeans.

When the last was laid out, Jamie realized that this was the closest he would ever be to Alex ever again, the nearest he had come to feeling loved by someone else.

Sniffing, he turned away and walked over to the drawer in the desk by the window and pulled it open. He saw the cheap second-hand camera he had bought in all the rush to get away now laid on top of the notebook he had bought Alex for his birthday that night.

He touched its cover, picked it up and let his fingers trail over the clasp. He almost clicked it open to look inside. But he couldn't. It was Alex and what, if anything, Alex had written inside on its pages was his and his alone.

So no, he wouldn't read it. Alex wouldn't want him to. Instead, Jamie tried to feel the words scribbled in secret on the inside, drifted back to that night he had given it to Alex, and remembered the surprise he'd felt when he saw the look on Alex's face, as if he had given Alex a million pounds as a present instead of a cheap notebook, a notebook that Jamie had almost decided not to until he had rushed back inside the shop and bought it after all. He hadn't known why he had done it, but perhaps something deep inside of him had, and now he placed the notebook back in the drawer beside the pen.

It was the last of the ritual, each part like the lock on another door. And there were no more to be closed.

Jamie was lost now. Scared. But he had been frightened before, hadn't he? Yet hadn't he also learned that no matter how scared he had ever been, no matter how often he had managed to put a brave face to the world, he was at least better off than some he had known at the homes.

At least he was still alive.

What was it he had heard Alex mumble to himself sometimes when he thought no one was listening? "Needs must."

Jamie thought he understood now what Alex had meant by it.

"Needs must, my friend," Jamie said. "Even when it's so hard to say goodbye. I'll never forget you."

Jamie only wished that Alex had let him say goodbye in person as reached down to the desk and gently closed the drawer.

CHAPTER 55

No longer with his life in danger, Alex had been transferred to another ward, a single room. As a private patient, travel insurance notwithstanding, he was treated like royalty.

Back from the morning's physiotherapy session, he limped back with his walking stick in hand, barely letting its rubber stopper touch the floor tiles he moved so fast. He smiled at everyone, greeted everyone on first name terms and entered his room.

Everything was neat and tidy. Everything was in place. He sat down on the edge of the bed.

Alone.

Tum tee tum tee tum, he sat twiddling his thumbs when one of the nurses came in holding a chart.

"Morning, Helena," he greeted her.

"Good morning, Alex," she said back without looking up from the chart.

"How are things?" he asked with a lilt.

"You, Alex, are getting along very well," she said, clipping the board to the end of his bed.

He pushed up his sleeve in readiness. Helena turned and walked towards the door; she opened it.

"Oh, Helena," Alex said. "Aren't we forgetting something, hmmm?"

Helena, hand still on the edge of the door, said, "and what would it be that *we* are forgetting, Alex?"

"My blood pressure!" Alex quipped indignantly.

Helena shook her head. "But your blood pressure is fine, Alex." Alex was crestfallen. His arm flopped down by his side. "In fact, Alex, once a day from now on should suffice."

Alex rolled down his sleeve. "I see," he said.

"Anything else, Alex?"

Alex picked up a glossy magazine, more for something to do. "A coffee would be nice, and maybe a wee scone to go with it," he said without looking at her.

Helena raised an eyebrow. "Café und kuchen?" she said.

"Aye, whatever," he said with irritation.

"I'm a nurse, Alex, not a maid."

Alex slammed the magazine shut. What was it about these people?

"Look, Helena, dear," Alex sad. "I am a very sick young man who is rehabilitating from a horrible assault. And ... I am a private patient. So will you *please* do as I ask?"

Helena let the doors slip from her fingers. She turned slowly to face him. Smiling, she walked up to the end of Alex's bed. "My dear, Alex. This is a hospital, not a hotel. And," she went on when Alex opened his mouth to speak, "you are a patent now in rehabilitation. That means doing things for yourself as much as you can."

"But ..."

Talk to the hand. Alex fell into silence.

"And apart from a slight limp in your left leg, Alex, there is certainly nothing wrong with your arms or your hands." Alex gawped. "Or anything else as far as every test known to medical science can determine. Now, is there anything else?"

Alex folded his arms and fell into a huff.

"Am I to be dismissed, Alex?"

Still nothing.

After a few seconds Helena turned to leave and reached out for the door.

"Wait!"

"Yes, Alex?"

"The post's late again," he informed her, nodding at the bare surface of his side table.

Helena drew in a deep, slow breath and turned to him again. "There is no post, Alex."

"Hmm," was all Alex had to say.

"Anything else?" Helena asked.

"Any calls?" he sniped, picking up the magazine again, flicking through its pages and trying to sound as disinterested as possible.

"None."

"Messages?"

"None."

"*None*?"

"None, Alex. The same as yesterday."

"Sure?"

"Yes, Alex. In fact, I am definitely sure," Helena said. "Why would anyone call and enquire about your welfare when you have given instructions that you do not want anyone to know anything?"

"You would think they cared enough to at least try," he said, slipping into a conciliatory tone.

Helena moved around the side of the bed and sat next to him. "Listen, Alex. Illness doesn't just hurt the patient, but everyone one close to him too. And when you push everyone away, it hurts them even more."

Alex didn't say anything.

"And what about your friend, Jamie?"

Alex jumped up off the bed at the sound of the name. "He hurt me!"

"Hurt you, Alex? I don't understand."

"He should have left me alone."

"What?"

"He should have left me with ..." *my gran*, he almost said, *the baby*.

Helena sat there with a questioning look on her face. "He should have left you?" she asked.

"Aye, left me!" Alex burst out. "I was happy. I wanted to stay and he brought me back. It's his fault. I've lost everything now. If it hadn't been for Jamie, I would have ..."

"Died, Alex?" Helena said. "You would have died."

The words were forcing themselves up from deep inside him now. "Aye! I would have died. And I would have been happy. It's *his* fault I didn't!"

"Just a minute," Helena said, slowly getting to her feet. "So now it's Jamie's fault that he saved your life, not the men who attacked you? They are your friends? You should be thanking those who nearly killed you?"

Alex began to shake with a rage. "Stop it. Stop it! You're making me confused."

Helena waited until Alex's rage began to subside. Red-faced, Alex blanched.

"You don't know what it was like, Helena," Alex said in barely a whisper. "I wanted to stay." He sat down again. "I wanted to stay," he said again, quietly.

She reached out and pulled him closer, felt Alex's shoulders begin to shake with emotion.

"I wish I had just stayed, Helena."

"Whatever it was, Alex, that made you want to stay where it was," Helena said slowly, "Jamie didn't know that. He did everything for you, you know? Not a lot of young men his age could have been so loving and kind. He slept at the side of your bed night after night, held your hand, told you stories. And even although he was smiling bravely, when the nurses were in the same room at the same time, we could see the pain he was feeling. He did his best not to let it show, you know, for your sake, Alex. He also played you music, did you know that?"

Alex turned away his face and sniffed.

"And each night," Helena said softly, "Jamie would kiss you on the cheek just before he fell asleep in the chair beside your bed."

Alex wiped the back of his hand under his nose.

"And sometimes he was very shy about letting anyone see how gentle he was with you. It can be very difficult for a young man to show his softer side in front of others. But he did, Alex. I thought Jamie would have made a very good nurse myself, the way that we saw him care for you, cleaning you up, making sure you were safe."

"He's only got a Duke of Edinburgh Award for something ..."

Helena shook her head. "I don't know what that is, Alex. But I can tell you this. There are no certificates to prove what is inside a caring young man's heart."

Alex turned away and looked at the blank wall. Helena went on. "And then Jamie would wake up each morning and go to work."

Alex turned to her sharply. "*Work*?"

"You didn't know?" Helena asked.

"What do you mean work? He's on holiday."

"But you were in a coma, Alex. For weeks. He didn't have any money and so he worked, here at the hospital."

"The insurance."

"Paid for your stay in hospital, your treatment. It didn't pay for Jamie."

"But ..."

"Jamie isn't your next of kin, Alex."

Alex's mouth dropped open.

"He didn't make much. Just enough for him to scrape by, enough so that he could stay with you."

"What did he work as?" Alex asked.

"A domestic."

"*A domestic*?"

"Yes."

"Cleaning bogs? I mean toilets?"

"Amongst other things, yes he did. He was good at his job too. And every minute he had left, he was back here, with you. And he didn't to get paid to clean you up either, Alex. He did that because he wanted to."

Alex sat down again. "He still should have left me alone. My Gran, the ..."

"Then you should send a letter of thanks to the attackers who almost murdered you," Helena said. She reached out and picked up the CD from the table. She looked at it. "Pretenders?" she asked.

Alex nodded.

"Jamie said they were your favorite," she said. "That you were a good singer too. He even told us that you had sung on stage once."

Alex sniffed. "That stupid ... laddie."

"Is that true?" Helena said, trying to catch his eye. "He said you were a very good singer. That everyone clapped and cheered when you sang."

Helena stood up slowly and walked towards the door. She turned back only once to look at him. Alex's head bowed with his back to her, his shoulders starting to shake. She walked out the room and left him to deal with his own feelings for a while.

A little while later, Helena sneaked back into Alex's room with a bulky folder under her arm. A sad looking Alex looked up.

She walked over and sat down beside him on the bed and opened the folder. "I shouldn't be showing you this," she said.

"What is it?"

"Police evidence. Anyway," she went on before pulling what looked like a mobile phone out of the folder. "The thing is, you see, no one knows what is being said."

She held up the phone. Alex looked at its screen. At first, everything was dark, a fuzzy blur.

"There!" Helena said. "That's your friend, Jamie."

Alex leaned in, concentrating on the fuzzy image as it steadied. He watched as a figure staggered along a dark street, carrying what looked like a rag doll in his outstretched arms. Jamie's face was bruised beyond recognition, and he swayed before falling to his knees.

"That's you he's holding up, Alex," Helena said.

A wave of emotion flooded though Alex's body as he watched Jamie struggle to pick up his lifeless body, Jamie's legs struggling to keep upright. Then he heard Jamie's voice.

"We can't make out what he is saying, Alex," Helena said. "The police think it's important, that it might help them to capture the men who attacked you."

But all Alex could do was look on, sadness in his eyes.

"It's his accent, Alex. It is too strong for anyone to make out. Do you know what he is saying, Alex?" Helena asked gently.

Words spilled out of Alex's mouth as he said, "Angel ... Jamie's saying 'you've killed an angel.'"

Then Alex broke down completely.

Helena placed the mobile back into the folder on the bedside table, stood up and left Alex to himself. A little while later Alex was in the corridor, speaking into the public phone. The nurses looked at one another, nodding.

"There is no answer," the receptionist at the hotel said down the line.

"Then try again?" Alex barked. "Harder this time!"

"I already have," the receptionist said. "Three times."

Alex put down the phone and hobbled off back into his room. He would call again later.

He sat on the bed, reached out and touched the compact disc. He hadn't played it since telling Jamie to go away. And now he cringed at how cold he had been towards Jamie. He slipped the disc into the little player, put the earphones in, picked a track and listened.

"... why do you look so sad?"

"Oh, Jamie," Alex said as he closed his eyes and listened, touching at the ring that had been taped to his finger so that it wouldn't fall off and be lost.

"Alex!"

But Alex wasn't listening, now dressed and with only but his walking stick as he hobbled past the nurses' station. The ward clerk reached for her telephone. Until Helena reached out and pressed down on her hand, placing the receiver back on its cradle.

Helena shook her head and smiled. "Alles ist in ordnung," Helena said. "Let him go."

"Aber, Schwester?"

Helena walked off, entered the changing room and unlocked her locker. Reaching into her bag, she pulled out her mobile phone and began tapping in numbers.

The network was informed.

CHAPTER 56

Shirley sat in the backroom, hair a fright, twisting and dragging curling tongs through her wig. Exasperated, she set the tongs down.

"It's no good," she complained.

"What isn't, love?" Jean said, turning around.

"The hair, look at it!"

Jean sighed. "Do you want me to give it a go, then?" she asked.

"It's just such a bloody mess," Shirley said. "I'll never get it right."

"Yes, you will. Here, let me," Jean said.

Shirley sat looking into the mirror while Jean worked her magic with the tongs.

"There," said Jean, standing back, sounding pleased with herself. "How's that?"

Shirley leaned in, prodding her coral shellac-covered claws into the strawberry-blonde candy floss crowning her head. She flopped back, disgruntled at the result. "I look like Carol Channing on acid."

Jean was about to tell her not to be so stupid when her mobile rang. So did Shirley's.

Without thinking, they answered at the same time. They both had the same message:

ALEX FRN ZUM HTL MERCURE

They let their arms flop down by their sides, eyes meeting in the mirror. Shirley ripped the napkin out from her collar, the one she'd used to stop her makeup session overrunning onto her new pink chiffon dress. Leaning forward too quickly, she bashed her head on the edge of the table when she'd bent down to look for her slippers. She clonked it again on the way back up.

Jean was already out of the door and searching around for the car keys.

"Don't leave without me!" Shirley called out, rubbing at her forehead with one hand while pulling a slipper on her left foot with the other. She flounced up from her chair in a puff of pink and purple and sprayed Madame Rochas onto her thrapple. She choked, coughed some more, and wheezed down hard on another.

Jean ran to the front of her fancy dress shop, a mere front for outsized women's clothes for men, and turned around the sign:

GESCHLOSSEN (We're shut!)

Shirley flip-flopped her way to join Jean, who was still searching through her handbag for the keys.

"Eureka!" Jean dangled them in the air. Her car keys as well. And they rushed out onto the dusty streets of the Reeperban.

By the time Shirley poked, shoved, gathered and stuffed herself—and her outfit—into the passenger side, she couldn't see out the windscreen. Neither could Jean from the over-spill of Shirley's pink and purple creation.

Unperturbed, Jean switched on the motor, tuned in, and rammed her foot on the accelerator. The wheels spun in a cloud of burning rubber, and the car launched backwards for ten feet.

"Wrong gear, dear," Shirley pointed out. Luckily for her, her dress had acted as an emergency air bag.

Jean ground the gears. And like her alternate, Jean Bond, the car provided a helpful cloud of black exhaust fumes that belched out from the back.

They were off.

As were half the skinhead lads and their lovers at the Fischmarkt, all of them patrons of Tom's Cabin from that night and more: the leather guys, now in smart business suits from the financial district; the paramedics from the krankenhause; the taxi drivers; the bakers; and candle stick makers; the off-duty cops; the motorbike fiends; the muscle guys; and the fans who had stomped their way through Alex's singing at der Titanic.

This was an emergency.

Even the reporters who had followed the story from the beginning made a rush for something that might prove a promising lead for the night's Zeitungen headlines.

Oblivious to it all, Alex was already out of the taxi and hobbling his way into Hotel Mercure, oblivious to everything but finding Jamie and going over in his mind what he was going to say to Jamie.

And every time he thought of how he would make up to Jamie, how he would apologize, he cringed inside, wishing that there were some other way. Except there was no other way, he realized. No way to squirm out of the obvious need to be up front and take full responsibility for how cruelly he had spoken to Jamie

He rode the lift to the third (really the second) floor, limped along the corridor and stood in front of the room door.

This is it, he thought, his insides shaking.

Alex pushed the key into the lock, thinking that knocking first, to warn Jamie, would have been silly. He opened the door slowly and looked around the side.

The place was empty, quiet.

Alex stepped inside and closed the door behind him. He wanted to call out. He checked the bathroom.

Another empty room.

The window was open. A cool, refreshing breeze blew back on the net curtain. A pile of clothes lay neatly on the bed.

Alex frowned and looked down at them, at the camera lying on top. Walking over to the little desk by the window, he hesitated for a moment before pulling the drawer open. His notebook was still inside, as was his pen. Nothing else.

He walked over to the tallboy and opened all of its drawers.

Empty.

Panic began to rise up inside Alex. He hobbled over to the wardrobe and pulled open the doors.

Empty wire coat hangers hung from the rail. Everything was gone. Everything of Jamie. It was as if he had never been here.

Alex looked around frantically, pulled at the pile of his clothes neatly folded on the bed.

Nothing of Jamie's to be seen. He rushed over to the telephone on the bedside cabinet and called down to reception. No one had seen Jamie. Of course, he might have left when no one was looking. Yes, the young gentleman had paid up the hotel bill for a month in advance. When? Yesterday.

Alex dropped the telephone back on its cradle. And it hit him.

Jamie was gone.

The song kept going through Alex's head. He dropped his walking stick on top of the bed, hunkered down and looked under it.

Nothing there either.

There had to be something.

Stand by me.

He looked up again, thinking, stood up, wining at the pain in his left leg.

The world took on a swimmy blur as his blood pressure sank, then rose when he stood up straight too quickly. He hobbled back through to the bathroom, pulling open the cabinet over the sink. Empty. Not a razor, toothbrush or paste left.

He hobbled back, stunned. The cold tiles pressed back at him. Alex shook his head. He looked down at the carpet, at the litterbin under the wash hand basin. Crouching down, he reached out and picked it up.

One single slip of paper. One ticket stub.

Alex dropped the basket and looked at the stub closely: Hamburg-Harburg. At 5:25 pm.

But where after that, Jamie? This isn't a ticket to Cuxhaven. Isn't a ticket to the ferry, either …

"Oh, my God!"

Alex looked at his watch. It was already 4: 56.

He limped and hobbled his way down the steps and into the long shadows that were beginning to stretch up a quiet Bremer Reihe. As fast as he could, red faced, huffing and hobbling, Alex made it onto the main street.

Alex raised his walking stick in the air. Taxis came and went. At last, one stopped. Alex threw himself into the back.

"Altona Haufbanhof," he shouted at the driver.

"Altona?"

"Ja! Und schnel!"

The taxi pulled out. Agitated Alex called out "*Schnel*! *Schnel*!"

~~*

By the time Shirley and Jean screeched to a halt, Bremer Reihe was jam packed with a motley crew of suits, Harleys, skinheads and drag queens.

"What the hell's going on?" Jean asked.

Cutting a divide through her chiffon, Shirley viewed the scene. "An accident?" she offered.

But Jean was already out of the car and making her way through the crowd. When Shirley opened the door on her side, an explosion of chiffon burst out.

The receptionist was backed against the schlussel wall. Questions were barked at him from all directions. Rottweilers sniffed and pranced around him menacingly.

Where was Alex? they demanded. "Wo ist er? Antwort jezt! Jezt!"

How should he know?

Every mobile in the place went off at the same time. Then silence as everyone elbowed and shoved for space to read the message: a picture of Alex clambering inside the back of a taxi.

Someone recognized the street. "Altona Tor! Altona Tor!"

As if reacting to a starter's pistol, everyone shoved and heaved to get out through the glass doors, which nearly snapped off, and back onto the street. Car doors opened and slammed shut, dogs barked, Harleys roared into life.

Shirley screeched to a halt and was pushed back. Jean whizzed past. Shirley followed, slippers slapping on the cobbles. "Where are we going?"

"Altona Tor!" Jean called back.

Shirley's hand slapped up to the beads on her neck. "Not the Tor!"

~~*

Alex threw the Euros at the driver, clambered out and ran for the haufbanhof on Altona Tor.

… stand by me … stand by me …

He was already inside the doors, looking around and wondering where the train left from. He was looking at the timetable when the roar of motorcycles and Trabants, skinheads and Rottweilers barked their way to a halt in the distance.

~~*

This time, Shirley, legs poking out the door with a flounce of chiffon, was ready to jump before Jean had a chance to stop the car.

Rush hour.

~~*

Alex pushed through crowds and found a timetable glowing with arrivals and destinations. The big hands on the clock read 5:15.

Come on, come on, where is it?

"Hah!" he yelped. "Hamburg-Harburg!"

Gleiss Five. Except the station was filled with hundreds of platforms. Which one?

Almost dragging his left leg now, he made for one of the escalators.

5:19.

Alex clambered his way to the top of the escalator, weaving past commuters. "Get out my way, will you no!"

At last, the top.

Now where? Gleiss funf, gleiss funf, gleiss funf, *stand by me* ...

He turned this way and that.

"Gleiss funf!" he called out in desperation. "Helfen mich," he cried out to the crowd of commuters.

"Bitte! Bitte!" He confronted one after the other. "Gleiss funf? Wo ist gleiss funf? Are you all dense? Eejits!"

A helpful arm pointed to another escalator. Alex spun around, tripping over his leg that wouldn't move as fast as the rest of him, and he fell, crashing down onto the concourse.

5:22.

Hands reached down and pulled him to his feet and dusted him down. In pain, face a grimace, Alex head for another escalator. At least it was down this time.

"Jamie! *JAMIE*!" He scrambled down the moving steps, clinging to the handrail.

The sound of rail carriages running heavily, quickly and slowly, rumbled through the station. Alex kept trying to see, craning his neck form side to side, looking down.

"Jamie!"

Tears stung his eyes. Gliess Five! The carriage, the train, Hamburg-Harburg.

Then where are you going, Jamie, then where?

"Jamie!" he cried out over and over. He called out again jumping the last few steps. The pain of the landing crunched up through his damaged hip.

5:23!

But the doors were closed on the train and it was already pulling out of the station.

"Damn blast it leg!" He gripped hold of a pillar and pulled himself to his feet. But he couldn't run fast enough and already he knew that it was too late.

He stopped and stood on the platform and watched the back of the train speed out into the early evening sunlight.

"*JAMIE*!"

The platform was empty. Silence and nothing but warm air, pillars and metal seats, metal bins and a few scraps of paper blowing in a gentle breeze, and Alex now alone.

He couldn't believe it. Jamie was gone now, and there was no way of finding out where he was going.

It was all too much. Alex sat down slowly on one of the metal seats, resigned, and lonely.

"Och, Jamie. Why did you have to leave? Why Jamie, why?"

Alex looked up at the tiled wall at the other side of the track. He already knew the answer to his own question as a tear fell from his eye. "Because I pushed you away," Alex whispered to himself.

But even as he hung his head, the pain in his hip was no competition to the pain and emptiness inside him, and he knew why. There would be no shame in it now, no one to see him as he cried.

Stand by me.

A shadow moved silently as his shoulders shook with emotion, a scrape of a footstep behind him, the gentle hand of a stranger on his shoulder. Alex, the world swimming all around him, slowly looked up.

"Jamie?" And the name came out in a mess even as he jumped to his feet. "Oh, Jamie, I'm sorry. I thought you had left me. I'm sorry, I'm sorry," Alex called again and again as he held on.

Jamie held him close. "I could never leave you, Alex," Jamie said. "Even if I thought you hated me for the rest of my life. Even from a distance, if that was the nearest I could ever be to you ever again, I would always stand by you."

Suddenly there was rapturous applause.

Like a slow moving waltz they both stepped around in a circle, looking at the crowd clapping, whistling, cheering, a strawberry blonde woman in a pink and electric frazzling-blue chiffon ball gown wearing fluffy pink slippers dabbing at her eyes.

"We're not invisible monsters any more, Alex," Jamie said quietly into his ear.

Alex looked into Jamie's eyes. "We're no monsters, Jamie," he said. "We never were."

CHAPTER 57

Hawks, doves, sparrows and angels, everyone mixed up in who was where in the pecking order, Jamie and Alex hugged and kissed on the platform as the cameras came out, the crowds rushed in, and the paparazzi piled down the escalators, clambering over each other and everyone else.

Microphones and notebooks appeared out of nowhere as the eye of the storm closed in. Lights flashed. Rottweillers wagged their tails, barked, and the rejected and shunned suddenly found themselves in the limelight.

Shirley's curlers began to lose their grip as she elbowed her way in. Jean ducked beneath the melee. Fame came with its own unforeseen consequences. The young pair might end up being crushed out of existence.

Shirley was there first, her biceps flexing as she snaked her protective arms around their thin, wee shoulders. Jean was next, barking orders in German for everyone to get back and give the fragile couple some room.

"Die Engel!" one of the reporters shouted. "Die Engel!"

More pictures. More flashes.

Jamie was crushed up against Alex. "What are they on about—dih ingil?" he asked.

"If we get out of this," Alex said, "I'll tell you."

Just as Jean, Shirley, Alex and Jamie found themselves being bustled into the street, the police arrived, lights flashing and sirens blaring.

The crowd bustled ever forward, until Jean's little Trabant was covered by them. Jean hauled open the back door and Shirley rammed Alex and Jamie inside.

"What's going on?" Jamie pleaded.

Shirley bundled herself inside the passenger seat. Jean managed somehow to clear a way through Shirley's chiffon to get to the ignition. The Trabant backfired twice, engulfing the crowds in smoke. A camera crew appeared through the fog. Jean pulled down sharply on the steering wheel, zipping a hairpin bend around tripods and yells and screams.

Shirley parted a wave through her ball gown and peered though the windscreen. "Where the 'ell are we?" she said, spitting out an ostrich feather.

"Yeah, where are we going?" Alex called out from the back. He inhaled a feather and started to choke. Jamie bashed him on the back. "All right! All right!" Alex said. "We've been, there done that!"

"Sanctuary, of sorts," Jean called out above the sound of the engine. "A breathing space."

The Trabant zipped up the dusty streets of St Pauli, then on to the Reeperban. Jean slammed on the brakes a little too hard outside of a shop front: Jean's Jollies, Fancy Dress.

Everyone piled out into the street. Jean and Shirley bustled the two lads to the front door. Everyone dived in, the last in a puff of shredded purple and pink.

Once inside Jean locked the door, pulled down the blinds and made sure the sign was the right way around still and against the glass:

GESCLOSSEN

Disney Land for adults was all the Jamie could think.

The place reeked of pancake makeup and dry cleaning. The colors came at him from every angle. There were wigs of every color and style, cowboy outfits, headgear sprouting giant eagle feathers for Indian chiefs, taffeta and crinoline, Marie Antoinette bodices and hooped skirts. Further back lay the more outrageous wear: giant tomatoes and every other fruit and vegetable one could imagine, all of them gigantic, as well as eye-masks on sticks fit for the Masque. And white and black naval officer uniforms—the only normal looking things to be seen.

"Tea, anyone?" Shirley asked, disappearing through a door at the back of the counter.

"Am I still in a coma?" Alex whispered to Jamie.

"If you are, then I am too," Jamie replied, turning around, eyes like saucers. It was like finding himself inside a toy box, one he never had.

"What are we here for anyway?" Alex asked.

"Actually," Jean said. "I'm not too sure about that myself. It wasn't until I saw Jack ..."

"Jack?" Jamie and Alex asked at the same time.

"Shirley," Jean elucidated. "When I saw him put his arm over your shoulders, I think we all got a bit carried away in the heat of the moment. As it is, I think you would have been crushed under that lot. The rest was just instinct. Anyway, I think we're safe for the moment. But once the papers get a hold of where you are ... Well, that's something else."

And as Jamie asked why, Jack—or rather Shirley—was already on her way out from the back of the counter. "You're both pretty famous, that's why," Shirley said. "And you, young man, being in the hospital, meant that they had to bide their time. Patient confidentiality. But when you left the hospital like that, it seems there was a free for all. Out of sanctuary and into the limelight. There's a lot of human interest about you two going on here."

Jean reached under the counter and pulled out a newspaper. She opened it. "Here," she said, handing it to Alex.

Tentatively Alex reached out and took the newspaper from her.

"Front page news," Shirley said, setting down the silver tray with its cups and teapot.

Jamie looked over Alex's shoulder, at the picture in the centre of the page. Alex could hardly keep the pages steady in his trembling hands.

"I saw this," he said quickly.

"When?" Jamie asked.

Alex lowered the paper and looked off to somewhere distant, somewhere beyond the walls. "Helena."

"The nurse?" Jamie said.

"Aye," Alex said to him. "But it wasn't in a paper like this. It was on a mobile phone. She said that I shouldn't have been seeing it because it was police evidence or something."

He lifted the page again and looked at the photograph. A video image turned into a single still photograph that was almost blurred beyond recognition. But Alex could make out the strain on Jamie's face, his mouth wide in a silent scream, the rag doll of Alex's body in his arms. It hurt too much to look at it.

"Nobody could make out what you were saying, you see," Alex said. "It was that thick accent of yours."

"I'm hardly able to remember, myself," Jamie said.

"Looking at this," Alex said, "and seeing the state you were in, I can hardly blame you. But I heard what it was off the mobile video Helena showed me. That's why they paper guys were shouting like that."

"Angel?" Jean asked.

Alex nodded. "Aye," he said, lowering the paper and looking at Jamie. "That's what you were shouting. 'You've broken the wings of an angel.'

"Ah, well, you see, I could have died," Alex sighed as he reminisced, putting on his best poetic-consumption demeanor. "No, no, don't worry about me." He coughed. "I'll live—I think. I could be wrong though."

Alex saw the less than pleased look in Jamie's face. He perked up. "Of course," Alex said, "had it not been for my hero here, Jamie, well ..." He sniffed quickly, regaining composure, but not quite fully. "... It doesn't bear thinking about, does it?"

Shirley wobbled in with more tea in the best china. Tiny tongs in the air with one lump of sugar hovering over the cup, she looked at Alex with eyes pleading for an answer.

"Oh, aye," he said to her. "I mean, yes. They're only teeny wee lumps, aren't they? So four should do just fine."

"Four!" Jamie squawked, his arms shooting back and true like a crow's wings in fright.

"Aye, well, maybe just three and a half lumps then," Alex corrected, "seeing as I've lost so much weight after being in a long, prostrated coma for endless weeks at a time and having had a *major* heart attack that almost *killed* me, I think that I need to build up my strength." He took the cup and saucer from Shirley.

Jamie's mouth tightened to a blister.

Jean walked in with a sponge cake. She cut it in half, then one of the halves into quarters as Alex's eyes widened. Jean cut one of the quarters in half again and held out the plate of Black Forest torte.

Alex reached out without a 'please' or a 'thank you', taking it all for granted, ignored the eighths and delicately scooped up a great wedge of a quarter. Jamie's lower jaw launched straight down to the deck. Alex didn't see this as his eyes had already had to close, what with the effort he needed to create enough space for the cake by jacking open his gob wide enough.

Jamie fumed as he watched Alex's mouth continue to stretch as wide as that woman on that old sci-fi program *V* when that alien woman had swallowed a whole rhinoceros!

"Poor thing," Shirley almost sobbed, listening to Alex's sorry story.

"He's quite out of danger now, you realize, miss?" Jamie cut in.

"Aye," Alex started. "Even the hole they drilled in my head has begun to close up nicely."

Jean straightened up, took a sharp intake of breath and slapped her hand over her mouth. She might have used her other to keep her eyes in, but she was too much in shock.

There was a crash as Shirley swooned back in a dead faint onto the floor.

"Well, ladies," Jamie said, scooping Alex out of his chair and it's too comfy, fluffy cushions. "We'll have to be going now."

Alex stood up with a demure, if pained, look in his face and hobbled, as if his left shoe was now suddenly made of barbed wire, at Jamie's side.

"Aye," Alex said to the two women. "Needs must, as they say. We better get back to the hotel."

Now recovered, Jean and Shirley shot a glance at on each other. As if a telepathic conversation had taken place between them, Jean stood up and spoke first. "Look, boys," she said. "Why don't you stay here for a bit."

"Yes!" Shirley jumped up and clapped her hands. She squeezed Jean as if this were the best present she had ever had.

"There's a big spare room at the back," Jean said. "All the privacy you need. Private shower, toilet, come and go as you please." She urged with wide eyes and a huge smile.

Alex looked at Jamie. "I'm no saying anything," he said. "But whatever you do say, I'll go along with it."

"But what about the hotel, Alex?" Alex reminded Jamie that he had already made the decision to leave. Not that Alex was blaming him for that. In light of the circumstances, it was entirely understandable.

"Though I'll never ask where you were really heading to, Jamie, because that was something private between you and yourself. But the fact is that you had already left the hotel anyway, so it can't be that much of a draw for you to go back to, can it?"

"No pressure, Alex. Ta," Jamie said, straightening up.

"Look," Jean began. "I'm not trying to tie you down. But it would be like a big happy family. Even for a little while. And Shirley and me, well, we're old hands when it comes to handling the public. I mean, look at this place. We have to keep everything secret from prying eyes."

"We can look after ourselves," Alex piped up.

"I'm sure you can, Alex," Shirley said.

"'Prying eyes?'" Jamie asked suspiciously.

"The clientele we get in here, love," Jean said. "All this, the fancy dress stuff, is just a front for the real thing."

"To be honest, what Jean is trying to say," Shirley said, "is that there are a lot of men out there, married men, who feel all wrong in this world, like me, and Jean helps us out."

"Men dressing up as women?" Alex asked.

"It's a bit more than that," Shirley explained.

"And the thing is," Jean said, "we understand what they feel like on the inside. They love their wives, and some of their wives love them all the more for it."

"Der Titanic?" Alex asked.

"A place where men ..." Shirley spoke up.

"Sometimes women too," Jean added.

"... can really be what they feel they are. What they really feel like inside. Anyway, a lot of those men have to be very secretive, about their careers, their neighbors. So you see, what with all the public interest in both of you, this would be the perfect place to hide for a bit of peace and quiet."

Alex asked for a few minutes alone with Jamie. When Shirley and Jean hustled off behind the curtain at the back of the counter, Alex sat beside him.

"Do you want to go home, Jamie?" Alex asked.

But at first, Jamie couldn't find the words to reply. Instead he reached out and held onto Alex. Alex put his arms around Jamie and hugged him tight.

"I thought I had lost you, Eck," Jamie said. "I thought you had died. I was so scared. I've never been so scared of being on my own before, no before I met you. And then I felt horrible and selfish because I was just thinking about myself. Then when they told me that you didn't want to speak to me, it was like something far bigger than me was giving me the answer that I should leave you be and let you go. That I had to face up to the responsibility of respecting your wishes in never see you again."

Alex pulled back a little and looked Jamie in the eyes. "It was me that was being selfish, Jamie. No you. And I've learnt my lesson. Anyway, the fact is we can't stay much longer in Hamburg anyway. So we can go back to the hotel, or we can stay here for a bit, with people who like us and without the papers breathing down our necks. That is, until it's time for us to go back home."

Jamie nodded, yes.

At least for a while, it would feel as if they actually belonged somewhere.

Jean and Shirley stood to attention, in front of the boys, as if they were on inspection parade.

"We still have to go back to the hotel, though," Jamie explained, "and pick up Alex's stuff. We're just worried about what will happen if we get seen? How can we get Alex's stuff out without being noticed?"

"Incognito!" Jean said, jumping up in delight.

Shirley clapped. "Jean, you're a genius. Of course, incognito."

"What do they mean by incognito?" Jamie asked Alex from the side of his mouth.

"Don't ask," Alex said.

CHAPTER 58

The doors of Hotel Mercure blammed wide open.

Matahari swished in first, wearing a jaunty hat and her face covered in black fishnet lace. Only one eye showed under the brim. Collar high, hand on hip, her other hand clutched a foot a long cigarette holder replete with silver ringed tip. Smoldering cigarette poking out the end of it thereof, she lifted it and sucked in smoke through her veil.

Behind her strolled in Jean Bond, in six-inch stilettos, for the authentic Sean Connery, seven-foot tall, tree topper look.

Fruit and Dessert followed.

The four strode up to the lift at the back. The receptionist craned his neck around the side. There was something familiar about that blamange.

The lift slid down to ground level as Matahari took in another long slow drag of her cigarette. After they all crammed inside the lift, she choked and spluttered just as the doors banged shut on the lot of them.

A little while later, the wee fat blamange struggled out past reception again, this time with a rucksack on its back. A banana followed on and smiled at the receptionist. Matahari and Jean Bond followed.

Out on the street, Matahari opened the back door of an authentic (because it was) Trabant. The blamange and the banana crammed into the back seat after having stuffed a gigantic rucksack into the boot.

"What do I have to be the blamange for, anyway?" Alex whined.

"Just get in," the banana snapped back.

The back wheels sagged and almost burst. Jean Bond's stiletto screeched on the cobbles, sending up sparks. Matahari climbed elegantly into the passenger seat, mile long cigarette holder poking out the door. She slammed the door closed. The cigarette holder was decapitated.

"Sheist!"

The receptionist approached the glass doors of the hotel and peered out. A cloud of fog enveloped the little car, but by then, the car and its passengers had already vanished magically anyway.

~~*

Alex and Jamie began to feel guilty after a week of living free in the flat above Jean's shop. Shirley and Jean didn't seem to mind though. They were happy that the boys had decided to stay for a while longer.

Eventually, Alex went back to the hospital with Jamie for a final check-up. Jamie sat in the corridor, terrified something would be found.

"I'm cured!" Alex called as he rushed out to meet him.

"Cured of what?" Jamie asked. "Being mental?"

"Epilepsy! ECG says there's no trace of weird brain activity. So that fat get of a skinhead, whoever it was, cured me!"

"You sure?"

"Aye, and I've told them to send all the results to that auld crow of a GP of ours back home. Best thing is, I don't have to come back here to the Krankenhaus."

Things had seemed to settle down into a steady routine. And with nothing better to do, and tiring of their eyes popping in and out of their heads at the sights of St. Pauli ..."The Beetles played in the ... well somewhere round here," Alex said ... and in the Reeperban, Alex and Jamie felt themselves spending more and more time at Jean's Jollies.

"What do you think of this, Jamie," Alex said, turning around with one of the white dress uniforms of a Naval officer, wearing the cap and gloves.

Except Jamie wasn't there. Or he could have been. The place was so stuffed with fancy dress and not so fancy dress that it was difficult to see if he was there or not.

"Entschuldigung Sie bitte?" a man's voice asked apologetically behind Alex.

Alex spun around. "Oh!" he said.

"Kann Sie helfen mich?" the man asked.

"Eh ... em."

"Diese," the man said, pointing to an emerald colored bejeweled Victorian gown complete with upstanding ostrich feathers dyed cobalt blue. "Haben Sie es in ...?" the man pointed at himself with an uncertain smile.

"Hmmm," Alex said, tapping one white-gloved finger at his chin.

And without thinking about it, Alex took a tape from the counter and began taking the gentleman's measurements. The man seemed to be perfectly delighted by Alex's attention. He smiled knowingly over at his Frau by the door, who breathed a sigh of relief and began to relax. She sat down on a chair and waved a lace hanky at her hot flush.

"Jean!" Alex yelled at the top of his lungs, making der Mann und die Frau jump.

"Yes, love," Jean called back from somewhere.

"There's a geezer out here that wants to know if we've got that green Victorian number in a size forty-fünf!"

The woman raised her eyebrows at her husband. The husband raised his eyebrows back at her.

Jean emerged through reams of ball gowns, feathers, streamers and netting. "Size forty-five?" Jean said. "Yes, Alex. We still have one, through the back. Would you be a dear and get it for me? It should be on the middle shelf, box twenty-six."

"Right. Box zecks und swanzig. Got it," Alex said, turning away.

"Oh, and Alex?"

"Aye?"

"We're not on different planets, love. We don't have to shout so loud." She smiled.

"Okay, Ma," Alex said, disappearing.

Jean's heart skipped a beat. Ma? Did that mean mother? Something happened to Jean then, but she wasn't sure what. Taking a deep breath, she smiled and approached the customer.

"Mein Herr, meine Frau," Jean said. "Guten tag."

"Er ist ihre sohn?" the woman asked Jean.

"Sorry for shouting earlier like that," Alex said. "Didn't realize I was being so loud."

"Don't worry," Jean said. "In fact," she went on, "I think der Herr was quite taken by the attention he received from a young, handsome naval officer. And one who wasn't being prissy about it."

"Eh?"

"These men, Alex," Jean said, "and some women too, are always frightened of the distain they think, and usually do, receive from others."

"Don't get you," Alex said, screwing up his face.

"He felt as if he was being treated as a human being for once. That's what I mean," Jean explained.

Alex frowned. "But he is," he said.

Jean smiled and laughed. "Yes!" she said. "You're right. He is!"

Just then Shirley appeared, her wig a fright. "Where's Jamie?" Jean asked.

"Through the back," Shirley said. "He wants to help so he's doing some stocktaking for me. Stocktaking I cannot stand. So I'm glad he's offered to help."

Alex jumped up. "I'll just go and see if I can give him a hand as well," he said.

Jean and Shirley stood side by side and watched Alex disappear through to the back. Jean wanted to hear him say something again, something he had said earlier. But he didn't. Something inside her sank a little. She looked at Shirley.

"What is it, love?" Jean asked.

Shirley sniffed.

"Oh, love, whatever's the matter?"

Shirley blinked her enormous, enormovibrolashed-mascara-smudged with a lava-flow-of-black-tears eyelashes at Jean.

"Shirley, what is it for God's sake?"

Dabbing at her eyes, Shirley could hardly speak. "Jamie," she said at last.

"Yes?"

"He called me Muuuuuummmm, uh huh huh huh huuuuuuh!"

When Shirley eventually lifted her tear soaked eyes from Jean's mascara-drowned shoulder, Jean said, "So did Alex to me."

They looked at one another, took in a deep breath, and burst into tears anew.

CHAPTER 59

Alex walked into the stockroom. Jamie stood on a ladder, tapping at boxes with a pencil, squinting at labels and ticking off items from a sheet.

"Jamie?"

"Don't break my concentration, Eck."

"Know this, Eck," Jamie said. "I'm surprised anybody knows where anything is in here, or anywhere else for that matter."

Alex looked around at the room, the shelves. Everything seemed to be stacked without any thought of order. "No very organized, is it?" Alex said. "Anniker's Midden, that's what this place should be called, no Jean's Jollies."

Jamie continued to count and tap at the boxes. He squinted at the sheet then climbed higher up the ladder, trying to see what was on the upper shelf.

"Jamie?"

"Alex, I told you, I can't stop just now."

"*Jamie*!"

Jamie peered down on him. "What is it?" he said. "Can you no see that I'm busy?"

"I need to talk to you."

After a pause and a sigh, Jamie stuck his pencil behind his lug and climbed down. "What is it, Alex?"

~~*

"Come on. Sit down for a minute," Jean said. "We'll be okay. The boys are busy through the back. Let's have a cup of tea."

Shirley sat down and caught sight of herself in the mirror. "Oh my God! Look at the sight of me."

"Darling," Jean said, leaning forward and placing a reassuring hand on Shirley's. "You can't be Marilyn ..."

"Manson?"

"Monroe, or Dusty or Carol Channing every day of the week," Jean said.

Shirley's wig collapsed. "You're right," she said quietly.

"Anyway, what did you think of the boys calling us both mother?" Jean asked as she poured the tea.

"Do you think they decided between themselves beforehand, to say it, as a joke I mean?" Shirley asked.

Jean looked out the window, at the sun, the way it was beating down on the dusty streets of the Reeperban. "I don't know," she said. "It sounded so natural the way Alex said it to me."

Shirley looked at Jean. "And it felt so natural when Jamie said it to me too, Jean."

"I know what you mean," Jean said. "And I felt it, here," she said, placing her hand on her heart. "I can't explain it. It was so unexpected, yet so overpowering. It knocked me for six straight out of left field, if you know what I mean. I feel as if I'm a mother whose long lost sons have found me." She shook her head. "I can't even have kids."

Shirley reached out and took Jean's hand, giving it a squeeze. Jean went on. "I don't even know where the feeling came from—comes from," she corrected. "There's nowhere for it to come from. It ..."

"Me neither," Shirley said, quietly dragging the wig from her head. "But it felt so natural, Jean."

They looked in each other's eyes, as if they were searching for an answer neither one of them had. Jean spoke first. "Are you thinking of what I'm thinking?" she asked.

"If you're thinking the same thing that I'm thinking, then yes."

"Well?" Jean asked.

"Jean?" Shirley said. "Before we say anything else about it, there's something I've been meaning to ask you."

"What's that, love?"

Shirley went down on one knee. "Will you marry me?"

~~*

"A show?" Jamie asked Alex nervously.

"Aye," Alex said. "It would be a way of thanking everybody, Jean in Shirley, for taking us in like their own kids. And for Helena and the guys at Tom's. And the women from the Titanic. What do you think, Jamie?" Alex said, his voice rising in excitement.

Jamie screwed up his face, still not convinced. "What kind of show?" he asked.

"Singing and dancing," Alex said. "You and me, up on stage."

"Awe, God!" Jamie cringed and stepped back.

"We can do it, Jamie. You and me, both together," Alex said. "Come on. Say aye. Even if we're both rubbish, it would at least be a way of giving something back for what everyone's done for us."

Alex stopped, eyes wide, jaws like The Joker, urging Jamie for an answer.

Jamie stood and thought about it for a few seconds. "I just wish somebody would find those gets that did it to us, Eck."

Alex looked serious for a moment. "I know, Jamie. And I haven't forgotten about them either. But I have to face up to the fact that they might never be caught. They know what they did to us, Jamie. So do we and everyone else. And if there's any kind of humanity in them, sooner or later, they'll no be able to live with themselves."

Jamie bunched up his fists. "I wish I could get my hands on them though, Eck. And sometimes it eats at me bad."

Alex put a hand on Jamie's shoulder and hugged him close. "I know," he said. "But we have to let it go, Jamie. Maybe even find it in our hearts to forgive them."

Jamie out of Alex's reaches. "Forgive them," he said. "Those neo-Nazi gets?"

Alex smiled wanly. "Think about it, Jamie. If we don't forgive them for what they've done, we're the ones who are going to end our days all bitter and twisted. We'll be the ones who will end up hurting ourselves for them."

Jamie still wasn't convinced. *Forgiveness my foot*! But Alex was right, he supposed. If they didn't let go they would be living with the bitterness in their hearts for the rest of their lives.

"What kind of show anyway?" Jamie asked, needing to change the subject.

Alex gave a sigh of relief. "Well, I was thinking about the name of the bar," Alex said. "*Titanic*! Then I had this brill idea for a show. And I've got just the right sang for us to sing."

Jamie's heart sank. "What song? What idea? And don't say Celine Dion!"

"Nah," Alex said. "Don't be daft."

Jamie sighed in relief.

"It's something even better."

~~*

"*Married*?" Alex looked confused.

"Yes," Jean said ecstatically.

"Congratulations," Jamie said.

"There's only one thing, boys," Shirley said, straightening her wig.

"Aye?" Alex asked.

"Yes," Jean said.

"We would like both of you to be the best man," Shirley yelped with a jump of delight.

~~*

News spread like wildfire throughout every nook and cranny in the Reeperban and beyond. But where was the reception to be held, the ceremony?

"The Titanic?" called out Alex when he heard Jamie saying it. "The bar?"

"No, the boat. The one that sank. Of course the bar," Jamie told him.

"It's all going to be so perfect," Shirley said.

And as Jean and Shirley made for the telephones to call all and sundry, Alex pulled Jamie aside. "We'll have to be quick now," Alex said.

"For what?" Jamie asked.

"Our show, what else?"

"Alex, lad, that's for by the by now," Jamie said. "We've got enough with the wedding to go on with now without thinking of singing and dancing. We're both the best man as well, remember."

"Don't worry," Alex reassured Jamie. "The wedding won't be for ages yet."

"Three days!" Shirley flounced through, feathers and fluff hanging from the rails.

"For what?" Alex asked.

"The wedding. Kirsche Kirche. Cherry church," Shirley said breathlessly.

"Three days!" Alex yelped. He fair fainted away onto the chair behind him.

"Alex! Alex!" Jamie darted toward him. "I've been feared this would happen. It's his brain. It must have exploded inside his head with the strain. *CALL AN AMBULANCE*!"

Alex sat bolt upright. "Three days?" he said.

Jamie staggered back in shock. "I thought you were dead again."

"No time for dying now," Alex said, launching himself to his feet. "There are things to be organized, Jamie."

"What!" Jamie lurched in fright.

"Come here," Alex commanded, disappearing into the back of the shop. Jamie followed on.

Almost immediately telephones began to ring. Shirley grabbed one of them. "Yes, it's true," she gushed. "Jean and I ... wunderbar ... ja ja."

~~*

"We've no much time," Alex said, getting down to the task in hand. He rummaged through the costumes.

"We've no time, never mind no enough time, Alex," Jamie said. "It's too much to do with the wedding happening as well."

Alex was having none of it. "We'll just have to kill two ..." *Birds with one stone*, he almost said. "... Never mind. I've got it for figured out." He reached into his pocket and pulled out a slip of paper. Unfolding it he gave it to Jamie.

Jamie squinted at it. "It's in German."

Buried in rummaging through boxes, Alex called back to Jamie with a helpful, "Learn it."

"I can't even read it, never mind learn it."

Alex yanked a black dress jacket out of one of the boxes. "Here," he said, holding it out to Jamie. "You can wear this." Titanic. Naval uniform. It didn't bode well with Jamie. Alex held up the matching trousers against Jamie. "They'll have to take them up a wee bit," Alex said. "Your legs are too short."

"Hey!" Jamie protested. "There's nothing wrong with the length of my legs."

"If you wear them like that it'll look like a bride's train trailing after you," Alex said.

"And I still don't know what this is about," Jamie said, waving about the bit of paper with the incomprehensible words on it.

"Jurgen Drew's song," Alex said.

Jamie spotted the word Titanic in the title. His heart sank faster.

Alex pulled a white naval officer's dress jacket out of another box and held it against himself. "Here, what do you think?" he said, chest out.

But all Jamie could say was, "How come I don't get the white one?"

"Because it doesn't suit you," Alex said.

"But I want the white uniform."

"Well, you can't have it," Alex said. "And that's that, *right*?"

Jamie lunged for it. "I want it."

Alex snatched it out of Jamie's grip. "Well you're no getting it!"

Thereupon followed the argument of the century. Both wanted the white uniform.

Neither wanted the black one.

Shirley and Jean crashed together in a headlong rush outside of the storeroom. They listened to the two lads arguing in a language neither of them could quite get the gist of. They moved closer to the door, faces scrunched up in concentration. Their hearts sang when they heard both of them calling out Jean and Shirley's new names at the same time.

"*Maaaaaaaaa*!"

CHAPTER 60

Everyone who was nobody was there. Nobody alive, that is. But dug up and reused. Marilyn Monroe, Stewart Granger, Boris Gay, Sally Bowls (twice), Marlene Dietrich (only one of her).

The music started. Everyone stood up in the pews. Jamie took Shirley's hand. She was so distraught her veil was sucked in with her sobs of joy. Dressed in white, her train followed her down the aisle mile after mile.

Jean came in as her favorite creation—Jean Bond—dapper in her top hat and tails, as were Jamie and Alex in theirs.

Alex walked one step behind because there was only supposed to be one best man after all, but Jean reached around and yanked him level with her. "Bugger tradition," she said into his ear.

There was something familiar about the priest, Alex thought, who stood before the alter in her white robe and golden miter, her raven black hair tumbling from under it seductively as her enormous eyelashes, accentuated with sloe-eyed eyeliner, opened wide as she clasped at her bible.

"Do I know her?" Alex whispered to Jean.

"Der Titanic," Jean said. "She sometimes sings there. She's a transsexual now in full holy transition."

The minister blessed the couple. I do's were said. Jamie reached out and took hold of Alex's hand when Shirley and Jean said them. Then they were married.

The bride kissed the bride.

The priest smiled down at her congregation like the virgin of holy sanctity she always claimed to be as everyone stood up and clapped, cheered and cried in joy.

Once it was over Jamie and Alex rushed outside. Pictures were taken.

Jamie was quite taken in himself with the attention until Alex grabbed his arm and yanked him off the steps of the church. Their long tails flapped after them as they raced towards the taxi waiting for them by the curb, and they jumped in before Jean and Shirley had a chance to notice they were gone.

And as Shirley and Jean walked arm in arm from under the eaves of the church, risotto was showered upon the newlyweds. Another cab was already waiting to take them to their reception at der Titanic.

~~*

Alex and Jamie's cab skidded to a halt. The doors swung open on either side and they jumped out and scarpered, already pulling off their clothes as they ran up to the front door of Jean's Jollies.

Jamie fumbled for the keys. "We're no going to make it," his voice waivered.

To which Alex snapped back. "We will!"

The door opened. They dashed in. The door slammed shut.

Once inside, they freshened themselves up and doused themselves in aftershave. The real stuff: Brut.

Alex made a quick call to der Titanic kneipe. Yes, their secret was still safe from the newlyweds.

"We're all right then," Alex said to Jamie. "They've still no Idea."

~~*

The sun was already dropping below the horizon and a golden evening light set Bremer Reihe aglow as Jean and Shirley entered der Titanic to rapturous applause, men as women, women as men, men as men, women as women, kissing and congratulating the happy couple.

"Lang may yer bum leak!" one muscle-bound, leather-clad number called out.

Every now and again Jean and Shirley would ask others if they had seen Alex and Jamie. They were supposed to be here already. Shirley caught sight of Jean biting her lip.

"Worried?" Shirley asked.

"Where are they?" Jean said.

"They must be around somewhere," Shirley said, trying to look over crowd.

They looked at each other with sudden shock. "You don't suppose?" Jean asked.

"No, they'll be fine," Shirley said.

"I can see our surprise for them is going pear shaped," Jean almost wept.

"Don't worry, Jean."

The lights went down. One of the leather boys climbed onto the stage at the back. It was Klaus, the surgeon who had operated on Alex all those weeks ago now. He grabbed the microphone. Madam Butterfly put another microphone, complete with stand, onto the stage making it two.

Jean looked at Shirley. Shirley looked at Jean and then back at the spotlight shining on Klaus. The beam narrowed down onto his crotch.

"Okay, okay," he laughed light heartedly, waving the light away. The beam widened up again. "Damen und Herren," he announced. "Wel*kommen*." Saying it the *correct* way.

The crowd fell silent. Klaus waited for the right moment. "Ich gebe Sie Jamie und Alex! Keine Panic auf der Titanic!"

The music started to rapturous applause. Jamie and Alex entered, one from stage left and the other from stage right. Jamie wore a black uniform, Alex a white one—he'd bribed Jamie with a Mars Bar for it.

They grabbed the microphones and gave it, as they say in Kelty, lalday. Everyone stomped and cheered along with the song.

"Oh, Shirley, look at them," Jean said, tears in her eyes.

But Shirley was too choked up to reply. She dabbed at her eyes. "They look so handsome in their uniforms." Jean, a black mascara of Niagara Falls running down her face, could only nod in agreement.

Leather muscle men in chaps and bulging jockstraps took the hands of Victorian ladies and bowed and danced and cheered. Alex and Jamie danced and spun around on stage in perfect rhythm to their singing. Then just as it ended they gave each other a quick A-line kiss.

The audience exploded and stomped their feet.

"Mehr! Mehr! Mehr … !" they called.

"Mare? They want mare, Eck?" Jamie breathed hard.

Alex unbuttoned his jacket, pulling it off to reveal a bare chest, skin glistening with sweat, now only in white gloves, cap and trousers. Jamie, not to be beaten, ripped off his jacket while they belted out another chorus.

Windows, bottles and glasses rattled on the gantry. Dusty Springfield rushed up and down trying to stop the glassware toppling off.

And suddenly it was all over.

Dusty sighed in relief, adjusted her wig and pulled her boobs from her back to her front where they belonged. Alex and Jamie stepped down from the stage and joined the crowd and went in search of Shirley and Jean.

~~*

Shirley was still dabbing at her eyes when she turned to look at Jean. "Jean? Jean? Where the hell are you?"

The spotlight fell on a lone figure standing in the center of the stage. The music began, and Jean sang her heart out for the woman in her life. "Pretty Woman."

Someone grabbed Shirley's arm, someone else her other, and pulled her to the front of the stage while Jean looked down and beckoned to her.

"Oh, I can't! I can't!" Shirley protested.

Oh, but she must. And with one final shove, she flew up onstage singing to along with Jean.

~~*

The crowd quieted down to just below ear-splitting level. It was a closed house, a private function, and no less busy for it. Shirley, Jean, Alex and Jamie stood close together at the side of the bar.

"Boys ..." Jean started to say. Jamie looked up. Jean then looked at Shirley. "Help me here with this will you, love," she said. "I don't know how to say this."

Alex looked up at Shirley, looked at Jean, then back to Shirley again. "Well," Shirley said, clearing her throat. "We know that you're both eighteen now, and with ..." she started to crack at the seams. "I can't Jean. I'm going to make a mess of it."

Alex and Jamie looked at each other. "Do you want us to leave the house? Is that what you're trying to tell us?" Jamie asked.

"Oh, God no, it's not that at all!" Jean cut in quickly, looking startled.

Jamie and Alex's eyes moved from one to the other as if watching a tennis match—though certainly not a squash match.

"We want to adopt you both!" Shirley blurted.

Alex and Jamie froze like statues. Shirley and Jean both smiled wide, nodding their heads frantically at the pair. Jamie and Alex turned to look at each other. "Eh?" Jamie said.

"Adopt you," Jean said. "Both you and Alex. Me and Shirley; we want to be your mother and eh ... mother to both of you."

"Adopt us?" Jamie asked slowly.

"Can you do that?" Alex asked.

"A real mum," Jamie said quietly to himself, looking down.

And the words he wanted to say were calling out from a secret part of his mind, from the past, as he lay there in bed at night, everything quiet, praying that someday, someone would love him enough to take him home ... someone who loved him, imagining what it would be like to have brothers and sisters, to go to school and holidays as a family, and ...

Jamie's bottom lip began to tremble. In all of his life it had been the one thing he had always hoped he would hear. That someone one day would care enough, someone who would want to be his mother. And now he was being offered two.

"Like a real mum?" he managed to blurt out without breaking down completely before the words were out of him.

"Yes, Jamie," Shirley said. "You and Alex. We both love you very much, Jamie, and we would like you to be our son along with Alex. We love you dearly Jamie ... Who couldn't?"

By then Alex was also finding it all too much to take. "A real mum, real mothers?"

He turned to Jamie and saw the pain trying to escape from him. "Come on, laddie," he said into Jamie's ear, pulling him close. "You don't need to hide your pain from me. You've done that for too long, and for too long you've been trying to be the strong wee man. But the abandoned baby's still inside you there, still hurting, isn't he? Don't let it hurt you any more, Jamie. Just let it all go."

Still holding onto Jamie, Alex looked up at Shirley and Jean. Then, after bowing his head slightly, he looked back up at them again and smiled before going on to say: "I think this means aye." Before adding, "Mum ... and Mum."

And then, oblivious to the rest of the world, all four hugged and kissed each other.

~~*

Barmaid Dusty was sure her heels had lost fünf centimeters already as she raced up and down the gantry. She had also been too busy to pay attention to the black and white CCTV camera displaying what was happening outside the entrance to the bar. The doors were locked.

One of the skinheads looked up and straight into the camera lens. He swung a baseball bat through the air and the screen went blank. A glass panel in the upper part of one of the doors shattered. Low, rhythmic thumping clashed with the music.

The music stopped.

The crowd fell silent and turned to the doors, at the shattered glass. Another security cam flashed up at the other end of the bar. Skinheads, nine or ten, perhaps more, were trying to crash through the doors. Confusion in the crowd gave way to fearful looks.

Alex looked round at them all. *What is everyone just standing around for?*

CHAPTER 61

Jamie jumped up on stage and grabbed the microphone. Someone had to take control of the situation. Naval cap half-cocked, he gripped the silver pole. "Listen. *Everybody*!"

No one listened. The floor heaved in a sea of sequins, Lurex, leather, aquamarines, fluorescent oranges and sherbet pink.

The hammering of the enemy at the doors was growing louder. The real monsters had arrived.

Alex clambered up on stage, on his hands and knees, cap askew, to join Jamie. Scrambling to his feet, he blew a feather floating down in front of his face away. It flew up in a flurry and fluttered back down. Alex's eyeballs crossed watching its trajectory. For a second, it distracted him, until Jamie's frantic calls into a microphone screeching feedback stopped him.

"*Shaaarraap*!" Jamie's voice yelled through the speakers.

That did it. Everyone stopped. The whirlpool of chiffon and brilliant colors stopped. Even the noise at the doors abated. With wide eyes, Alex turned to Jamie.

"Listen up everybody. This is an *emergency*!" Jamie yelled, and then, trying to reassure the audience: "We could all *DIE IN HERE TONIGHT*!"

You don't say, Alex thought, grabbing for the fluttering feather once again.

And it just as well no one could understand quite what Jamie had just said either. His finger wagged in the air, his face transformed into a mask of grim determination. "We're all running round like headless chickens in the slaughter house. Nobody's going sink us, Titanic or no!"

That turned some heads, crash helmet hair dos or not. Still nobody had a scheiße-ing clue what Jamie was saying. But it sounded good. The air was electric with expectation.

Alex's stomach churned at the thought of headless chickens in a slaughterhouse.

"We need coordination," Jamie yelled. Murmurs of approval. "We need someone who can *TELL* us how to deal with the enemy!" More murmurs and nods. "We need *leadership*!"

"Ja!" someone yelled.

Alex's eyes grew dreamy. Here was a hero in the making, his very own Jamie. And Alex was standing on the same stage as him. His heart beat with admiration.

"This calls for someone who's clear-headed and determined," Jamie yelled. "Someone with the answers we *need*."

"Ja! Ja! Ja!" the crowd yelled back.

Jamie drew in a huge breath then bawled into the microphone. "WE NEED *ALEX*!"

"Eh?"

Silence.

Alex looked at Jamie, then at the expectant crowd. A wan smile crossed his face.

"Here's a man who *knows* what to do," Jamie screamed into the microphone.

Alex wanted to slink off the stage quietly unseen, unnoticed. *I'm only a wee laddie*.

"And he, *heeee*, ladies and gentlemen, hims and hers, this man here knows all the answers to everything in the *UNIVERSE*!"

Alex's jaw dropped open. *What*?

Jamie beamed with pride, chest out fit to burst. "I give you *Alex McMullen*!"

The crowd erupted. Stilettos and Carmen Miranda platform wedgies stomped out in rhythm to their chanting. "ALEX, ALEX, ALEX!"

Alex tried to smile. The microphone flopped with a thunk in front of his face. He smiled at Jamie, at Jamie's hero worship of him, the wrong way around as Alex could see it. Jamie smiled back and nodded at him enthusiastically.

Awe, God!

Alex looked at the crowd for a second, a painful effort to smile cranked up the sides of his mouth. It was an effort. He glanced at Jamie, who had his fists on hips, his elbows out, chest out in pride.

He opened his mouth to speak. The microphone was suddenly whipped away from his gob.

"A big cheer for our man of the moment," Jamie yelled into the great big mic. "Alex, the man who knows EVER ..."

Alex grabbed the microphone back. Suddenly the strength came to him, though from where he didn't know. The crowd hushed itself into silence, expectant. Mile long eyelashes fluttered at their heroes on stage. Chiffon-clad sisters and their wives huddled together.

"Ladies ..." Alex's voice wasn't more than a whisper. "... And gentleman," he said, squinting at two Billy Jean look-a-likes in white Wimbledon gear, clutching their tennis racquets. He then looked at a star struck Jamie. "It gives me great pleasure ..." Alex said.

A sudden look of confusion fell over Jamie's face. Alex bit his lip. He turned back to the crowd. He looked over beehive hairdos. The doors were now hanging by a thread. The invisible monsters were out there, waiting.

Alex took on a steely-eyed look. He raised his arms in the air as if to silence the crowd. But no one was talking anyway as their looks of rapture began to give way to ones of desperation.

What do I say?

You say what you need to say, Alex, he heard in his grandmother's voice. *Do what you need to do. Needs must.*

And suddenly he knew. This was their last chance, he realized. And the words screamed out of his mouth, down on through the wires at the speed of light, and hit the crowd with a current that jolted them all into action.

"*Get the bastards!*"

Confusion gave way to cohesion. The crowd turned from the stage as one and charged for the doors. The doors swung wide—*out* of the way—taking half the lintel with them as pink and purple and aquamarine flooded through a breech in the hull and gushed into the street.

Alex jumped down from the stage. Jamie followed. He ran up behind Alex, grabbed him by the shoulders and spun him round.

"I knew you would know, Eck," he said, taking a Davies' locker deep breath of pride. "I just knew you would."

And with that he planted a great big smoocher on Alex's mouth. "My laddie!" Jamie said. "I'm so proud of you."

Alex quickly gathered himself together. There was a job to be done, an enemy to be beaten.

And he remembered the last time, the kicks, the punches, then the coma, and how he almost lost Jamie forever. The bastards had got away with it once. They had almost destroyed everything Alex ever loved.

Jamie looked at him now. Alex's eyes had grown deeper somehow.

"Never again, Jamie, never again," Alex said.

Both their heads turned at the sounds of the whoops and yells, the clatter of spiked heels on the stone steps up to street level.

"Let's get them, laddie," Jamie said.

Alex made his Red Indian warrior call, his hand batting *woo woo woo* sounds bursting from his mouth. Jamie took a deep breath in admiration as they rushed after the others to the outside world. Stilettos screeched on the pavement.

Sparks flew up like tracer fire as they skidded around the corner. Ladies of the night stepped back into the shadows of the doorways as the tsunami of color flooded by. Four skinheads belted down the strasse, running scared. With Boris Gay at their heels and a six foot four Elsa Lanchester, dressed in her greatest incarnation as The Bride of Frankenstein, chasing after them it was no surprise.

A lady of the night stuck her foot out of a doorway. The first skinhead tripped over it and did a cartwheel imitation as he flew into a wall. The second, a wee fat get, crashed into his back flattening the first one into a pancake. Another even fatter one crashed into the other two, ricocheting off and spinning around into the middle of the road like a dancing hippo.

Boris caught up.

The fattest skinhead tripped over his own feet in fright. He crashed to the pavement. In a split second he turned to look over his shoulder. Like a woman screeching, the skinhead yelled and tried to crawl away.

Too late.

Boris Gay, followed by the other ladies, was already on him. No way was Boris going to let *this* one get away.

"*Timber!*" She leaned forward full tilt and let nature do her best. Gravity was a great deterrent to escape.

Crunch!

Alex grabbed one of the racquets from Billy Jean; Jamie took the others. "Eck? Eck!"

Jamie picked up a rock from the side of the pavement, ran and whacked it through the air to Alex. Seeing it coming but closing his eyes anyway, Alex swung his racquet hard. The rock flew and thudded into fatso's back, sending him flying.

Alex and Jamie quickly, followed up in the rear as sisters manhandled two other skinheads. Alex broke through. Claws swooped down on the captives.

"Wait!" Alex yelled. "Don't kill them."

The crowd stopped. The skinheads look relieved.

"*Yet!*" Alex looked around. Where was the other one?

The street was silent. He looked up at the doorways they had already ran passed. An arm stretched out, mile-long fingernail pointed from a mercy angel of a hooker to the other side of the street. The two skinheads now safely captured, everyone's head turned in unison to where the finger was pointing: A doorway opposite.

Someone began to say something. Immediately Alex's finger went up to his mouth. "Sssh."

No one spoke. The world fell silent. The dark of the night closed in on all sides.

Crouching, now on the hunt, Alex moved across the road swiftly. Jamie followed up in the rear. Alex's ark looked good even in the dim streetlights.

A shadow darted out from the doorway. A bald headed fatso in jerkin and bleachers.

But Alex was quick. He jumped on the gorilla's back. The skinhead spun round and tried to shake Alex off. Jamie closed in. The skinhead reached up and tried to rip Alex off his neck.

Alex gritted his teeth and held on tight. "Oh, no you don't," he said.

The skinhead spun around and slammed backwards into the wall behind him. Unfortunately, Alex was the buffer zone in between. The wind punched out of him, seeing double, he still clung on. A fist swung up and thumped into Alex's eye.

Alex let go and slid down. His legs buckled. His prey escaping, Alex lashed out and grabbed at its ankle. The skinhead spun around, glaring down at Alex. He swung out with his free foot. Alex rolled to the side, the cold and grit of the pavement cutting into him.

His eye ached like hell and for an awful moment he thought that the monster had blinded him in the eye. He tried to hold on but the skinhead ripped his leg free. There was something about that face.

But it was too late. The skinhead had already turned away and was now running up the street.

No no no.

Someone gripped Alex under his arms and yanked him to his feet. It was Jamie.

"Jamie, that face," Alex said, dazed.

"Don't worry, laddie. We got the other two at least."

"But *that* one's getting away!"

Two dark shadows, low and swift, darted out, silhouetted against the streetlight.

"*Schnel*!" a gruff voice yelled out.

The skinhead's Doc Martins slithered to a stop. The rottweilers took up stances on either side of the skinhead, slavering, growling and looking damn mean.

The dogs were the same.

Alex ran up the road. Jamie called out to him and followed. Some of the sisters caught up with them.

Now all of the monsters had been caught. Hands fell on the skinhead, holding him tight. Alex took a close look at the face. Fury built up inside him.

"We meet again," he said close to its face.

The skinhead pulled back in disgust. Alex leaned in closer.

"Well," he said, "we'll just have to make sure."

The look fell off the skinhead's face."

"Get its knickers aff!" Alex commanded.

Everyone was taken aback. No one moved. Hands held onto the skinhead tight. The rottweillers kept their distance.

Right eye almost closed, Alex lurched in and struggled to rip the skinhead's bleachers down.

"What's going on?" Jamie asked.

Once he was stripped of his bleachers, Alex pointed. "That's what's going on," Alex said. "There. The bite mark on its fat ark! *He's* the one." The skinhead looked shocked. "Attempted murder then, isn't it?" Alex said.

The skinhead gave him a sneer.

"Remember forgiveness, Alex?" Jamie said.

"I want to clobber it!" Alex replied.

"Come own, Alex. What would that give you?"

Alex fist flew up and hit the skinhead in the eye. Whack!

"There's your answer," Alex said. "*Satisfaction*, that's what it gives me!"

Only now there were as many hands dragging Alex back.

The police arrived. The skinheads were arrested, handcuffed and taken away.

"I didn't think you had it in you," Jamie said.

"Neither did I," Alex said, wincing when he dabbed at his eye.

"Did you see the tattoos on it?" Jamie asked.

Alex looked with his one good eye at Jamie. "Aye," he said. "The Union Jack. They were Brits. Skinheads from our own country. And it makes me sick."

CHAPTER 62

They all split up into two camps. Some stayed on at der Titanic to help mop and scrape up and drink themselves into a well-earned oblivion. The rest followed Jean and Shirley, Alex and Jamie to Jean's Jollies for a private party.

Everyone was laughing and cheering, patting the boys on their backs. The lads, still dressed as officers, were the most requested dance partners.

"Jean—I mean, Ma?" Alex asked.

Jean smiled. "Yes, love?"

"Is it all right if I was to use your computer for a bit?"

Jean looked taken aback. She wasn't even sure that she had heard Alex's request properly above the noise of the crowd. "That old clonker of a machine?" she said. "I don't have any games on it, Alex."

"No, no, that's no what I'm wanting to use it for."

Jean shrugged. Alex thought he should explain things her a little more. "It's just that I had set up an email account thing when I wiz back home in Kelty, just before Jamie and me came on holiday to Hamburg. And since we've been here, I'd forgot about it till now. Is it all right if I was to use your computer see if there's any email for me?"

Jean shrugged again. "Why, of course you can, love. It's not a fast internet connection, I'm afraid, but yes, you use it all you want."

And with that, she gave Alex the password.

Two doors between him and the rest of the universe, Alex walked down the quiet hallway into Jean's office. Opening the door, he flicked on the light switch, walked over to the Jean's desk, sat down on her chair and listened for a moment to the silence while he looked at the lifeless computer screen.

Reaching over, he pressed the on button and the computer hummed into life. Sitting back, he took a few slow breaths, reached out for the keyboard and tapped in the password that would allow him to connect to the Internet.

The connection was slow. Jean had been right about that. But at least it was working.

Alex looked at the screen and just hopped that he remembered how to do it. He typed in his email address.

Seconds ticked by. His breath caught.

There was one message waiting. The date on when it had been posted was more than a month old. Alex bit his lip as he sat there looking, wondering what to do next. There was only one other person on the whole planet who knew that Alex even had an email address.

He reached for the mouse and moved the cursor over the waiting message and clicked:

Dear Mr. McMullen,

It took a while and some rather tricky negotiations, but I managed to find what you are looking for.

It wasn't that there was anything particularly difficult about it, just a few clerical errors that had been made by administration years ago. Unfortunately that caused a series of mix-ups in a chain that ended up being broken and reconnected elsewhere by mistake. After I found that to be the case, I unpicked everything and reconnected all to their rightful places. After that, it was all rather simple really.

Alex frowned as he continued to read the message.

> *One of the dates was wrong. That was the first clerical error. The month was wrong specifically. It should have been a one not a seven. No accounting for some peoples' handwriting. It should also have been January and not July.*
>
> *The second break in the chain was the place name. That was why it proved so difficult for you, or anyone else for that matter, to find what you were looking for.*
>
> *There was nothing mysterious or even secret about it; just another mistake on handwritten documents. After that they were placed in a different folder to where they should have really been put, which naturally only further exacerbated the problem.*
>
> *However, I have scanned and attached the file that you were seeking.*
>
> *If I can be of further assistance I'll be only too happy to be of assistance.*
>
> *Mssrs. Jameson and Co.*

Alex peered down at the little icon at the bottom of the screen. He sat back, heart thumping.

Reaching out for the mouse again, he moved the cursor over it …

<OPEN>

… And clicked.

CHAPTER 63

"Hey, Eck, where have you been?" Jamie called out from the middle of the crowd, the party now in full swing.

Alex let go of the door, let it close behind him and steadied his breathing as much as he could as he pushed his way through the partygoers to where Jamie reached out and grabbed his arm.

"Come on," Jamie said. "Let's dance. Everybody's dying to watch us do the sloshed. I'll give you my last Parma Violet."

"Later, Jamie," Alex said.

Jamie stopped. "What's up with you?" Jamie said. "You're looking a bit serious. Something wrong?"

Alex could hardly hear Jamie above the din. "I need you to come with me for a bit, Jamie," he said.

"Come on," Jamie said. "Stop being so serious looking. Let's get partying, man."

Alex reached out and put a hand on Jamie's arm. "It'll only take a minute, Jamie, please," he said.

Jamie shrugged and blew out a breath of resignation. "Okay then," he said and followed Alex through the crowd to the back of the shop.

"Where are we going?" Jamie asked as they stood in the hallway.

Alex pushed open the door to Jean's office, stepped inside and held the door open for Jamie.

"What's going on?" Jamie said stepping inside. It all sounded too quiet now except for the hum of the computer's fan.

Jamie turned to Alex. "What is it?" he asked.

"Sit down, Jamie," Alex said pulling out the chair from Jean's desk.

"Eh?"

"Just do me a favor, Jamie, and do is I ask," Alex said.

Jamie pulled a face and sat down, still in his officer's uniform.

"Here," Alex said, giving Jamie the mouse. "Just move it over to there on the screen then click it. The connection's a bit slow so it'll take a wee while."

"Eck, what's going on," Jamie asked. "What is all this about?"

"Just do it, Jamie, for me."

Jamie huffed and faced the screen and moved the cursor over to the little icon at the bottom. "This?" he asked.

"Aye, that," Alex said, taking stepping behind Jamie.

Jamie clicked the mouse it. From top to bottom, like a scroll being slowly unrolled down the screen, shapes and colors emerged, a little out of focus looking until it was revealed. Jamie sat saying nothing until he saw the words at the bottom of the screen.

Alex leaned forward and spoke closely into Jamie's ear. "You see, Jamie," he said. "I told you all babies are bonnie, even you." He stepped back again as Jamie looked at the old picture before him, at the toothless smile, the bright laughing eyes, happy.

"Al ..." but the word was cut off in Jamie's throat.

"Aye, Jamie?"

There was a pause and then Jamie tried again. "Alex, could you give a man five minutes with himself? I'd really appreciate it."

Alex reached out and gently touched Jamie's shoulder. "Of course I can, Jamie," Alex said. "Take as much time as you need."

Already feeling Jamie's shoulder trembling under his hand, Alex let it go and slipped away. At the door he turned and took one last look back, at Jamie's shoulders bowed over, shaking, and gave the man the time he needed to be by himself.

And after he stepped into the hallway and closed the door, he heard Jamie break into muffled sobs.

"See, Jamie," he whispered quietly, knowing he couldn't be heard. "Somebody did love you enough to take your photograph after all.

He touched the door. Then let his hand slip down and quietly walked away.

CHAPTER 64

"It's a bit weird," Alex said.

"What is?" Jamie asked, squinting into the sunlight as they sat at a table in St Pauli park.

"Knowing now that I'm older than you are," Alex said. "That I'm no two months younger than you, but now I'm three months older."

"Aye," Jamie said stretching. He took a look around at all the other empty tables. The park was deserted.

Alex picked up his coffee, thought about it, looked at it, and suddenly lost the taste for it. He put it back down. He'd hardly touched the stuff in the past few days.

"Hey," he said. "How come you've got a driver's license then?"

Jamie shrugged, raised an eyebrow. "I passed, didn't I?" Jamie said. "But it doesn't matter now since I'm older than seventeen in a half anyway."

His rollup tobacco and papers still sat in his pocket. At the same time that Alex had grown a dislike for his usual favorite brew, Jamie had lost the notion to inhale poison. Still, maybe he would find some use for it. Like at the bottom of a bin. Or maybe he would just keep hold of it in case he had a notion for it sometime in the future, or never again, as a relic from the past.

"And they'll be no drinking for you after this as well," Alex said, "at least not until your eighteenth birthday."

Jamie turned to him. "You make it sound like I'm an addict or something," he said.

"Actually, there's something even worse than that about you now," Alex said.

"Like?"

"That you're English, no Scottish after all. God help me, but I think I'm going to be sick."

"Funny ha ha," Jamie said.

They sat there in the silence, still no one else around. And no helicopters this time either.

Alex spoke first. "It's been good too though, Jamie?"

"Well, apart from getting our heads bashed in aye, and you almost being murdered by British Nazis, it's been a load of laughs."

Alex leaned into the table between them. "Jamie?"

Jamie, one eye open in the heat of the morning sun, looked over at him. "Aye, Alex, I know that we can't stay here any longer, pal. I knew we would have to go home someday." He shrugged.

"How'd you know that was what I was going to say?" Alex asked, taken aback.

"And that wasn't what you wanted to say to me?" Jamie said.

Alex slumped back. The look of his cold coffee in the cup was making him feel queasy.

"I can hear a 'but' somewhere in there in your voice, Jamie," he said.

Jamie sighed. "*But*," he said, "I just didn't want to think about it, I suppose. I knew it would have to end, but somehow I thought it never would, that's all."

"I know what you mean, Jamie," Alex said dreamily, looking up at the clear blue sky as a wren flew over their heads. "It's all been that different to how it is back at home in Kelty."

"Aye, really different," Jamie agreed, nodding. He looked at Alex. "When do you think we should tell them?" he asked.

Alex looked off into the distance, at the grass, the trees. "Now, Jamie. I think we should tell them now."

And at that, not another word spoken. They stood up and walked away.

~~*

Shirley and Jean were in floods of tears. Everyone was hugging everyone else. Jamie and Alex had agreed that they didn't want a big fanfare leaving do. The truth be told, Alex and Jamie just wanted to slip away quietly, unnoticed in the night, telling no one.

But they owed it to Shirley and Jean.

Yes, they really did have to go now, and yes, but sorry, they already had a home to go to.

Jean had wanted to drive them to the train station, but Alex and Jamie didn't want that. It would have only made saying goodbye take all the longer and be more painful for it. It was better this way.

And suddenly Jamie and Alex were back out on the dusty streets of St Pauli waiting for a bus. Jamie had organized the tickets for the train and the ferry.

It was time to go home.

CHAPTER 65

They walked from the sun into the terminal building, which in reality was nothing more than a series of wooden slats on posts, all enclosed in clapboard. The outside sported a matte, colored blue, washed out, sun bleached. Inside it was cool.

Jamie looked out the fretted windows on his side, Alex on his. Their footsteps echoed dully back at them on the concrete as they strode forward, rucksacks on their backs like seasoned travelers.

Already there were a few stragglers, other travelers, weekenders and long haul aficionados in front of them. Everyone seemed to be talking in whispers, heads leaning in close to one another. Alex looked down, past the central galley, once used for customs checks but now no more.

"This is it then," Jamie said.

Alex nodded, looking at the other travelers in front of them waiting to board. "You got the tickets?" he asked.

"Aye," Jamie said.

Alex's legs took him forwards as if by their own volition, for it was like everything was in a dream to him, slowing down, the check-in growing more distant instead of closer. He looked out one of the windows again as he passed it by and saw the ferry, hardly believing at it steadiness, that it was floating on water and not bolted down on rock.

He spoke without looking at Jamie. "Where are they?"

Jamie turned his head and looked at Alex. "In my pocket," he said.

"Right," Alex said.

The straps of the rucksack felt heavier than when he'd first walked through this same terminal building only a few short months ago. "Let's see them," he said.

Jamie took a quick sideways glance at Alex then away again, at the gathering line of passengers a few hundred yards away.

"What do you want to see them for?" he asked.

"Because I want to see them," Alex said.

"Alex, they're in my pocket," Jamie said, sounding a little exasperated.

"Then all you have to do is take them out and let me see," Alex said.

"What for?"

"Cat's for!"

Jamie kept on walking as he struggled with the strap of his rucksack, pushing his hand into his inside pocket. He pulled out the tickets and held them up. Alex reached out and took them from Jamie, stopped walking and turned the envelope over. He looked at it front and back.

Jamie stopped walking a few paces up ahead and turned himself sideways on to Alex. He bit his lip, hoping Alex wouldn't notice what was on the tickets.

Alex opened the envelope and pulled out the tickets. He looked at them. He hadn't seen them yet and still it seemed as if he knew what he would find.

"What's this?" he said.

"Tickets?"

Alex looked up at Jamie then back to the tickets in his hand. "What were you hoping for, Jamie? That I wouldn't find out until it was too late?" His voice was steady, calm.

"Och, Alex," Jamie said.

"I've got two tickets here," Alex said. "One for a foot passenger and one for a single cabin."

Jamie looked away shaking his head.

"Well?" Alex said.

"It's all they had left," Jamie said, "okay?"

"So why did you no take the single cabin for yourself then?" Alex asked.

"Awe, for God's sake, Alex, does it matter?"

"Aye, it does." Jamie remained tight lipped.

"I'm waiting, Jamie."

An older couple passed them by, one on either side of them.

"Because it was the only one left," Jamie said, "and I know that you like your creature comforts."

Alex looked behind them. A young couple stood handing over money at the check-in. "The only ones they had left?" he said, turning back.

Jamie looked at him for a moment. "Alex, don't do this to me."

Alex looked at the tickets again and sighed. "Is it really because you didn't ..."

Jamie closed his eyes. Suddenly the air seemed too thick. "Aye, you're right, Eck!" Jamie blurted. "It's because I didn't have enough money left for a double cabin, okay? Satisfied now? We've nothing left. I've nothing left."

Alex looked at him. There was a look in Jamie's eyes, a look that said 'I'm vulnerable—you don't have to shoot me.'

He separated the two tickets then sighed. And if the weight of his rucksack would have let him, he would have shrugged as well. "You better have this then," he said, handing the foot passenger ticket to Jamie.

Jamie half-nodded, not wanting to keep eye contact with Alex any more than he had to. He took the ticket. "We'd better get going then," he said.

"Aye," Alex said. "We'd better."

They stood at the end of the short queue in silence while others jabbered in front. Jamie held back, but Alex waved him in front and watched as Jamie handed over his passport and ticket and took his boarding pass.

Jamie looked over his shoulder quickly to make sure that Alex would follow and do the same.

CHaPTer 66

"No, don't go now," Alex said, dumping his rucksack down in the cabin.

Jamie turned around inside the tiny cabin, his rucksack, the same old silver forlorn Apollo moon mission looking thing still on his back.

"Close the door, Jamie," Alex said.

"What is it?"

"I need to speak to you."

Jamie closed the cabin door and laid his rucksack down next to it. He looked over at Alex standing looking out the porthole. "What is it you want to talk to me about?" Jamie said.

"Come over here," Alex said.

Jamie walked over. Alex opened the porthole and the warm air breezed in.

"Better with the window open, you think, eh?" Alex said.

Jamie nodded. "Aye, I think so."

"See, Jamie, when I was a bairn I was always taught that if there was a bit cake left and you cut that bit in two, you always took the wee-ist bit for yourself." Jamie said nothing, except raise his eyebrows and shrugged.

"But," Alex went on, "in my experience, in reality that is, if I've been offered anything, I was always given the wee-ist bit, except for when it was my gran. She always gave me the biggest bit. Even although it always made me feel guilty taking it, I have to say."

"What are you telling me this for?" Jamie asked.

Alex turned to him, the warm breeze blowing softly though the window. "Because, Jamie, nobody else since ever gave me the bigger bit of the cake. That is until now."

"But?"

442

"No, hold your wheesht for now, Jamie. I've got something else I need to say to you."

Alex turned and looked out of the porthole and down onto the dock where men in orange overalls scurried around on the quayside, their arms waving every now and again, shouting in German, sometimes holding walkie-talkies to their mouths.

Everything began to take on a distance that hadn't been there for Alex a few moments before when they had arrived. He looked up and over the port town of Cuxhaven, at the gulls circling high above, some swooping down then away again.

"I can hardly believe we were ever away, Jamie" Alex said softly. "And I'll tell you this. If it hadn't have been for you, I don't think I would ever have come here, or anywhere else. In fact, Jamie, I know I wouldn't have."

"Aye, you would have, Eck," Jamie said, "sooner or later."

Alex kept silent for a moment. A gull swooped down past the porthole and away again. Alex followed it with his eyes until the bird disappeared behind a crane.

"No, Jamie," Alex said. "No without that great big shove you gave me. You see, I couldn't see any practicality in it. And that's all my life has ever been concerned about, with practicalities, trying to find the place that's safe and how to keep it safe from everything. But it's a con, Jamie. A great big con. There aren't any safe places, no really. Some maybe safer thin others for a wee bit of time, but no forever.

"All I could think of was, what's for dinner, or having to get ready for work in the morning, or thinking about what's going to happen if I can't get to the shops in time. Always thinking about bills, thinking about buses and timetables as well. It was like being jailed inside a cell inside a great big prison with invisible bars on it, or being a tree growing roots behind a wall. Always trying to fix things so the next thing will work. About making money and worrying about paying even more bills, worried about getting up in the morning in time, worrying about Thelma in Derek. Aye, I was even worrying about them as well.

"Never once did I think about going away own a holiday. It was all just about surviving and scraping by from day to day, working towards something and no idea what that something was.

"But I kept thinking there has to be something at the end. Except I was that lost being so busy all the time that I couldn't see what that something was either. And a still don't know what it was supposed to be.

"We're are like that, Jamie, I think—being too busy, that is. Only the problem is that nobody ever sees what's happening to them. Sometimes maybe we never get to see. Or when we do, it's too late, when our roots have grown too deep, then suddenly, when we take a look in the distance we can't free ourselves to get to it, and it's even worse, because now there's a wall that's been built around us as well, Jamie. A wall that we never noticed was being built around us until it was too late.

"What I'm trying to say, Jamie, is that in your own way, you saw that wall when I didn't. And it was you who helped me jump over it to the other side before the wall was built too high and make escape impossible. No, I had to be pushed. Really pushed over it to freedom, Jamie. And it's still there, Jamie. That wall, back there in Kelty, waiting for us to jump back over it, back to the other side to where we were before. Only our roots are going to grow even deeper this time. Deeper and older, and that wall is going to grow higher and higher until we're too weak to even try the next time. And all this, this, will be just like a dream, something that never happened. And that scares me, Jamie."

"We can always go on holiday again, Alex." Jamie said. "People go on holiday all the time."

"You're not getting what I'm meaning, Jamie," Alex said. "Going away for wee short holidays is all part of the root system, all part of the busy-ness, all part of being too busy to see what's really happening to us. It's part of the same trap where we end up having too much else to think about to even notice it.

"But you know what, Jamie. Now that I've had this break away from it all? I can look back and see it for what it was when we were living back home. We were being tangled in a web. And the more we struggled to survive, the more we tried to get things right, to keep a roof over our heads, fighting to keep things together, the more we were getting stuck."

"I think you're giving me more credit than I'm due, Eck," Jamie said.

Alex sighed, looking out to the sun falling towards the horizon, behind the spires, the rooftops. "My gran died in that house of hers, Jamie. Near sixty years she was in it. Paying bills, worrying about things, worrying about neighbors and paying for the privilege of staying in a concrete box all her life. All she had was her telly, a couple windows, four walls and one bill to be paid off after another. And all that effort for the privilege of buying a hole in the ground at the end. And she didn't even get that! Just before she died, Jamie, she made me think."

Jamie reached out and slipped an arm over his shoulder.

"It was like a light, Jamie. Just a tiny wee light in the dark. And I'd almost forgot about it.

"You see, all that darkness, darkness of thinking about … surviving in that environment, thinking that I'd end up my days doing the same thing as her, and that that would end up being my fate as all. That was all I thought I was going to end up with in life. And then you came along, Jamie. And giving me that push that you did has been like striking a match in the darkness for me."

Alex turned to Jamie. "I'm feared, Jamie. Feared that I'm going back and that I'll forget all about what it was like. And feared that I'll grow old and decrepit. I had one rotten mother, and there's too many rotten memories back there to go with it. But I found that there's something better, Jamie, something that's been there all the time, but that I couldn't see for being too busy and blind to notice before now."

"What are you talking about, laddie?" Jamie said.

"I'm talking about our real mother, Jamie," Alex said. "A mother who's been there all the time for us. That's what I'm talking about."

"What mother? I still don't get what you're talking about, Eck."

Alex looked seriously at Jamie. "All I know is that's she's out there waiting for us, Jamie," Alex pointed at the open porthole. "And you know what? She's always been there for us. And she's been waiting for us all this time, only I was too blind to see. She's our real mother, Jamie, outside, out there. No back in Kelty. No in that place where we'll be scrimping and spending and getting ourselves into debt to build a concrete box like my gran did, working to buy another cage just to bury ourselves in. And you know what, it wasn't until you handed me that ticket for this cabin that I realized it."

"Alex, lad, I don't know what you're talking about. What are you trying to say to me?" Jamie pleaded.

Alex heart beat faster. He slowed his breathing, steadied himself and looked Jamie in the eyes. "What I'm trying to tell you, Jamie, is that I'm no going back."

CHaPTeR 67

"You're leaving me?" Jamie asked, shocked.

Alex was silent for a moment. "No, Jamie, I'm no leaving you," he said. "I'm asking you to come with me. I need you, Jamie. There are too many invisible monsters still out there. And you saw them when I couldn't. Come with me, Jamie. You and me."

"But we *are* gone back home," Jamie said. "We're on the ferry. We'll be back in Kelty by the morning!"

Alex stepped up to him. "Come with me," he said. "But if you don't want to … well, I was going to say that's fine … Except it won't be fine. Because no matter where I'll find myself … I'll never forget you, Jamie."

"Awe, Alex, don't do this to me. You keep doing stuff to me and I don't understand."

"And, Jamie?"

"What?"

"I'll never forget something else, either. You didn't just give me the biggest bit of the cake, you gave me near enough all of it, only leaving yourself with enough and no more to no starve. And I'm no so sure that you wouldn't have even done that for my sake as well."

"Och, Alex, you're no thinking right," Jamie said.

"I would never forget you, my Jamie," Alex said. "Even as I grow to be an old man, I would never forget you for a very good reason."

"Because I got you the cabin, for God's sake?"

"More than that, Jamie."

"What?"

"Because I didn't realize how much I could love another human being until half an hour ago. That's why. Come with me, Jamie. We can be together no matter what happens to us, always. Our mother's always there, like she's always been there for us, and we didn't even know it."

"What mother are you talking about?" Jamie said.

"Out there." Alex pointed at the porthole. "Mother Earth, Jamie, our real mother, the whole planet, ours."

Jamie looked out the porthole. "Awe, God!" he said. "I think they're about to pull away the gangway."

"Another thing," Alex said. "This is the ferry's last sailing here. So if you do decide to come with me, there'll be no going back, ever."

The ship's horn sounded. Jamie looked frantically at Alex.

"Damn blast it!" he said. He lurched at his rucksack and threw it over his shoulder. Alex did the same with his. Jamie wrenched open the cabin door and threw himself into the corridor. "Come on!" he yelled at Alex over his shoulder. "They'll be yanking up the anchor!"

"What floor's the door out of this boat on again?" Alex shouted, his rucksack swinging from wall to wall.

The floor rumbled beneath them.

"God! They're starting up the engines," Jamie cried out. "Deck four!"

They ran, slithered and jumped down two flights of stairs. Alex rushed up to the reception desk, crashing into it. "Stop the boat!" he screamed at the receptionists.

The perfectly coiffed receptionists looked at them, puffing and panting hanging onto the edge of the desk in front of them.

"We have to get off!" Alex yelled. He turned to Jamie. "They're no listening to me!"

The engines beneath them rumbled louder with increasing power. The ship's horn sounded again.

"Think of something, Jamie, quick!"

Jump?

Swim?

Give up?

"Medication!" Jamie yelled.

Brilliant.

"Aye, I forgot my medication," Alex yelped.

The receptionists looked at one another, then back at Alex and Jamie.

"Aye," Jamie said out of breath. "He's a nutter. He needs his pills." Alex shot him a look. "He's had a hole drilled in his head," Jamie said. "Quick, show them, Eck."

"Owe, aye," Alex said, bowing his head over.

"Here, see?" Jamie pointed at Alex's wound. "They had to drill a hole in his head. ZZZzzzzz! ZZZzzzz!"

A receptionist fainted away beneath the desk. The other stepped back, talking frantically into her walk-talkie. Two security guards appeared out of nowhere. The receptionist jabbered away at them in Danish, pointing at the doors. The bulkhead doors clanked and opened slightly. Alex and Jamie flew at them and squeezed through.

Someone shouted behind them. Alex and Jamie didn't stop. They lurched down the ramp, metal clanging and twisting as if in agony beneath their feet as they headed down the endless ramp.

It began to sway under them. Alex tripped over his feet and crashed down on his hands and knees.

"Run, Jamie!" he yelled. "Save yourself. Go without me or you'll never escape!"

Jamie skidded to a stop and slammed back against the metal wall as the ramp sung sharply to the right then left, then dipped down.

He scrambled back up the steepening slope, grabbed Alex by the arm and pulled him to his feet. "Never!" Jamie yelled above the twisting metal. "I'll never leave you. Now come on!"

The ramp lurched downward and there, at the bottom, was sunlight shining on the quayside swinging off to the right.

"Jump! *JUMP*!"

The leapt through the air, arms and legs wheeling then crashed onto dry land. Alex rolled over with his rucksack under him, skating along the concrete as he looked up to watch the ramp swing over the edge of the dock. Rolling to a stop he sat up and looked around for Jamie.

"Eck! Eck!" Jamie cried, tumbling over, scrapping backwards until his legs fell over the quayside, his fingers grasping uselessly, green water raging below his dangling feet as the ship's propellers tore up the surface.

Alex turned to see Jamie's hand grasp a rope, sliding down, his other hand losing its grip on the algae-covered concrete.

"Jamie!" And as if his rucksack had become a feather from Heaven, Alex flew over, hunched down, and looked down at Jamie's terrified eyes. Jamie's hand slipped until he was hanging by one arm, his legs dangling above the ferry's propellers churning up raging waves.

Alex snatched down at Jamie's T-shirt, and closed his eyes tight. "God help me now and give me the wings that I need to fly!"

Teeth gritted, Jamie's T-shirt stretched into string cutting into his fingers, holding tight, Alex pulled up with all the power he never knew he had in his legs and dragged Jamie up and back over the edge.

The ship's horn sounded, the waters boiled, and they lay gasping on the side as the sun beat down on their blood pounding faces. Men in orange overalls scratched their heads, shrugged and let Alex and Jamie go on their way.

Only when they were walking back through the warm interior of the old check-in building with its sun faded-blue painted sides did their legs begin to start shaking as they walked along in silence and in solitude.

Jamie looked up at one of the monitors. Then did a double take. He stepped back.

"Eck!"

Alex walked back and looked up at the screen. Except it wasn't a monitor now, but a television. The language was unintelligible, as were the subtitles. German, thought Jamie.

"I think it's Dutch," Alex explained.

And there sat Thelma, smiling behind her big black shades. Snippets of video were being inter-spliced with what looked like an interview. Then the words appeared along the bottom of the screen: *Het Colossus auf Kelty!* it said in German. And then there was that guy with the big goofy grin wearing an even goofier green hat and big rubber yellow hands.

"Derek," Jamie said.

Shouted over the commentary running came the words: "*Amsterdam yah bass!*"

"Oh, my God," was all Alex could say.

There were snippets of Thelma dancing her heart out in front of an audience, clapping and cheering as they wondered at the size of such a woman who could actually spin and jump around with such energy, never mind walk. And this all done to Irene Cara singing *What a Feeling...*

"Fame at last then," Alex said. "In Amsterdam of all places as well."

Jamie smiled. "They made it then," he said. "What do you think?" he asked, still looking up at the screen.

Alex turned to him. "I'm happy for them, Jamie," he sighed. "I'm happy that they made it."

Jamie put an arm around Alex's shoulder.

"I still love them, Jamie," Alex said, his voice threatening to break. "But I know now that I can only love them from a distance."

"Aye," Jamie sighed, giving Alex's shoulders a reassuring squeeze.

They readjusted their rucksacks and started to walk away when Jamie heard the voice. Not a voiceover this time, not in Dutch, but in English, a version of it anyway.

It was Derek talking, subtitles moving along the bottom of the screen in German. Alex walked back and stood beside Jamie, listening.

"Fate's a funny thing," Derek said to the unseen interviewer. "Things happen, and then unexpected things happen because of them. And in that light, I would like to say this if I may, a message from both my sister and myself."

Derek looked straight into the camera. "Alex, pal," Derek said, "wherever you are, let it never be said that both your sister, Thelma, and me, will ever forget what you did for us all those years. We've sent a message to the flat, but please don't take it too hard when we say that we'll be staying here in Amsterdam. And just one other thing, and this concerns fate here: There's also a very special guy out there who I want to thank as well. For if it wasn't for him, Thelma and I would never be as successful as we are today."

Looking straight into the camera, Derek smiled. "That special guy's name is Jamie McFarlane. If it wasn't for him, if things hadn't happened the way they did because of him, well, where would Thelma and me be now? Still at home."

Thelma pushed her face into the picture. "From the both of us," she said. "Alex *and* Jamie, thanks for making this happen."

"Aye," Derek said. "We love you guys and always will, wherever you are."

Thelma blew a big kiss at the camera before the picture faded out.

CHAPTER 68

The whole world seemed to invert, to come up on all sides and surround the boys in a protective bubble. And all at once they were connected and isolated at the same time.

Each sat in silence in the warmth of the early evening sun as it steadily intensified its brilliance to a deepening orange. They would have to stand by their lives wherever they took them moment-by-moment now, decision by decision. Mistakes would be made, corrected, joys and exhilarations were still to be had.

They sat on their rucksacks, their world crammed into such little spaces under them as they leaned back on the railings, the canal behind them, its waters still—the calm before the storm, perhaps, waiting for the floodgates to open, for everything to rush in.

Alex sighed and closed his eyes to the heat of the dying sunlight. "This is nice," he said in a whisper.

Jamie turned to him and saw the beatific smile on his face. "Aye," Jamie sighed himself and felt everything inside of him melt away, the tension, the fear of the unknown fading away for the moment at least.

It was a dream, of course, to be free, forever free. And there would be prices to pay for it along the way.

There would be no one to but each other to turn to now if anything should go wrong. There would be no one to utter words of consolation and solutions except each other.

No authoritarian bureaus to turn to. They would be on their own, making their own decisions, and that somehow frightened him.

The melting wax feeling inside Jamie's chest began to solidify again, molding into something, something tight.

He closed his eyes against it. *Everything will be fine*, he thought, *everything will be okay*.

And he thought of their old home once more, that little flat, and told himself that that would be for the last time he would ever think about it.

He felt Alex's hand slide into his own, holding tight. Jamie squeezed Alex's fingers with his own and smiled to himself, and the tension, the fear that might have been, melted away again.

Alex whispered into his ear. "I love you, Jamie."

And this time it was Jamie's eyes that stung. Reaching around, he pulled Alex close.

To be loved unconditionally, for someone to tell him that he was loved, was too much to find the words that he wanted to say to Alex.

Alex held onto him, whispered and hushed the child who had been forced to grow up to quickly because of something that had been forced upon him, and rocked the weeping child who at last had been set free, holding him tight, holding him safe. "That's all right laddie," Alex said quietly into Jamie's ear, "you can cry all you want to now, that's it, sssshhhh ..."

Jamie's buried his face in Alex's shoulder as years of silent emotional pain finally their way out him. "Alex, Alex, Alex, what would have happened if I'd never met you that day ..."

Then there was silence again as the shadows around them grew longer as another day drew to an end.

"Then, I think," Alex said, holding Jamie tight, "that I would have been the sadist wee laddie alive."

That was the real seal that bound them together, that more than any other, a seal unbreakable in its emotional strength. That out of everyone else on the planet, it had been pure chance that had actually met one another.

~~*

"I feel stupid," Jamie sniffed pulling his rucksack onto his shoulders again.

"Why?"

"For greeting like that. I've never cried in front of anybody like that. I feel daft."

Alex looked at him. "Daft?" he asked.

"A bit," Jamie said, hitching up his rucksack.

"It proves one thing though," Alex said.

"What?"

"That you're human."

"A snortering human, then," Jamie said. "That's what I am. Anyway, where to now?"

Alex looked around. "I'm no sure myself," he said. "It's not exactly hooching with activity around here, is it? God, and I'm starving as well."

"Me too," Jamie said. "What's with the look?"

"Nothing," Alex said. "I just thought that you would be at me for wanting to eat. Considering that I'm a fat get."

"You're hardly fat, Eck," Jamie said. "No now you're no anyway."

"You always told me I was, "Alex said, raising an eyebrow and sticking his tongue in his cheek.

"I was only having you on," Jamie said. "You were never fat."

"Never?"

"No, you weren't. Anyway, I never wanted you to lose weight. I was always feared of something if you did."

"Feared of what?"

"Your ark."

"Eh?"

"I was always feared that it would shrink."

Alex's eyebrow dropped. "Pray tell why?" he said.

"You know."

"I don't know."

They walked towards the town of Cuxhaven, the ground dusty under their feet.

"Well ..."

"Aye?" Alex said.

"You always went on an eating binge when I went on about you needing to lose weight. So it stopped it shrinking."

"What?"

"Your sexy ark."

~~*

"I was just thinking," Jamie said.

"What about?"

"You know how you were talking about us having a bairn?"

"Aye, what about it?" Alex said, hardly needing to be reminded.

"Well," Jamie said, "we could get a dog." Alex froze at side of dock, his hand gripping the rail. Jamie thought Alex was having an epileptic fit. "Alex? Alex!" Jamie panicked and rushed over to Alex, fearing the worst and wishing he had a pair of pliers to prize Alex's fingers off the railing.

"A dog?" Alex said, his eyes sliding to the side at Jamie.

Jamie stepped back, feeling relieved, then indignant. "Eh, well, aye," he said adjusting a shoulder strap.

"A dog!"

"Aye, a dog. What's wrong with a dog, like?"

"You equate a bairn with a dog?"

"Awe, forget it," Jamie said. "I should have kept may gob shut."

"A dog with three legs," Alex said. "A dog with big ears and a snout like Concorde, no doubt!"

"Eck, I just thought," Jamie pleaded.

"Thought what?"

"That you've no changed."

A little while later, the sun dropped below the horizon.

"What will we do for dosh now?" Jamie asked.

"We work, of course," Alex said. "A job here, a job there. You've done it before, Jamie. At the hospital, remember? You can do it again. And me too."

"Hey," Jamie said as they walked along. "I could teach English as a foreign lingo. Teach stuff about Robert Louis Jameson, and Sir Walter Scot ..."

"Burke and Blair?" Alex suggested.

"Arthur Conan Boil, Sean Connery."

"Sawny Bean?" Alex said.

"All *right*!"

They walked off into the distance, two shadows, voices fading, just legs and arms now and again, showing around rucksacks that were too big.

There was laughter.

Then there was silence.

~~*

Alex never did tell Jamie about the letter, the one that Jameson had given him at the reading of Alex's grandmother's will. It wasn't until Alex opened it later that it became clear why the old solicitor had sounded so helpful that day.

It was the deeds to his grandmother's property. She hadn't been renting it for years, as Alex had thought she had. She had been buying it and had ending up owning it outright. No wonder she had been so pleased when Alex had helped renew the wiring or did the painting. She had been letting Alex feather his own future nest egg, investing in his own future without him even realizing it.

He had gone back with the letter to the old solicitor a few days later. Did Alex wish to put the property up for sale? Grab the cash and run in other words? Alex had sat there biting his lip. No, he wouldn't be selling it.

"Wise decision, Mr. McMullen, and a very astute and mature decision if I may say too," Jameson had said, sitting back in his big leather chair.

That way, Alex had explained, he wouldn't be tempted to throw money away at whoever gave him the biggest sob story, which Alex knew was his weak point. And the only ones who knew about his grandmother's house were himself and Jameson.

And yes, the old solicitor would be only too pleased to take care of Alex's property for rental purposes. Thus the money collected had gone into an investment fund. Would there be anything else?

"Aye, Mister Jameson, there would be," Alex had said. "I need to write a will."

"Another wise decision."

Alex had reached into his pocket and pulled out a slip of paper, then read from his little list. When Jameson had finished Alex's will he had looked over his spectacles at him.

"Benefactors?" Jameson had asked.

Alex sat himself up straight in his chair. "There's only one, Mister Jamieson, and that would be someone I love very very much," Alex had said. "If anything should ever happen to me then I would like everything to be left to Mister Jamie McFarlane."

FIN

about the author

Michael Sutherland lives in Edinburgh, Scotland. He writes fulltime, has had several stories published, and is currently writing a speculative fiction novelette titled *Revolver*.

His standalone short stories, *Skinz* and *Another Journey,* have been published by Musa Publications. Several of his other stories appear in two collections: *Passport to Phelamanga* and *From Here to Hallucigenia*, where a spin-off of *Invisible Monsters* can be found in his story *What Goes Around Comes Back Weird*. His short story *The Photograph* (Jupiter Magazine) has been described as "Atmospheric … revolutionary in its style and delivery. A thoroughly good story" by CFnest, and "Something you won't see coming" by SFRevu.

He has a Bachelor of Science and studied creative writing at university.

Lightning Source UK Ltd.
Milton Keynes UK
UKOW042014290513

211457UK00003B/485/P